THE BASQUE DILEMMA

A NOVEL

BY

M. BRYCE TERNET

The Basque Dilemma

ISBN-13-978-1978092334
ISBN-10-1978092334

Also by M. Bryce Ternet

A Basque Story

Diplomatic Weekends in Africa

Strohm Alley

The Yellow House on Maloney Grove

The American Middle Class Revolution

Rock Creek

The Stevenson Plan,
A Novel of the Monterey Peninsula

To the Basque people, who make the world a more interesting place.

Etorkizuna, kontakizuna.

&

To my wife, Renata, who makes my world a better place.

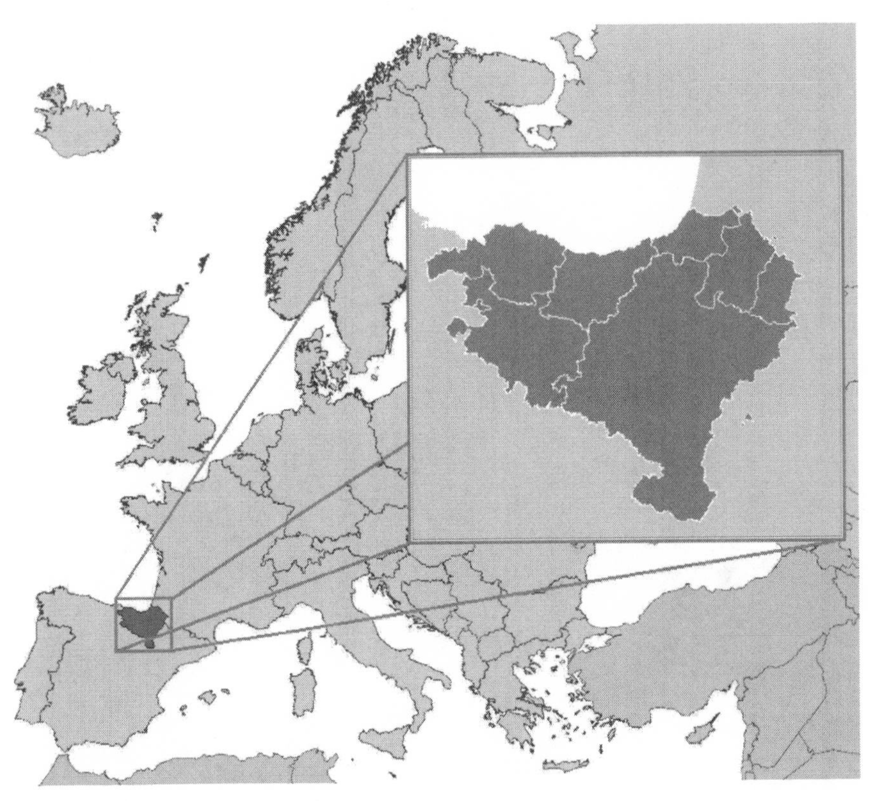

The Basque Country

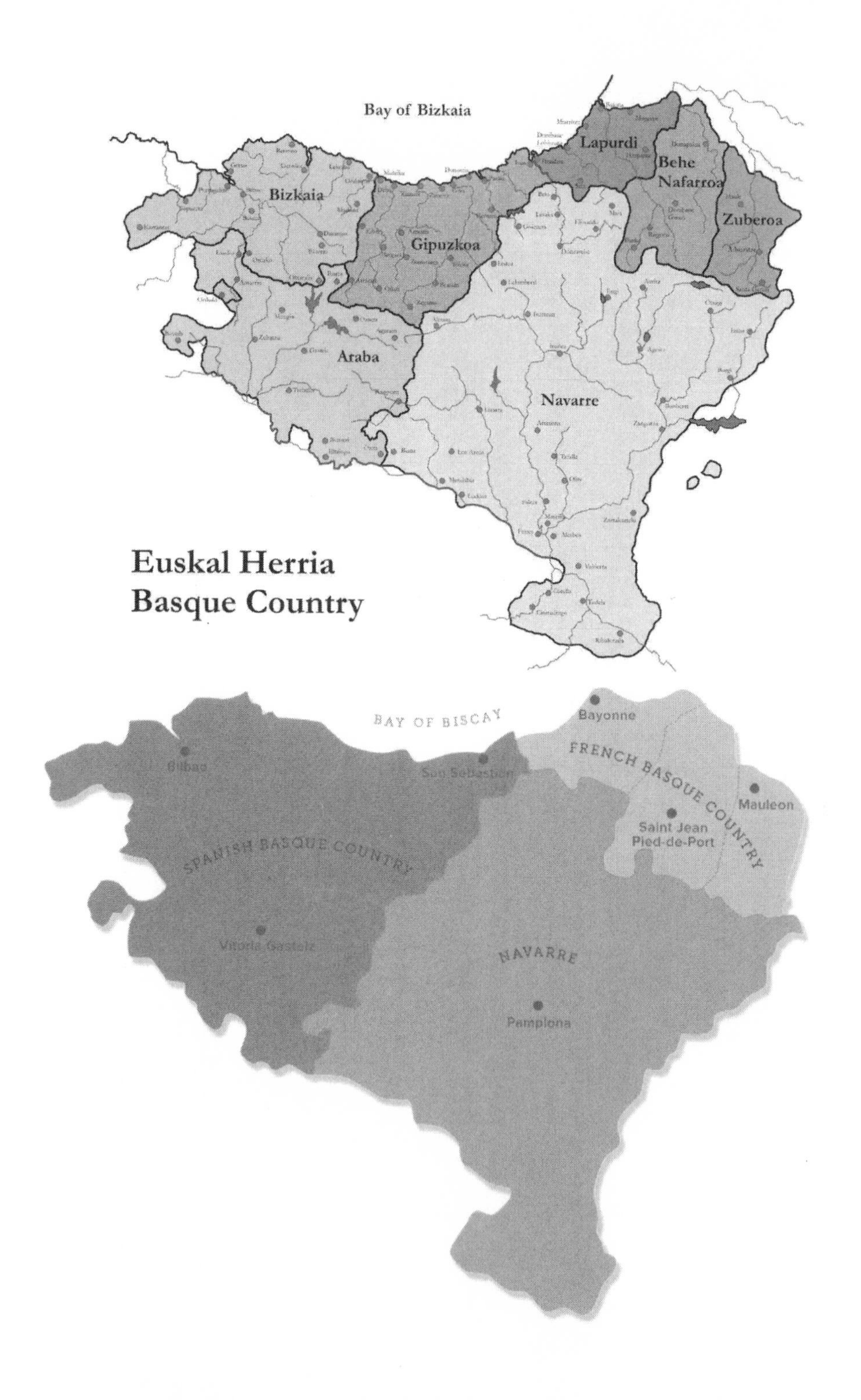

Bay of Bizkaia
Lapurdi
Behe Nafarroa
Bizkaia
Gipuzkoa
Zuberoa
Araba
Navarre
Euskal Herria
Basque Country
BAY OF BISCAY
Bayonne
Bilbao
San Sebastian
FRENCH BASQUE COUNTRY
Mauleon
Saint Jean Pied-de-Port
SPANISH BASQUE COUNTRY
Vitoria Gasteiz
NAVARRE
Pamplona

There is not a Basque problem in France,
but a French problem in the Pays Basque…
The struggle of the Pays Basque will endure as long as there are Basques.

—Henri Pérez

Ser damira ardiac otsoari ihes ari badira?
(Is it surprising that the lamb should flee the wolf?)

—Basque proverb

SUSPECTED TERRORIST ATTACK AT MONTPARNASSE TOWER

PARIS, FRANCE: An explosion occurred at 4:00 PM GMT at the Montparnasse Tower. The blast struck the Tower's 59th floor roof viewing platform; a popular place for tourists to take in views of the surrounding city. Over thirty people have been declared deceased. More are reported to be injured.

Among known killed and maimed are individuals from France, England, Spain, Germany, Russia, India, China, and the United States.

Unconfirmed sources claim numerous bombs were detonated on the viewing platform. The Tower has been evacuated while French security forces search the building for additional explosives.

A French official, speaking on the condition of anonymity, stated the French Government is treating the incident as a terrorist attack. No group has yet claimed responsibility. However, preliminary assumptions are that the Islamic State, also known as ISIS, orchestrated the attack, based on similar recent events in Western Europe.

Roadblocks have been established throughout Paris as authorities search for suspects. France's security level has been raised to high alert.

The French President has called the attack an act of cowardly barbarism and declared a national emergency. French officials are reportedly urging the President to temporary close the country's borders.

Top ranking officials throughout Europe have condemned the attack. The U.S. President has expressed condolences to Parisians, the French people, and the friends and family of those killed or injured.

Part I.

(Three Days Ago)

I.

Lake Annecy, France

TOO MANY PATRIOTS HAVE GIVEN THEIR LIVES for the Basque homeland to end like this. The traitors may have pledged the occupying governments of Spain and France to end violent actions in support of an independent Basque Country. Patxi Irionda had pledged nothing. Unlike others, he hadn't forgotten the original pledge.

No rest until independence.

He would never have betrayed Euskal Herria, betrayed the Basque people, like the cowards supposedly representing ETA had done in 2011. Now, five years later, it was time for things to change.

Because in five years, nothing had changed. Nothing.

The Basque Country still fully occupied on both sides of the false border between France and Spain. The Basque people still forced to live under the tyranny of these false representative governments. The Basque culture was still repressed. Declaring the ceasefire, and then actually complying with that *putain* joke, had done ETA and the Basque people nothing. Nothing. Public opinion polls conducted after the ceasefire indicated that support for independence had been at an all-time high. Even so, no one did anything.

It was time for something to happen.

And, in Patxi's view, the only way anything would change would be a return to killing. No one paid attention to independence movements anymore. People were only interested in Islamic terrorist groups doing their pointless murderous deeds in the name of a silly religion. Recently, ETA had even been initially blamed for one of their cowardly attacks in Barcelona.

But Patxi had to admit that these fanatics had proven one thing: if you wanted to capture the world's attention, random people needed to die. Simple as that.

No more words. No more declarations. No more pledges.

Patxi believed he heard the voice of the great Sabino Arana whispering the very words into his ear. It was time, once again, for action.

Time for Patxi Irionda to come out of retirement.

Time for violence.

Time for the return of ETA.

He sliced a few pieces of saucisson and chewed them slowly while overlooking the majestic snow-capped alpine peaks surrounding Lake Annecy. Lake Annecy wasn't as beautiful as the Pays Basque, but was definitely one of the nicer corners of France. And having the Swiss border only fifty kilometers away and those country's hazy extradition rules to France or Spain was a definite added bonus.

A good place to plan.

II.

San Francisco, California

CAPITAINE NIVELLE OF THE FRENCH Division Nationale Anti-Terroriste, or DNAT, was never the most forthcoming with information. Once Special Agent John Gibson was able to get him on a call after returning from his investigation on the Monterey Peninsula, Nivelle offered very little explanation as to why exactly it was *absolument nécessaire* that Gibson get to France. As soon as possible. Nivelle said Gibson needed to return *tout de suite*, whatever that meant. Under any other circumstances, Gibson would have told Nivelle to stick his *tout de suite* up his smug arrogant French ass.

After all, Gibson was in the FBI, not the CIA. The CIA was supposed to deal with the French DNAT, not him. In theory, anyway.

His not so long ago adventurous foray into the world of the Basque terrorist group ETA had proven that jurisdiction can cross lines, even international ones.

But what little Nivelle said to him was enough to get Gibson packing. Nivelle told him that Gibson's former partner, Sebastian Parker, was in serious danger. Gibson needed no other reason to immediately book a flight to Paris.

"Any idea how long you'll be gone?" Rachel Dowling asked him.

Gibson packed a shirt into the travel bag he had placed on his bed. "I don't know, honestly," he absently answered. "I need to find out whatever the hell Nivelle is talking about. But knowing Parker, it's not hard to believe that he's in some sort of trouble."

"That's your friend who lives in the south of France, right?"

Despite the seriousness of the situation, Gibson couldn't hold back a slight chuckle. "Yeah, it's the south of France all right. But if he were here, he'd quickly point out that he lives in the *Basque Country* before saying he lives in France."

"Oh yes, I recall how the Basque Country crosses the Spanish and French border, although most people think the region is only within Spain," Rachel remarked.

Gibson respected her intelligence. When he first met Sebastian Parker and began learning about the Basques, the Basque Country, and the Basque conflict, he'd needed numerous lessons. His girlfriend, if the two of them were not too old for him to refer to her that way, clearly needed no such lessons.

"As Parker would no doubt point out, there is a significant portion of the Basque Country population who would like it to only be known as the Basque Country, and not regions of Spain or France."

"But I remember a few years back that the Basque terrorist group had agreed to a ceasefire and that the conflict was really over this time," she added.

Gibson folded a pair of khakis and placed them in the travel bag. We'll see, he thought. He considered how ETA had notoriously agreed to ceasefires in the past, only to later once again restart their violent crusade to establish an independent Basque Country. Many believed these periodic ceasefires had only been covers for the organization to recover and regroup. Could the most recent 2011 ceasefire have been just the same old ETA song and dance? Even for ETA, the amount of time that had passed from the ceasefire declaration and the stop of violent actions had been significant. Significant enough for most people to believe that peace had finally come to the Basque Country since ETA began a violent campaign in the late 1960s. Many believed that Europe's last armed conflict had come to a definitive end.

After a pause, Gibson replied. "True, but with groups like ETA, one can never be sure. Sometimes after trying out peaceful negotiations, frustration with a slow process boils over into violence once again."

The wooden *lauburu*, or Basque cross, which Sebastian Parker sent him as a gift and Gibson had hung on his bedroom wall, caught his attention while he spoke. "And there's always a danger that some splinter group could form, trying to reignite the fire," he added reflectively. He wondered if that could really happen with ETA.

"But with all of the global terrorism acts occurring these days, wouldn't this be a bad time to come out of retirement, so to speak, for a group like that? Seems like calling attention to themselves all of a sudden would backfire, as European countries, like France and Spain, are already on high alert for terrorist activities."

A valid point, Gibson had to agree. But there was another way to look at the situation. "That's true, but a radical nationalist could see it is as the opposite, and is a perfect time to announce a rebirth. With governments preoccupied with Islamist terror groups, someone may see this as a time when a resurgent ETA would be able to become more powerful than ever."

"Let's hope not," Rachel said as she walked up next to him and touched him on the shoulder. "And I hope your old partner is not mixed up in anything having to do with that."

Gibson zipped his travel bag shut. "Me too. Because he's not just a partner, he's a friend."

III.

Sare, French Basque Country

IF SEBASTIAN PARKER EVER HEARD complaints about a mother-in-law, he would remind people that they didn't have a Basque one. Although he had nothing to compare to the experience, having a mother-in-law within a twenty minute drive from one's home had to be a challenge for anyone. His was relentless and Basque. He wasn't sure which of the two was more aggravating.

Every time she visited, she had a way of commenting on things that needed to be done around the house, always making Parker want to punch something. *You need to repaint the house. You need to redo these floors. You need to clear the back yard of brush.* On and on. Parker would fall back on the excuse that one didn't exactly buy an eighteenth century farmhouse without expecting work to be done, but with his mother-in-law, the argument would have no standing. After all, her house in Saint-Jean-Pied-de-Port was constructed in the sixteenth century.

But she was right that there was a lot of work to be done on the house and property. A seemingly never-ending amount, in fact. Since he and his wife, Alaitz, had bought the house over a year ago, the perpetual list of things to do hadn't dwindled. Parker loved the house and appreciated how fortunate they were to buy the place. The Basque tradition of only passing down homes to the eldest child in the family was as strong now as hundreds of years ago. Fortunately, his overbearing mother-in-law had used her considerable influence to coerce the previous owners to sell to them. Somehow he imagined that she left out telling the previous owners that her Basque daughter had married a foreigner, especially an American. Considering she'd helped them get the house, and that he'd grown to love the place, he tried to not let her comments unnerve him.

One didn't get this kind of house back in the States. Back there one could maybe find a home from the 1800s in the older parts of the country, like New Orleans, but most houses were rarely more than a hundred years old. And their Basque farmhouse was over three hundred years old.

But historic character comes with challenges, and Parker had been busy with home improvement tasks from the moment they moved in. The constant chores distracted him from his goal of writing a book about living in the Basque Country for a year, but he planned to get writing eventually. There would definitely be a lot to describe.

Where they lived outside of the village of Sare, like the Basque Country's rural areas in general, was far from the cosmopolitan setting in the coastal enclaves of Biarritz or San Sebastian. Even with the massive influx of summer tourists from Paris, Germany, and elsewhere, the Basque countryside remained largely untouched. One could still go for a walk and not see a moving vehicle. Somehow, the Basque countryside remained unspoiled.

Americans hadn't really discovered the Basque Country. They preferred to stick to the other coast in southern France. That was okay with Sebastian Parker. If Americans knew the Basque Coast, the Basque Country would likely no longer be unspoiled.

He wasn't ashamed to have been born in the States. But somehow American tourists perpetually stuck out in crowds. Whether the most annoying common trait was the unnecessary loud talking, the failure to attempt foreign languages, baseball hats, or overweight midsections, he wasn't sure. But, rightly or wrongly, the popularization of a tourist destination anywhere in the world often meant that a place had become popular with American tourists. Typically this occurred after a place was initially discovered by Western European travelers, normally German or French late-teen or early twenties backpackers, followed by affluent Asian tour bus groups.

But by choosing to live in the rolling hills of the Basque Country, Parker left America behind and moved to the only place in the world where he truly felt he belonged. After a short career in the American Central Intelligence Agency, living abroad was a haven. But he wasn't exactly living in a *safe* haven. As a CIA analyst, he'd been assigned to cover Basque nationalist groups, such as ETA, IK, Haika, and Irrintzi. Now he was literally living in the back and front yards of these groups. On any given day when walking into the village, he was guaranteed to pass by someone who'd been affiliated with one of these groups in the past. Or still was.

While these groups would label themselves as nationalist groups, others, such as the French, Spanish, and US governments, labeled them something else: terrorist organizations. And they were not likely to see someone who had once worked to help destabilize their efforts in a pleasant light. In fact, if a total ceasefire hadn't been declared, and actually sustained so far for once, his life would surely be in danger on a daily basis. It could easily still be.

There were no more killings or assassinations in the name of Basque independence these days. But that didn't mean that some former radical could feel the need to take out pent-up aggression on him at any time. Yet, he was sure his mother-in-law's status in the French Basque community guaranteed him a large, strong safety net, even if he didn't like admitting this painful truth. Most of the time, she was fairly insufferable. But he knew she proclaimed that he wasn't to be harmed, even if someone felt repressed anger for his former position in the CIA.

And they didn't try to conceal his former profession. Parker insisted on not trying to hide from his past, not wanting to live his life in constant fear of being discovered. However, if there ever was a return to violence, the situation would undoubtedly change. Considering that he loved the old Basque farmhouse they were renovating and cherished living in the French Basque countryside, he hoped nothing ever changed.

But with Basque separatist groups, and especially with ETA, Sebastian Parker knew he would never be completely safe.

These ominous thoughts occurred to him while walking back from Sare's quaint downtown. He'd picked up a baguette at the boulangerie, brebis cheese at the fromagerie, and paté de compagne at the charcuterie. As everywhere around the world, times were changing. Even in the remote corners of France, visits to huge supermarkets were becoming more frequent than buying groceries directly from small shops such as the village baker, cheese maker, or butcher. Parker felt fortunate that they still bought the majority of their food from the local village shops and weekly market.

As he walked up the pathway to their traditional Basque countryside house—whitewashed stone exterior accented with exposed red-painted timber trim and shutters and an orange tile roof—Alaitz opened the front door.

"Did you get the paté?" she asked in English as he stepped closer. Most of the time they spoke French, other times English, other times Basque, and occasionally Spanish.

"Hello to you too, *mon amour*, my wife," he quipped as he put an arm around her waist and kissed her check.

Alaitz pulled away from his embrace and grabbed the bag he was carrying. "Your wife has been starving for paté all day." She kissed him and walked to the kitchen.

"At ten in the morning?" Parker commented as he followed.

Alaitz spun around quickly to cast him a menacing glance. "You'd better be nice to me, Sebastian, or I'll call my mom to come over for lunch."

"Oh, that'd be fantastic. I'd love to hear how I'm not Basque and don't even have any Basque lineage."

Alaitz set the bag on the kitchen counter and turned to look at her husband. "Deep down she adores you; she just has a hard time expressing her feelings. You know that Basques aren't the best at showing emotions."

"Yeah, yeah. I know. She clearly doesn't despise me as much as she acts. But saying she adores me is probably going a little too far. More accurate would be that she adores that I adore you." He positioned himself behind Alaitz and let his hands rest on her stomach.

"To have the word *adore* in the same sentence with my mother is quite an accomplishment." As she spoke, Alaitz lowered his hands to her buttocks. "And your wife is also starving to have her husband. So consider yourself lucky."

Parker kissed her earlobe gently as he felt her unbutton his pants. Even if they had their differences, at times such as these he definitely considered himself lucky.

IV.

Paris, France

THE TEN HOUR FLIGHT from San Francisco to Paris was manageable for about half of the time. John Gibson had never enjoyed flying. Too difficult to relax in a setting where one had no control. And being confined in a chair was not how he'd ever choose to spend half a day. In years past, he may not have minded the food that was served, but his newly discovered culinary appreciation made him see the food as equivalent to oversalted microwave dinners. Somehow he had Sebastian Parker to thank for all this. And thinking of Parker made the time pass even slower.

What the hell had he gotten into now?

From the moment the plane touched down at Orly, Gibson wanted nothing more than to get to the French Basque Country to do whatever he could to help his young friend. But his years of experience in the FBI had taught him to always go into a situation as prepared as possible. Before he did anything, Gibson needed to know the situation.

And Capitaine Nivelle was probably the only person who could really give him an accurate assessment. He first encountered Nivelle during his investigation into the murder in San Francisco of a Basque-American City of San Francisco Councilman tied to a radical Basque nationalist group leading back to France. The investigation also introduced him to the wily Sebastian Parker. Initially, Gibson didn't care for either, but Parker had considerably grown on him over time. Nivelle, on the other hand, was not the kind of person to ever grow on anyone.

But Gibson did respect Nivelle. Arrogant and irreproachable as he was, Nivelle was devoted to his profession. Gibson suspected that the cold and steadfast Nivelle liked Parker more than he would ever confess. And if Parker was to remain safe living in the heart of the Basque Country, Gibson knew that Nivelle would likely need to be involved. He was, after all, the French equivalent of an FBI department head, and his department was anything to do with Basque nationalist movements.

As promised, Nivelle had a driver waiting for Gibson when he exited from the airport's customs area. The driver, who Gibson assumed was a plainclothes officer in Nivelle's department, said his instructions were to take Gibson from the airport to meet Nivelle. Gibson asked where he was being taken. He received no reply.

Typical Nivelle.

The driver took them south after leaving the airport, before eventually turning north into the heart of the city. After his previous time spent in Paris with Sebastian Parker hunting for a dangerous young radical named Lopé, he'd managed to get his bearings on the city's layout. He recognized signs with directions for the Sorbonne and the Jardin du Luxembourg. They were somewhere in the area of the Latin Quarter, in the fifth or sixth arrondissement.

When he began seeing signs for the Cathédrale Notre-Dame, he recognized they were approaching where the Seine River traversed the city, separating the downtown into two sides, the left and right bank.

The driver turned left on the wide tree-lined and elegant Boulevard Saint-Germain. This direction would take them to the Invalides, the final resting place of France's controversial hero, Napoleon Bonaparte. The thought occurred to Gibson how it was ironic that this man who united France, terrorized Europe, and for a time was the most feared leader in the world had actually been born in Corsica. And like the Basque Country, Corsica had been fighting for independence for decades.

And Sebastian Parker had a habit of annoying him by saying he didn't know anything about history...Gibson told himself he should remember to share this historical observation with Parker when he saw him again.

Hopefully that would be soon.

The driver took a right turn off of the Boulevard Saint-Germain. He brought the car to a sudden stop in front of a café with a large space of outdoor seating in front spilling over onto the sidewalk. Nearly all of the outdoor tables were full with people chatting, sipping coffee, and eating from small plates. Waiters in snappy outfits weaved among the tables carrying trays like trapeze artists. Café scenes such as this didn't seem to exist in the States. Even living in San Francisco, perhaps the most European-like city in the country, the cafés on Columbus Avenue didn't have anything close to a vibe such as the scene on display. He thought it could be a painting.

Something else a lot of the people were doing was smoking. That was one thing about Europe that he didn't miss. He never could understand why anyone would think deliberately inhaling the byproduct of fire was a good idea.

He was glad Parker had quit smoking. That kid used to smoke like a goddamn chimney. As the thought occurred to him, he was briefly transported back to a dark night in Paris while he and Parker were trying to track down José Aldarossa Arana, more commonly known as Lopé. That night he'd very nearly mistakenly shot and killed Sebastian Parker. Ironically, lighting a cigarette that night may have saved Parker's life.

Lucky son of a bitch.

"Hey, you. You get out and go inside now," the driver said in a thickly accented and annoyed tone. The order snapped Gibson from his thoughts. The driver said something else in French, but Gibson didn't understand. Gibson wished Parker were there to respond to whatever curse word the driver had uttered. The driver didn't bother to turn around in his seat to face Gibson. Instead he just waved his hand flippantly in the direction of the café.

Sometimes the French could annoy the shit out of anyone.

Stepping out of the car, Gibson took in the warm Paris air. After a night spent in a plane, the fresh air felt miraculous. He closed the door of the car and was about to turn and ask the driver for any further instructions, but the driver gunned the car into gear. Gibson caught a quick glimpse of the car screeching back onto Boulevard Saint-Germain.

Remember to ask Parker what the French word for asshole is when you see him.

When he turned back to face the café, he read the sign above the entrance. Les Deux Magots. *Magots*? Must be some weird French thing.

As he walked into the café, the scents of the outdoor air blended with the smell of freshly brewed, strong black coffee, cooking eggs, freshly baked bread, wine, and sugary pastries. French cafés always offered a hell of a combination of smells.

But also noticeable were less pleasant odors. There was a noticeable smell of sweat whenever a waiter passed by. Not entirely unexpected given that the month was August and Paris definitely sizzles in summer, as the song says. And despite becoming more *Americanized* in many ways, apparently the use of deodorant had not yet caught on as much as fast food. But with the whiff of body odor hitting one first, a blast of cologne or perfume followed, another French tradition Gibson was not entirely fond of. A dab of the stuff would be okay, but the French seemed to take things to an entirely other level.

And then there was the inescapable cigarette smoke perpetually floating in the air above France in a cloudy sheen. Even with the passing of laws forbidding smoking in restaurants and other public places, the stench of the gray cloudy monster was always around. Gibson could see smoke flowing in thin streams from the outdoor patio through the large open windows of the café.

When in Paris.

Scanning the room, he spotted Capitaine Nivelle seated at a small bistro table in a far corner. Nivelle was staring directly at him, apparently having been watching him the entire time but doing nothing to signal him. As he walked across the room, Gibson noted Nivelle's same crooked smirk punctuated with a thin dark mustache and narrow eyes that he firmly remembered. Nivelle just needed a stiff dark blue hat and he would look like a French military officer in an old movie.

"Agent Gibson, how good to see you again." Nivelle stood and extended a hand. His English was lightly accented, and from the ambiguous manner he spoke Gibson could not be sure if Nivelle genuinely was glad to see him or not.

The fact that Nivelle had chosen to address him as *Agent* so openly in a public setting struck Gibson as odd. Even if not there on official business, fellow nonuniformed law enforcement officers typically would elect to not announce themselves or others. After all, Nivelle was not in uniform and instead wore a dark gray suit. An impeccably tailored suit, Gibson observed.

Nivelle sensed Gibson's unease. As Gibson shook his hand he quickly added, "Oh, it is okay. This is August in Paris. There are only tourists in the city now too concerned with getting to the Tour Eiffel or the Louvre to notice anything else. Even when not summer, this café is always packed with tourists thinking they are going to feel the presence of that old drunk American author of yours who was wise enough to live in Paris for some time."

Gibson had noticed a lot of Asians and Americans in the café when scanning the room for Nivelle. The Americans in the room were blatantly obvious in their baseball hats, baggy clothing, and loud voices. He remembered Parker told him once that there was always a great exodus of locals leaving Paris during the month of August for vacations.

"Old drunk American author?" Gibson questioned.

Nivelle rolled his eyes in response. "*Quel con*," he responded, shaking his head in disgust. It is not surprising that you Americans do not even know one of the finest authors your country has ever produced. This café used to be a favorite place of Ernest Hemingway when he lived here." Nivelle didn't pronounce the *h*, so the author's last name came out as *Emingway*.

Gibson felt like kicking himself for not knowing that one. Rachel would have known. And although he had never been much of reader, he recalled enjoying the few books he had read by Hemingway, despite not caring for the author's political views.

He wanted to say something clever in response and not let Nivelle think he'd gotten to him. "Ah, Hemingway. But clearly that was long before this place was popular with tourists. Otherwise, he would have stayed far away."

Nivelle's smirk twitched slightly, indicating recognition of a counterattack. He changed the subject. "Would you like to order something? Since this place is such a favorite of Americans, they even serve American style coffee."

Back on the attack, Gibson said to himself. "How's American style coffee?" he asked, pulling out a chair from the table and seating himself.

Nivelle sat back down. "American style coffee is weaker coffee served in big, how do Americans say...*mugs*, with lots of milk. This is a style of coffee some French children enjoy."

As Nivelle spoke, a young, pretty waitress wearing a loose blouse and short skirt walked up to their table carrying a notepad and pen. "Excuse me, sir, would you like to order anything?" she asked Gibson.

Nivelle started to speak in French to the waitress, no doubt ordering him an American style coffee, whatever the hell that was, before Gibson interrupted him. "I'll have an espresso. *Merci*," he said.

Nivelle's gaze turned from the waitress to Gibson with a look of mild appreciation. "*Alors*, *Monsieur* Gibson, I see that it is not true that one cannot teach new tricks to an old dog."

Gibson was about to correct Nivelle's misphrasing, but decided not to. What he really wanted to do was tell the arrogant French prick to go to hell, but he also decided against this course. Nivelle knew something about Sebastian Parker, and, like it or not, Gibson needed Nivelle.

At least for now.

The tension between them was palpable, as always. Gibson figured this was caused by a combination of mutual respect and a shared sense of competition. Similar to competitive athletes, no one wanted to admit that someone else was better at their craft. The same held true for busting criminals. If he was going to get anywhere with this guy, he needed to lighten the mood.

"Listen, let's start over. How have you been, Nivelle?" Gibson asked, attempting a friendlier tone.

Nivelle momentarily eyed him suspiciously as he raised his small espresso cup to his lips. He tilted his head back and took the espresso shot like a shot of whiskey. His demeanor became noticeably more relaxed. He shrugged his shoulders in the manner that only someone born in France could do and replied, "*Vous savez, c'est fou comme toujours.*" As he spoke he puffed his mouth and exhaled, another mannerism Gibson believed only a French person could do. "Oh, *pardon*. I forgot for a moment that you do not speak French," Nivelle added.

"I don't speak much, I admit. But I've come to learn a little and can understand some. For instance, I understood that you said something about things being crazy as always."

Another look of mild admiration appeared on Nivelle's face. "At times, you have a way of impressing me, Agent Gibson." He let a moment linger before repeating, "At times."

The waitress returned and placed a saucer with a small porcelain espresso cup in front of Gibson. "If you're so busy, how do you have time to meet an American for coffee?"

"You Americans never cease to amaze me. You think you have life so much figured out and that your way, your fast food and being in a rush all the time and all *cette merde* is the only way. But you do not recognize the truly important things in life."

"Such as?"

"Such as making time for a coffee with someone. Such as making time to step away from your little computer screen and get outside during the middle of the day and smell the air and feel the sun on your face and have real food for your *dejeuner* instead of some fast food *merde* at your desk."

Gibson slowly sipped his espresso, drinking half of the small cup. The coffee was strong and dark and delicious. "So you believe you French have figured out the secrets to life then?"

Nivelle shook his head. "No secrets—*secret*." He raised two fingers and touched them slowly together to demonstrate his point. "More than anyone else in the world, we French respect the importance of one appreciating life every day. Not just after work. Not just at *les week-ends*. Not just during *les vacances*. But every day. We still take time to take a break during the work day to have a coffee with a colleague, or to have lunch with our wives. And we know and respect the importance of having good, real food, and to have good, real wine. You Americans, you don't seem to understand how important this is to life. These are all essential elements of what it is to be French."

"And it works?"

"*Mais, bien sûr*, it works! Look at us. We have one of the longest life…oh *merde*, what is the word." Nivelle then raised his hands in accomplishment as if he just scored a goal. "Life expectancies in the world. Unlike you Americans who live your stressful lives eating bad food and drinking Budweiser and have massive *crises cardiaques* in your fifties and die. You don't know how to live, *mon Dieu*!" Nivelle had partially risen while speaking, and Gibson thought he would stand on top of his chair and start singing the French national anthem.

I wish Parker could be here to see this, Gibson thought.

"You don't even know how to take time to be with women like we French do. And when you have sex you just jump right. Here in France we prolong the moment to gain even more satisfaction. Why do you think our women spend so much money on lingerie?" Nivelle slyly said as he watched their waitress crossing the room.

"Hey, we don't know each other that much, pal," Gibson said out loud.

Nivelle shrugged his shoulders heavily and blew air out of his mouth, making his top lip tremble. "You Americans are such puritans. Afraid to talk about sex. Afraid to show the woman's breast in your magazines or on your televisions."

Gibson felt like pointing out that the whole French puff, as he called it, when the French blew air forcefully out of their mouths and made their lips vibrate, was the mannerism of an infant.

Just keep Sebastian in mind. Nivelle said he was in some sort of trouble.

He bit his tongue, literally, and grinned. "Yes, you are probably right, Nivelle. Americans need to learn how to live better."

"Like the French." Nivelle raised a finger to exemplify his point.

You are really pushing it, Frenchy…

Gibson bit his tongue a little harder. "Yes, like the French."

Nivelle smiled as widely as Gibson had ever witnessed. Nivelle slammed a hand down on the table and exclaimed, "*Formidable*! We agree on something!" Although his hand slam and voice were loud, no one surrounding them even appeared to notice.

"Now, let us get to the matter at hand," he suggested after composing himself.

Gibson felt his pulse quicken. "Yes, Sebastian Parker."

Nivelle flashed his trademark smirk, undoubtedly contemplating how much Parker meant to Gibson. To his credit though, he did not. Most likely because he'd capitulated on the whole French way of life thing, Gibson thought.

"Yes, Monsieur Parker. A young man pulled between different worlds. And now one of those worlds may betray him."

"Which world?"

"*Eh bien*, clearly not the American one. And I am happy to say not the French one. No, *mon brave*, his Basque world has placed him in serious danger."

"How so?" Gibson quickly countered.

"By marrying into a family *légaux*."

"I may recognize a French word here or there, Nivelle. But you're going to have to help me out on that one."

"This is the word we use to describe ETA collaborators who are unknown to police forces, living normal lives, except, in this case, we know his *belle-mère* is a strong supporter of Basque nationalism, including the movement's radical front."

"Bell mare?"

Nivelle smirked at Gibson's botchery of the word. "His *belle-mère*. His mother-in-law. I would also say his father-in-law, but Parker would have never met him. He was killed under particular circumstances in 1986. I doubt Parker is even aware of this."

"Particular circumstances?"

"You have to understand, the mid-1980s was a volatile time for the Basque radicals, on both sides of the border, in France as much as in Spain. I personally experienced this madness. There were various groups, ETA, IK, Irrintzi, and for once they actually functioned together, which has not happened much in the history of the—" Nivelle paused to absently wave a hand "—so-called *Basque movement.* And the GAL was operating in France in full force. Everything was *absolument fou.* I know, because I was stationed there at the time in charge of tracking ETA members hiding in France. And all these groups were very dangerous. I almost lost one of my best men. A man named Caudet. Almost killed during an attempted car bombing meant for me."

"I'm sorry to hear about the injury to your man," Gibson genuinely offered, having nearly lost and indeed lost colleagues in the line of the duty during his law enforcement career. "Of course, I know ETA and remember discussing IK in the French Basque Country, but the other one is new to me." Gibson also didn't recognize Nivelle's reference to something called *the GAL*, but this didn't seem as important. He made a note to ask Parker about the GAL.

"*Irrintzi.* This is the name of the annoying Basque war cry of theirs. But this was also the name for a splinter group devoted to stopping tourism projects and the selling of traditional Basque houses to wealthy foreigners to use as holiday homes. They called these acts the ridiculous name of *folklorice.* They were opposed to anything related to tourism, such as TGV connections to the French Basque Country." Recognizing Gibson hadn't picked up on the TGV comment, Nivelle added, "TGV is our high speed rail network. They tried many times, and succeeded on a few occasions, in destroying portions of the track."

"From what I've seen in my time down there, they didn't exactly do a bang-up job stopping tourism," Gibson remarked.

"Yes and no. Places such as Biarritz and Saint-Jean-de-Luz have been attracting the rich and famous for centuries. But during this time, high profile tourist projects were either stopped or were severely altered. One of our most famous chefs, Alain Ducasse, was behind a major restaurant resort project on the Basque coast in Bidarray, but after running into major opposition, including repeated bombings of his site, he pulled out."

Gibson noted how Nivelle spoke of this chef as one would a movie star in the States.

"The resort was eventually built, but never how Ducasse had planned the project," Nivelle continued.

Gibson held up both of his hands, needing a time out. "Wait, what's all this have to do with Parker's deceased father-in-law?"

"It is known that his deceased *beau-père,* Claude Etxegaraya, was a member of Irrintzi. He was killed by a car bomb left in front of a tourism office in central Bayonne. The assumption is that the bomb went off while he was arming the device, but we do not know exactly what happened. All we know is that a bomb detonated within the vehicle with him still inside. The explosion blew the hell out of the entire front of the tourism office."

Gibson was confused. "But I thought all these Basque groups turned such people into martyrs for their cause?"

Nivelle appeared mildly impressed again and held up one finger. "*Précisément,* Agent Gibson. You are *absolument* correct. Normally, his photograph would have been plastered on the sides of buildings and they would carry signs in the streets with his image as part of his funeral procession *et toute cette merde.* Normally his wife would have held his ashes in some sort of vessel above her head as a symbol for one of their own dying for their beloved cause. But none of this happened with Etxegaraya. He simply was no longer in the picture." Nivelle raised his hands in front of his face and extended them outward with a puff of air to demonstrate his point. "This is why I say that the circumstances of his death were particular. And the girl's uncle, her mother's own brother, was a prominent ETA operative. He was killed in Biarritz by an unknown assassin. Probably a member of the GAL."

"While this is all interesting, what does it have to do with a potential threat to Parker today?"

Nivelle slowly lifted a hand. "Patience, *mon brave,* patience. We are getting there."

That was the second time Nivelle called him that—*mon brave.* Gibson would have to ask Parker about that one again. He hoped the expression wasn't an insult.

"While it was known that Etxegaraya was a very active member in Irrintzi, the activities of his *belle-mère,* Zurina Etxegaraya, are far less certain. And as you know, any of these Basque movements have always included women on a near equal basis as men, a testament to the original socialist roots of the movement."

"Brothers and sisters in arms," Gibson commented.

"*Exactement.* And she may have been more dangerous than her husband, as many believe she was in charge of logistics for relocating and hiding ETA operatives in France."

"Wow, impressive. Reminds me of our Graciana."

The mention of Graciana Etceverria clearly agitated Nivelle. He became visibly tense and raised a hand to signal the waitress. When she arrived, he ordered two *pressions*, which Gibson remembered was the word for draft beer in France.

"I do not wish to speak of that little *salope* right now."

"But don't you think you should track her down one of these days?" Gibson provoked.

"*Je vous dis, NON!*"

Gibson wanted to inquire more, but decided against after seeing how worked up Nivelle had grown when he mentioned Graciana. Must be the hypercompetitive nature coming out in Nivelle having to admit that he was never able to catch her in their previous collaborative investigation. Had to be. Unless maybe there was something else?

Two tall glasses of beer suddenly were set in front of them. Nivelle quickly grabbed one, touched the glass against the other, said *santé*, and took a long drink. After swallowing, Nivelle closed his eyes and took a few deep breaths. When he opened his eyes, he appeared calm and collected.

"Beer in the morning right after coffee," Gibson observed as he grabbed the other glass.

"Welcome back to France, Agent Gibson," Nivelle said with a wide grin and outstretched arms.

Gibson took a slow drink. The beer was crisp, full bodied, and delicious. Not so bad being back in France, he had to admit. But he was here for a purpose. His last investigative adventure in California may have begun as such, but this time things were different. This time he was beginning with a clear purpose.

"But I thought you said something about this family being unknown to the police?"

"You see, ETA logistics operators were some of their most secretive assets. The reason they were so effective for so many years was because no one really knew who they were, not even other ETA members. So while we are very certain his mother-in-law was one of these people, this was never proven and she has never been charged. But we believe she was tied to the elite commando unit called *Biscaye*. In more recent years, she has taken on a new role, a public role, as a spokesperson for the Basque nationalist movement."

What a family to marry into. "So she's never been convicted of anything?" Gibson asked.

"No, but that does not mean she is innocent. And your young friend married into a very volatile situation."

Suddenly the thought occurred to Gibson that he didn't realize Sebastian and Alaitz had actually been married. The last he knew, they were still planning a wedding.

Another thing to ask Sebastian.

"Why volatile if she's only a public spokesperson?" he asked.

"Volatile because she now openly advocates an end to systematic violence in the name of Basque nationalism. Perhaps losing her husband changed her mind, or having a daughter, or who knows, but the fact is that she took a dramatic turn in her views on the Basque movement."

"Okay, but sounds like she made this turn some time ago. Why so relevant now?"

"As you undoubtedly are aware, ETA declared a permanent ceasefire in 2011 after a regional summit in San Sebastian involving mediators such as Kofi Annan. This time appears to have been legitimate."

"However?" Gibson inquired.

"However, ETA did not state in their ceasefire that they would lay down their arms. This piece of the puzzle seems to have been overlooked all these years as the violence has stopped. But this does not mean that at any moment the violence could not start again. In years past, ETA used ceasefires to reenlist and rearm until they decided to start again."

"Yes, but 2011...that's getting to be a long time now. Don't you believe it's possible that this time the ceasefire is legitimate?"

Nivelle was quick to answer. "No, history has proven that ETA is never to be trusted, in Spain or in France. I have never believed they were going to stop. Possibly the primary players grew tired of the fight in 2011 and gave up, but that does not mean that there were no others who disagreed and were ready to keep their dream alive. Frankly, I am surprised they have been quiet this long."

"Do you have proof?"

"*Non*, not exactly. But I have enough evidence to believe that something is about to happen. There has always been the potential for some small group to form which could do something to reignite the entire movement. We have been monitoring the situation very carefully, but with the passage of time, it is possible that we have not been able to track everything. And, as I mentioned before, ETA deliberately left this door open when they declared their ceasefire, but did not agree to a plan to lay down their arms. I have always believed that it was only a matter of time."

"And so you think that the position of Parker's mother-in-law on an end to violence endangers him?"

"The facts that he is ex-CIA and that he's married into an important Basque family are no secrets. Many believe he still works for the CIA."

"Hold it right there," Gibson firmly instructed, holding up a hand. "Not true, Nivelle. I know for a fact."

Nivelle shrugged. "All the same, what is fact or not does not matter. What is important is perception, and most people still see him as a threat...and a target."

"A target?"

"*Mais oui, bien sûr*. A high profile target. If he were to be killed, this would be a motivational calling for a rebirth of the radical and violent Basque independence movement. And if this were to be coordinated to take out his mother-in-law too, this would be an even grander statement."

Gibson felt his pulse quickening. "And how certain are you that they are targets?"

Nivelle held up his hands. "I tell you this out of respect for you. I recognize that you are not here on official business, so there is a limit to how much I can tell you. All I can say at the moment is that your young friend is in danger, and the wisest decision would be for him to leave the Basque Country. *Franchement*, the wisest move would be for him to return home."

Gibson shook his head. "You don't understand. To Parker, the Basque Country is his home. Where he was born doesn't matter. He's home there."

Nivelle puffed once again, causing his lower lip to tremble. "That is not wise, but if that is what he wishes, *c'est la vie*."

"So what exactly are you advising me to do?"

"You should travel to the *sud-ouest*. Find out if *Monsieur* Parker suspects anything. Ask him if he has noticed any new faces around the village where he lives. Ask him about his *belle-mère*. Ask him about his wife and his wife's relationship with her mother. Ask him—"

Gibson cut him off. "Hold on there, Nivelle. Sure sounds like you're trying to give me orders, and as you pointed out earlier: I'm not here on official business."

The Nivelle smirk reappeared. "*Comme vous voulez*, John Gibson. But remember, I am trying to help you and Sebastian Parker."

"I appreciate that. I do." Gibson stood up and extended his hand. "Thank you for the intel. I'll get down there and be in touch with what I can uncover. In the meantime, if you happen to learn of anything new that you are able to share, *unofficially* with me, I trust you will do so."

Nivelle stood up and shook his hand. "*Bonne chance, mon brave*."

"You know, as much as we've been through, we could probably be on a first name basis by now," Gibson suggested after realizing that he honestly did not know Nivelle's first name.

Nivelle's only response was to flash his smirk.

The French.

Although he was anxious to head south after parting ways with Nivelle, John Gibson realized the hour was already midday. The trip down to the Basque Country would take a half-day, and since he was planning to surprise Parker anyway, he didn't want to show up at night.

He decided to find a small hotel in the Saint-Germain-des-Prés district, as he was already there after meeting with Nivelle. He planned to leave for the southwest in the morning. He was tired from the overnight travel and the thought of lying down in his hotel room was tempting after taking a hot shower, but he remembered something Sebastian Parker had told him about international travel. Instead of giving into exhaustion and sleeping, thus getting off of a normal day and night schedule, the better thing to do was to push yourself as long as possible. So Gibson decided he would walk the streets of Paris until he could walk no more.

It was hot and humid, but nothing like the DC summer heat he remembered from the decades he'd lived there. Living in San Francisco, one could easily forget what a real summer day felt like. But the legitimate summer weather didn't bother him too much. He changed out of the button-up shirt and pants he'd been wearing since leaving San Francisco and put on a pair of khakis and a polo shirt.

Wandering the streets of Paris didn't sound like such a bad way to spend an afternoon, although an even better situation would be to have Rachel by his side.

V.

Perpignan, France

ALMOST A GOOD PLACE to be, thought Garikotz Auzmendi. *Almost.* Not quite France. Not quite Spain. Similar to his hometown of Hondarribia across the Bidasoa River from the town of Hendaye in France, the French city of Perpignan is near the border with Spain. Both areas are on the water, one on the Atlantic Bay of Biscay, the other on the Mediterranean Sea. Both are on the fringe of the Pyrenees Mountains, at the opposite ends of the range. But only one of these areas was his home, as only one of these areas is in the Basque Country.

And it was not Perpignan.

Unlike Perpignan, Hondarribia had resisted a lengthy siege. That happened in the year 1638. A century and a half later, they were not so fortunate, as the city succumbed to the overwhelming force of the French Revolutionary Army in 1792. But Garikotz couldn't completely hate the French for destroying a large part of his hometown at that time, which they did by blowing up nearly all of the city's former surrounding medieval ramparts, sacrificing only one section. After all, they were merely following the voice of their own revolutionary cause, and that was something he had to respect. And soon thereafter, the French returned across the river and stayed there. Even with a short occupation, Hondarribia remained itself. Even when the French tried renaming the city *Fontarrabi.*

But throughout its history, Perpignan had wavered between identities. Although once a Roman settlement, the medieval town of Perpignan really began to shape the future city in the tenth century. Since then, the territory including Perpignan had changed hands between the Spanish, as capital of the Kingdom of Majorca and later part of the territory of Barcelona, and the French when King Louis XI attacked and annexed the city in 1463. The city famously later revolted in a violent uprising against French rule after ten years, but after a long siege by French forces the uprising was quelled. However, twenty years later, a new French king, Charles VIII, returned Perpignan to Spanish rule in a conciliatory gesture. Yet during Europe's destructive Thirty Years' War, the French besieged and captured Perpignan yet again in 1642, ending over one hundred and fifty years of Spanish rule. Another seventeen years had to pass for the territory to officially be ceded by Spain to France, but since that time the city had remained within France.

Perpignan suffered from a perpetual identity crisis. As did Garikotz Auzmendi.

Born to a Spanish mother and a Basque father from the other side of the river from Hondarribia, raised in the Spanish Basque Country within the greater Basque Country, a stone's throw away from the border with France...self-identity had always been a challenge for Garikotz. And it didn't help that his full name was Garikotz-Ernesto Auzmendi, the Ernesto part having been handed down from his grandmother, rumored to have been *friendly* with the American writer Ernest Hemingway while he stayed in Hondarribia at the castle, now a hotel, but once a tenth century fortress. Local lore held that Hemingway wrote the majority of his novel *The Sun Also Rises* while staying at the castle. Local lore also suggested that the author found special comfort in the company of a Hondarribia *señorita*...and that señorita was, according to the tales, his grandmother.

Although he had mixed feelings about his grandmother consorting with an American, he had no mixed feelings concerning her choice of men. Garikotz had read *The Sun Also Rises* several times throughout his life and admired the author's ability to portray vibrant scenes and situations, such as those found everywhere and every day throughout the Basque Country, in simple, approachable words and sentences.

Garikotz had never been able to find much ability in fictional writing, but he considered himself an intellectual. He had a dual degree in cultural studies and history from the University of the Basque Country in Bilbao, spoke seven languages (Basque, Spanish, French,

Portuguese, Italian, English, and German), and was a frequent author of political articles on affairs in the Basque Country. Prior to being banned by the Spanish government in 2003, he was Batasuna's, the nationalist party's, primary voice, albeit under pseudonym.

If not for the anonymous publishing name, he would have undoubtedly been jailed with the rest of the party's leaders for having been found supporting a terrorist group, as the Spanish labeled Batasuna the political wing of ETA. He had to admit that the allegation was not entirely untrue. After all, Batasuna would never condemn violence conducted by ETA in the name of achieving Basque independence. But the Spanish fascists had no right to ban and outlaw political parties. Outrageously, they had done so, and done so in full view for the world to witness. The world seemed to see Spain as a glowing beacon of democracy in the post-Franco era, but fact was that Spain was far from *glowing* and the world only wanted to see Spain this way, as anything was improvement over the terror that Franco inflicted. And that terror was felt more harshly than in any other region of Spain than the Basque Country.

Even speaking the Basque language was outlawed. And punishable. This was something the policing forces had no problem enforcing.

But that was the past. The present was that the Basque Country, at least the Spanish Basque Country, now had some level of autonomy within Spain. The Basques were allowed to elect their own ruling parliament, collect their own taxes, provide their own police force, and speak their own language. But it was not enough.

Even if the Spanish side had some autonomy, the Basque Country was still occupied by imperialistic powers and divided into parts of Spain and France.

"When we stop to eat?" a pudgy Chinese tourist interrupted Garikotz as he was in the middle of describing the city's uprising against French rule in 1473.

A few women huddled around the man asking the question, nodding their heads in agreement.

Garikotz was perplexed. *Not even an hour on the tour so far—how can these people possibly be hungry already?*

Normally he only conducted tours for high profile groups, not this current group of Chinese tourists who booked through a third-party budget tour reservation company. That tour organizer contacted his company for the day-long city tour job. But neither of his two young tour guides, history students at the University of Perpignan, were available to do the tour. As owner of the company, Garikotz was left with no other option than to do the tour himself or pass on the job.

The two women flanking the apparently starving man raised hands to their open mouths. The translator they'd brought with them, a young man Garikotz guessed to be in his early twenties, roughly a third of the average age of the thirty person group, leaned in closely to Garikotz. "*Monsieur*, please, they are very hungry," he said in crisp English.

When he first encountered the group, pouring groggily out of their oversized charter bus, Garikotz was told the bus had been driven overnight from Nice. He informed the group's translator that he preferred to be called *Seignior* over *Monsieur*, but the translator clearly hadn't understood.

Garikotz tried not to show his annoyance. Although it was normal while conducting tours to feel as if part of the group was not paying attention, he found Asian groups to be particularly challenging. Not too long ago, the majority of his tour groups were Germans. Old, young, middle-age—the Germans didn't seem to mind traveling together, as long as they were all German. The German groups may have been particular at times, wanting a precise schedule of a tour's planned stops and time duration at each place, but being meticulous and punctual were not characteristics that normally bothered tour guides. Demanding and high maintenance groups were far more difficult.

But German groups were becoming less and less, and Asian groups were becoming more and more. There had always been some Japanese groups mixed in with the rest, but in recent years, most of the time the Chinese and South Korean groups dominated the tour industry in Perpignan. And from what he heard from other tour operators, the same was true throughout all of France and Spain. Garikotz didn't mind the Asian groups, as any good tour operator needed to have patience and understanding to serve all nationalities, but year after year, he missed the Germans more.

There were even fewer American groups these days, and he didn't mind leading a herd of loud overweight cowboys in baseball hats around every now and again. Especially today he wouldn't mind. The Americans may have been loud and obnoxious at times, but they at least followed orders.

His group today had spent more time breaking away to take photographs with their cell phones or cameras than listening to him or the translator. And after walking under two kilometers, now they were apparently on the verge of succumbing to starvation, even though before beginning the walking tour of the city, Garikotz had asked to confirm that the elderly group had eaten breakfast. Garikotz saw older people in a similar light as children. They needed to be fed or they would start complaining. But this early start to the complaints surprised him.

"Fine, we will rest here for five minutes," Garikotz said. He spoke in English at the request of the translator, who told him that most of the group had some English language capacity. They appeared to understand his capitulation. No translation needed. Before the translator even began speaking to convey the instructions into Mandarin, a ripple effect had started among the group, and they eagerly reached for their backpacks to pull out bags of snacks.

As he observed the group separating to find a place to sit around the center of the Place de la Republique where they'd stopped, he noted the food items the Chinese people ate. The spread was an odd assortment of what looked like dried fish products, small sausages, buns, and hot tea poured from liquid containers. The French in particular were known for the variety of options they would include as typical *casse-croûte* items such as this, but this was more than a light snack. The Chinese group was eating a serious late breakfast or early lunch. He watched as they stuffed their faces with the contents of a bag one of them was holding while still searching for the next bag to raid.

Like children, Garikotz thought. *But what do I really know of children?* Now in his late forties, Garikotz had no children and had never been married. He considered his continual devotion to the cause his only spouse and only child.

Although this hadn't always been so.

Nearly thirty years ago, things were very different, and he would have never imagined that he would spend the rest of his life working a cover job as a tour guide operator in Perpignan, so far from the Basque Country. Back then, in the mid-1980s, Izaskun was nearly as important to his life as his commitment to seeing a fully independent Basque Country.

Izaskun.

Even now, with so many years in between, he felt the bite of saying her name to himself. It had been the most difficult decision of his life to turn away a future with a wife and family in exchange for a life with purpose. But he never doubted that he made the correct decision.

Staying with Izaskun would have only complicated matters, and would have increased the risk of both of them being discovered by Spanish, or later, French police. Back then, she was as radicalized as he was, and together they were the very symbol of Basque strength and tenacity. He was the voice of a movement. She was one of movement's best assassins.

They lived in refuge on the other side of the border, in the French Basque Country in the city of Bayonne. For years, the French Basque Country had been a safe haven for Basque political exiles such as themselves. They could live in relative security and still carry out their activities. For Garikotz, this involved many days seated in their apartment on Rue des Tonneliers in Petit Bayonne in front of a typewriter. For Izaskun, this time involved forays across the border into Spain to carry out missions, often returning to France by way of ancient Basque trails passing through the Pyrenees. Everything was good and the movement was at its height.

Then came the GAL. The so-called secret army covertly enlisted by the Spanish government to hunt down ETA members in France.

At that time, everything changed. The French Basque Country, or anywhere in France, was no longer safe territory. The actions of the GAL changed all that.

With their security shattered, Garikotz began to realize they would never be able to retreat to a countryside *baserri* to raise a family. Izaskun liked to talk about such a future as they drank patxaran and smoked hand-rolled cigarettes on the roof of their apartment building and looked down on the normal weekend rambunctiousness going on below in the streets of Petit Bayonne.

As the GAL intensified its actions, with unstoppable targeting and killing of Basque nationalist exiles in France, certain things became abundantly clear. Izaskun had to leave Western Europe. Together they would represent a more difficult target to conceal wherever they went. Gariktoz would no longer be able to make his contribution to ETA, to the cause.

This was long before the time of computers and internet and cell phones. In the mid-1980s, current global news was still limited and communication was challenging. A week, at minimum, would be required for a written piece Garikotz sent from South America to reach Spain or France, and the cause needed much faster turnaround if his work would retain and reflect the support and pulse of the people.

And so, Izaskun went into exile in Argentina.

Garikotz stayed.

They never spoke again.

Garikotz still had the long, straight hair, round-frame glasses, and slender build of his youth. But everything was different. He was sickened by how the primary core of ETA had given up.

No rest until independence.

But hope remained. Patxi Irionda represented the figurehead of that hope.

Garikotz had no real desire to kill anyone himself; he never had. But he had no moral qualms about others killing in the name of the Basque cause. The people that would die would merely be casualties of war. That was all. ETA may have been down, but not out.

And ETA was no terrorist organization. ETA was an army fighting for the freedom of its land and people. Always had been. Just as ETA was still at war with the Spanish and French governments.

No rest until independence.

The French had not always been a target for ETA, but after the GAL, the French were no longer allies or even complacent hosts. As long as they continued to collaborate with the fascist Spanish government, they were also the enemy of ETA.

And once they were back, once they announced their rebirth with such a show of force, there was no doubt that ETA would see a total resurgence in new members wanting to join the struggle. Garikotz was no fool with a cause. Unlike others, he knew the difference between rhetoric and reality. And the reality was that membership in the organization and numerous associated groups was far below historical highs.

A fool he was not, but he did have a cause. And he was not going to stand by and watch the Basque movement die a slow and agonizing death while succumbing to the encroaching imperialist powers of Spain and France.

The real fools were the so-called leaders of ETA in 2011. *What the hell were they thinking at that fucking San Sebastian conference*?

ETA's membership may have been down after the fascist governments of Spain and France collaborated to arrest and imprison so many, but Basque nationalist sentiment was still as high as ever. Garikotz admitted that with all of the arrests slicing apart ETA ranks at the time, a point could be made to consider other options. *But fully surrender*? That was absurd. And unacceptable.

Of course, those so-called leaders at the time left a back door open, in theory, by delicately saying that they were not completely committed to laying down their arms, even if they were declaring a permanent ceasefire. But it was a bitch move. Nothing but a feeble attempt to save face within the ETA organization. It was even more a bitch move because those who called themselves leaders clearly never intended to raise arms again. Now, years later, nothing had happened except for the Basque movement to continue a disappearing act, more and more every year.

That would soon change.

"*Monsieur! Monsieur*! We are ready to go," the young Chinese translator impatiently said to him.

Garikotz nodded his head, accepting his duty and confronting his fate.

Fuck Kofi Annan and his damn San Sebastian peace conference. This thought made him smile. The prospect of his immediate future seemed more bearable.

VI.

Biarritz, French Basque Country

PATXI, GARIKOTZ, ITXASO—they all thought Aitzol Rubina was a fool for refusing to ever leave Biarritz. Patxi, in particular, always gave him a hard time whenever he had the chance to tell him that he was putting their group at risk by staying in such a high profile place. But he disagreed. He may not have been as smart as Garikotz or as clever as Patxi, but he realized something they did not seem to understand.

By staying in Biarritz instead of hiding out in some tiny village somewhere, or moving to another region like Gariktotz, or going to another country like Itxaso or Patxi, he was actually lowering his risk of looking suspicious. Instead of running or trying to keep a low profile in the countryside, he was living his life as he always had: free and completely in the open.

And his life was just what he loved: food, beer, rugby, and women—though not necessarily in that order. But even in his late forties, Aitzol could kick the asses of kids half his age up and down the rugby field and then drink them under the table at the bars in Petit Bayonne.

He never went out hard-core drinking in Biarritz though. His nights out in Biarritz were reserved for one thing and one thing only: picking up and banging the hell out of foreign chicks.

Aitzol had nothing against women, not at all. He loved women. He loved them so much, he could never even think of spending his life with just one. *Why would anyone want to ever do that?*

But he hated foreigners. Always had. Growing up in Biarritz, there was no escaping the masses of foreigners that invaded the city and greater Basque Coast every summer. The Parisians were bad too, but at least they were French, for the most part. But the foreigners, they were the ones that bothered him most. The snotty British, the loud Americans, the bitchy Russians, the stubborn Germans, the crazy Swedish. From childhood he'd grown to hate them all equally. They came in summer and thought they owned everything, forgetting they were only visitors. They clogged the roads with traffic and filled all the cafés and restaurants.

Foreigners also crowded the beaches, especially the Grande Plage. But Aitzol didn't mind their presence there. For some reason, young foreign woman visiting France thought every woman in France always went topless at the beach. He was glad that myth stayed alive. Perhaps because after foreigners returned to their homes from a holiday in France, they told everyone about topless French women on the beach, or showed photos they discreetly took with their cell phones and posted on their *putain* social media sites. Yet, ironically, aside from a few old French women who didn't mind letting their sagging breasts hang in the open, the majority of the topless women they'd seen were really other foreigners.

No matter. If the dumb foreign *meufs* wanted to show off their *nichons*, he was more than okay with seeing bared perky breasts. At times he could even pick up women straight from the beach and take them back to his place in downtown Biarritz. He was not the most handsome of men, and a lifetime of playing rugby left his nose battered and a little crooked, but he was muscular without a gut, still had all his dark hair, and had the darker complexion of a true Basque. His greatest asset, though, when picking up women, was his practiced overpronounced French accent when he spoke English. At times, he only had to utter a few words and he could almost see their legs opening for him.

Not long after, they would learn the meaning of the legendary Basque strength as he relentlessly rammed into them while they cried out: *Yes! Ja! Da!*

Women and rugby kept him occupied, but his devotion to ETA gave him purpose. Thank God for Patxi, he often said to himself. Without Patxi, there would be nothing after the cowards gave up. Patxi may not have been a rugby player, but he had *couilles*, and having balls was something Aitzol respected in any man. Actually, he could even respect women who apparently had *couilles*, such as Itxaso, but that was a different matter.

Patxi Irionda had brought them back into the fight, and Aitzol believed every word Patxi said. They would be a spark for the entire movement to regain momentum, regroup, and take the fight back to the streets. No, no mere spark. Their announcement back into the fight would be a fucking explosion that no one in France, Spain, or the entire world could ignore.

The way Aitzol saw it was in comparison to a rugby match. Up until the so-called ceasefire had only been the first half of the rugby contest that was ETA's fight for total Basque independence; the time since the ridiculous ceasefire was a long half-time, too long of one. But now was time for the second half of the match. The second half would end in ETA's victory.

Garikotz always had some fancy names to call the Spanish and French governments, such as the *imperialist occupying forces*, or some other term.

Aitzol just saw them as bastard foreign invaders. And bastard foreign invaders needed to be beaten back.

He was aware that the reality was that they would never be able to expel all the foreign invaders from Basque lands. Garikotz had some elaborate explanation for why this, unfortunately, would never be possible. But as Garikotz and everyone else truly devoted to the cause knew, achieving full independence was no unreachable dream. They just needed the right person to lead the way. That person was Patxi Irionda.

Aitzol remembered the last time the entire group of them had gathered for a meeting at a remote hunting cabin in the Pyrenees. At that meeting, Garikotz had gone off for a long time on how one of the faults of the previous leadership of the organization had been too many leaders—a leader of military operations, a leader of logistics, a leader of recruiting, but never one true leader. Now ETA would have that leader.

And Aitzol was anxious to return to what he'd been trained to do decades ago. Older or not, he knew he could still kick some ass and was more than willing to kill for the cause. In the mid-1980s, he'd been tagged at a young age to become not only an enforcer within the organization, but also an assassin.

At that time, fear swept through the French Basque Country as the GAL operated without restraint during the Dirty War, murdering ETA partisans on French soil, at times right under the nose of the French security forces, who should have been protecting refugees in their land from being executed in their streets.

But they didn't.

Basque refugees were murdered on the streets in broad daylight. Executions were carried out in the middle of popular tourist areas with French police and gendarmes within the immediate vicinity of attacks. Yet those same French police forces were never able to capture any of the GAL assassins. It was all such *putain merde*.

The GAL—the *Grupos Antiterroristas de Liberación*—the Antiterrorist Liberation Groups, was what they called themselves. But they should have just called themselves what they were and what everyone knew they were: death squads. These death squads were illegally financed by the Spanish government to hunt and kill ETA partisans and other Basque separatists in France. From the early 1980s until 1987, they reigned unrestrained terror until the cowardly French government capitulated to what everyone seemed to forget was state-sponsored terrorism and began arresting and imprisoning Basque exiles who had for decades found legal refuge across the border from Spain in France.

But in 1987, attacks by the GAL suddenly stopped. And this happened just as Aitzol was gaining ground on tracking down the most infamous GAL assassin of them all—the *woman in black*. The *putain salope* disappeared from the scene just as mysteriously as she had entered. This cold-blooded killer, rumored to be French and possibly even French-Basque, and reputed to have carried out more assassinations during this time than any other GAL operative, was never identified.

Almost thirty years later, she still had not been.

Aitzol was trained as an anti-assassin. His charge to hunt down and kill the killers before they were able to execute any more Basques. But he had strict instructions to not cross the border into Spain. The ETA leadership wanted certain members to never again cross the border in order to restrict possible identification by the Spanish government's security forces in Spain. This was long before the internet facilitating people searches or hand-held phones able to quickly take high quality pictures. Back then, it was a lot more difficult to identify someone, and the leadership wanted its promising young assassin to stay in France.

Infuriatingly, after the *putain* GAL stopped operating in France, Aitzol's mission lost importance. Due to the leadership's desire to keep more of a low profile in France to maintain as much of a safe refuge for members there as possible, even if the French government had given into the demands of the Spanish to start incarcerating Basque refugees, operatives with similar mandates, namely to carry out assassinations in France, were essentially put on hold. The leadership conveyed that they wanted to reassess ETA's presence in the northern Basque Country before reengaging in major actions in France.

For Aitzol Rubina, this meant a lot of waiting to be contacted with a mission. He anxiously waited for one, but never was given one. Years passed, and Aitzol filled his time with rugby, booze, women, and target practice high in the Pyrenees or deep in the pine forest of the Landes. Waiting for action. Waiting to prove his devotion to the cause. Waiting to show his worth.

But a mission never came.

Then, one day, Patxi Irionda called a meeting and informed a group of members, both covert and not, that the leadership decided to declare a permanent ceasefire. Clearly holding back tears of frustration, anger, disappointment, and the pain of a thousand souls departed in the name of Basque independence, Patxi told them the fight for an independent Basque homeland was over.

Thank God that Patxi had changed his mind. Thank God that Patxi had the courage and strength to continue when others had given up. Thank God for Patxi Irionda. *Eskerrak Jainkoari.*

VII.

French Basque Country

GIBSON COULD HAVE FLOWN FROM Paris to Biarritz very easily—there were multiple daily flights. But taking the train was so much more appealing. Besides, taking the train wasn't going to be much slower than flying. And the train was so easy and convenient, as he'd discovered on his previous visit to France.

After departing with Nivelle, he hopped on the Metro and was quickly at the Montparnasse train station. Just as quickly, he booked a ticket to Biarritz and was arranging himself in a comfortable windowside chair. The train compartment was clean, inviting, and spacious. Unlike on the plane ride over, his knees were not jammed against the seat in front of him. And in a relatively short time, he'd be at his destination, thanks to the modern efficiency of the French high speed passenger rail network. *If only we could figure this out in the States...*he thought for not the first time.

When the train was approaching the city of Dax station, within an hour's distance from Biarritz, he decided to call Sebastian Parker. Up until that moment the possibility hadn't occurred to him that Sebastian and his wife might not even be home. He didn't expect to stay with them. Probably wouldn't be a good idea anyway, as he was a federal law enforcement officer and, for all he knew, Parker was being watched, staying with them would draw even more attention to Parker. He knew Sebastian and Alaitz lived outside of the village of Sare, and he vaguely remembered driving through the village and the surrounding area during his last trip to the Basque Country. He figured if he was unable to reach Parker, he would get a taxi from Biarritz to some inn in the village and wait to make contact. But it would be better if could immediately reach Parker.

He navigated on his cell phone to Parker's name and pressed the "call" button. He was relieved when he heard Parker's voice answer after the second ring.

"*Quelle surprise! Comment ça va, mon vieux?*" Parker had a habit of speaking French to Gibson, knowing that Gibson had only a rudimentary understanding of the language.

The old him would have told Parker to cut that shit out, but Gibson's once steely demeanor had softened in recent years. "Hello, Parker. Do you think you can pick me up at the Biarritz train station in an hour or so?"

"Biarritz? Are you fucking serious?"

"Yup, I'm on the train now and about to reach Dax."

"Holy Jesus, Gibson! You sure do know how to catch one off guard."

"Listen, Parker, I'm sorry if this is a bad time—"

Parker cut in quickly. "Are you kidding? You could call me in the middle of the night and I'd be there for you."

Gibson felt touched. He never imagined growing so fond of Sebastian Parker. "Thanks, Parker. Good to know."

"On second thought…" Parker started to say. Gibson knew the young man enough to realize Parker was about to add some smart-ass quip. "My wife is a light sleeper and has a Basque temper like you can't believe. So it may be better in those situations to wait until morning to call."

"Noted," Gibson replied.

"So what brings you here? Not that I'm not delighted to hear from you, and, of course, I'll be at the train station."

Gibson hesitated in responding. "How about let's get to that later?"

"Ah, sounds juicy. But fine. Have it your way and keep me in suspense. I've got to get ready to drive up there to meet you anyway, and driving while talking on a cell phone is even more treacherous here than in the States."

Memories of witnessing French drivers darting in and out of traffic lanes at obscene speeds popped into John Gibson's head. No further explanation was required. "Sounds good. See you soon then."

"*À bientôt*, Gibson."

"Yes, see you soon."

"No, no. You're back here now out of the comfort of the good ol' USA. So say: *à bientôt*."

"Fine, fine. *À bientôt*, Parker."

"*À tout à l'heure*, Gibson," Parker gleefully said and hung up.

Son of a bitch, Gibson said to himself, not caring that he didn't know the French translation for the expression.

Gibson recognized Sebastian Parker standing on the platform as the train pulled into the Biarritz train station. He looked the same as the last time as he'd seen him: above-average height, slender, longish light brown hair, and youthful.

"I was beginning to wonder when I'd see you again," Parker said as Gibson stepped down from the train on the platform.

"What can I say, Sebastian. I missed you," Gibson admitted. He extended a hand to Parker. Parker shook his hand, but also put his other arm around Gibson's shoulders in a half hug.

"All right, all right, that's enough." Gibson pulled away, pretending to be annoyed. "Don't go kissing me on the cheeks or anything."

Parker stared at him for a moment without speaking. "I missed you, Gibson. It's good to see you," he eventually said.

"Good to see you too, Sebastian. Now let's get out of here. I'm starving."

Parker grinned. "Spoken like a true Frenchman. Food comes first."

Such a simple sandwich, yet so delicious and utterly fulfilling. A thin, crispy on the outside, soft and flaky on the inside baguette sliced in half with a thin slice of ham and butter. That was all. And it was delicious.

Parker said the ham was called Paris ham. But the magic of the simplistic sandwich was not just the ham. Gibson was sure French butter was somehow better than any butter in the States. Aside from the succulent ham, the bread made the difference between this sandwich and the same kind he'd order from any San Francisco deli.

"Why do baguettes never taste this good in the States?" Gibson asked. After leaving the train station in Parker's small Peugeot car, Parker stopped at a bakery on the outskirts of Biarritz. Somehow Parker always seemed to know how to find good food.

Parker shrugged and shook his head as he switched gears. "You know, that's seriously one of life's greatest mysteries, and I wish I had an answer. You can have a French *boulanger* relocate to the States and open a bakery, but somehow even they will not be able to replicate a true French baguette. I've heard said that the flour makes a difference, but that theory should be tossed out, as one can easily obtain French flour in the States these days. I honestly think it's something to do with the water. But who knows?"

"Whatever the mystery, it's definitely noticeable. Any time I get a baguette back home, my jaw gets tired from chewing." Gibson took another bite of sandwich.

Parker laughed. "Yeah, true. I just stopped trying to find a real French baguette when I was back there because I was constantly disappointed. But don't get too full from that. My wife has pledged to make you a full-blown Basque dinner tonight."

Gibson eyed the sandwich in his hands suspiciously, now wondering if finishing the whole thing was a good idea. He decided the sandwich was too good to go to waste and took another bite. Gibson was looking forward to meeting Parker's wife. He'd only seen her while Parker was recovering from the gunshot wound from a sniper in a Petit Bayonne alley. They never spoke, but her demeanor told him a lot. She was stern and would do anything for Parker. Unfortunately, if Nivelle's information was accurate, even with Alaitz's firm resolve watching over Parker, Gibson didn't believe she'd be able to protect him this time. He wanted to tell Parker the real reason for his visit, but not yet. Although his typical approach would be different, Gibson wanted to ease into the moment and wait for the proper time.

"So, before we head home, I need to drag you with me to my mother-in-law's in Saint-Jean-Pied-de-Port. Just a little out of the way and I promise it will be a short visit. She doesn't like me very much anyway, so I'm sure we can make things quick."

"Why doesn't she like you?" Gibson asked, although he recognized that Parker's manner had a way of irritating some people at times. Himself included.

"Because she's Basque and her daughter is Basque. I'm not."

"That's the only reason?"

As far as I can tell, yes. But who knows? Women are unpredictable and inexplicable most of the time to begin with, but when you add Basque temperament into the mix, things get even more complicated."

"But things are good with you and your wife?" Gibson remembered having a phone conversation with Parker months ago while he was spending time with Rachel in Carmel Valley. During that call, Parker was talking about getting married. "So when did you get married?"

Parker smiled in response. "Ah, yeah, I guess I forgot to tell you. We didn't do any formal ceremony or anything. I mean, we did—but no guests were invited. Alaitz and I hiked up to this monastery in the Pyrenees and had a Basque priest marry us on the mountainside. I'd show you pictures, but we didn't take any. We decided to keep the memory just for us."

"Sounds amazing, Parker. And congratulations."

"Yeah, it was. And thanks." Parker paused, briefly glancing out of the window at the passing landscape, which had turned from residential areas into rolling hills shortly after they were out of Biarritz. "But as for how things are between us, that's a bit more complicated. Let's save the discussion for later."

There's going to be a lot to discuss, Gibson thought. "No problem," he said. He noticed that Parker's normal cheery demeanor had become a bit sullen. "I thought you'd own your own vineyard by now," he said in an attempt to lighten the mood.

Parker laughed. "Not a bad idea, I have to say."

The next half hour of the drive passed with the two friends catching up on each other's lives. Gibson talked about his recent case turned adventure tracking down a group of affluent bank robbers in the Monterey Peninsula area of California's Central Coast and how the heist had been amazingly tied to California's Spanish colonial history. Gibson was not surprised to find Parker especially liking the historical and cultural aspects that Gibson relayed, having delved into the Monterey area's complex historical society. He left out mentioning his newly found young friend in Monterey named Isidro de la Vega—the two of them would not get along. Isidro's social awkwardness would annoy Parker. Parker's brashness would offend Isidro. He also left out having received help from Detective David Chiles in San Francisco during the investigation. Chiles and Parker had never clicked.

He told Parker of his developing relationship with Rachel Dowling. Being typical Sebastian Parker, he took his line of questioning a little too far into the personal realm, but Gibson recognized Parker meant no offense.

Gibson noted that Parker skirted around the issue of describing any more relationship details between him and his wife. Instead, Parker described his still somewhat recent Basque village and countryside life experience. After recovering from the rifle shot to his shoulder, Parker resigned from his position with the CIA and never returned to the US. Instead, he stayed in France and initially moved into an apartment with Alaitz in Bayonne, followed by buying an aging Basque farmhouse outside of the village of Sare.

"You should have seen this place when we first moved in, Gibson. It was something else. There was literally still straw on the floor in a room adjoining a kitchen where some farm animals were kept overnight during winter; typical of the old-school Basque farmhouses. "But can't complain. The fact that we even ended up with that house is a miracle."

"Why's that? Too expensive?" Gibson asked.

"That's part of the reason. And I can understand how some of the natives of the area get disgruntled about how high property values have skyrocketed in the Basque Country. Unfortunately, in many cases you can have a house that is a holiday home to some British family that only comes over a couple of times a year. The Basque villages and countryside already have emptied due to a lack of jobs, especially for young people, but adding empty vacation homes only adds to growing emptiness."

"Is this anything new?"

"Not at all. This has been going on since the 1980s. A British holiday home not far from ours was nearly burned to the ground in an attack. And back then a lot of holiday homes would be spray-painted with slogans like *The Basque Country Is Not for Sale* or *Let the Basque Country Live.*"

"Do you see it happening again?" Gibson began to feel concerned. If what Parker described was noticeably escalating, it could be an early indication of a greater awakening, one in which Nivelle sensed Sebastian Parker would find himself in grave danger.

Parker shrugged his shoulders and turned the corners of his mouth downward, proving Gibson had been wrong to assume only people actually born in France could pull off such a mannerism. "Honestly, I don't know. There've definitely been some continual antitourism attacks here and there—a busted front window of a realtor's office known to solicit foreigners, or a sign with an English translation spray-painted over with *No to Tourism.* I mean, these things are probably just done by drunk teenagers hoping for a rebirth of ETA so they can feel better about destroying things."

"Do you think that's possible? I mean, after all, the last time we dealt with something related to ETA, we had a group of young adults not much older than teenagers behind a particular brutal execution."

Parker turned his head to flash a grin. "*Touché, mon vieux.*" Parker glanced toward the rolling Basque countryside passing by. "But there's more to the issue than just rising property values, and Alaitz's mother helped us out with actually buying the house. A bigger aspect is related to Basque traditions. They even all have their own names. Ours is called *Muino*, the Basque word for hill. The *baserri*, as a Basque house is called, is an essential component to Basque culture."

Gibson considered pointing out that Parker changed the subject, which bothered him as he couldn't tell if Parker had done so deliberately or accidentally. "How so?" he asked.

"A tradition in Basque families is to hand down the family *baserri*, including all lands, to the firstborn. With rising property values from foreigners willing to pay far more than what locals could ever manage, combined with a lack of economic opportunity for young people, this tradition is simply vanishing. At this point, it's debatable that the situation could ever change."

"So why would they blame foreigners if this is such a foregone conclusion?"

Parker grinned. "Old habits die hard. And this is one place in the world where people really want to hold on to those old habits."

"So I take it your house wasn't in your wife's family?"

"No, it was not. And we bought the house from an older couple who could have given it to their eldest son instead."

"Still, seems unfair that they'd blame you. They at least got one Basque in there, even if she is married to some American."

Parker huffed in response. "Yeah, *some American* is spot-on. This is also a culture that is unforgiving to those perceived as outsiders, regardless of where they come from. I know a guy who moved to our village years ago from Mauléon, the capital of the French Basque region of Soule. And despite the fact that he's lived his entire life in the Basque Country, just because he's from a different region he's treated like an outsider. And another guy I know who's half-Basque, with a Basque father and a Portuguese mother…he's lived his entire life in our village. But because his father decided to marry an outsider, the son is treated as one. So, as you can imagine, I'm not so popular around town."

"You do have a way with people, Parker."

The two men laughed.

VIII.

Lisbon, Portugal

BACK IN THE 1980s, ETA maintained a commando unit in Lisbon. Like in France, one had only to cross the border with Spain to find sanctuary. At least until the GAL started taking down her people in France. Itxaso Harinordoquy was surprised that the anti-ETA bastard GAL units were never sent into Portugal. Maybe the explanation had something to do with relations between the governments of Spain and Portugal at the time. Politics and history—none of that stuff was important. Those were Garikotz's things. Itxaso's thing was blowing shit up.

She was recruited by ETA while still in lycée. But having grown up during the 1970s in the Basque Country, she needed little encouragement to join the nationalist cause. Being raised in that hostile environment where their own language was outlawed was more than enough. But Itxaso had even more reason to hate the repressive fascist Spanish government. Her father was imprisoned for being an ETA sympathizer when she was ten years old and died in prison not long after, under suspicious circumstances.

After high school, she was moved from Donostia to Baiona, where she was trained in the art of bomb-making. Once her training was complete, she was again moved, this time to a unit in Lisbon.

The electric tram she was on began an ascent up one of the city's steep hills. Everything was going just as Patxi predicted.

IX.

French Basque Country

"IF MY MOTHER-IN-LAW DIDN'T LIVE HERE, I'd probably spend more time in Saint-Jean-Pied-de-Port," Sebastian Parker commented.

He and John Gibson walked down a sloping narrow cobblestone street lined with two-story white stone buildings with red wooden window shutters and red roofs. Flower boxes sat below many of the windows on both floors of the houses and they were overflowing with red geraniums. Some of the houses had a business of some sort on the first floor. Many of the stone doorways had the age of the house etched into the stone above the entrance. Most houses dated back to the sixteenth and seventeenth centuries.

"This place is definitely charming. And these houses are incredible," Gibson observed.

"Yeah, seeing dates like 1601 on a house makes me think our house is not so old. And there may have been even older structures here, if not for Richard the Lionheart and his soldiers destroying the town."

A group of backpackers passed by as they walked. "This is also a starting point for a lot of people who do the *Camino de Santiago*—or the St. James' Way trail, as the trail is called in English, leading through the Pyrenees to Santiago de Compostela in Spain. It's an old Christian pilgrimage route, but these days the trail is a popular backpacking route. That gate we walked by earlier, the Porte Saint Jacques, is a UNESCO World Heritage site, marking the start of the trail.

"This was also the ancient capital of the Basse-Navarre region, or Lower Navarre, which is now one of the three French Basque regions. But originally this area was part of the Kingdom of Navarre, more rightly associated with Spanish history than French. And this region was actually the last of the three to become part of France, only happening when Henri IV became King of France. Labourd and Soule, the other two French Basque provinces, had already passed to France as part of the Treaty of Ayherre at the end of the Hundred Years' War."

"Navarre, Labourd, Soule. I don't know how you keep all these names straight."

Parker chuckled. "What's interesting is to know all of the names in English, French, Basque, and Spanish. And then when in conversation with locals, one must be careful when referring to a place, as it can sometimes indicate that you're taking a certain political position. Anyway, we're almost there, so here's the deal with Alaitz's mom. She could either be intense or unfriendly, neither would surprise me. I just need to pick up something from her for Alaitz and should hopefully be in and out."

"You lead the way, amigo," Gibson replied.

Parker smiled. "Nice one with the *amigo*, Gibson." Then he came to a stop in front of a doorway with 1653 written in the stone archway above the heavy wooden door with thick iron hinges. "Okay, here we go," he said as he knocked on the door.

A smallish woman with short dark hair, who Gibson guessed to be in her sixties, opened the door and initially stared sourly at Parker. But once she noticed the presence of Gibson alongside, her impression immediately changed into a wide grin.

"Sebastian, who is this nice-looking man you have brought to my door?" she asked.

At first, Parker was speechless. Not only had his mother-in-law instantly changed her expression upon seeing Gibson, but she'd also spoken flawless English. He didn't even know she spoke English. When Alaitz first introduced Parker to her mother years ago when he was an exchange student in Bayonne, her mother hadn't even spoken French to him. Instead she only spoke Basque, even though he only knew a few words of the language.

"You do not speak to me now?" his mother-in-law asked, placing her hands on her hips and staring at him intently.

Parker tried responding, but the words from his mouth were an incomprehensible mixture of French, English, and Basque.

His mother-in-law shook her head and turned to face Gibson. "I don't know what my daughter does with this young man. He does not even know how to properly introduce people. So, I will do it myself. My name is Zurina. Please come in." Zurina opened the door all the way and gestured for them to step inside.

"Thank you, Zurina. That's a beautiful name. My name is John." Gibson entered the house first, followed by Parker.

Zurina lightly slapped Parker as he passed by and quickly muttered in Basque, "Where are your manners, boy?"

Parker was tempted to respond something along the lines of being so shocked at her bizarre pleasant behavior that he didn't know how to react, but he held back. Besides, he thought, this was an interesting development. *Zurina kept the fact that she spoke English a secret from me all these years? And my own wife never thought to mention this little tidbit either?*

"Please, please. Sit down. Sit down. Would you like something to drink, or maybe something to eat?" Zurina ushered Gibson through the entranceway into her kitchen. She pulled a chair out from under a heavy wood table and gestured for Gibson to have a seat. He complied.

"This son-in-law of mine…he should have called me first to let me know you were coming. I would have been so happy to make a nice Basque lunch for you. Have you had Basque food?" Zurina placed her hands on Gibson's shoulders.

Gibson was embarrassed by the amount of attention he was receiving. He noticed Parker languishing in the doorway between the kitchen and the entranceway, looking confused, shocked, and amused at the same time. "I'm okay, really. I had a sandwich once I got off the train in Bayonne, and Parker, I mean, Sebastian, tells me that his wife, your daughter, is going to prepare a large Basque dinner for us tonight. But thank you for the offer."

Zurina shrugged her shoulders and blew air from her mouth, making her cheeks vibrate. "*Un sandwich*? *Quelle catastrophe*!" she said with unveiled disgust, turning to look directly at Parker.

"What do you want me to do? He called me from Dax," Parker replied, annoyed at the accusation. "*Putain de bordel*," he said to himself, just loudly enough for his mother-in-law to hear. She scowled at him in response.

Turning back to Gibson, the grin returned to her face. "Ah," she said, holding up a finger, "but you did not say no to a drink. How about a pastis? It is not Basque, I must say, but we are an open-minded people. We even sometime allow our daughters to marry foreigners."

"Sure, I would love a pastis. Thank you very much," Gibson responded.

Parker countered with a huff and puff of air from his mouth shaking his cheeks. "Open-minded in terms of alcohol, maybe…sometimes. And I don't think Basques would like pastis if it was associated with somewhere north, like Paris."

"We like cognac and armagnac, do we not?" Zurina suggested.

"Cognac and armagnac are produced not very far north of here. If they were out of the Basque preference range, then Bordeaux wines would have to be removed from the list, and I don't see that happening. Basque wines from both sides of the border are wonderful, don't get me wrong, but sometimes we need the strong backbone of Bordeaux wines too."

Zurina breathed in deeply through her nose and exhaled. Her eyes quickly widened. "Calvados! I do not know one Basque person who does not like calvados. What do you have to say to that, Mr. Smarty Pants?"

Mr. Smarty Pants? Where the hell did she learn that one? "Okay, okay. You've got me there. Basque people do love calvados, I concur."

Zurina patted Gibson on the back in acknowledgement of her apparent victory. "I will get you a pastis, Monsieur John." She opened a cabinet by the table and pulled out a bottle of Ricard.

"Although I do have to say that the Basque love of calvados probably stems from the fact that while the Basques in Spain make a lot of cider from apples, they don't really make any stronger apple liquor, explaining why Basques from both sides of the border like calvados, made in the north of France."

Zurina breathed deeply again. She turned from the counter where she'd set down the Ricard bottle to look and grin at Gibson, not at Parker. "This son-in-law of mine...I admit that he is very clever." She turned to gaze at Parker. "This must be why my daughter is so fond of him."

Putain de bordel, Parker said to himself.

After leaving his mother-in-law's house, Parker told Gibson they'd take scenic back roads to get up and over to Sare. They passed by a farmhouse and Parker mentioned that the idyllic countryside farm had once been raided by French authorities, turning out to be one of ETA's main command posts in France.

"You know the Basque wine Irouléguy?" Parker asked Gibson.

"Sure, I remember having it once or twice."

Parker grinned knowingly and cast a quick glance at Gibson. "Remember that night in Petit Bayonne when we went out to that nice dinner?"

"Good Lord," Gibson said, recalling the evening, filled with wonderful food and lots of wine. Too much wine. "No, I don't remember everything, but I remember that awful hangover the next morning."

"We were having red Irouléguy wine that night." Parker motioned out the window to a sprawling vineyard carefully planted along a steep hillside. "The grapes are grown right over there."

"Wow, pretty steep."

"There's actually a requirement for the vines to be grown above a specific elevation, so I imagine the vineyard managers look for anyplace they can make work. A place around here also makes pear and prune eau-de-vie."

"I think I read somewhere that the Basque Country is known for cider, but I don't remember ever having any or you mentioning it."

Parker peered sideways at Gibson as he drove on the narrow road. "Interesting cultural observation, Gibson. Making cider used to be popular through the Basque Country, on both sides of the border. For whatever reason, making cider fell out of favor on the French side of the Pyrenees sometime in the last century, while remaining popular on the Spanish side."

Soon thereafter, there were no more signs of habitation. When Gibson asked just how *back road* they were going, Parker responded by saying that he'd be surprised if they passed another car. He added that they were much more likely to run into a herd of sheep.

And they did.

"Wow, that's a lot of sheep," Gibson commented. They were at a standstill, with at least a hundred sheep mindlessly blocking the small mountainous road in front of them. After a few moments of silence, Gibson asked, "Why don't you just honk the horn to scare them off?"

"That would be disrespectful."

"To the sheep?"

Parker shrugged his shoulders. "Yeah, to the sheep, but also to the Basque shepherd who is probably around here somewhere. And to the mountain, and to the countryside, and to the Basque people. These are brebis sheep after all, and they produce the milk to make that unofficial Basque national cheese."

Gibson looked at Parker curiously. "You know, you've grown up a hell of a lot since we first met. That Sebastian Parker would have plowed through this herd with a blaring horn and then flicked his cigarette butt at the sheep while passing."

Parker laughed. "I guess almost getting killed and getting married will do that to a person."

Gibson also laughed. "So that reminds me—when did you actually get married? Last I knew, you were talking about it, but you said you were going to send us an invitation. And if you had, I would have been there."

"Ah, yeah. That's right. Sorry I didn't explain that earlier. Yet another reason why Alaitz's mother hates me. We did plan on having a larger wedding, but Zurina refused to approve of our marriage unless I converted to Catholicism. Which, as I'm sure you would assume, knowing me as you do, I absolutely refused to do. I love Alaitz and wanted to marry her more than anything else, but there are some things I could never do. That's definitely one."

"How did you get married then?"

"Like I said before, just the two of us hiked to a remote monastery in the mountains and had one of the monks marry us. The whole event was actually pretty amazing. But, of course, her mom thinks I'm the spawn of Satan for marrying her daughter without permission."

"The spawn of Satan?"

"Yeah, really. She actually called me that again today while we were over there. But she said that proving I have an uncle means that maybe I'm not descended from the dark one after all. I guess I should thank you for that. She seemed to really like you."

"*Uncle?*"

Parker hesitated before responding. "Yeah, about that. Alaitz's mom, and family actually, has some pretty deep-rooted ties to the Basque nationalist movement, and I didn't think it best to announce we had a sudden visitor arrive who happens to work for the FBI. She doesn't take kindly to law enforcement types, if you know what I mean. That reminds me—What you are doing here anyway?"

Gibson didn't enjoy holding back from telling Parker that he was aware of Alaitz's family history. He also noted that despite what Parker might say about not liking his mother-in-law, he clearly protected her by only saying that the family had ties to the Basque nationalist movement, instead of directly implicating the family's history with more radical components, as Nivelle had told him.

And he didn't enjoy lying to Parker. But the time was not right to reveal the true nature of his visit. "Oh, the bureau decided to send me last minute to this international law enforcement collaboration conference in Paris. I actually skipped out on the last day to come down to see you."

Parker eyed Gibson curiously. "I'm not the only one who's changed since we first met. *That* John Gibson would have not missed one minute of that conference."

"Probably right. Here's something else *that* John Gibson would have never done." Gibson got out of the car and instantly began running into the herd of sheep with his arms raised, yelling like a madman. The sheep quickly scattered and Gibson turned around to see Parker laughing hysterically.

X.

Paris, France

PATXI IRIONDA WAS PLEASED. The plan he and Garikotz formulated a little more than six months ago was finally coming to fruition.

The world would be reminded of the Basque struggle and the fierce determination of the Basque people. The Basques would never be subdued. The Romans, the North Africans, the Visigoths, the Franks, the Fascists, the Nazis, the Spanish, the French—no force in history had ever been able to overthrow the Basque spirit. Although they had all tried.

He was seated by himself in the corner of a dark tavern. At least for the moment. He was sure the dark-haired woman standing alone at the end of the bar was eyeing him as she sipped on a martini. She wore a red dress, the dress clinging to her body like a glove, accentuating her breasts and putting her little ass on display.

He was certain she was watching him, waiting for him to approach her. He was also certain she was a *pute*. Women didn't dress like that and go alone to a dark bar in a back alley of Montmartre if they were not prostitutes. Patxi didn't mind. Her being a *putain* only simplified things.

Sure he would have to pay, but there would be no unwanted questions. She would have a job to do, nothing more. After months of planning the attack now coming to a close, he was dying for a piece of ass.

Even better, with her being a prostitute, he wouldn't have to put in any effort. She had clearly noticed his interest. And being a working girl, eventually she would ditch her modesty and walk over to his table and sit down.

He would then order another whiskey, maybe even one for her. After that, he would take her back to his hotel room and play the game of letting her do her job to him while also having his way. When he was done, he'd send her on her way. If that meant an hour or four hours, he didn't know. Tonight he was feeling a strong passion for life.

In the meantime, he sipped his whiskey, an Irish whiskey. He drank it without ice, as always. The Basques really needed to make their own whiskey, he thought. Another initiative he promised himself to look into once he moved to the top. Maybe someone smart like Garikotz could figure out how to get it started. After all, everyone knew that once the Basque Country achieved independence, they would need to look for ways to strengthen their economy. Economics was not a strong area of Patxi's talents, but being a leader meant that he needed to always see beyond to the bigger picture. And then what needed to happen to achieve that end goal would fall into place.

The dark-haired woman sat down in the booth next to him and placed a hand on his thigh. With his prediction proving true, he felt even more confident of his plans.

XI.

Vilnius, Lithuania

"HEY YOU! WHY YOU NOT ASK US IF WE NEED ANYTHING?" a man barked at Graciana Etceverria in accented English as she walked by the table where he was seated with a woman and another man.

She kept walking, pretending not to have heard his rude outburst. It was true that Graciana didn't pay as close attention to her Lithuanian customers at the restaurant as she did to foreigners, especially Americans and English. And why would she? Lithuanians never tipped.

And besides, she had been in many Lithuanian restaurants since moving to Vilnius. She treated her Lithuanian patrons just as they would be treated at any other restaurant.

The difference was that the restaurant where she worked was in the primary tourist corridor of the city, just off the Town Hall Square in the city's Old Town, and her restaurant made no secret of being a tourist oriented restaurant.

Menus written in Lithuanian were only provided if requested. Otherwise, they were all in English. And that wasn't just for the benefit of the Americans and English. The Germans and French tourists all seemed to understand English, even if they pretended to be offended at there being no menus in their own languages. And the Asians…well, Graciana wasn't always sure they understood English, but at least they could point to what they wanted.

Although, for her own sense of self-worth, she was glad that she didn't work at one of the other tourist restaurants in the area that also had pictures of all available food items on the menu. Even being a fugitive in hiding, her sensibilities at having been raised in a Basque-French culture that fully appreciated good food and drink wouldn't allow her to stoop so low on the cuisine ladder. To her, that would be comparable to working in a fast food restaurant.

"Hey, it is to you I am talking!"

Graciana picked up an order she knew was ready and turned. As she walked back to the table of three Lithuanians, she noticed the two men openly eying her figure, even the one sitting next to a woman who was clearly with him. And even, Graciana noted, with the woman sitting next to him being very attractive, especially compared to her very unattractive male companion. But being gawked at like a piece of meat, and especially *pork* for Lithuanians, based on all the pig products they ate, was nothing surprising. The persistent act seemed to be an accepted cultural trait. The Lithuanian guys were even worse than French guys, and she hadn't thought that possible.

"Yes, can I help you?" she slowly asked when she reached their table. She didn't force a smile as she would when annoyed by foreigners, though—Lithuanians didn't smile.

"*Taip*, Jurga. We would like to order more food," the man said gruffly, causing the other two at the table to laugh.

Calling her *Jurga* was another non-surprise. She'd been told on numerous occasions that she shared a resemblance with the popular Lithuanian singer. Graciana had seen the singer's picture and wasn't sure why people thought they looked so alike. Maybe the short black spiky hair sparked the resemblance? She was glad to at least be compared to a good-looking woman. But from what she had seen in her time there, Lithuania had no shortage of those.

"Would you like more potato zeppelin?" she asked.

She deliberately used the ridiculous sounding English translation of Lithuania's national dish instead of calling the treasured potato and meat creation by the proper name: *cepelinai*. She also purposefully made the grammatical error of pronouncing the words in singular form, a component of the English language, along with articles, which were difficult for Lithuanians to grasp. This was similar to how native French speakers often had trouble pronouncing the letter "h" when speaking English, and how native English speakers could never seem to get either the French or Spanish "r" quite right. As for speakers of other native languages attempting to speak Basque—forget about it. Always so many problems.

The gruff Lithuanian grinned. "*Taip*! Yes, we want more zeppelin. And bring us more *alus*."

"*Alus*?" Graciana asked, even though she knew this was the Lithuanian word for beer.

"*Kurva bled*! Yes, *alus*. Beer!"

Graciana liked how when Lithuanians cursed they did so using words from different languages. The erupted explicative just used by the annoyed Lithuanian man, for example, was a combination of Polish and Russian words. But she thought the mix of curse words was fitting, at least for Vilnius. A group of foreign students studying at Vilnius University once had a going-away party at her restaurant, and she overheard a discussion a few of them had regarding the history of the city. Apparently, the city had been a multicultural destination stretching back to the Middle Ages and had always been a melting pot of regional languages. Lithuanian wasn't even the primary spoken language in Vilnius until less than a hundred years ago.

She acknowledged the order with a slight grin and walked away. She overheard the woman at the table call her a *pizda*.

Overall, it wasn't such a bad place to be. Lithuania even reminded her of France, at times, although the differences between Western and Eastern Europe were hard to miss. Eastern Europe was definitely a different world.

But there were a lot worse places she could have ended up starting a new life after escaping after the fallout of Lopé's plan to entice American-Basques to contribute resources for Basque independence. After that young American was shot, she had no choice but to get out and go into hiding. She heard that he didn't die and she was glad. He was charming. For a *mec*, anyway.

Of course, she was still in touch with some contacts in ETA, or ex-ETA since the ceasefire. But she was no longer considered a potential asset. She felt she was treated more as a liability. Being the only member of the group involved in the killing of the US politician in San Francisco still alive and uncaptured, her not being caught was in the interest of the organization. Even if the organization didn't really still exist.

But even with a new name, new passport, and new haircut, keeping a low profile wasn't going to last forever. Eventually she would move again. Maybe she would try Minsk or Saint Petersburg? Vilnius had not been her choice. The destination had been chosen for her and she was supposed to stay there indefinitely. But fuck that. She wasn't going to be caught or used as some political trade. She recognized that she might never be able to stop running and hiding. Committed to a torturous life of not being able to ever return to her home; this was a fate she accepted.

XII.

Sare, French Basque Country

"LOOKS LIKE QUITE THE PLACE." Gibson said as Parker parked the car in a dirt driveway.

"Yeah, for sure. We got a great deal, but it's an old Basque farmhouse and needs a lot of work."

Parker opened the house's front door and motioned for Gibson to enter. Gibson noticed how even though the house was clearly over a hundred years old, there was an open floor plan with no walls between the house's kitchen, dining room, and living room area; as now popular with new houses.

Once inside, Parker asked Gibson to take off his shoes—even in farmhouses, one didn't wear shoes inside the house, he said. But one didn't walk around in socks or bare feet either; that would be a big faux pas. Instead, one always changed into a pair of slippers to wear inside the house. Parker admitted that he didn't know where the tradition started, from the French or the Basques, but explained that this was a fairly universal practice in any French or Basque home. As they were in the Basque Country, the slippers they used were espadrilles, and Parker handed Gibson a pair of the rope and canvas slippers. Just as Parker was explaining how the Basques had first invented espadrilles in the Basque province of Soule, Alaitz walked into the house from a back door in the kitchen area. She had a handful of green herbs she set down on a counter.

"Great to finally meet the man I've heard so much about," Alaitz said, approaching Gibson and Parker. Gibson held out a hand to shake, but Alaitz ignored his hand and brushed her cheeks against his and made a small kissing noise in the typical French greeting. As always, Gibson was surprised and didn't know how to react. He didn't believe he would ever get used to the *kissing but not kissing cheeks* thing.

Blushing, Gibson replied, "Oh, hello. Nice to finally meet you too. Although I hope Sebastian has left out any bad things about me."

Alaitz did the same brushing of cheeks and kissing thing to Parker. "My mother called me earlier to tell me about you."

"*Ah bon*?" Parker questioned, genuinely surprised.

"Yes, she was very impressed with your uncle," Alaitz smiled mischievously as she said the word *uncle*. "By the way, Sebastian, that was very clever of you. Not very honest, but clever." Parker started to respond, but Alaitz held up a hand to stop him. "It's okay, I understand."

Alaitz turned to face Gibson. "And besides, from all that you have told me about John Gibson, he seems like he could be your uncle anyway. You must understand, John, for my mother, family is extremely important, and you are the first family member of her only daughter's husband she has met, so the occasion was very important to her."

"Am I no longer the spawn of Satan then?" Parker asked.

Alaitz flashed him a quick scowl but did not address his question. Turning back to face Gibson, she asked, "Tell me, John: Do you like Basque food?"

"I've never tried any that I didn't like," Gibson truthfully admitted.

"Wonderful. Because tonight you will have a true Basque country dinner. But in the meantime, you and my husband must leave me alone. As Sebastian can tell you, one of the things about Basque women is that you never want to get in their way in the kitchen."

"Good to know," Gibson replied.

"We'll drop off his bag in his room and then head out for a walk," Parker added.

"Okay, that sounds good. Just be sure to return hungry," Alaitz said.

"Just FYI, when a Basque woman says to be hungry, you'd better be ready to eat an entire chicken," Parker said as they walked down the road. "So I hope you are, or will be very soon."

"Based on the Basque food I've had in the past, even if I wasn't hungry I would make myself hungry," Gibson replied.

"Alaitz is an amazing cook. You'll see." Parker paused, glancing at the horizon where the sun was setting behind a line of low hills. "You know, if the land was flat here, you'd see all the way to the coast." "Ah shit, I may as well just come out with it," he added nervously. "Alaitz and I are going through something. I'm not sure what's happening, but it's not great, whatever it is."

"What's going on between you two? You seem really happy, Sebastian. And I mean that."

Parker kicked at some stones in the dirt road. "Yeah, that's just the thing. I am happy and I think she is too. But her goddamn mother. That woman." Parker shook his head in disgust. "I swear, she drives me crazy. And that would be okay if that was all of her issues, but the fact is that she really influences Alaitz. So any time I'm not in the highest regard, her mother magnifies the situation."

"That's how mother-in-laws are," Gibson commented, suddenly trying to remember if he'd experienced such a thing with the mother of his ex-wife in what seemed like ages ago.

"Yeah, the fact that her mother helped us get the house kind of sucks, as that's always over me. As if I wasn't already so much less of a man already, according to her, on top of that, Alaitz really wants to have a baby, and that's not working out so far. Not for lack of effort. So this just creates another reason for her mother to view me as inadequate."

"Ah hell, Parker. I'm sorry to hear that."

Parker shrugged and waved a hand in front of his face. "*C'est la vie*," he said. "So how was your time in Paris?"

Gibson recognized the abrupt change in subject, but didn't mind. Discussing feelings and relationships had never been a familiar area. "I've been meaning to ask you. I came across this place where Hemingway, I guess, used to hang out called the two maggots—how is a café named after maggots?"

Parker laughed, slapping his side. "*Merde*, that's hilarious. The two maggots," he said, not pronouncing the *t* in the word, "doesn't refer to fly larva, but to trinkets. That café was once owned by a collector of Asian trinkets, and the place came to have the name. Although I do agree that for an Anglophone it does appear to sound disgusting."

"So Hemingway used to actually go there?"

"Oh yeah, definitely. He was big into the Latin Quarter, St. Germain-des-Prés, and Montparnasse. Although I'm not sure what he would think of any of the places nowadays. They aren't exactly the untouched inner-urban enclaves they once were. Paris is even such a different city than when I first lived in France as a student."

"How do you mean?"

"I know this may sound weird, as Paris always been a huge city, but the place feels even more crowded these days. And the cultural face of the city has changed too, perhaps as a result of more people moving there."

"You mean all the new immigrants?"

"I'm not saying I'm opposed to immigration or anything, but the growing presence of Muslims in Paris, and throughout France, has been very noticeable. I remember when I was a student in Paris, one rarely saw a veiled woman walking the streets of the main downtown areas. These days this is a very common sight on the Champs-Élysées."

"You think it's a bad thing?"

"I don't. We're an open world and things evolve. I'm fine with change. As long as people respect one another's traditions, where they live shouldn't matter. I think culture is stronger than nationalism, honestly, although I know that's a minority view."

"Hard to swallow these days with Islamist extremism happening."

"The way I see things, I live in the Basque Country, which has had the odds stacked against it for centuries. Yet, somehow, these people have retained their culture despite all the obstacles put up against them. And the appreciation for Basque culture just continues to grow. Every year a new Basque-language school seems to open somewhere."

Parker gazed at the horizon. "And it's amazing to see, honestly. There's so much to love about Basque culture. These fields here," he said, pointing outward toward the grassy fields stretching into a line of hills, later stretching into a line of mountainous peaks, "they used to be all part of the traditional open land of this Basque village. Anyone could graze their sheep out there as much as they wanted. Now that's all gone. But knowing this and standing here and seeing it—that's a sensation no book could ever convey. And I love that stuff. Don't get me wrong, I know we have some culture and traditions in the States, especially in a few specific pockets, but the setting is nothing like this and I honestly don't know if it ever will be."

"I would go so far as to say you, Sebastian Parker, are helping to conserve the Basque culture. You have chosen to live here and, from what I've seen and know about you, you are a careful observer of Basque culture and traditions. Therefore, I'd have to say that you yourself are testament to the survival of Basque culture."

Parker stopped walking and shook his head. "Damn, I wish my mother-in-law were here to have heard you say that, especially now that I know she understands English."

"She really doesn't like you that much? Don't get me wrong, you have the tendency to annoy the hell out of people, Sebastian. But for someone to totally dislike you—I'd think that to be a rare occurrence."

"Except for my mother-in-law, apparently. I don't know what the deal is, but she's never approved of me. There's been constant tension, seriously from the time we first met in high school. It's like her mother has this inherent dislike of Americans."

"Funny, as you are probably one of the most *un-American* Americans I've ever met."

Parker laughed. "I know. Hilarious, right?"

Gibson laughed too.

"So a conference in Paris?" Parker suddenly asked, making Gibson feel uneasy.

"Just another boring conference."

"You're absolutely staying a few days with us. I insist. If you have a flight booked, you need to change it."

"I don't mean to sound presumptuous, but I didn't book a flight out of Paris until next week." Gibson didn't like once again lying to Sebastian Parker. In reality, he'd booked no return flight.

"Fantastic," Parker said, slapping Gibson's shoulder. "Then for a couple of days I'm going to thoroughly immerse you in Basque food, drink, country, and festivities."

Gibson smiled uncomfortably. "Sounds good, Parker."

Parker toured Gibson through the village of Sare, pointing out some of his favorite places in the quaint, picturesque Basque village.

"This is not a bad place," Gibson commented as they strolled through the central square area of the village centered around, like most Basque villages, a church and a large *fronton* wall used for different variations of the game of pelote. Gibson hoped Parker and his wife would be able to stay there as they planned. They seemed to have a great life ahead of them, even if they were going through a difficult stretch. Maybe Nivelle was wrong. During Gibson's last time in France, Nivelle did, after all, think he was cornering an active terrorist training camp that turned out to be a long-abandoned one in the region to the north called Les Landes.

Parker suggested that they head back to the house. Once there, Parker reminded Gibson to take off his shoes and put on his designated espadrilles. He told him to feel free to settle in the guest room before dinner.

Gibson didn't take long to arrange his suitcase on top of a wooden dresser in the room on the second floor. He changed into a different shirt. Unlike at home, he didn't need to put on a sweater or sweatshirt. It was a midsummer evening, and it felt like one. Not something he was used to now living in San Francisco.

He walked down the stairs to the first floor. Parker was seated at the old-looking wooden table in the dining area of the house. There was a bottle of rosé wine on the table, three wine glasses, and a plate of something resembling paté surrounded by toasted slices of baguette.

"Ah, perfect. Now we can drink some wine together," Parker said as he noticed Gibson approaching. He poured three glasses.

"Is that a Basque wine?" Gibson asked.

"*Mais, bien sûr*! We probably drove past the vineyard where the grapes for this wine were grown earlier today. Probably sometime before you made friends with the herd of sheep." Parker grinned widely, handing a glass to Gibson.

"Made friends with a herd of sheep?" Alaitz asked as Parker handed her a glass.

Parker and Gibson laughed. "Yeah, he's a natural *berger*," Parker added.

Alaitz shook her head. "I don't even want to know. But I do want to officially welcome you to our home." She raised a glass in the direction of Gibson.

Gibson raised his own glass of wine and clinked glasses with Alaitz and Parker. "Thank you for having me. I'm glad to be here in your beautiful home."

The three took sips of the crisp, deeply colored pink wine. "With some work, hopefully this place will be beautiful." Alaitz took another sip of her wine and set the glass on the table. "Now, you two feel free to chat while I finish making dinner."

"Here, help yourself to some pepper mousse," Parker suggested, pointing to the plate on the table. "It's basically just puréed red pepper, and spreading the mousse on slices of the toasted bread is really good."

Gibson had barely finished a piece of bread with the pepper mousse when Alaitz set a bowl down in front of him. The bowl was filled with a steaming green soup.

"Garlic soup. A Basque favorite," Parker commented as Alaitz set a bowl in front of him.

Alaitz brought a bowl to the table for herself. Once seated, she said, "*Bon appétit.*"

There were slices of bread in the soup with a white melted cheese on them. Garlic soup didn't sound appetizing to Gibson, but he tried to stay open-minded. When he tried a spoonful of the soup with a piece of the cheese-covered bread, he was pleasantly surprised. The garlic taste was not overpowering at all as he'd suspected. Instead the soup had a tangy earthiness coupled with the bread and melted cheese. A wonderful combination.

After soup, a new wine was brought out—this one a tangy white wine that Parker said was also from the Lower Navarre region where they had driven earlier. With the wine came a salad of dandelion leaves and bacon. This also sounded strange at first to Gibson, but turned out to be a delightfully tasteful combination of bitterness from the greens, mixed with the rich saltiness of the bacon.

"For some reason when I hear Navarre, I just think of Spain," Gibson admitted after reflecting on Parker's mentioning the name of the region in the French Basque Country.

"Yes, a province in Spain named Navarre can be traced all the way back to the Kingdom of Navarre, which actually started as a Basque kingdom called the Kingdom of Pamplona. This kingdom stretched across the Pyrenees into what is now France," Parker noted.

"But then I remember that Navarre isn't considered an official Basque province in Spain?" Gibson questioned.

Alaitz huffed in apparent disgust.

"Oh, you're treading on shaky ground there, *mon vieux*. Better save that one for later," Parker carefully suggested.

Once Parker cleared the table of the small salad plates, there was a pause in the meal to sit and chat. Whereas in other cultures people having dinner guests may just get through the food phase and then take time for conversation, here the conversation did not wait. Instead, they inserted conversation directly into the dinner plan, as if just another course of the meal.

Like her mother had shown earlier in the day, Alaitz took great interest in John Gibson. She admitted that it was strange to have never met any of Parker's family. And despite the fact that this man was not an official family member, she sensed a clear kinship between the two and found John to be very fatherly. Long ago she'd learned that Sebastian had lost his mother at a young age and that his father was nonexistent in his life. But he often spoke fondly of John Gibson.

"How is the Basque dinner so far?" she asked him.

"Great. The last time I was over here, Parker...I mean, Sebastian, introduced me to Basque food and I've liked pretty much everything Basque I've ever tried."

"Pretty much everything?" Parker asked.

"Rachel and I have found some Basque restaurants in Northern California, and there are a few upscale ones in San Francisco we go to from time to time. I tried the inky squid thing once and wasn't the biggest fan. I'd have to say the same for cow tongue, which Rachel dared me to order once."

"Ah, *txipirones en su tinta*, baby squid in black ink sauce—that's a Spanish Basque specialty. But as for the cow tongue, I've lived in the Basque Country my entire life and have never had such a thing or heard of this being a Basque dish," Alaitz commented, looking over at Parker.

"Cow tongue is a Basque-American thing, not something popular here. Actually beef, in general, isn't really in Basque cuisine here," Parker offered as explanation.

"And coastal Basque cuisine is different from interior Basque. Even though we are less than thirty kilometers from the ocean, we don't eat as much seafood as people do in Saint-Jean-de-Luz or Hendaye," Alaitz offered.

"To make things even more complicated, there are not only differences in French Basque versus Spanish Basque cuisine, but also regional differences in the three French Basque provinces," Parker added.

"So I'm guessing then that the way Basque food is presented in the States, outside of fancy San Francisco restaurants, is probably not traditional?" Gibson asked.

Alaitz brought a new bottle of wine to the table. Gibson recognized the label. It was an Irouléguy wine, from the area outside of Saint-Jean-Pied-de-Port.

"I think Sebastian told me about this. How is the food presented?" Alaitz asked.

"They make a big deal of calling it family style," Gibson responded.

"*Family style*?" Alaitz asked.

"Yes. When they bring big bowls or plates of food to a table and then let everyone serve themselves," Gibson said.

"That is what we do at our homes, so I don't see a lot of difference. We Basques love our food, but a difference between a Basque person and French one is that unlike the French, we are not concerned with the presentation of food. For we Basques, that is just a waste of time. Some of our most delicious dishes do not look attractive, but they are delicious." Alaitz rose from the table and returned to the kitchen area.

"I think the difference is that what became traditional American-Basque cuisine was an evolution based on circumstances," Parker suggested.

"You had Basque immigrants in the western United States who were spending months out on the range as sheepherders and when they went into town, they found a Basque boarding house. True to Basque character, most likely the first thing they wanted was to eat, and eat a lot. So they would be seated at long communal tables with other herders in from the range and local Basques. Then the boarding house keeper would just bring in multiple trays of food all at once. Soup, salad, beans, potatoes, steamed vegetables, and then some sort of meat, typically lamb.

"Basques here eat all of these things, but in different forms and not all at once, and lamb is not as popular with Basques here as the Basques in the western states. But again, that was most likely a circumstantial thing, as there were a lot of sheep in those areas of the US and not as many chickens or pigs, more traditional Basque meats. That's not to say that Basques here don't eat their fair share of lamb though. Basque lamb stew is one of my favorite Basque dishes." Parker finished his glass of white wine and nodded that Gibson do the same. Then he filled their glasses with the red wine.

"This is a Tannat and Cabernet Sauvignon blend, a very common grape blend for Irouléguy red wines," Parker said as he swirled the wine in his glass.

"The wine should taste very nice with this salmis of pigeon," Alaitz added as she placed a large bowl in the center of the table.

Gibson peered into the bowl. The contents appeared to be a sort of stew with small pan-fried birds sticking out of the bowl. "*Pigeons*?" he skeptically asked.

Parker grinned at him from across the table as Alaitz brought another bowl to the table with roasted potatoes. "Don't worry. Not what you think. These are wild pigeons called *palombes*, not the pigeons you see in city streets."

Alaitz placed two of the little birds in a bowl and then used a ladle to pour over some of the stew. She added roasted potatoes and set the steaming plate in front of Gibson. "You'll love it. I promise," she said.

Gibson tried a bite, carefully cutting away a piece of meat from the little body to have with a spoonful of the stew. It was excellent. The stew was earthy and rich and added an entirely different taste to the small bird, which may have otherwise tasted like chicken.

After the main course was over and more glasses of wine were poured, Parker cleared the table and brought back a plate with a large cheese round and a jar of jam. "This is brebis cheese, made from sheep's milk. Alaitz has a cousin who makes brebis cheese up in the Pyrenees we get directly from him. The cheese has a nutty flavor and a lot of people like it with jam. This one Alaitz made herself from local cherries."

After the cheese course, Alaitz brought a dessert to the table. Parker explained the dessert was a kind of baked cherry pudding, also made from local cherries. Parker poured them small glasses of patxaran, which Gibson remembered was a Basque liquor made from berries called sloe berries.

"Normally I'm not into desserts, but this cherry tart is amazing," Gibson acknowledged.

"I'm glad you like it. Would you like more?" Alaitz asked.

"Good Lord, no. Thank you. I feel like I'm about to burst already," Gibson said, patting his stomach.

"I'll make *piperade* for breakfast tomorrow. Normally we would never eat eggs for breakfast, as we have them for lunch or dinner, but I know Americans love eggs for breakfast."

"That's kind of you, but please don't go out of your way for me. Honestly, I think I'll still be full from this meal tomorrow morning."

"I understand we only have you with us for a couple of days, so I'm going to be sure you eat nicely while you are here," Alaitz sternly stated.

Gibson held up his hands in surrender. "Okay, I give up. If you insist."

Alaitz smiled at him. "I do."

Gibson was about to say that he was ready for bed when he pulled his cell phone from his pants pocket to check the time. He was not someone glued to his cell phone and didn't use his too much, but his phone's screen instantly caught his attention. He had four missed calls from a number he didn't recognize, but the calls clearly came from someone in France based on the country code of 33. Who would possibly be trying to call him? He gave Nivelle his cell phone number, but he didn't think even Nivelle would be calling him so soon.

But opening a text message from the same number erased any doubt that Nivelle was trying to reach him. The text message read: "Do not believe reports. Tour Montparnasse not ISIS. ETA is back. Return call. -Nivelle."

Gibson felt a chill race through his body.

"Something wrong, Gibson? You look like you just saw a ghost on your phone," Parker said.

Gibson struggled to speak. "Have either of you seen any news reports today?"

"Nah, as you can see, we don't turn on the television often and neither of us have smart phones. Usually we read about the news on our laptops."

"I think we should look at one of them now. Something has happened in Paris," Gibson slowly said.

Parker's wide grin suddenly faded as he sensed the seriousness in Gibson's tone and demeanor. "Sure, Gibson. Hold on." Parker went into another room and returned with an open laptop. He set the computer on the table. He opened the BBC World News homepage and the main story's headline left them speechless.

"*Mais, c'est quoi*, Sebastian?" Alaitz asked when she saw Parker staring in disbelief at the screen. When he didn't reply, she walked up behind him to see for herself. "Oh, *mon Dieu.*"

SUSPECTED TERRORIST ATTACK
AT MONTPARNASSE TOWER

Extraditing is contrary to all the traditions of France
especially when it concerns political combat.
—Gaston Defferre, former French Minister of Interior

Killing here in Euskadi is part of the landscape,
as it rains, there are trees, people are killed.
—Basque Country citizen

Part II.

(1985)

I.

Biarritz, French Basque Country

"Because of the increase in the murders, kidnappings and extortion committed by the terrorist organization ETA on Spanish soil, planned and directed from French territory, we have decided to eliminate this situation. The Grupos Antiterroristas de Liberación (the GAL) founded this object and put forward the following points:

1. *Each murder by the terrorists will have the necessary reply, not a single victim will remain without a reply.*
2. *We will demonstrate our idea of attacking French interests in Europe, given that its Government is responsible for permitting the terrorists to operate in its territory with impunity.*
3. *As a sign of goodwill and convinced of the proper evaluation of the gesture on the part of the French Government, we are freeing Garcia Diez, arrested by our organization as a consequence of his collaboration with the terrorists of ETA.*

You will receive news of the GAL."

The decree was published in every major newspaper in France and Spain after they spared the life of the coward Diez. The dual-faced act had the chilling effect the leaders of the GAL hoped it would.

For too long the ETA terrorists were able to find safe refuge by just crossing the border between Spain and France. Someone could murder a politician or policeman in Bilbao and be safe in Biarritz by the end of the same day. And they didn't even try to hide. Instead they lounged freely on the beaches and sat sipping coffee or wine in cafes. All within clear view of anyone paying attention.

But the French authorities apparently had no intention of bringing these murderers to justice. For some reason, letting the ETA terrorists find refuge was okay with the French government. Was this some ill-conceived ideological farce that somehow these terrorists were revolutionaries?

Marie-France Etceverria was glad to join the GAL. She didn't even need to be recruited. She volunteered. She may have been Basque through her family's heritage, but she saw herself as French. No one in her family could even remember the last member to speak Basque. Like many other Basque families, hers had assimilated into the broader French society, and she didn't feel any connection to the Basques or their ridiculous cause.

And she believed in what the GAL was doing. They were not only hunting down the ETA murderers in their so-called French sanctuary, they were also sending a message to the French government that these criminals could no longer be allowed to continue living freely and unpunished in France. Some people labeled what they did as terrorism, but the real terrorists were ETA. If France would not stop them, the GAL would.

Besides, working for the GAL paid nicely. Very nicely. She didn't know where the money came from. She suspected the funds originated from the Spanish government somehow, but she didn't care. Money was money. And after her bastard husband left her on her own with their daughter, she needed money.

She was seeing someone, and he seemed to really like her, but she was no schoolgirl with romantic dreams. She saw the relationship as what it was—they were sleeping together. She was a single mom and couldn't rely on him, or any man, for anything more. Besides, she would never be able to tell him she was a hired assassin.

Becoming an operative for the GAL in France was an excellent job. Most of the time she was either paid to be on-call as needed, or was assigned to conduct surveillance of known *etarras* living in France. And keeping an eye on the careless ETA morons was easy work.

But sometimes she was asked to kill. She had no problem killing. And although she believed in the purpose of the GAL, this was just a job like any other. Her icy demeanor surprised even her GAL counterparts.

She received no training of any sort and she didn't understand why training would ever be needed. She didn't use complex bombs or assault rifles to execute her orders. She didn't get involved with hand-to-hand combat. She merely walked up to her targets and pointed the small .38 revolver she was given at their heads or chests and fired. Perhaps being a woman helped her in her efforts, as she didn't look threatening. She could approach one of the *etarras* during the middle of the day on a city street and execute them. It was easy.

And this was actually her preferred way to handle her assignments. With her assigned driver, a different one for each assignment, always nearby, she would be in and out before the first phone calls were ever made to the police. Though she also realized that the French police forces took their time in responding to hits on ETA members in France these days—a great benefit to her and all members of the GAL.

For her first execution she'd worn an all-black outfit. The outfit felt right, as she was bringing death with her. And from that time on, she always wore the same black outfit to carry out her killings. The fact that she'd gained notoriety as a lethal assassin pleased her.

She was known as *the Lady in Black.*

Her blonde hair contrasting against her black outfits must have also made an impression, as she knew some people referred to her as the *blonde assassin*. But she preferred Lady in Black.

Sitting at a crowded café on the Avenue Reine Victoria in downtown Biarritz, just blocks up from the city's famous Grande Plage, she watched her next target at a table in the corner. He was having a glass of wine with a female companion. He smoked and laughed as if he didn't have a worry in the world. And to everyone else in the café—the bartender, the waiter, the other patrons seated at tables—he was just another Spaniard living in France. But Marie-France knew differently.

She knew who he really was: Juan Manuel Irigaray, a senior member of ETA who'd been responsible for the bombing of a shopping mall in Madrid killing numerous innocent people. And now here he was…clearly not at all worried about being detected. *But he should be.*

Soon he would meet the Lady in Black.

II.

Bayonne, French Basque Country

JEAN-PIERRE NIVELLE WAS QUICKLY MOVING up the ranks. He was proud to be serving his country, to be serving France. But his current assignment troubled him.

He'd been sent down from Paris to track the activities of Basque radicals in France, and specifically in the border regions with Spain. There was activity all the way down the Pyrenees to the border on the Mediterranean, but his real focus was on the French department of Aquitaine, home to the three French Basque provinces.

His charge was mixed. He was to not only provide surveillance and reports on the activities of known French Basques, but also identify and watch the Spanish Basques hiding out in the French Basque Country. Most of whom were members of the Basque separatist group ETA.

However, the politics of the situation were a *bordel de merde*. Whereas he was to not only monitor, but also apprehend French Basque criminals, he'd been given strict orders to do nothing to Spanish refugees, as they were officially labeled by the French Government. How were murderers considered refugees?

And then there was the GAL—the group kidnapping, torturing, and at times executing Spanish ETA members in France. The orders from headquarters were not so clear on what he, or any French policing force, should do with them. Officially, they were to investigate any GAL activities and arrest perpetrators of crimes. But Nivelle didn't understand why he, or anyone, should stop what the GAL was doing, as the French Government was clearly not addressing the fact that terrorists were getting away with murder in Spain by crossing the border into France. There were others who disagreed, even within his own unit. A colleague of similar rank named Roman Guerin particularly disagreed with Nivelle's views on the situation. If Guerin had his way, they'd arrest anyone suspected of being tied to the GAL and detain or deport them. Guerin seemed to have no problem letting suspect, and sometimes even known, killers live freely in France.

But Nivelle knew the political reality was that his government still didn't completely recognize the legitimacy of the Spanish government's transition into a democracy after decades of a military dictatorship. Therefore the French government was not willing to join the Spanish in the fight against the Basque separatists. But the day to day reality was something different. That reality had murderers being allowed to freely roam in his country. In his view, if he could do nothing and his government was not willing to do anything, by all means they should allow the GAL to act with impunity. They were merely doing what no one else could.

Even though he realized that such a proclamation would never happen, he wished the president could declare that France didn't mind the so-called *Dirty War* being conducted by Spain on ETA members in France. After all, everyone knew that the French conducted their own less than legitimate actions against the Greenpeace radicals protesting the nuclear testing program in France's South Pacific territories.

As for the French Basque radicals, those he had no problem busting. France was France. *Mon Dieu*, the greatest country in the world. There would no *putain* separatist regions such as Brittany or Corsica or the Basque Country. There would be no dividing of *l'Hexagone.*

Jamais.

There was a knock on his office door. Nivelle called out to enter. Philippe Caudet, a junior officer assigned to his team, stepped inside his office. "Sir, we just received a call on the whereabouts of Garcia Diez. He's somewhere up in the mountains," Caudet reported.

"Alive?"

"Yes, apparently. At least that's what the caller said."

"Have you told Guerin?"

"*Non, Chef.* I came to tell you first."

"*Bien joué.* Let's keep him out of this for now. If we take him along, his emotions may get in the way and get us killed."

"How do you think?" Caudet asked, looking confused.

"There may be some *etarras* still up there looking to make an even bigger statement by engaging us in a gunfight once we find what they've left of Diez."

Caudet smiled knowingly. "Ah, that's why you are the boss," he said, tapping his nose.

Ever since the GAL's very public announcement the day before about freeing Garcia Diez, they'd been waiting for such a call. Although Nivelle would not have been surprised if by saying "freeing," the GAL meant they killed Diez. This would not have been the first time that they employed such use of words to describe their actions.

Diez had been reported missing by his wife over a week ago and was assumed to have been kidnapped by the mysterious GAL, but there'd been no identification of the hit until the public announcement included his name. Often with the GAL, if they kidnapped an ETA operative there would be one of two outcomes. Either the dead body of the kidnapped person would be left in some public place on display, or there would be no trace of the person ever again. They would simply vanish.

Caudet drove them in their black Peugeot 505 squad car. He took the A63 highway south from Bayonne in the direction of Saint-Jean-de-Luz. Nivelle didn't bother asking where they were going. Once Caudet got behind the wheel of a car, he transformed into another human being altogether. The transformation was a mix of racecar driver and maniac, accelerating to obscene speeds and weaving in and out of traffic as if they were in a hurry to save someone's life. Which, Nivelle had to admit, in the current situation could be true.

Another of Caudet's driving habits which annoyed Nivelle was that Caudet refused to drive without one of his unfiltered Gauloises cigarettes hanging from his lips. The smell of smoke wasn't what bothered Nivelle—*after all, how could the smell of smoke ever bother a true Frenchman?* He himself had never been a smoker, but he had no problem with others smoking wherever they wanted to smoke. Smoking was as natural to the French as wine and cheese.

But how Caudet always seemed to forget to ash his cigarette out of the window while driving annoyed Nivelle. After getting out of the car with Caudet he would always have cigarette ash on his uniform. And if smoking was an accepted French trait, so was being presentable at all times.

At Saint-Jean-de-Luz, Caudet exited from the A63 onto a smaller roadway, the D918, muttering something about the foothills outside of Ascain being their end destination. But Nivelle knew the regional geography enough to know there was really only one foothill outside of Ascain—the mountain known as La Rhune.

The mountain's 900 meter peak was prominent from the entire Basque Coast. The mountain was a symbolic and realistic barrier between France and Spain and had even served as a gateway to smuggle downed Allied pilots and others across the border into Spain from occupied France during World War II. Nivelle was aware of reports of certain paths across the mountain now being used to not only covertly bring ETA members into France, but also to smuggle goods between the two countries.

A small train carted tourists up to and back down from the summit, where there were radio antennas and a café with an overlook of the countryside and coast. Someone once told him that the mountain was considered mythical by the Basques. Apparently, there were ruins strewn around the mountain alluding to ancient Basque pagan worship sites. *Crazy Basques.*

He didn't understand them. One minute they were claiming to be devout Catholics, not even letting their women sit together with the men during mass. Yet the next minute they were paying tribute to the spirit of the trees or some *putain merde*. The extreme opposites didn't make any sense. He'd even heard that the Basque cross, their *lauburu* or whatever they called it, wasn't even a Christian symbol at all. Even though this Basque cross looked like a Christian cross, the symbol dated back to their pagan heritage.

The Basques just didn't make any damn sense. None at all. They complained about being a part of France, yet from what he'd so far witnessed, none of them even spoke the Basque language. So how could they really say they were so different? He remembered from his history studies in lycée that France had always been many regions that merged together to form one, similar to Spain, Italy, and Germany. So in his mind, the time for all these so-called independence movements had come and gone. Their ancestors had decided to give up their regional differences and joined together to create something grander. This was something those of the present should never be so selfish to forget. His own father had died fighting for the glory of France while trying to protect against the breakup of the country in Algeria. France not being able to hold on to the country's southernmost region was a disgraceful shame.

But something was happening here in the French Basque Country; Nivelle could feel something was amiss. He didn't expect anything near the level that the Spanish Basques had raised with their own independence effort, but Nivelle sensed the situation was close to breaking open.

He, *and France*, couldn't let that happen.

The road began gradually to ascend, passing through a rolling pastoral landscape of farmhouses and hillsides. Handwritten signs at the end of unpaved driveways on the roadside advertised products available for purchase: cherries, Basque cakes, paté, plums, saucisson, country bread, brebis cheese.

Caudet turned onto a narrow rocky road leading into the forest. The road immediately rose steeply. "This road leads to trailheads on the mountain," Caudet commented as he downshifted with one hand and somehow lit yet another cigarette with the other. "Our guy is somewhere on the trail where this road ends in about a kilometer."

"According to the caller, that is," Nivelle clarified.

Caudet shrugged. "*On vera.*"

"Yes, we shall see."

The road ended abruptly at a small parking area near a trailhead. "Should we wait for the others?" Caudet asked once he had stopped the car.

Nivelle considered the situation before replying. Standard protocol would have him play the scenario safely and wait for the other officers, due to arrive shortly. Nivelle ordered the backup just in case this turned out to be some sort of a trick and they needed additional firepower. Caudet told the others where to go, and even with Caudet's racecar driving style, the other two police cars would not be too far behind.

But if Garcia Diez was really out there somewhere, he might be in danger, and every minute counted. Once again, Nivelle had mixed feelings about his duty. Officially, the GAL were criminals and were to be treated as such. But they were taking care of the terrorists, who were even worse criminals. And Garcia Diez was clearly a criminal posing as a political refugee and living freely in France. In Spain, Diez would be captured and imprisoned for his crimes after taking one step across the border.

And now Nivelle's job was to find and protect this known terrorist, as the French state still recognized the plight of the Basque separatists in Spain and their persecution by the Spanish government. But still—he would not be disappointed in the least if they discovered a dead body down the trail instead of a live one.

The biggest doubt in his mind was that he didn't know if he would shoot at GAL suspects, if there were any waiting for them. Although doubtful they'd still be present, there was a possibility. Of course, if fired upon, he'd return fire. But his heart would not be into firing at these people. He was glad he'd deliberately left Guerin out of the investigation. Of course, the man would be pissed off as hell later when he learned that he'd not been involved, but Nivelle didn't trust Guerin. Somehow Guerin seemed too close to the Basques.

"No, let's go on ahead. Once they see the car here, they will know to follow," he said, deciding.

"*Très bien, on y va.*" Caudet tossed his cigarette butt out of the car window. He opened the car door and stepped out, pulling out his revolver as he did.

Caudet was the best kind of officer, Nivelle thought. Fearless. Loyal. Always ready to follow orders.

Nivelle stepped out of the car and assessed his surroundings. The road had ended above the tree line. From this heightened elevation there was a sweeping view of the landscape all the way to the ocean. Turning back to the mountainside, he noted that there were various boulders on the slope one could hide behind, but he didn't sense any ambush awaiting them. The trail led around the side of the mountain though, so he couldn't know for sure what to expect. He pulled out his own gun.

"*Allons-y*," Nivelle instructed and the two men began walking on the trail.

Garcia Diez didn't take long to find. Just as they rounded the corner of the mountain on the trail, past a few grazing *pottocks*, the wild Basque ponies roaming the Pyrenees, they saw him on his knees by the side of the trail less than a hundred meters in front of them. He was naked and had both hands on his head. Nivelle noticed he was swaying slightly.

As they approached, they could hear him sobbing. A blindfold covered Diez's eyes. Nivelle expected to discover Diez's hands bound and one of legs shackled somehow. But Diez was not restrained at all. He was on his knees with his hands on his head apparently by choice.

Scanning the perimeter, Nivelle felt confident that Diez's capturers were long gone. And although his resentment for Garcia Diez remained, Nivelle couldn't help feeling sorry for the broken man before him. Whatever torture he endured to be reduced to such a pathetic state must have been unimaginable.

But at least he was alive.

The last *etarra* kidnapped by the GAL had not been so lucky. Parts of that unfortunate former ETA military strategist were found alongside a mountain road. The funeral procession after was elaborate with hundreds of cars honking their horns throughout the French Basque countryside until reaching the Spanish border. Once there, the Spanish Civil Guard reportedly separated the hearse carrying the deceased from the rest of the motorcade so that the procession could no longer proceed together, carrying the spectacle across the border.

The Spanish didn't even try to be politically sensitive with anything related to ETA or Basque nationalism. And they didn't care about any repercussions for their actions, from what Nivelle had seen. Must have made dealing with the Basque troubles over there a lot easier.

III.

Petit Bayonne, French Basque Country

THE BASTARDS WOULD PAY for what they did to Garcia Diez. This was a personal promise Patxi Irionda made to himself on a daily basis ever since they were informed of what the son of a bitch GAL members did to Garcia Diez. Patxi had known him for years. Diez had been his mentor within ETA, in fact, and Patxi attributed most of his understanding of the organization, its history and purpose, to Diez. What could they have done to break such a powerful figure? In his prime, Garcia Diez was the most feared man in all of Spain. And he had been reduced to crying? Like a baby?

Patxi hadn't seen Diez since the brutalization by the GAL. Honestly, he didn't want to. He wasn't certain how he would react to seeing this former hero who had, frankly, now become an embarrassment. Would he embrace him or slap him? Patxi didn't truly know and didn't care to find out.

Whatever he'd been reduced to, Garcia Diez was still responsible for setting Patxi on the course to become a great leader in the organization one day. And there was a price that had to be paid for targeting his mentor. Patxi was determined to make this known.

He glanced around the room, surveying his assembled team. His old friend, Garikotz Auzmendi, was the most dependable and intelligent person he'd ever known. The combination of these two characteristics made Garikotz an important asset. Patxi would make sure Garikotz remained in his growing inner circle within the organization.

Garikotz's girlfriend, Izaskun, was also devoted to the cause like Garikotz, yet not quite as much, Patxi always thought. To her credit, Izaskun volunteered to become an assassin. Early on, Garikotz made clear that he preferred to remain as an intellectual and logistical contributor to the organization. Patxi knew that both Izaskun and Garikotz were equally prepared to kill in the name of Basque liberation. But there was something else about Garikotz. As if he had no other purpose. Patxi often wondered if Izaskun's actions were more intended to impress Garikotz than anything else. When Garikotz was into writing something political for the cause, for example, Patxi always noted that he didn't even seem to recognize Izaskun was in the same room, even though he knew they had been intimate for years. Yet Izaskun was always there for him, even if Garikotz didn't notice her.

Garikotz was presently hunkered over a typewriter with a cigarette dangling from his lips. Patxi didn't know for sure, but he assumed Garikotz was writing an announcement of the attack they were planning and the provocation that was its cause. Everyone knew the Spanish government was funding the GAL—this was the only way they could pursue ETA members across the border into France. And if they continued doing so, clearly not respecting international laws, they would be made to suffer.

During the first wave of GAL attacks in the early 1980s, ETA had not adequately responded to this threat on their northern refuge, in Patxi's mind. Now that the GAL was active again, they could not be allowed to continue their cowardly intimidation tactics. And although the way to directly cut the head off of the snake would be to hunt down the criminals in France, the situation was more complicated.

They could not just kill freely in the French territories. Doing so would draw too much attention to their presence in France and could easily instigate a response from the French authorities who, for years, had more or less looked the other direction. Besides, the IK group was doing enough, more than enough, to draw attention to the French side of the Basque territories. Those fools were almost as damning to ETA as the *putain* GAL.

And the GAL were going to have to face another member of his team, Aitzol Rubina, still in training. If they thought they could just stroll around the northern Basque Country picking off ETA members at will, they were in for a surprise. Patxi had no doubt that once released on his own, Aitzol was going to become a formidable foe. The bastard mercenaries would learn the true meaning of what the French feared and called *la force Basque*.

Lastly, but truly not least, there was Itxaso Harinordoquy. She was honing her craft as an expert in explosives and would one day be among ETA's finest. The attack they were planning on the Spanish Civil Guard barracks in Irun would be her first solo bombing. And it would be one always remembered.

Colonel Antonio Molina was stationed in Irun, and they'd recently uncovered that he was the GAL's primary contact across the border in Spain. The suspicion was that he was in fact the primary representative within the Spanish government paying GAL members for their services. It was even rumored that Molina was involved with recruiting new mercenaries to join the GAL.

Of course, Molina would be replaced by someone else. Some other heartless Fascist killer. But his death would send a clear signal to the *bastardos* that members of the Basque movement knew what they were up to. More importantly, the hit would send a message that ETA could strike down any one of them, even a colonel in the Civil Guard. Patxi wanted to make sure this was heard loud and clear. Not by just the Spanish, but by anyone standing in the way of a free Basque homeland.

And they couldn't just kill Molina. That wouldn't be enough. They needed to make a spectacle of his death. Nothing less than a huge car bomb explosion lighting up the streets of Irun would do.

"Okay, let's go over the plan," he announced to his crew in French. French was the language they decided to use among themselves. They all spoke varying degrees of Basque, an unfortunate but not uncommon reality with Basques on both sides of the border. Everyone except for Aitzol spoke Spanish fluently, and everyone except for Izaskun spoke a decent level of English. But they all spoke French, so this was the natural choice for their common language among themselves.

Garikotz often pointed out how the French and Spanish governments were to blame for the suppression of the Basque language, but

Patxi would not let him go off on any tangent tonight. It was not a time for words. It was time for action.

"Garikotz's contact in Irun has been tailing Molina, and our informant within the Civil Guard has provided Molina's schedule for this week. In two days, he's going to be attending a meeting off the base, in downtown Irun. The meeting is to be held in Irun's city hall at eleven in the morning. We could not ask for a better opportunity to take out our target and inflict a blow to the Spanish government at the same time."

Patxi paused, letting everyone be fully prepared for what he was going to say next. He closely watched the expressions on each of their faces.

"When I formed this commando unit, I clearly conveyed to all of you my position on the potential for collateral damage in our operations. As our attack will be midday in a crowded area, with many people leaving offices for lunch in restaurants or at home, there is no doubt that the attack will have civilian casualties. And while this is regrettable, we need to send a message to Madrid to stop paying the bounty hunters to blindly execute our people in France. I see no better way to do this than to execute our strike in a public setting. An attack on only Molina himself would be easily forgotten. No one will easily forget what we will do. Now, I know you all pledged to me from the start that you were willing to sacrifice civilians if we have to, but I want to reconfirm that you are all prepared for this reality."

No one moved in the room. The stillness was stifling.

Aitzol sprung to his feet, alarming everyone else. He quickly pulled out his box of Gauloises from his jacket pocket. "I say fuck it. The Spanish government is responsible for anything else that happens. Not us." He lit one of his cigarettes.

"I agree," Garikotz said, standing.

As soon as Garikotz stood, Izaskun quickly did, saying nothing.

"What my bomb destroys is beyond my hands. If people are there, they should not be," Itxaso said as she stood up.

"*Bien.* I'm glad you all have upheld your resolve in the name of our cause," Patxi said as he stood himself.

"According to our informant, Molina's car is scheduled to be serviced by an off-base garage tomorrow. Garikotz has arranged with the service station's owner to have a half hour free with the vehicle. During this time, Aitzol will be there to install Itxaso's bomb underneath Molina's car."

Aitzol nodded in agreement.

"Then Izaskun will be nearby city hall the next day, the day of the meeting, to detonate the bomb once Molina exits from his meeting."

Izaskun nodded in agreement.

"My advice is to not be too close," Itxaso suggested.

"Where are you coming from?" the border guard asked Patxi in French. The guard stood outside the car door peering in beyond Patxi to clearly check out Izaskun seated in the car's passenger seat. He had on the blue uniform of the French border guards.

The plan was for Patxi and Izaskun to return to France in the car, pretending to be a couple. Aitzol would cross the border in the mountains. There was no need for Garikotz or Itxaso to be in Irun for the attack.

The strike they orchestrated had been a thing of beauty. The bomb underneath Molina's car was detonated by Izaskun's hand just after he and his driver closed their doors. And the blast occurred just as a group of men in suits were walking by. Once the bomb detonated and Patxi was sure Molina had been hit, they didn't wait around to witness the aftermath. But he was certain the bomb claimed a few other victims in addition to Molina and his chauffeur.

He didn't feel nervous at all responding to the fresh-faced border guard questioning him. The guard was now intently looking at their passports, fake passports that Garikotz made just for this particular mission. Tomorrow the fake passports would be useless. Tonight they were going to help them return to their safe haven in the north.

"We went on a late honeymoon to San Sebastian for a few days," Patxi replied, laying a hand on Izaskun's thigh next to him. "We were married last year, but you know how it is," he added, in a quieter voice, as if not wanting Izaskun to overhear. "I needed to save some money first to make sure she had a good time." Patxi winked at the young officer, hoping his attempt at male camaraderie would be appreciated.

It was.

The young border guard peered once again through the open car window at Izaskun, and Patxi saw the guard's gaze fall to Patxi's hand on her thigh. The young guard grinned sheepishly and handed Patxi back their fake passports.

"*D'accord. Bonne nuit les amoureux*," the guard said, trying to sound affirmative and older. He waved a hand for Patxi to pull forward, and they passed underneath a sign stretching across the roadway stating that they were entering France.

IV.

Bayonne, French Basque Country

"I DON'T UNDERSTAND WHY WE MUST ALWAYS MEET HERE," Marie-France said to him, clearly displaying her frustration. "You know I prefer being across la Nive in Petit Bayonne."

But this was only partially true. Marie-France did prefer the narrow streets and alleys of Petit Bayonne more than the wider streets of Grand Bayonne just across the river. She had since a child, when her father used to take her on long walks around this city where she'd been born and raised. But there was more to her preference.

Most of the targets Marie-France was given orders to kill would be found in Petit Bayonne. In fact, they were all foolish *cons* to hang out there in one place. There was an unbelievable number of bars they all frequented, all located within roughly a four block radius. The Basques liking to have a good time was legendary. That worked in her favor. She always knew where to find her targets.

Any occasion to spend time there in the lions' den of the ETA bastards only gave her an enhanced knowledge of the area—especially now that she was carefully noting how certain alleys led to certain streets, or how certain doorways were deep enough for one, especially one petite such as herself, to hide in while anyone chasing her would pass by and not notice her in the shadows.

"*Ma chère,*" Jean-Pierre Nivelle said as he reached for her hand across the small round table. "Over there is too dangerous for us to be seen together. If they find out who I am, it could be bad for you."

Would it be? Marie-France wondered. After all, Jean-Pierre was not posted to Bayonne as an undercover agent. He might not wear a uniform like the other *flics*, but he made no secret that he was French police.

And how ironic identifying her consorting with the French police would be. She, the feared *Lady in Black* assassin. Openly collaborating with the very police forces ETA members thought were there to safeguard their exile and protect them from the Spanish government following their cowardly asses across the border into France. Maybe the discovery would actually send yet another signal to ETA that the old days were quickly coming to an end.

The signal that ETA members were no longer safe in France.

And the Spanish government wasn't even making an effort to conceal their knowledge of what was happening. Of course, they denied supporting the GAL. Marie-France found this especially ironic since she made her living off an income from the Spanish government. She saw an article in *le Monde* with a senior Spanish official stating that even if accusations of a group of mercenaries tracking down and killing Basque exiles in France were true, there was nothing the Spanish government could possibly do, as whatever was happening was occurring in France.

But no one would recognize her. Her hair was naturally blonde, as one of her infamous titles attributed to her, but once she accepted a position within the GAL, she started dyeing her hair dark brown and only wore a blonde bob wig when she carried out her assignments. She also always wore dark sunglasses. Even if she wore one of the all-black outfits she was known for, the chances of anyone recognizing her were slim.

Besides, she didn't think the fools would ever suspect one of their killers would be bold enough to eat in the same restaurants and drink in the same bars as them. The Basques weren't clever enough to consider the possibility. They may have been around for a thousand years before the French or Spanish, or whatever history they claimed, but she thought this was due more to their insular mentality and brute strength than anything to do with intelligence.

After all, she'd been married to one of them.

That big Basque bastard left her alone with their daughter, saying that he felt compelled to join ETA and the Basque cause. He said the

French Basques weren't radical enough, even with IK's escalation of violence under Philippe Bidart. He said he needed to join the fight and stop sitting on the sidelines. He said he needed to go to Spain and leave his life behind to find a new one with purpose. He said he was first Basque, second French. To him, Marie-France and their daughter were and always would be French—even though Marie-France's grandmother was Basque and their daughter was at least half-Basque. Even though Marie-France was his wife.

He left her broke and with a child to care for on her own. He left them both. She never heard from him again. But she hoped that one day when a target was assigned, she would see the image of his face on the photograph handed to her. The photograph that would identify who she was to kill next.

Marie-France prayed for that day.

And what did this French police officer sitting across the table and delicately holding her hand think of her? That she did not yet know.

Clearly, he found her attractive and engaging. He wouldn't chase after her the way he did if he didn't. French men were like that. This was a difference from Basque men. Not to say that French men were not arrogant and stubborn, nearly as much as Basques, but French men appeared to appreciate women beyond carnal instincts.

Maybe not, she concluded as she considered the comparison further.

But at least they were more suave and romantic about everything, at least initially anyway. On a first date with a Frenchman, they took you to a fancy restaurant. A first date with a Basque assumed you were cooking dinner and revealing all the cooking secrets your mother had told you while serving him.

With Jean-Pierre she still wasn't sure. They first met when he approached her while she was sunning herself on a beach in Anglet, the *Sables d'Or*, a favorite place of hers. One afternoon a week she devoted to spending time on the beach by herself. Eventually, she planned to also bring her daughter. But for now, she needed these few hours once a week all to herself. Paying a babysitter for the time was completely worth the cost.

Even then, Jean-Pierre didn't try to hide that he was a policeman. He wore pants and a shirt to the beach where everyone was wearing swimsuits or bikinis or less.

He had approached her full of confidence as she sat on her elbows looking out at the ocean in a skimpy outfit. He made no attempt to conceal his gaze wandering to her breasts and abdomen as he approached. He didn't even have on sunglasses.

He walked up to her, smiled, said hello, and sat down without invitation. The moment happened so quickly, she didn't know what to say. And then, so confidently, so arrogantly confident that it was appealing, he just kept talking. Everything moved in a blur. She couldn't recall later much of what he said. Only that he told her his name, Jean-Pierre, and that he would be calling her soon. He said he hoped she would answer his call and accept his invitation for a social outing together.

And just as abruptly as he arrived, he stood up, astonishingly easily for a person standing up in loose sand, and walked away.

Marie-France knew that despite his ultraconfident demeanor, he was still just a man. If he'd been something more, despite all other appearances, if he'd been something different, he would not have turned back for one last glance at her before leaving the beach. She saw him look back. He played being caught coolly, as with everything else.

But she liked it. She liked it all.

His narrow, squinty eyes. His chiseled cheekbones. His thin mustache. His thick, dark hair. His thin physique. This was a man she could be into. He may have been a little stiff like many French men, but he was completely opposite from her hulky, broad-nosed, wide-faced former Basque husband. Although they never divorced, she considered him dead.

But how the hell was this *mec* going to call her? Although she didn't remember the entirety of their conversation, or, rather, the entirety of what he said to her, she was certain she did not give him her phone number. And she was certain he had not asked.

Yet, the next afternoon, he called her at home. When she realized who was calling, she allowed herself to feel a brief moment of girlish giddiness. *Allowed herself*, as in her current profession she didn't have time to be girly or romantic or even sentimental. Her situation was hard enough just to maintain a certain level of motherliness for her daughter.

But she couldn't deny the interest she felt for the dashing French *flic*. Not only was he attractive, but the simple call of biological need had been building in her for some time. She had not allowed herself the pleasure of being with a man for quite a while.

She wasn't forbidden to socialize, or have companions. But she had no misconceptions regarding the level of danger she had put herself, and her daughter, in by accepting her role as a hired killer. Officially, the French government vowed to chase down any of the GAL operatives, provided they were given good reason. Marie-France didn't know if she believed this proclamation. At times, the French police forces appeared to care about the ETA scum she and her comrades were hunting down in France. In practice though, they didn't seem to care too much. She had even heard of some of her fellow GAL operatives actually running by French police after carrying out a hit the French police didn't even bother to chase after them—even with the screams from the other direction clearly indicating that the person running away from them had been the cause.

Marie-France never ran. She walked away from her assignments, casually ditching her wig, coat, sunglasses, and firearm. If she were to walk by a French policemen after one of her hits, she was sure she would attract their interest, but not as a suspect. Her actions would not be of interest. Her short skirts and tight tops would be under investigation.

"I hope you understand. I'm in a difficult position here. If the people who I aim to keep an eye on suspect me of more than just watching them, things could become dangerous," he continued, still gently holding her hand.

The look in his eyes was honest and she felt a little sorry for him. She did like Jean-Pierre, but their relationship would never be anything more. She loved herself and her daughter. That was all the love she had left.

She looked directly into his eyes. "Jean-Pierre, you are a good man." She looked away. "You shouldn't worry so much about me," she said, still not looking at him.

"But I want to worry about you. These are dangerous times, even here in the French Basque Country. This is my job, so I know."

You don't know everything. Marie-France concealed a smirk by biting her lower lip. And what if he did? she wondered. *Would he be like the French police who looked the other way?* She still didn't know. In their time together, she'd learned that Jean-Pierre was a complex individual who selectively voiced his opinion only when he felt he needed to make a statement. Otherwise, he could have anything hurled at him and his expression and demeanor remained unchanged. This was a characteristic she found both admirable and was annoying.

She was also annoyed that he was starting to see their relationship as more than what it was—or more than what the relationship was to her. She had no desire to ever be attached to another man.

Her ex-husband had seen to that. *Quel espèce de connard.*

But she was still a woman. And, like men, women needed sex. "Let me show you something," she suggested, gripping the hand touching hers.

They were done with dinner. The *poulet basquaise* they shared was perfectly seasoned with just the right amount of *piment d'Espelette*, the legendary pepper spice originating from the French Basque village of Espelette. Per her usual dinner routine, Marie-France refused both an hors-d'oeuvre and dessert. People always commented on how she was able to eat so much and remain so thin. But this biological fact was no mystery to her. She only ate what was necessary. Appetizers and desserts may have been tempting, but they were never necessary.

She'd heard of the whole French paradox theory, but didn't understand why people found difficulty, especially the British and Americans, understanding that if one didn't wish to gain weight, one had to pay attention to what and how much one ate. And besides preferring to walk most places, Marie-France never really exercised. Just by being aware of her food consumption and being active, she didn't need to worry about her weight or body.

Marie-France led him to a walkway following the path of the medieval ramparts surrounding the city of Bayonne. Portions of the walkway had been converted into public park areas with landscaped greenery and benches. The line of lampposts produced a romantic glow in the Bayonnaise air as they walked hand in hand along the path, with the former ramparts mounting a formidable defensive wall on one side.

"*Je pense que je suis tombé amoureuse avec toi*," Jean-Pierre confessed after they walked in silence for a few minutes.

Marie-France dreaded hearing the words that he had fallen in love with her. She wanted nothing to do with love. He was staring at her as they walked and she felt his eyes on her. She nervously grinned and squeezed his arm. "Let's go up there." She pointed to a stairway leading to the top of one of the ramparts.

She liked Jean-Pierre. She just didn't want this. Her life was already complicated enough.

Jean-Pierre, thankfully, didn't press the issue further and only grinned like a schoolboy. She hoped he would not say such a thing again. And she knew how to keep him quiet.

At the top of the stairs, there was a grassy area overlooking the walkway below and the spires of the Cathédrale de Sainte-Marie prominently looked down upon them. Marie-France recognized that Jean-Pierre was a law-abiding man. His chosen profession demanded this of him. But she was not going to give him a choice tonight.

Once they walked to the point of the rampart where a wooden bench was located, she abruptly turned and pushed him back onto the bench. Before he had time to react, she lifted her skirt and mounted him. As soon as she leaned in to kiss him, she knew she'd won the moment. There would be no further resistance. His kiss was on fire.

The cathedral spires were going to get a good show.

V.

Petit Bayonne, French Basque Country

GARIKOTZ DIDN'T KNOW WHAT TO DO. Izaskun meant a lot to him—more than he ever expected a woman would. But his first devotion was to the cause, and he expected that would never change. She had thrown herself into the movement after meeting him, and he didn't question her own dedication to Basque independence. She'd even volunteered for the most dangerous position of being an assassin for ETA, crossing the border in secret into Spain and carrying out attacks on targets and then returning to live clandestinely in the French refuge. The position was extremely dangerous not only for the risk of being captured, or even killed, while carrying out the operations in Spain. But also because one had to increasingly fear being hunted down like a dog by the *putain* GAL in France.

Since they lived together, this obviously put more of a target on him. But he'd never tried or even wanted to hide his true identity. As a former journalist with a proven record of suppression by the Spanish government, he applied for and received official refugee status by the French government. Although there were thousands of Spanish Basques living in exile in France, there were few who actually received such official recognition by the French government.

His documented physical abuse at the hands of the Spanish government was hard to deny. He formerly had been employed by the newspaper *Egin* in San Sebastian. Refusing to obey orders to stop publishing articles with Basque cultural themes, he'd been beaten on numerous occasions. Each time had always been the same—as he would leave his office at night, a group of men would pull him off of the street into some dark alley and beat the piss out of him. Of course, they never had on uniforms, but Garikotz knew they were from some branch of the Spanish police force sent with specific orders to pound a message into him.

Others may have eventually given in to the demands and stopped publishing articles that resulted in severe beatings. And he was sure they believed he eventually would too. But unlike some of his counterparts in the Basque journalism world, Garikotz wasn't concealing his name for the articles he wrote. Furthermore, he wasn't even writing what could be perceived as radical articles for *Egin*. He was writing about subjects such as Basque food, dance, and sport traditions, and supporting the movement to have more Basque-language schools and dual-language signs in the Basque Country.

He became a poster child for the antidemocratic movements covering the Basque independence movement, and they always happily published pictures of his battered face after each beating he received. The image of a beaten cultural journalist spoke a thousand words to the world on the extent of Spanish repression and brutality.

Of course, Garikotz had a double life and double career and was secretly scribing pretty much all of ETA's written materials, but no one knew about that part of his life. After so long, and after so many beatings, his good friend and fellow ETA member Patxi Irionda finally convinced him that he would be able to better serve the movement not living in constant threat of being beaten, or worse. After all, the more Garikotz's face made international news, the more of a target he became.

Izaskun was no refugee living in exile. She'd been born in Anglet, not far from their apartment in Petit Bayonne. Both of her parents identified as French Basques, but she did not receive a strict Basque upbringing.

No reason to doubt her level of devotion by any means, as rarely did one find a French Basque who actually spoke Basque, especially with the younger generation.

But he did question Izaskun's motives.

He'd come to know her too well. If she never met him, he assumed she would have been a supporter of Basque cultural identity, and to a lesser extent, Basque independence. He did not believe, though, that she would ever have volunteered to be an ETA assassin.

These ponderings ate at him daily. On one hand, as a devout follower of the cause, he should feel fortunate to have such a talented—as he heard her described by many—operative on their side. And he should be proud for having been responsible for introducing her to the cause in the first place. On the other hand, it was difficult to get beyond the fact that he felt responsible for whatever would happen to Izaskun. As with all of the special operatives, as she had become, it was only a matter of time before she would be captured, imprisoned, or killed.

"You're looking too serious again. Here, take this," Izaskun said, handing him a glass of red Irouléguy.

"But this *is* serious business we are involved in, Izas," he said, calling her his nickname for her. "The moment someone stops remembering that fact, that is when they get caught or killed."

Izaskun abruptly blew air from her mouth, causing her lips to unattractively vibrate. "Of course, I know this, Gara," she responded. "The last thing I would ever want is for something to happen to keep us apart."

Even though Izaskun had spoken innocently, there was something unsettling to Garikotz about her words.

"And I'm always very careful. Everything in Irun went smoothly, just as we planned," she added.

Garikotz couldn't deny this point, as everything had progressed perfectly. The high profile target of Colonel Antonio Molina was eliminated in a public setting for all to see, and they even managed to take care of another Spanish Civil Guard soldier escorting Molina to his car, Molina's driver, and a few civilians in the vicinity of the explosion were wounded. The killing of only Spanish police forces and the wounding of civilians could not have been better planned.

He couldn't have predicted such positive results. Garikotz had the perfect ammunition for the propaganda pieces he'd already written and distributed, describing how ETA never intended harm to civilians, but that their struggle against the heavily armed Spanish oppressors left them no choice but to use guerrilla warfare tactics. With each attack, as he stressed repeatedly, they attempted to avoid civilian injuries and causalities, but the Spanish government's continued occupation of the Basque Country left them no choice. The possibility of injuries to the good people of the Basque Country was unfortunately something they could never completely rule out.

Of course, this was all a fabrication. They chose the locations to hit their targets precisely because they would be in public settings, where an attack would be prominent and visible and the Spanish government would be unable to conceal or weave their own lies in the aftermath.

As typical practice, most of the time ETA warned of attacks prior to a bomb detonating by placing anonymous calls to the police through one of their supporting journalist contacts in the Basque Country. This would allow an area to be cleared beforehand and still had the high profile of grabbing people's attention by occurring midday in an urban setting.

But the problem with these warnings was that often they only resulted in a car exploding on a city street. And ETA had blown up a lot of cars already. Patxi had been preaching for some time that if they were ever to make any progress, they needed to accept the potential for harming civilians. An unfortunate, but necessary, reality.

Garikotz cautiously agreed with Patxi. He agreed that nonlethal bombings had lost the impact they once had for inciting fear, but he recognized the alternative was a dangerous path. There were many supporters of the cause in the Basque provinces, but if they became seen by the Basque people as murderers, they could expect that support to dwindle. That could not happen.

And for as strong of a leader as Patxi Irionda was becoming, Patxi's brash tactics concerned Garikotz at times. One day, he feared, his friend would go too far.

VI.

Biarritz, French Basque Country

PEOPLE WOULD THINK THE HIT was retaliation for Colonel Antonio Molina. Marie-France was sure. Although no one except for herself and the top leaders of the GAL would know the truth. The truth was that Juan Manuel Irigaray had been marked as a target a month before Molina's assassination in Irun. And since that time, Irigaray had the unfortunate distinction of being assigned to the Lady in Black. She'd been patiently observing him and tracking his movements. Waiting to strike.

That time had arrived.

She received word that she was to carry out the attack as soon as she felt she could most efficiently execute. The timing just happened to be after the Molina hit. She wanted to wait until she knew exactly where he would be and everything about the area before striking. After six weeks of following him, she had complete confidence.

It was Wednesday and she was going to take out her target at approximately ten in the morning. She knew right where he would be. She was so sure she didn't even bother tailing him beforehand to ensure he would be at her target site. Instead, she decided to take a casual stroll in Biarritz before *work*.

She gave instructions for certain items to be left in a vehicle for her at an exact location near the site. She also gave her driver a specific location where and when to be parked waiting for her afterward. Everything was in place. Now she just had to act.

But there was no rush. She wanted to savor the moment for as long as possible. Her feelings were always this way before an assignment. Marie-France felt calm and serene and powerful. She was about to execute someone in the middle of the day in a popular area of a major resort city. And nothing was going to stop her. She just knew it. The day was hers.

The sun was dazzling and warm. She was wearing a short black skirt and a white blousy top with an oversized red belt. She accented her outfit with large dark plastic sunglasses and a pair of low black heels. Her fake brown hair was pulled back into a loose ponytail. She would later ditch the heels for more appropriate shoes.

In her first attacks, she hadn't even run after walking into bars or cafés and shooting one of her targets. She calmly, but quickly, turned and walked away, meeting her driver at the nearest intersection. At first, she imagined people were so shocked to see a petite blonde woman dressed in a short skirt and a black overcoat casually pull out a gun and shoot a person in such a public place that they were left shell-shocked after and had no capacity to pursue her, even if they wanted to.

But with more hits lately by the GAL, times were changing.

One of her GAL counterparts had been pursued by a mob after a hit at a bar in Petit Bayonne. Although what happened was partly the fool's own fault, as he'd chosen the Bar Lagunekin on Rue Pannecau as his site—a serious mistake. This favorite bar for Basque radicals was located on a stretch of road without side streets or alleys. The location was pretty much the only place in all of Petit Bayonne where this was the case. Picking such a site without nearby escape routes was suicidal. And it nearly had been.

After he fired at his target in the bar, he was followed by a group of men, and the fool wasn't able to even run, as he picked a weekend night to carry out the attack and Rue Pannecau was normally packed with people. As he was pursued, the group yelled at him and called out for help. Quickly a group of ten turned into fifty as other Basques poured out of bars to join the pursuit. The GAL member would surely have been beaten, strangled, and tossed into the Nive to drown had he not been fortunate enough to make it across the river. There he saw a French police car and ran to it, literally tossing himself on top of the hood of the car and surprising the hell out of the two French police officers inside. Being arrested that night for attempted murder, as the *con* had not even managed to kill his target, saved the idiot's life.

Marie-France could not ever let such a thing happen to her. She had her little girl to look after.

She felt sexy in her short skirt. She liked noticing men sitting at the outdoor cafés along Biarritz's central Grand Plage staring at her as she sauntered by. Just as she could feel the warm sun touching her skin, she could feel their eyes on her body. She wondered if all men were like French men and made absolutely no attempt to conceal checking out women, even in front of their wives, girlfriends, or mistresses.

The beach was just beginning to fill up with the usual mix of retirees, local families with little kids, Parisians, and other foreigners. The British were always easy to identify with their pasty skin. Old German couples seemed to love wearing Speedos and bikinis long after they should have stopped doing so with their bulging bellies and saggy breasts. Italian guys stuck out with their hairy chests and thick gold chains around their necks. Parisians were easy to spot too, always looking uncomfortable and overdressed for a day at the beach.

Sunlight glared off of the brilliantly blue water and small waves lapped at the shore. There was no breeze and the smell of blooming flowers blended with the salty smell of the ocean.

Rocky cliffs curved inward slightly and framed the beach to the north, with the white lighthouse towering above. To the south, large rock outcroppings were scattered along the shore as if some giant had decided to throw boulders into the water from the shore. She understood why Biarritz had been a popular beach resort destination for hundreds of years. The glitzy city had once been limited to European royalty, as evidenced by the former baroque palace of Napoleon III, now an elegant hotel. These days, Biarritz was accessible to everyone. Thankfully, Americans hadn't really discovered Biarritz yet.

She stopped walking on the esplanade bordering the beach area and stared out at the ocean. The vast expanse of water extending to the horizon looked so calm and peaceful and inviting. But the ocean was unpredictable and dangerous. The moment you stopped respecting the ocean, it could kill you. She closed her eyes and inhaled deeply. After a few moments she opened her eyes. Marie-France didn't need to see a watch or clock. It was time.

The car, a small black Renault, was right where it was supposed to be, at the intersection of the Avenue d'Ossuna and Rue Marie Hope Vère. She would find Juan Manuel Irigaray at the Café de Pyrenees, seated outside at the same table he sat at every Wednesday morning. He'd be reading a newspaper, sipping coffee, and smoking cigarettes, just as he did every Wednesday morning between approximately nine-thirty and eleven-thirty. At eleven-thirty, he'd order a glass of white wine, just a pre-lunch *apéritif.* She'd ventured close enough to hear him ask the waiter for the glass of wine on numerous occasions. After he finished his glass of wine, he'd walk to one of half a dozen different restaurants where he would meet someone for lunch. There was no pattern to his lunch location selections, as far as she'd observed, but his Wednesday routine of morning coffee followed by an early glass of wine remained unchanged. She'd seen him visit other cafes for a similar ritual. He even visited the Café des Pyrenees occasionally on different mornings. But for whatever reason, his Wednesday routine was unwavering.

Such arrogance. A perfect example of how lenient the French government and French people had been with these terrorists living as *refugees* in France. Even one of the alleged leaders of ETA didn't deem varying his schedule as necessary to avoid becoming an easy target. Even when he knew the GAL was after them, and very potentially, after him.

She admitted that the GAL did normally target lower level members in the organization. Rank and file members who somehow ended up in France. Or the occasional mid-tier hit man or woman. But the upper-tier members were usually left aside. They were considered as too high profile targets.

The GAL was walking on a tightrope. They wanted to make a statement by tracking down and killing ETA operatives hiding in France. The group wanted to firmly catch the attention of the French. They did not, however, want to overexpose themselves by becoming the assailant killer of individuals who were supposedly under the protection of the French government. Individuals somehow granted official political refugee status. Individuals like Irigaray.

But the situation needed to change. They were getting away with too much. The French people may have seen them as idealistic, if not misguided, radical revolutionaries, but the truth was that they were killers trying to overthrow a democratic government. If the French would only wake up from the illusion of seeing a reflection of the Parisian barricades of 1792 when they considered the Basque independence movement in Spain, they would see things as they really were. The majority of Spanish Basques had voted against complete independence for the three Basque provinces from Spain. Clearly, ETA was only a lingering menace needing to be eliminated.

She was now nearly beside the Renault. She quickly glanced around to see if she was being watched. Just a few people walking in the vicinity heading wherever, minding their own business. She opened the side door to the Renault and removed a blanket from the passenger seat. Marie-France grinned. Everything was there. Black overcoat, flat shoes, and the Molotov cocktail in a glass cylinder she was going to use to kill Irigaray. From what she was told, the bomb was an improvisation that the Spanish military had designed, with a self-igniting fuse that would explode it like a mini firebomb upon shattering its glass with force.

The force part would not be a problem. Although Marie-France had not been overly interested in politics in the past, she was increasingly becoming passionate about her job. Of course, the money was nice—so much better than begging for a part-time job or having to live off of social welfare from the government. Some French women might have tried to take advantage of a situation like hers and claim that their husband, the father of their child, the provider for their household, had run off and left them hopeless. But Marie-France had no way of even proving he was alive or dead, and even when he had been working, he'd done under-the-table construction work and had joked about how he always cheated on paying taxes. The government was going to be no help to Marie-France. She didn't want it to be.

She quickly changed shoes, leaving the pair of low heels she'd been wearing and the brown wig inside the car. The car would be untraceable anyway. And no one would notice or care about a pair of black heels and a wig in a random car near a crime scene. There were a lot of old women in Biarritz wearing wigs, and as for the heels—everyone knew that French women love heels.

Even though the temperature was rising, slipping the black overcoat on was comforting. She grabbed the glass canister and placed it in a pocket of the coat. She'd moved on from the serene, peaceful state at the beach. This was a new phase of the process she came to know in carrying out her assignments. This was her power phase. This was when people died.

Marie-France once read an article describing her hits. Witnesses at scenes made such a big deal about how calm she always appeared, before and after she walked up to a man and shot him in the chest. The combination of a petite blonde woman with such a calm demeanor removed any possible suspicion of her true intentions when people first noticed her.

Marie-France didn't understand the big deal made about remaining calm. What good of an assassin would one be by arousing suspicion before even getting close to the target? And she didn't let herself think of her actions as committing murder. Some may call what she did that. But, before anything else, this was just a job. She openly admitted that her situation may have subconsciously contributed to her level of ease at carrying out assignments, knowing that she was striking back at a terrorist organization. An organization that robbed her of a husband. But she wasn't in this for ideology. Like many of her GAL counterparts, she was in for the money. Those in Spain running the show seemed to have enough ideology about the whole thing for everyone.

Today was no different than any other. Her icy resolve cut through the mounting heat.

The Café des Pyrénées was just down the block and within a minute she saw her target, seated at a table outside, just where she knew he would be. But something was not as planned. Irigaray was not alone.

Ordinarily, there would be no issue for Marie-France. More often than not, her targets were in the company of others. The difference this time, however, was that she wasn't using a gun. She was armed with a handheld bomb. With a gun, there'd be no problem. She'd walk up, point, and shoot Irigaray without the slightest hesitation. If the man seated at the table made any move, she'd effortlessly shoot him. In her experience, though, people were so shocked to see an act of violence suddenly occur in front of them that they were petrified.

With a firebomb, now clutched inside one of the overcoat's inner pockets, there would be no way to direct the blast solely at Irigaray. She didn't know much about the explosive device she was gripping with her left hand, but she knew enough that in order to cause self-detonation she had to slam the device against something hard to shatter the glass. Something such as the cement at Irigaray's feet or the steel bistro table.

She'd already ruled out the sidewalk—the blast might spread underneath the table and only hit his legs. He would surely not die from burned legs. And her bonus after the assignment would be half as much if Irigaray wasn't killed. She didn't want to use the explosive from the beginning and clearly conveyed that she was not comfortable switching her ways, especially for such a high profile target. But the bosses, whoever they were—she only was given direction, assistance, supplies, and money from her assigned middle man—insisted that Irigaray go down in flames. Literally. Apparently, they wanted to make a glaring example of Irigaray. They wanted to clearly demonstrate that the GAL could take down anyone. Any time. And in any form.

This was all fine and good with Marie-France. But they failed to advise what she should do in a situation where it was obvious that if she carried out her assignment there would be collateral damage. As she decided that in order to make a definite strike at Irigaray she would have to throw the glass canister at the top of the bistro table in front of him, there was no doubt that the resulting fuel and fire burst would spray onto not only Irigaray, but whoever was seated next to him.

The two men were close enough now that she could make out specific details. Irigaray had been in the sun too much the previous day and his face was slightly sunburned. The other man had not shaved for a few days and had the start of a grizzled gray beard.

She didn't know what to do. Should she abort her assignment? Due to the inner dialogue she was having as she walked closer to the café, she failed to retain her usual habit of appearing inconspicuous. She didn't realize she'd been staring at Irigaray the entire time and he had not failed to notice an attractive young women approaching with her eyes set on him. He probably thought she was into older men. But what this meant was that he would definitely remember her face.

Her cover was blown. Now or never. If never, she'd lose the bonus commission. And maybe the bosses would not give her another assignment if she messed this one up. This high level target. After all, they had already paid her upfront fee and expenses for observation time, which her middle man pointed out repeatedly.

She couldn't have that. She couldn't lose this job. Her daughter needed her. Whoever was sitting with Irigaray was out of luck. His mistake was being friends with a terrorist bastard.

Everything happened so quickly. Marie-France didn't miss a step. Didn't hesitate for a moment. She approached the two men, Irigaray now leering, and smiled. When she was nearly within arm's distance, she quickly pulled the canister from the overcoat and threw the device with all her strength down at the top of the table. As she did she pivoted her body away from the oncoming blast and turned to start running down the sidewalk.

She didn't see the explosion. She didn't need to.

She heard it. She heard the sound of the glass shattering on the table top. She heard the hiss of the gas explode into flames outward from the point of impact. She heard the instant screams of terror from the two men.

She'd later see the images of them on the cover of an international news magazine. Irigaray and the other man ran into the street screaming wildly, tearing at the flaming clothing not yet burned from their bodies.

The other man turned out to be another senior ETA operative who secretly crossed the border to meet with Irigaray. This turned out to be a great advantage for Marie-France. Neither man died from their burns. But with her hit on both, and her site selection in the heart of an international tourist destination, in the middle of the day, with beautiful blue skies and sunshine in the background of the two burning men, her assignment reverberated further in the world press than any other GAL hit in France.

The GAL had been known in international circles before, but now they would make international headlines. And Marie-France was to thank for this. For her effort, she would be substantially rewarded.

But she didn't know this at the time. At the time, she just wanted to get away as quickly as possible. She may have approached calmly, but based on the location and time of day, there was no walking away calmly. She ran.

She pulled off the black overcoat as she sprinted down the block. At the end of the block, the intersection with the Rue de Frias, she saw her driver in the gray Mercedes-Benz, just as he was supposed to be. Before reaching the intersection, she made herself stop running. She heard the screams of the two men in the background, and now a police siren. She calmly opened the side door of the Mercedes and sat down. As soon she closed her door, her driver drove to the Avenue de Verdun, leading directly out of the city to the D260 and onto the D810, leading to the much larger A63 highway. Just as she had planned, within minutes they were out of Biarritz and into the countryside. They would drive to the rendezvous spot where the vehicle would be abandoned and they would each be taken by different drivers to different locations.

By midafternoon, Marie-France would be home with her daughter.

VII.

Louhossoa, French Basque Country

LOUHOSSOA WASN'T FAR FROM THE VILLAGE where Patxi had grown up, Saint-Pée-sur-Nivelle. He was staying in a safe house with an older French Basque couple helping keep him concealed in their house just outside the village. He didn't live in secret all the time, but at times he would suddenly change his routine or go into hiding for a couple of months. Just to keep moving and be difficult to track.

Being in the old Basque farmhouse in the countryside almost felt like returning to his childhood home. But there were some things from his childhood he would never be able to revisit. His parents.

They were executed by a GAL hit squad during what was considered the first wave of GAL attacks on exiles living in France five years ago. His father had been a senior member of ETA, considered by many to be one of the organization's top leaders and known for his appeal to both the military and nonmilitary factions within the organization. After years of harassment and growing fear for their safety in Bilbao, his parents left Bizkaia to cross the border with their son and settled in the charming village of Saint-Pée.

Patxi's father introduced him to the ETA organization, and Patxi admired his father's role. He hoped to one day be as revered of a leader.

But the fucking GAL henchmen got to his father. One night, a pair of them snuck into his parents' country home and cowardly shot them in their sleep. The hit was meant as a warning in the early days of the GAL—to display their ability to operate in France as freely as they did in Spain.

The cold-blooded assassination had a different effect though. Instead of striking fear into the hearts of the Basque political exiles in France, the attack reinforced their resolve. After all, Patxi's father made publicly known that while he remained an ardent supporter of Basque independence, he'd decided to retire from all militant activities. His mother never played any part in ETA. Over a thousand people attended Patxi's parents' funeral at the old church in Petit Bayonne, with many people waiting outside, as all the benches within were occupied. The funeral service was conducted in Basque, and there was no one in the entire quarter of Petit Bayonne that didn't hear the haunting chorus of voices singing the *Eusko Abendaren Ereserkia*, the anthem of the Basque Country. This anthem was closely followed by another. *Eusko Gudariak* was a hymn of Basque soldiers from the 1930s adopted as ETA's own nationalist anthem.

The killing of his parents had another impact. It set a fire within their son.

Even with his father's gradual tapering, and eventual retirement, from ETA, Patxi was raised knowing where he came from. From the time he was a boy, he knew he would join the cause.

His progression into the movement started with his participation in the urban street struggle called *kale borroka* by the Basques. This low level form of resistance was mostly carried out by youth, breaking the windows of banks, setting fire to realty offices, or spray-painting slogans on walls or signs such as *Eusal Herria ez Dago Salagai—The Basque Country Is Not for Sale.*

Eventually he joined a Basque youth cultural group. That's what they called themselves anyway. By claiming they were just a cultural group, they could legally sponsor rallies and events and not have the police on their asses. But in truth, they were in training, both politically and physically, to officially join the movement after high school.

The French Basque radical group, IK, was an option, but they seemed so unorganized compared to ETA. They pulled off a few interesting operations though, such as planting a bomb in a public square in Paris. And they almost pulled off an attack which would have been huge even by ETA standards. They planted a bomb on the TGV high speed rail line between Paris and Biarritz with the intent to detonate just as a train would pass by, surely derailing the train and inflicting a huge number of casualties. If they'd pulled off this planned attack, the shift of Basque radicalism may have moved into France instead of staying in its more traditional home in Spain. But, perhaps prophetically and indicative of the perpetual secondary status of IK, the bomb did not detonate and the plot was uncovered by French authorities.

This failed event also had other far-reaching impacts. Up until recent years, the only violence in France related to the Basque independence was the low level *kale borroka*. But now that IK had begun a new campaign of higher level violence, including killing a couple of French *gendarmes* on different occasions, French support for the Basque struggle was decreasing rapidly.

IK may have thought they were doing good to bring the fight north, but as Garikotz often described in the correspondence reports he distributed describing affairs in France, IK was doing far more harm than good to the overall Basque independence movement. There were multiple reasons why. For one, the French government had always supported the Basque struggle in Spain. For political reasons in consideration with their neighbor to the south, they may have never made official public statements in support of the Basque movement or the armed resistance in response to Spanish occupation, but the reality was understood that the French government never trusted the Franco regime and still didn't believe that post-Franco Spain was a free democracy. To that end, the French government had supported refugee status, both officially and unofficially, for Basque political exiles seeking refuge.

And as for Spain's claim that these refugees somehow made routine trips back across the porous border to conduct attacks in Spain...the French government routinely stated an unawareness of such activities originating in France. So the French government was fine with violence occurring outside of the country's own borders. But IK's misguided actions were making the situation more complicated. Now the French government couldn't say that all violence associated with the Basque movement was south of the border. The violence was happening in their own country.

Of course, the violence was being carried out by a different group than the *etarras* living in France, but there was no way to separate the individual identities of IK versus ETA at a macropolitical perception. At this broad level, the two groups were one and the same. Both armed wings of a cross-border independence movement. Now that the French government had to extend its own police forces to protect the country's citizens from these perceived domestic terrorist acts, granting refugee status and looking the other way were both rapidly coming to an end. And they had IK to thank for this unfortunate turn of events.

Furthermore, IK's actions were having a broad impact on French perception of the Basque movement in general. France, even more than Spain, had multiple ongoing independence movements. The Pays Basque was one, but there were also firm separatist movements in Brittany, headed by the Union Démocratique Bretonne (UDB), and Corsica, with its Fronte di Liberazione Naziunale Corsu (FLNC), among others around the hexagon. The revolutionary spirit of the French never seemed opposed to these movements achieving some level of regional autonomy. But once people started getting killed in the name of these independence movements, the mood changed. And with a loss of public support for the Basque cause, there would eventually be fewer safe houses offered to those exiles who wanted to remain clandestine. There would eventually be more people reporting to authorities of suspicious persons. There would eventually be more scrutiny of identification papers at border crossings. And, perhaps worst of all, there would be more cooperation between the Spanish and French governments.

Patxi respected the frustration of the IK members and other Basque political and paramilitary groups in the French Basque Country. It was undoubtedly true that they did indeed get treated like children compared to the concentration of activity in the Spanish Basque provinces. Probably didn't help that some people did refer to the northern Basque Country struggle as literally the *little brother* compared to the struggle in the south.

And they had every right to be upset at the French government for not being allowed independence. Especially since numerous powerful politicians, including President Mitterrand himself, vowed to grant the

Basque Country more autonomy, even going so far as to claim the area could be its own department instead of being part of the lager Pyrénées Atlantiques Department. But as with others, Mitterrand's promises faded away after he was elected.

But the fact was that the French Basque provinces hadn't endured the horror experienced in the Spanish Basque provinces. They'd experienced nothing remotely like the atrocities in the south. The Basque language in the French provinces was dying out, but not because the language had been forbidden and illegal for decades as Basque had been in Spain. In the French provinces, the Basque language was dying due to lack of interest in keeping it alive by the majority of the population. Cry as much as they wanted, but the French Basque provinces had let Basque culture fade over the years when the language could have flourished.

Besides, the view was near universally accepted by the Spanish Basques that the northern provinces were part of the bigger picture, part of the overall plan for the future of an independent Basque Country. But first things needed to be settled in Spain, where there was a direct threat to the survival of the Basque Country, even without the old bastard general in charge. And they needed things to stay calm on the French side of the border. If not, the traditional refuge in the north could come to an end.

That end had already started. Not long ago, two young *etarras* had reported to French police officers that they were being followed and believed their lives were in danger. The French officers didn't bother to investigate. A day later, a witness saw the two young men forced into a vehicle after exiting a bar in Petit Bayonne. They disappeared that night.

The GAL were growing bolder every day. And that *salope* Lady in Black—she was worst. In response to their attack on Molina in Irun, the GAL struck again, and she carried out the attack. She didn't even bother to wait for night. She struck in the middle of the day, in the heart of Biarritz. The lethal bitch had struck and escaped when there must have been at least ten French policeman in the general vicinity. The two men she hit were miraculously not going to die from their injuries, but the psychological toll of the attack was profound. *She lit them on fire.*

Patxi planned to make them pay for the attack. With Garikotz's help, he was strategizing a coordinated attack hitting back directly at Madrid with the dual purpose of reminding Navarre that the province was part of the struggle. A coordinated attack such as this would capture everyone's attention.

The Madrid attack would be a bomb in the city's international airport. Like France, Spain was highly dependent on the tourism industry, and striking the primary arrival point for international visitors to Spain would send a clear message. Patxi wanted to plant a bomb in one of the airport's terminals and order detonation at night, when there would be less activity. He didn't mind some collateral damage of injuring or killing people, but he recognized that too much display of force would harm their international image.

Garikotz convinced him to change direction and suggested they instead plant a car bomb in the airport's parking garage and detonate during the middle of the day. Garikotz requested a member of the Madrid commando unit conduct a site reconnaissance. The Madrid contact reported that a segment of the main parking garage was undergoing construction and off limits to the public. Consulting with Itxaso, Garikotz predicted they could detonate a bomb inside a parked vehicle directly adjacent to the area closed off for construction. With the proper placement of the explosives, it would be possible to direct the force of the explosion toward the unoccupied portion of the parking garage. Therefore, the attack would be very high profile, demonstrating ETA's ability to strike at the epicenter of the Spanish establishment, and it would have an extremely destructive impact. Furthermore, the attack would inflict fear in the minds of potential travelers to Spain, yet have no casualties.

It would be perfect, Garikotz assured him.

Patxi would not change his plan for Navarre though, and Garikotz didn't disagree. The province of Navarre had long been a thorn in the side of the other three Spanish Basque provinces of Alava, Biscay, and Gipuzkoa. While the province was clearly a Basque province and should be grouped with the other three, the Spanish government had kept a firm grip on Navarre.

Although never proven, a long suspicion was that Spaniards from other parts of the country were relocated to Navarre and set up nicely. The situation was outrageous, but similar to the stance on the northern Basque provinces in Spain. Most people saw the full incorporation of Navarre as a secondary issue to be dealt with later. And it absolutely would be dealt with. Not only for historical reasons, but also because the province's incorporation into a newly formed independent Basque Country would more than double the size of the existing three other provinces combined.

The organization's leaders may have been afraid of making statements in Navarre, but Garikotz was firm in his belief that more needed to be done to influence Navarre to join the fight. A bombing in the province's City of Pamplona would send a wake-up call. Patxi wanted to set off a bomb at the university, partly because of its central location and partly because the university continued to openly reject offering courses in Basque. Garikotz had no objection.

But, unlike with the planned attack at the Madrid airport, Garikotz didn't agree with Patxi's plan to not call in the attack before the explosion. The campus of the university was located directly in the *centre-ville* of the city, and an attack there would be sure to have casualties at any time of day, considering the proximity of classrooms, dormitories, and cafés and bars, popular day and night.

Patxi said he'd call in the attack, but he wasn't sure he would. He wasn't bloodthirsty and wished there was another way, but they were left with no other options. The GAL couldn't keep getting away with it. They murdered his parents and they were lighting his people on fire!

These attacks would be good. Very good. Once they secured independence in the southern provinces and acquired Navarre, they would next regain the northern provinces. If the French refused to grant Basque independence, he would plan similar attacks in places such as Paris or the tourist favorite, Côte d'Azur.

Someday, the Basque Country would be united and free. And Patxi Irionda knew his destiny was to help make this happen.

VIII.

Saint-Jean-de-Luz, French Basque Country

CHARLES MARTEL WAS ALWAYS LATE. Always. Garikotz didn't know why he even bothered to be punctual when they arranged meeting. But punctuality was a fundamental quality to him; breaking from his own foundation of character would be an effort. He sat in the Café Bittor and waited.

A half hour after their planned meeting time, Charles stepped in through the doorway of the café, looking as smug and full of himself as ever. Charles fit the description of a sophisticated French radical very well. Always immaculately dressed with his short dark hair perfectly in place. A silk scarf wrapped around his neck and tucked into the front of his shirt. The two made an unlikely pair, with Garikotz in his jeans, loose sweater, flat cap with his longish hair sticking out of the sides, and glasses.

"Ah, my friend, how good to see you," Charles said as they shook hands.

"You're late," Garikotz replied.

Charles glanced at the watch on his wrist and shrugged his shoulders. "*Eh bèh*, what is time for people like us? Don't tell me that you didn't take advantage of your time to reflect on how to craft your next piece? Perhaps you even started writing?" Charles asked, lowering his eyes to the paper tablet on the table in front of Garikotz.

Self-obsessed prick. Damn him for being right, Garikotz thought. He didn't bother responding directly to Charles' observation. "We have some items to discuss," Garikotz suggested.

Charles waved across the room at a middle-aged waitress. "*Un café, s'il vous plait,*" he called out, obnoxiously loud enough for everyone in the café to hear him.

Charles made an event of being seated, gracefully pulling the chair from the table and sitting down slowly. At times, he annoyed the hell out of Garikotz. But Garikotz and Charles shared an important role for their respective organizations. Garikotz was ETA's contact with IK. Charles was the same in reverse. They each provided the primary communication link between the two groups. Even during times of dispute, Garikotz and Charles stuck with meeting monthly to inform and be informed.

They picked a different location for each meeting, always choosing Basque nationalist friendly places where they could speak freely and not worry about being overheard. But having a welcoming location came with a price. This very café had been the scene of a brutal attack just months ago, when two GAL members had walked in and sprayed the interior with semi-automatic machine guns. There'd been only one ETA member in the crowded café at the time, but the GAL members shot everyone indiscriminately, including women and children. *Les sales connards...*

Garikotz couldn't wait for his friend Aitzol to track down GAL killers in France. His training was almost complete and he was going to be good. He'd become one of ETA's hunters of hunters. There were already a few that he knew of on assignments in the French Basque County, but not enough. The GAL was too prominently funded and supplied to be just some random assortment of mercenaries looking to cash in by tracking down ETA members in France and then jockeying for a bounty from the Spanish government. Mercenaries they were, clearly all of them, but they were no random group—they were highly organized. And they were highly orchestrated. Garikotz had no doubt that the maestro leading them was within the Spanish military. He doubted the truth would ever be proven. But decades from now, the whole world would know that the GAL was just a paramilitary wing of the Spanish government.

But the fellow Basque separatist now sitting at his table didn't have to worry about the GAL. The GAL didn't give a damn about IK. The

GAL issued statements that potential targets would be expanded to include any French citizens known to provide cover, collaborate with, protect, or employ any ETA member in exile. But Garikotz doubted this would ever happen. The GAL wouldn't risk pissing off the French government.

And besides, not one IK member had ever been targeted by the GAL, despite the fact that both groups, ETA and IK, were fighting for the same ultimate goal: total Basque independence. Garikotz didn't mind the existence of IK, not nearly as much as many of his ETA counterparts. They saw the parallel group as a nuisance, if not worse. Many didn't want IK operating at all. Anything they managed to do took away the focus from the real fight for the Basque Country in Spain and also made life more difficult for ETA members living either openly or clandestinely across in France.

Garikotz's duty was to stay informed of IK's actions and maintain a connection between the two organizations. Another duty was to try and influence those actions, or nonactions. Garikotz wasn't opposed to IK's low level violent activities, the street struggle they'd always conducted and encouraged in youth groups.

All of that was okay. The French Basques didn't have nearly as much to revolt against as their brethren locked in struggle across the border in Spain. If they wanted to make their war focused on tourism and foreigner home ownership in the Basque Country, this was a fine goal.

But lately, IK had been trying to turn up the heat.

"The airport? You guys really thought that was a good idea?" Garikotz asked, not trying to hide his annoyance. Charles didn't speak Basque and his Spanish was poor, so their discussions were always in French.

The expression on Charles' face instantly turned from grin to grimace. "That son of a bitch lied—he said he'd give us our own department after he was elected. But did he? The subject was never even mentioned again and he refuses to address the question when confronted on his dishonesty. We should have never believed him."

There might be some validity in Charles' position, Garikotz considered. After all, President Mitterrand had lied about his intentions to create a separate Basque department. But setting off a bomb at the Biarritz airport as the President of France's plane landed was a risky endeavor. The attack would undoubtedly bring global attention to the French Basque Country, but there was no way of knowing what kind of reaction the French would have after such an attack. Not that this all really mattered though, as the attack failed when the explosives didn't ignite. IK didn't have the same skill level as ETA, proven yet again. Just a couple of months ago two IK members killed themselves after the car bomb they were attempting to set ignited prematurely. They were still amateurs, but dangerous amateurs.

"Something of this magnitude would be counterproductive for the ultimate goals of the cause," Garikotz said.

"But things are moving too slowly here in the north. We need to make our presence known now or the French are never going to acknowledge that the Basque struggle is not limited to what happens in the south. If we don't act, the French Basque Country is going to become home to retirees and foreigners. If we want our own rights, if we want our liberty, we have only one path: struggle."

"I agree with you Charles, to a point. But more than likely the idea of a French Basque department was a sacrifice the French made to the Spanish in the name of diplomacy. The French may say they are not supportive of the Spanish state, but they are still direct neighbors sharing a long and porous border. The Spanish would not approve of the creation of a Basque department, as this would further provoke Basque separatism in Spain."

"Even if that's true, we cannot let the momentum pass. Pierre is leading us in a new direction."

Pierre Sartout. Called the *Pyrenean Mesrine*. Garikotz had met the charismatic IK leader once. Sartout was the type of person so in love with his image that he forgot everything else.

From the beginning, Sartout didn't deny that he was pro-violence. There were even rumors that at IK's beginning, he undertook a few attacks on his own without general consent of others, including a failed attempt to set off explosives on one leg of the Tour de France passing through the Pyrenees. Garikotz and most others who found out about the failed attack later cringed at the thought of what might have happened had Sartout been successful.

"The time for sitting on our hands is over. We can't wait forever for you all in the south to get something done," Charles added.

Garikotz didn't take the bait, though he felt the sting of Charles' words. He calmly took a sip of his coffee and grinned without speaking. Of course, he could have responded that ETA had been fighting for Basque independence for decades against a brutally repressive government, while IK and the various other French Basque nationalist factions were all relatively new to the game and faced a much less repressive occupying government to counter. But he needed to be diplomatic.

"Can you tell me what exactly happened to EHAS?" Garikotz asked, changing the subject. Although he knew exactly what had happened. Sartout had coerced, purportedly using any means available, to have EHAS disbanded. The organization had been a direct threat to IK, as EHAS did not condone violence as a means to achieve Basque sovereignty in France. EHAS pursued nonviolence in their cause, stating that the situation in France was vastly different than in Spain, that use of violence in the French Basque Country could result in less support from the overall French Basque population, and that by resorting to violence in France they would provoke a formidable foe, the French government, which in all honestly had been mostly accommodating to the Basque cause.

Charles instantly recoiled at the mention of the former rival group. He shook his head dismissively. "Oh, they didn't have any support anymore. Only we have the support of the people," he responded.

Now you do...after eliminating your competition, Garikotz thought. "You know, most people agree that the Basques of the north support violence in the south, as they believe there is no other choice to achieve our goals in the face of such adversity. I wonder if one would say the same for Basques of the north believing the same for the struggle in the north?"

Garikotz's use of one of the words Charles so often put in his own press releases, speeches, and handouts made him smile. But Charles was no dimwit. He recognized the deliberate use of the word to deflect the true intent of the question Garikotz asked. "And tell me, what do you think the majority of our people in the south would say regarding our struggle here? Do you believe they would say that violence is *not* justified in order to achieve total Basque independence?"

A solid counter question, Garikotz admitted. The Basque people had a reputation for being passionate about life, more so than the French or the Spanish, which is saying a lot. And there was no way he could say that the same people supporting violence in the south would not feel the same for the Basque cause in the north.

"But you recognize that the escalation of the level of violence in the north is directly jeopardizing the safety of those from the south seeking refuge here," Garikotz asked.

Charles waved a hand, shrugged his shoulders, and blew a puff of air from his mouth. "Yes, yes, these are difficult times. But why should the Spanish Basques be considered more privileged than the French Basques?"

"Perhaps unlike you and your organization, we don't see ourselves as Spanish or French Basques, just Basques. And we see our struggle as universal, on both sides of the border. And we see this as a situation where the use of force is more justified in the south than in the north. The escalation of violence in the north only risks blocking the overall objectives of the movement."

"That's bullshit, you hypocritical son of a bitch, and you know it. You and your group have always treated us like the retarded cousins, and now that we are showing how capable we are of replicating your actions in Spain, you get scared that attention may shift northward instead of being all about..." Charles stopped himself short of announcing the name of ETA. After all, even though they were in a friendly environment, there was no way of knowing for sure if the safe location had been infiltrated with a spy. Everything that they said to one another could be considered hearsay, but by directly saying the name of one of their active organizations they could implicate themselves beyond reproach.

What Charles was saying was not entirely untrue, Garikotz thought. But he would never admit such a thing to the arrogant asshole sitting in front of him. Although Garikotz liked Charles, there were times when Charles pushed the line too far. After all, IK was just a junior player in the game compared to ETA, and everyone knew it. Even members of IK knew this, although they would never admit so much.

"And I'll tell you something—" Charles almost slipped and said Garikotz's name, something they agreed to never do during their meetings. "We are soon going to do something that will be far superior to anything that has ever happened in Spain. Nothing, in fact, will compare. In one sole event, we will surpass you in our devotion to the Basque cause." Charles raised a finger to exemplify his point. "Remember me saying this to you: We will become the dominant Basque independence group."

Charles lowered his finger and lifted his small coffee cup. He leaned back in his chair, content to see the look of bewilderment on Garikotz's face, and took a long sip of the strong coffee. These Spanish Basque pricks will have to respect us now, he said to himself. A sly grin slowly appeared on his face. He had Garikotz right where he wanted him.

Garikotz felt a jolt of panic run through his body. *What were these idiots going to try next?* "Charles…I think you should reconsider. A major statement now is not advisable. We are working on big plans in the south and we need calm in the north."

The current situation was that ETA members could relatively safely live on the French side of the border and still be wholly involved with operations, and even take part in those operations, across the border. The GAL was a total bitch, no doubt there, but they were still only getting a relatively small percentage of the overall ETA presence in France. No one really knew how many ETA members, direct or indirect supporters, were in France. Not even Garikotz—even he could only guess. The Basques had a history of being a secretive people, and nothing about that characteristic had ever changed.

"Listen, we are stronger than you or anyone realizes. We've very nearly pulled off some attacks that would have reached a magnitude far greater than blowing up a supermarket."

What a smug delusional prick. Charles' reference to what many considered ETA's most known attack of a bomb detonating in a

Barcelona supermarket was a not-so-subtle dig at the organization's track history. But to even think IK could be considered as equal to ETA was ludicrous. Garikotz's jaw tightened. "That may indeed be the case. But the fact of the matter is that if you continue to maintain this level where you have been reaching lately, eventually it's going to come down on you."

Charles waved a hand in the air and sighed. He reached into his jacket pocket and pulled out a pack of cigarettes. Lighting a cigarette, he said out of the corner of his mouth, "The GAL is not after us. You know this is true."

Garikotz tried to smile, though it was difficult, as his teeth were firmly gripped together. "Did you see the press release this week? They warned French Basques to stay away from places popular with refugees…"

"Yes, yes, so they are sloppy with their machine guns. So what?" Charles absently responded through a cloud of smoke.

Garikotz didn't immediately respond. Their discussion was beginning to get heated, and if he didn't tone things down, the meeting was going to come to a premature end. He took a long sip of coffee.

"Didn't you once state that your primary enemy was the development of tourism, calling tourism just a new form of imperialism? Shouldn't that be your primary target?"

"This is one target, yes. But a vacation war to drive away summer tourists and the *roast beefs* from buying holiday homes here is not enough. We also want a statute for the Basque language, a new form of economic development installed not based on tourism, a new institutional entity for the Basque people, and amnesty for all our prisoners. Since your Herri Batasuna is no longer inviting us to meetings, we have to assume that you do not believe the French Basque Country is sufficiently Basque for you. So you cannot expect us to sit around and do nothing while you try and carve out a country all for yourself down there."

Garikotz could have responded that ETA's overall objective was to have a unified, independent Basque Country across all four provinces in Spain and the three in France, but he'd said the same thing so many times before to Charles and others like him that he didn't have any desire to repeat again. But Charles made a valid argument about feeling rapprochement from the primary political wing of ETA. They recently toned down their rhetoric regarding the northern Basque provinces, mostly because they didn't want to fight a war on two fronts."

With the absence of a response, Charles continued. "You know, what you guys also don't seem to understand is that you come across the border and act like you are conquering heroes on a much-deserved vacation and you see us as crazy cousins or something. But you haven't conquered anything. And you come here and preach reformism in the north, while practicing radicalism in the south. I'm sorry to say this, but this is fucking hypocritical bullshit." Charles waved his burning cigarette in front of him as he spoke. "And you have been coming here, what, since the early 1960s? Ever since you attacked that train carrying Franco supporters?"

"Yes, that's true. But the train was not only carrying the bastard general's people. The train was traveling to Guernica to commemorate the Republican's victory in the civil war. And do you know what happened at Guernica? One of our sacred Basque places?"

Charles shrugged and put out his cigarette. "Yes, of course, I had history class in school. The town was destroyed and a lot of people were killed."

"A lot of Basque people," Garikotz added. "And do you know that after that attack the Spanish arrested and tortured hundreds of people who could have had nothing to do with the attack, but were targeted just because of their pro-Basque sympathies?"

Charles lit another cigarette. That part they will leave out of history books," he commented.

Garikotz laughed. "I'm sure they will. Along with many other things having to do with the Basque movement and this goddamn Dirty War the Spanish are waging by sending assassins to track us down. Someday maybe the truth will be known that they didn't just hire Spanish ex-military, but also French mafia, former Portuguese secret service agents, Italian neo-fascists, and they even recruited anyone they could find in France who would appear unsuspicious. I doubt those details will be included in any history books either."

Garikotz finished his coffee and set his cup down. "But, do you honestly believe that you are going to win over the people and have public support for a path of violence? By taking this route, you are putting yourself in a dangerous position of losing the firm support you have maintained with a path of low level violence. Escalation could mean the end to you."

Charles grinned in response. "Could be the end to you, I think you mean. You are worried you will lose your future safe haven over the mountains."

"Of course, we are worried about that. But what happens to us will be tied to what happens to you. If not now—eventually. The French government is already granting fewer and fewer refugee status approvals. Even when granted, some individuals are being sent to the far reaches of the French territories around the world, far from our motherland."

"You gained your support by demonstrating your force. We will do the same." Charles forcefully stubbed out his cigarette.

IX.

Bayonne, French Basque Country

NIVELLE SENSED SOMETHING WAS BOTHERING CAUDET. And he suspected whatever this was had something to do with Marie-France. Nivelle had been seeing her for months and whenever he mentioned her, Caudet became agitated. Caudet was not a man to hide his feelings. He also wasn't a man for small talk, but when two people spend as much time together as he and Caudet did, they were bound to find out about each other's lives.

Caudet suspected Marie-France was a GAL asset, Nivelle knew, but he never openly made the accusation. But the two had an argument after Nivelle discovered that Caudet ordered a background check on Marie-France without Nivelle's knowledge. That he'd done this behind Nivelle's back was unacceptable.

Yet, it was plausible, Nivelle admitted. After all, they knew for a fact that GAL had at least one female on their assassin squad, the infamous Lady in Black. Not long ago that minx had carried out a very high profile attack on two ETA members in downtown Biarritz during the middle of the day. While investigating the scene, Nivelle found a pair of heels and a wig in a parked car nearby. He couldn't be certain, but he figured they were related to the attack.

Could Marie-France really be the Lady in Black? *La Dama Negra* as the *etarras* called her? After all, even after months of sleeping together, most of her life was still a mystery to him. And even though he was displeased with Caudet's background check on her, he later reviewed the file. But there was nothing extraordinary in the file hinting at any involvement in radical right wing activities.

Actually, there was nothing at all indicating anything out of the ordinary. She had an estranged husband whose whereabouts were unknown, but Marie-France told Nivelle long ago how her husband had abandoned her and their daughter. No secret.

And she had a day job as a secretary at a small exporting company in Biarritz. Records indicated she'd held the position over a year.

Caudet could go to hell with his doubts. As plausible as the possibility might be, it was not possible. Nivelle was sure.

Now Caudet was bringing up the subject again. They were seated at a café on the Nive in the center of Bayonne. The sun was bright and although still morning, the day was already warming quickly. "*Chef*, I know you like her, but I think maybe your affections are clouding your judgment," Caudet cautiously suggested.

Nivelle fought back his initial desire to respond with hostility. He didn't like his girlfriend being accused of being a ruthless killer, but Caudet was, after all, only being thorough.

"What makes you believe she is the Lady in Black? Just because she fits the physical description of being a petite and pretty woman? If you want to find one of those, all you have to do is look around," Nivelle said, opening his hand at a pair of women walking by in summer dresses.

Caudet looked into his coffee cup. "Yes, that's true. But, tell me, *Chef*, what would you do if it was her? Would you arrest her?"

A good question, Nivelle reluctantly admitted. Officially, they were obligated to arrest anyone breaking the law. But, unofficially, Nivelle's mandate concerning GAL operatives was not so defined. Orders from Paris were vague, and one didn't know what to believe. Some thought they were supposed to try and stop GAL operatives; others thought they were supposed to help them. His personal opinion on the matter was conflicted. After all, they were targeting terrorists who were claiming to be refugees. But none of this included his growing feelings for Marie-France.

"I don't know, Caudet," Nivelle admitted. "But it doesn't fit, even if she does match the physical description of this GAL assassin. The bosses believe this Lady in Black is motivated by one of two things: money or revenge. Marie-France has a good paying job. I've confirmed her employment with official records. And somehow I imagine you've conducted some sort of surveillance on your own of her movements, without my approval or knowledge, and can confirm you've seen her walk to and from her place of work to her apartment in Biarritz?" Nivelle asked.

Caudet looked downward and didn't respond. Instead he lit a cigarette. He shrugged his shoulders through a cloud of smoke, his eyes still averted. "Just thought I was doing my job, *Chef.*"

Nivelle sighed. He couldn't be too upset with his devoted partner. After all, Caudet was doing his job. Although their official orders from the top were vague, they were charged with not only keeping an eye on Basque refugees in France, and in particular on known and suspected ETA members, but also trying to identify members of the GAL in France—although they didn't have specific orders to arrest any GAL operatives even if they were to identify them. Nivelle wondered if this vagueness was in response to a recent deal between the French and Spanish governments he read about, with the Spanish government purchasing a large number of tanks and armored vehicles from a major French company. If so, then the French government knew the best way to handle the situation.

"*Ça va*, Caudet. But let's work together from now on. I have a feeling things are about to drastically change here in the Basque Country, one way or another."

Change was in the air, as was a new direction in how the French people and government viewed these *refugees* that had been freely streaming across the border for so long. Just a week ago, French police forces had been ordered to raid the home of a French primary school teacher in Anglet suspected of supporting ETA. The police discovered an arsenal within the school teacher's home, including rocket launchers, hundreds of kilos of ammonal explosives, plastic explosives, AK-47s, and grenades. The arsenal cache was meant for a military outfit, what the Basques called a *zulo*, and the secret stash was hiding in the middle of a quiet residential neighborhood. And Nivelle knew of plans to raid a farm outside of Saint-Jean-Pied-de-Port where a farmer was suspected of hiding explosives for ETA. And then there was a factory in Saint-Jean-de-Luz run by a respectable businessman under similar suspicion.

"Seems to me, Caudet, that ETA's days of freedom here in France are quickly coming to an end."

Caudet raised his head to face Nivelle. "That may be true, *Chef*, but I think there will still be IK here to deal with," he said while exhaling smoke from his mouth.

IK, the bastard stepchild of ETA, Nivelle thought. The *terroristes locaux*, as French police forces referred to them. Like a child jealous of a sibling receiving all the attention. He agreed with Caudet though—even with ETA's presence removed or at least concealed, there would be some vacuum that IK or other French Basque radical groups might attempt to fill. But something they would never have compared to ETA in Spain would be a large percentage of the population supporting Basque independence at the cost of violence. That would not happen in the French Basque Country. The Spanish Basque Country may be more Basque than Spanish, but Nivelle sensed the French Basque Country was more French than Basque. And the French government and policing forces were ready to deal with IK.

"As for my girlfriend, leave her to me. Not only does she not fit the description of our assassin for hire, but she has no call for revenge. Her husband was not gunned down by ETA, he simply left her. If she had any revenge to take out, it would be on the *fils de pute* who left her and her little girl."

Caudet dropped his cigarette and ground the glowing embers out with his foot. "*Oui, Chef.*"

A couple of months had passed since they first starting seeing one another, and Nivelle believed everything was superb between him and Marie-France. They saw each other a few days every week, meeting for lunch or dinner or going for walks on the beach, and Nivelle often stayed over at her apartment. If not for her infant daughter, Nivelle was sure that Marie-France would want to stay over at his place.

Not one to often fall for a woman, his experience with Marie-France was new. He hoped to one day get married and have a family, but he didn't plan to find himself in the right place with the right woman until later, when he was more established in his career. He was still on the rise and having attachments now would make things difficult. Despite recognizing this point, Nivelle couldn't deny the strong attraction he had for Marie-France. The timing may not have been exactly right, but could he really let her slip through his fingers just because he wanted to excel in his career? She also came with a baby daughter, but this was not an important factor to Nivelle. Besides, he really liked her little girl and would not mind becoming a father.

Nivelle increasingly considered that he would not be able to live without Marie-France. He could still advance in his career. Perhaps not as rapidly as he'd hoped. But it would be worth the sacrifice.

He suddenly swerved the car to get back into the lane, seconds before he would have rammed into an oncoming truck. *Merde. Concentrate on driving instead of your love life, connard*, he scolded himself.

He really went out of his way to impress her tonight. Marie-France was led by the restaurant's hostess to a solitary outdoor table in a courtyard. Only one table was set with a white tablecloth and there were two candles lit on top. Soft lighting illuminated the area from outdoor lamps hidden among the tall plants enclosing the courtyard. This was obviously the restaurant's most exclusive table and one only used for special occasions. Reserving the table must have been expensive.

He was seated at the table, dressed in a nice suit. Even from a distance and in the dimmed light, she could see his eyes gleaming as he watched her approach, led to the table by the hostess. He was handsome, and he was good to her. And he probably would continue to be good to her, and her daughter, if she desired.

But she didn't. In fact, she'd been pondering calling things off with him for weeks. The comfort of having a good man beside her whenever she wanted had prolonged inaction on her part though, and she now regretted having not acted sooner. A good man he was, but she didn't need any man in her life.

At first their relationship was just what she wanted: fun, easy, and noncommittal. She enjoyed spending time with him, he was good to her daughter when she wanted him to be around her, and the sex was great. He was very polite and considerate and never asked for too much. When she would tell him that she didn't want him to stay over at night, he would leave without question.

Unfortunately, after a couple of months things began to change. He started asking to see her more; to spend more time with her daughter; to have the three of them go on a trip together. And the sex changed too. From the exciting sex of a fresh relationship, full of mystery and passion, into sex where there's more to the act than just pleasure. This sex was wonderful when mutually shared, but not when only one partner viewed the experience this way.

And now he was going to propose to her.

It was her fault for not ending things sooner. She was going to have to speed up her plans. She knew who he was and what he represented. The French *flics* may have been largely leaving GAL operatives alone, even when they knew who they were, but that didn't mean this would always be the case. And, besides, things were changing. More and more GAL operatives were being identified and killed by ETA. The situation was getting too dangerous, despite the paychecks.

She had planned one more hit, one more to have enough money saved to relocate her and her daughter and start a new life. But if she stayed any longer after tonight, he would keep following her and by doing so would lead ETA to her. Last night was going to have to be her final job for the GAL.

At least she'd ended her appearance with a particularly impressive hit. Not as good as her recent work in Biarritz, but one that would not be forgotten nonetheless.

Francisco Otegi was a well-known ETA operative living openly in Petit Bayonne. Somehow the French had granted him official refugee status after Otegi supposedly proved that he'd received threats against his wife and child while living in Spain, apparently traceable to a Spanish government official. So unlike many of his counterparts, he didn't even bother pretending to be someone else or shying away from recognition.

He did, however, exercise caution. He did not go out with groups and spend late evenings in Petit Bayonne like many of his fellow *etarras*. Those were the easiest to pick off, in Marie-France's opinion—just wait for them to be drunk enough to make some bad decisions and they were open game. But Otegi was different. In fact, in all of the time watching him, she never saw him overindulge in drink like many of his friends he met for lunches or dinners. But that didn't mean that he was without other indulgences. And although he didn't go out frequenting bars late into the night, that didn't imply he was at home with his wife and child.

Whatever else he was, Otegi was an unfaithful husband. Apparently even in exile he was able to easily find and maintain mistresses. In just a few weeks of tracking him, Marie-France could identify two women he was intimate with outside of his marriage. And when she witnessed Otegi with his family, he appeared to be the most loving husband and father one could imagine. All smiles, kisses, and tenderness.

Clearly family life was not enough to satiate his appetite though, as a few nights a week he left their apartment on Rue Bourgneuf and walked straight to one of his mistresses' places. Marie-France was sure he told his wife that he was only going out so often to meet up with other exiles for both social and professional reasons. It was a perfect cover-up. Everyone knew the *etarras* hung out in the bars pretty much every night in Petit Bayonne.

Although he wasn't stumbling home alone in the narrow, dark streets and alleys of Petit Bayonne late at night with his senses numbed by alcohol—he was still walking home alone through those same streets and alleys. That was enough of a window for the now seasoned assassin that Marie-France had become. She had only to plan differently.

She would not be able to sneak up on him once he was walking alone with no one around. As he was never inebriated, his senses would not be dulled enough for her to be able to ambush him from a frontal position. She had to improvise.

Marie-France was small and light on her toes, thus already not one to make much noise when walking. But in the still of the night, when nothing else is moving, the footsteps of another are easily distinguishable. And even her light steps would be noticed.

But not if she had on ballet shoes.

Even though she was certain no one would be around to witness the hit, she still wore her trademark black overcoat and wig. While Otegi was walking home after a visit to mistress number one, she stealthily ran up behind him and put a bullet in the back of his head before he even had a chance to know she was there. She was turned in the opposite direction at a full sprint before she heard his body crumble to the ground. At the corner, she ditched her black coat, wig, and gun as always, but this time added the ballet shoes. At the time, she didn't realize the hit would be her last job, but now, on reflection, she decided that this part of her life was over. Time to move on.

She needed to end things with Jean-Pierre, which she would now do. He would beg and plead, but she would not be swayed. Her mind was set. She had a friend in Mauléon who worked in one of the city's largest shoe factories. With the money she'd made from the GAL, she would disappear from the coast and move inland, deep into the Basque Country. In Mauléon, she and her daughter would be safe. Unlike in the provinces of Labourd and Basse-Navarre, there was not much violence in Soule. There were not even any *etarras* there that anyone was aware of, and that would be good for her. Some might be in hiding as *liberados*, those known ETA members in France living clandestine lives, but they would not be a problem. As long as they wanted to stay hidden themselves, they would not be asking many questions about new faces.

Odd that this smallest province of the French Basque Country had not attracted more refugees. Soule was the most rural and remote, by far, of the provinces, and she'd read that it had the highest percentage of Basque speakers. She'd heard that the inhabitants of the Soule province called non-Basque speaking foreigners *kaskoinak*, while other Basque people, especially in the French Basque Country, were referred to as *manexak*, the name for a common breed of sheep in the greater region. So she would become a *kaskoinak*. There were worse things she could be called, she thought.

She'd never really believed in any anti-Basque movement, but to be separated from all the craziness would be good. She'd been told by her contemporaries that there was a mighty bounty placed on her head. In Mauléon, under a new identity where no one knew her except for one person, she could remain unfound.

And so could her daughter. Graciana.

X.

Hendaye, French Basque Country

A GENTLE BREEZE BLEW IN FROM THE OCEAN, carrying the salty scent of the sea. It was still early in the day, not too hot yet, and Hendaye's beach, *la plage d'Hendaye*, was still relatively empty. The sun was warm and Garikotz gazed longingly across the Bidasoa River at the buildings of Hondarribia's *centre-ville*. The river was the border between France and Spain, splitting the Basque Country into two halves.

Garikotz noticed Patxi approaching. Patxi raised his hand to shake. "Do you miss Hondarribia?" Patxi asked, following Garikotz's eyes southward across the river.

"That's my hometown, so part of me will always miss Hondarribia. But I was just thinking how ridiculous it is that a river divides our Basque Country. They may call our lands Spain or France, but to us all of this is just the Basque Country, as it always has been. But to go there we have to stop at the border crossing and show our passports and be asked questions to be allowed entry. Hopefully one day things will change."

"Hopefully. That's what we are trying to do, right? Let's walk while we chat," Patxi suggested. They began walking along the promenade between the beach and the Boulevard de la Mer.

"Yes, of course. A united *Euskal Herria* is what we need to achieve. And, for the moment, I'm quite content to be over here rather than over there. Our brothers and sisters over there must be very careful."

"I fear that we are only going to have to become more careful on this side too though," Patxi predicted. "The *putain* GAL is relentless and I'm beginning to feel that the French are less supportive of our cause than they used to be. And those IK fools are making things more difficult for us. Did you convey our concern to your IK contact?"

For the safety of all, no one knew the identity of Garikotz's IK contact except for Garikotz. He didn't even reveal Charles Martel's name to Patxi, his unit commander and old friend. "Yes, I conveyed very clearly that we do not approve of their escalated tactics and that they need to tone down their actions." Garikotz stopped walking and turned to look outward at the calm ocean extending to the horizon.

"You don't sound confident that they'll comply."

Garikotz took a deep breath. "Because I'm not."

"Goddamn idiots. They will kill us all," Patxi said angrily.

"We should have taken out Sartout when we had a chance. Now he's too popular among their ranks and his removal would only make him a martyr. Someone else would rise to fill his place."

"You're probably right. Although I'd love to take the selfish asshole out myself," Patxi replied.

Garikotz laughed and they started walking again. "As much as I agree with you, I understand where they are coming from. Our leaders could have brought them into the movement more so that they didn't feel left out."

"A mistake, yes, but there have been many mistakes made during the cause." Patxi now stopped to turn to the ocean. "One day though, Garikotz, one day you and I are going to be able to set this movement in the right direction."

"You make it sound like a prophecy."

Patxi turned to face Garikotz. "I hope it is prophecy. You and I were brought into this movement for a reason. Just a matter of time until we are the ones in charge."

"And then?"

"And then we unleash hell on those who would deny us our unification and independence," Patxi coldly snapped. He punctuated his words by slapping Garikotz's shoulder.

Living in the French Basque Country is also my country, but it is different.
—ETA member

France is determined to expel the Basque terrorists from our territory, but the main problem is finding them.
—French official

Part III.

(Present/*Gaur*)

I.

Paris, France

THE ATTACK IN PARIS at the Montparnasse Tower was being called the worst terrorist attack in France's history. Other attacks may have cost more lives, but the fact the attack occurred in the heart of the city at one of its most distinguishable landmarks made the attack all the more horrific. The entire country was considered on high alert and the borders were being watched more closely than they had since the creation of the European Union and the dissolution of national borders. The attack was initially blamed on radical Islamists, but through an anonymous posting, ETA definitely claimed responsibility.

"How surprised are you?" John Gibson asked Sebastian Parker.

The high speed train to Paris jolted slightly. Anyone else could have assumed that Gibson was asking for an opinion on the attack in general. However, considering Parker's long association with the Basque culture and radical movements within, including ETA, there was no doubt that Gibson was specifically asking his thoughts on the apparent reemergence of the violent separatist group believed to have been disbanded.

Parker was still a little bitter at Gibson and didn't know if he felt like having a conversation. They hadn't spoken much in the last day. After the news broke, Gibson admitted that his entire visit was based on information he received from Capitaine Nivelle within the French DNAT regarding a potential threat to Parker. These days, a potential threat to Parker was a potential threat to his wife.

Parker was furious at finding out Gibson withheld his true intentions. But he did admit that Gibson had been wise to wait until the morning after their feast and the generous amounts of alcohol they consumed to break the news. Learning of Gibson's deception would have been much worse while inebriated.

Besides, the fact that Gibson went out of his way in the first place over concern for Parker, and therefore Alaitz, was heartwarming. But Parker's stubborn nature didn't like knowing he'd been left in the dark.

Then Gibson and he argued some after Gibson suggested that Parker needed to run and hide, for the sake of himself and his new family. Gibson believed the reemergence of ETA as evidenced by the attack in Paris only solidified any vague intelligence Nivelle may have discovered about increased activities. And any verification of a return by violent Basque nationalists could make any detected threat to Parker real. Very real. Gibson strongly encouraged Parker and Alaitz to consider moving somewhere safer. He also was initially opposed to Parker's idea to offer to assist Nivelle in indentifying the culprits behind the Paris attack.

Although Gibson wasn't comfortable with Parker's proposition, he reluctantly admitted to himself, and then to Parker, that they could be of help to Nivelle. Together, as a team, anyway. And this way, Gibson would be able to keep a close eye on Parker for at least the short term instead of being across the world during what would likely be a turbulent few weeks. He'd request a leave of absence from work. He wasn't currently directly involved in any high profile cases back in the States and after three decades of service, he was sure his request wouldn't be denied. He'd miss Rachel, but Parker needed him—even if the stubborn punk would never ask.

"At least two full ceasefires, and a few other partial ones, have been proclaimed in the past by ETA. None lasted. There was always a return to violence. And this group has always been hard to predict. Yet, I'm sure I'm not alone in believing that this time was going to be different." Parker slowly shook his head as he turned to look out of the train's window at the passing countryside. "Maybe we all just wanted to believe it too much."

Gibson considered adding comforting words suggesting that de-escalation could still be possible before a full return to armed struggle, but he would not say anything so naïve. Especially not to Sebastian

Parker. Very much especially after he'd already pissed him off by not telling him everything he knew from the start. Which wasn't much, but he understood Parker's disappointment. Partners, even unofficial partners, are not supposed to keep secrets from one another.

But the fact of the matter was that if an organization such as ETA wanted to end a ceasefire and reassert violence as a means to carry out their mission, there would be no stopping them. And by selecting such a prominent tourist target with no political symbolism beyond inflicting pure terror, the act had clearly displayed the extent of their resolve. From his limited experience with ETA and other radical Basque nationalist groups, blatant attacks on civilians as occurred in Paris were rare. Everyone would now fear not just a return of ETA, but the emergence of a new, more radical, lethal, and uncompromising ETA.

Parker broke the silence that had fallen between them. "And somehow no one seemed to notice that in this last ceasefire the terms and schedule for disarmament of ETA were very poorly defined. When I read the terms that came out of San Sebastian, I was frankly shocked. It was as if everyone was so excited to get ETA to proclaim a complete end to violence that they neglected to map out how they would remove the means to cause violence."

"So you think that's the explanation? That they just decided to revert to violence even though the organization appeared to have ended?"

Parker smiled inwardly. Gibson had become much more astute on ETA and the overall Basque separatist movement since they first met. Now he was making references that only those most familiar with ETA would know. True, at the time of the ceasefire announcement at the summit in San Sebastian, membership in ETA was at an all-time low. That was how everything appeared on paper, anyway.

Parker and others most familiar with the group knew that although the cooperation and crackdown on ETA operatives by Spanish and French forces had severely crippled ETA in the years before the ceasefire, the group was far from finished. Their numbers may have been low, officially, but they still had a large support base from the overall public, especially in the Spanish Basque Country, where people had always believed that they were the only alternative to Spanish domination of the Basques.

Ironically, ETA's influence with younger generations of Basques, on both sides of the border, was extremely high at the announcement of the ceasefire. Accordingly, eventually ETA's ranks, depleted as they were, would have been filled with a new generation of Basques willing to pick up the snake and hatchet—ETA's feared symbol. Therefore, only safe to assume that if they had held out a little longer, a new generation of radicals would have swelled their ranks and brought new life into the Basque separatist cause.

Parker turned to face Gibson. "Possible. Everything is always possible with the Basque people. They held off the Romans and the Visigoths and the Moors. They sailed across the Atlantic long before any Italians. They survived the French Revolution and Franco. They were effectively doing economical migration in the form of sheepherding in the Americas long before this became a modern day practice. They're an amazing people and I would not put anything beyond them, even some morphed version of separatist terrorism."

Parker paused, turning back to the window. "But there's something else."

"What else?"

Parker was lost in thought and didn't answer.

"Parker? What else?" Gibson asked again.

Parker shook his head quickly, snapping himself from an inner reflection. "I don't know yet, Gibson. I don't know yet."

Gibson decided to give up. Knowing Parker, eventually he would say whatever he was thinking. They were getting close to Paris and he had to start thinking of what he was going to say to Nivelle. After all, Gibson was in France on unofficial, personal business and Parker wasn't even in the CIA anymore.

The reasons they had for wanting to assist in the investigation for the Montparnasse Tower attack would be understandable to Nivelle, given their past experience working with the Capitaine. But as far as explaining the situation to anyone else—that could be difficult.

And if they were going to get anywhere, they needed Nivelle's help. Gibson hated recognizing that already he had to keep something else from Parker. But he knew that Nivelle and Parker would prefer kicking the other in the balls instead of talking to one another, and there was no way he could reveal to Parker how vital it was that Nivelle support their efforts.

Not an ideal situation by far, but it was the only way. They needed Nivelle.

Capitaine Nivelle didn't know what to think of his present situation. Agent Gibson called him the day after the attack asking if he and Sebastian Parker could meet with him, saying that he thought they would be able to help track down whoever was responsible. Now he had the two Americans sitting in front of him, wanting something from him, at the same table in the Les Deux Magots he had sat at with Gibson only a few days ago. Or, at least, there were one and a half Americans. Nivelle always considered the young man as more French than American most of the time. And now that he had married a French citizen, Nivelle saw him even more as *un Français*. Although he would never admit this to Parker.

"I apologize for being blunt, but why the hell do you want to be involved in *toute cette merde*?" Nivelle brusquely asked. "Neither of your organizations are involved, your country is not even involved. And he doesn't even work for your country anymore!" Nivelle gestured to Parker.

"Oh, how impressive. I didn't realize you knew the word *hell* in English," Parker responded before Gibson had a chance to say a word. "You know I thought of you the other day. My wife and I live not far from the Nivelle River. Do you realize that during the Napoleonic Wars the Battle of Nivelle between the allied powers against the French was a decisive victory for the allies and led to Wellington's armies being able to push north? Just another irony that goes along with your name."

"*Va te faire foutre, petit*," Nivelle said slowly with a grin.

Gibson raised his hands at both of them. "Hold on, you two. Everyone's a little on edge right now. And, Parker—we need to recognize that Nivelle has gone out of his way to meet with us. I'm sure he's needed elsewhere."

"Bravo. A fine display of diplomacy," Nivelle commented.

Nivelle could have added that in reality, he was not doing much. Although his department was still assigned to keeping an eye on Basque nationalist groups, with the fizzling out of IK long before the ceasefire announcement of ETA, violence from Basque separatist groups had all but disappeared and was limited to young drunk idiots occasionally throwing bricks through the windows of tourist offices. No one saw what was coming. No one even had imagined this turn of events. Even if someone had, they would not have pictured such a thing happening in Paris. There was no pattern and very little to trace. Whoever had pulled off the attack made sure to leave no bread crumbs to follow.

That left Nivelle with little more to go on than a hunch. Even if he didn't prefer asking for help from some John Wayne American and his aggravating young quasi-French-American counterpart, there was no denying that they had helped him before. Perhaps they could be just as useful again. The beauty of the situation was that they had come to Paris to ask for his help.

"Yes, this is true. I am sacrificing my valuable time to meet with you to discuss your thoughts on this terrible event and who may be responsible," Nivelle smugly added.

"*Putain merde*. You're not doing this out of the kindness of your heart. You don't have a clue who did this, do you?" Parker immediately shot back.

Quite possibly the most infuriating person I have ever met, Nivelle thought. "*Bien sûr*, we have a clue," he responded, although all that was really known was that ETA claimed responsibility. "But we French are resourceful," he added. "And if I'm offered free intelligence, I'm not going to turn this down."

"*Parfait*. So you see us as a charity now. Just what I always wanted to be," Parker quipped.

Nivelle grinned. "You know, you have quite the mouth on you."

Gibson chuckled, breaking the growing tension at the table. "I've said that to him myself a few times before."

"So here's the deal. We're offering to help do some investigating for our own reasons. Gibson here can't help himself when it comes to chasing down criminals and I would like to help because I believe I can.

And I'm personally involved now, apparently, since you seem to know of some threat to me and my family," Parker pointedly said to Nivelle.

Nivelle shifted in his chair. "*Je vois.* You are bitter about that and this is why you are being so hostile."

"I'm hostile because you could have gotten in touch with me directly instead of contacting Gibson. I'm a big boy and can take care of myself."

Nivelle shrugged. "*Oui, oui, d'accord.* I promise to keep you fully informed in the future of any threats to you I become aware of."

"So let's start with that right now and you tell us all that made you contact Gibson in the first place."

Nivelle leaned back in his chair. "I have to admit—I wish I knew more. And there's no way of knowing that the intelligence that made me contact Agent Gibson has anything to do with this new attack, but it could. *Je ne sais pas. C'est possible.* For the last few months though, we have heard mention of your name. I don't know if this is because of your former employer or due to the family you have married into, but you have been, *comment dis*...on someone's radar."

"I have never tried to hide that I used to work for the CIA. I've also never tried to hide that I am a friend to the Basques."

"*Oui, oui...tu as les couilles, toi. C'est sûr.*"

"But what do you mean about the family I've married into?"

"You don't know your family's history?"

Parker shifted uncomfortably in his chair. The subject of Alaitz's family history was not an open topic of discussion between them. Whenever Parker brought it up, Alaitz quickly changed the subject. He knew her family, including her mother, had a history connected to Basque radicalism. Her mother was always suspected of having a connection to ETA, but there was no doubt about her deceased father's involvement with Irrintzi and his death during a car bomb hit. Out of respect for Alaitz, he avoided the subject. "Some, yes. But maybe not as much as I should," Parker reluctantly admitted, looking away.

"Sebastian, you should discuss this with your wife," Nivelle suggested.

"Yes, douchebag, I will."

"*Douchebag? Qu'est-ce que ça veut dire?*"

"It means you're an asshole."

"Parker, relax. Let's keep things pleasant," Gibson butted in. "Nivelle, what else can you tell us? We're happy to help. I'm off-duty, but consider it a pro-bono offer. I can access whatever resources I am able to assist in tracking these bastards down before they strike again. I may not have any jurisdiction here, but I do share a personal passion to help rid the world of goddamn terrorists. From my limited exposure to the Basque culture, they don't need ETA to rise again. I think that's something we can all agree on. Yes?"

"*Oui.*"

"Yeah."

"Okay, so let's work together. As you know, Parker has an intimate knowledge of Basque and ETA affairs. So everything is in your best interest to let us assist you. But we need an open line of information sharing among us, and that starts with you."

"We don't know much. *Je dois le dire.*"

"Awesome," Parker sarcastically said.

Gibson was about to scold him before Nivelle continued.

"*Mais,* we heard that there may be a connection to some rugby player in Biarritz or Bayonne."

"A connection to the attack or to a threat to my family?" Parker asked.

"To the attack. I am sorry, but as for the threat to your family, I have no specifics. We only received vague intelligence that you were being watched."

"Fine. We can start there. Now, unless you have anything else to offer, we're done here," Parker said.

"Somehow I forgot how charming you can be," Nivelle said with a smug smile.

"Glad to know you missed me," Parker answered, puckering his lips at Nivelle.

Parker knew of a cheap hotel in a Latin Quarter back alley where they could stay for the night. After their meeting with Nivelle in Saint-Germain-de-Prés, he told Gibson the Latin Quarter was only a short walk away.

A young woman suddenly stopped in front of Parker and placed a cigarette between her lips. "*Tu as du feu*?" she asked.

"*Non, desolé*," Parker responded. The young woman flashed a look of disappointment and continued along her way.

"Why is it that French women who smoke never seem to have their own lighters?" Gibson inquired.

"This is a cultural phenomenon, I agree. As with other things, French women just expect men to do certain things, including having lighters. I also think it's an excuse for French women to feel sexy by randomly asking strange men to light their cigarettes for them."

"Is the act an attempt to, I don't know, pick a guy up? Clearly she targeted you instead of me."

"Honestly I don't think so. They don't expect to strike up a conversation, just to show their confident sexuality by having a man do something for them. But I'm sure they take some pleasure in selecting their targets. In general, French women just have a sexuality that seems unique. Even if they are not the most attractive by traditional standards, something about them makes them very sexual creatures."

"I've heard that they spend more on their lingerie than any other nationality," Gibson said, after an attractive older woman passed by on the sidewalk.

"And I think that's part of their confident sexual awareness. They feel sexy from the moment they get dressed in the morning."

Gibson was pleased that Parker had apparently forgiven him and that all was good again between them. And he was happy to be in Paris again with his young friend. After they checked into their hotel, Parker suggested they walk around until they found an enticing restaurant. He said there would be no shortage of options and there was not. Egyptian, Lebanese, Kurdish, Senegalese, Brazilian, Nepalese, Vietnamese…even living in a diverse city such as San Francisco, Gibson had never seen so many different global cuisine options in one place. Parker left the decision to him and Gibson selected a small Burmese restaurant.

"Good choice. I haven't had Burmese food in years," Parker said as they were seated, proving Gibson wrong that he'd picked something Parker was not familiar with.

"Since you're familiar with this food, I'll let you do the ordering."

Parker agreed and ordered tea leaf salad and Shan noodles. The tea leaf salad was a unique combination of tea leaves, shredded cabbage, garlic, chili pepper, tomato, dried peas and beans, topped with ground peanuts. The salad was spicy and tart and wonderful. The noodles dish was a plate of thin rice noodles topped with ground chicken, onion, chili pepper, and bok choy. The combination was flavorful yet light and didn't make Gibson feel full, as he did normally after eating anything with noodles. Parker ordered a Tunisian rosé wine, which paired nicely with the spicy food.

"So what are you thinking about all of this?" Gibson asked as the server cleared their table.

Parker poured the rest of the bottle of wine into their glasses. "I think Nivelle doesn't know anything. Although it's never going to be said or confessed, I think the French really dropped the ball by assuming that ETA was really gone for good."

"There's something else though you're thinking, I know it. I saw you about to tell Nivelle back there, but you held off."

"I don't want to share my thoughts with him yet, but I believe there's a strong possibility that this was not an action by ETA as a whole."

"What do you mean?"

"I mean that it's not typical ETA. Throughout their history, they rarely targeted civilians with their bombings and they normally called in their attacks beforehand, limiting the number of people injured or killed."

"Okay, but you just said *rarely* and *normally*..."

"Yeah, I'm aware of what I said. I'm not sure yet where I'm going with that. But I do believe that this could be the action of some splinter group. Maybe not even ETA at all. I think automatically labeling the bombing an ETA attack was a mistake, even if someone did claim it to be."

"So what do you suggest we do?"

"The rugby connection."

"What?"

"Nivelle mentioned there may be some link to rugby in the French Basque Country. We can pursue that angle to see if we can uncover anything."

"How?"

Parker downed the rest of his glass of wine. "I have my own rugby connection in the French Basque Country."

II.

Sare, French Basque Country

“HOW WAS PARIS?” Alaitz asked, handing Sebastian Parker a glass of rosé wine.

Parker and Gibson had taken the train back from Paris the day after their meeting with Nivelle. Gibson was surprised when Parker suggested they head back to the southwest. Parker said that there was nothing more they could really do in Paris, but this was only partially true. The full truth was that Parker was eager to get home to his wife.

Gibson was also shocked when after dinner Parker suggested they head to bed for the night instead of going to some bar. Gibson asked if this was one of Parker's old tricks, to say he was turning in early to only sneak back out again when Gibson wouldn't see him, as he'd done to Gibson numerous times before. Parker told him he was no longer interested in staying out late.

But Parker was the one actually surprised—surprised to have become so attached to another person. Alaitz had always been important, his closest friend and greatest love. But he'd come to terms with being on his own most of the time and only seeing her on occasion. And as for others, he liked people and had many he called friends and some family members scattered around the world, but he never felt attached to any of them.

“Oh, you know, lots of people and dog *kaka* on the sidewalks, *comme toujours*.” He took a sip and agreed with the description of rosé as the taste of summer in a glass that he'd once heard.

“Once we get this finished out here, we're going to have quite the patio.” Parker referred to their plan to build a wooden patio area behind their house. He hadn't had time to start the *bricolage* project yet, but he was looking forward to one day. Do-it-yourself home improvements. Another new thing.

Alaitz sat down in a chair next to him with a glass of rosé. The view overlooked rolling hills of the Basque Country leading all the way to the Pyrenees.

"Someday I'm going to make our *boules* court out here too. And I'll teach our kids how to play," Parker enthusiastically added.

His mention of children made Alaitz slightly shudder, although Parker didn't notice. Everything had happened so fast. Being together constantly. Marriage. Buying a house, a big house, a house meant for a family. And now home improvements and picturing children running around their back yard. Not long ago there would be months, even years at times, when Alaitz and Sebastian would not see one another. And the entire reason they had never been together was because of her, not Sebastian. He may have liked to tell himself that he was the one always needing distance, but Alaitz was who never wanted to get married. To anyone.

Her views on marriage had nothing to do with Sebastian. She loved him dearly and had ever since they first met when he was an awkward American exchange student in her lycée. He had always been a wonderful friend and lover, and he was an attentive and sweet husband. But she never wanted to get married. She remembered how much her father controlled her mother. Only after her father was out of the picture was her mother able to become the strong, independent woman she became.

But almost losing Sebastian when he was shot triggered a change in her. Seeing him so helplessly lying in a hospital bed with tubes coming of him. Knowing that there was a good chance he would die. It changed her. And it had led to them being together.

She wanted to bury the feelings and thoughts of any doubt managing to occasionally make an appearance, but she couldn't make them go away. She was sure that Sebastian sensed there was something bothering her at times. To his credit, he never said anything. She hoped these feelings would pass. Alaitz did want to be with Sebastian, and she wanted all of the things he wanted for them. Everything just happened so suddenly.

"Are you going to be involved in the investigation?" she asked, glad to have an excuse to change the subject. Sebastian made no secret of the reason for his journey to Paris with John.

"Yes, are you okay with that?"

"I never liked what you did before. You did it anyway. Why should you stop now?"

"We weren't together."

"We weren't? I thought we were always together. That's what you used to say to me."

Parker took a sip of wine and looked away from Alaitz to the mountains. "You know what I mean. We weren't living together. We weren't married."

"Why is now so different?"

Parker continued gazing at the mountains on the horizon, even though he knew Alaitz was staring at him. "I don't know. It just is. And I'm concerned about your safety. Whatever I do now can be directly linked to you. That wasn't the case before."

"That may be true, but you shouldn't worry so much. My family has been involved with this struggle for centuries. There has never been a time when we were not in danger, even when no one expected anything to happen. I have an uncle who was murdered in the 1980s who'd been out of ETA for years, yet he was killed all the same. To this day, no one knows if it was the GAL or ETA itself who killed him for something he did in the past. Or maybe for just leaving them? Who knows? We Basques don't easily forgive."

"Which uncle was that?" Parker turned to face her.

Alaitz took a sip of wine and grinned mischievously. "You really don't know, Mr. CIA Man?"

"*Former* CIA man," Parker clarified.

"Yes, yes, former. All the same. I'm surprised you don't know his name and other things about my family."

"Out of respect for you, I never researched your family in depth. I only know about what happened to your father, as he was such a prominent figure in the French Basque Country before his death, and that your mother has always been a colorful figure. Otherwise, I really only know that your family has had a history of being connected to pro-Basque sentiments. Even if I wasn't looking into a family name specifically, names come up. At times, repeatedly, which is the case with your family name. And, of course, I've heard of the mystery regarding your uncle."

"*Tout de meme*, it doesn't matter. I barely remember him. And, according to my mother, he was not the most likable person and probably deserved whatever happened to him."

"What did happen to him?"

Alaitz's eyes narrowed. "I thought you were not interested?"

"I guess I am now."

"He disappeared one night in Saint-Jean-Pied-de-Port. Apparently having dinner with friends, then, *poof*, gone. No trace whatsoever. Until months later a *berger* with his sheep came across a partially decomposed body in a pit somewhere high up in the mountains. The body turned out to be my uncle."

"The 1980s sure were a violent time in the Basque Country," Parker commented.

"They were. The 1990s weren't any safer though, especially for a family with ties to the nationalist movement. Once the French government started cracking down on refugees from Spain, a lot of people were suddenly in danger and they had to keep moving around and changing their identities. According to my mother, this included a few of my family members."

"But never your mother, apparently?"

"I think the Spanish, the French, the GAL...they were all afraid of my mother."

They both laughed. "I don't blame them," Parker said. "But, you know, me taking this on, I may have to be away from home some. As in overnight away. I'm pretty sure I'll find a lead here in the Pays Basque, but I don't think what I find will lead to anyone or anything here. What has definitely changed from the 1980s and 1990s is that the world has become a much smaller place, and the Basque Country was never very large to begin with."

"What's that mean?"

"Means that if these really are Basque radicals, they are not going to be in a place where they may be easily recognized. If they are even in France, probably doubtful, I suspect they are far from the Basque Country. Anyway, what I was saying is that I may be gone quite a bit in the next couple of weeks."

Alaitz wasn't sure how to respond. Obviously Sebastian was saying this as he was concerned about leaving her alone at the house. Touching, yet also unjustified. Alaitz could take care of herself. But the truth was that she didn't mind that they would have time apart. She had been feeling smothered lately. Not smothered by Sebastian, but smothered by the concept of *them*. A break would be welcome.

She also didn't want to inquire about any details of his planned investigation. Better for both of them if she knew as little as possible. She hoped he understood.

"Where is John?" she asked, once again glad to have an excuse to change the subject.

John Gibson was anxious as he called Rachel Dowling on his cell phone. *How would she react?*

From the moment they met, he informed her he was an FBI agent. There was no need to describe his profession further. Movies and television shows made it clear that the job was potentially dangerous, even if exaggerating the life of agents to make every day appear an adventure in crime solving.

But this was different. This was not the murder of a politician tied to a new branch of a movement. This was not an elaborate robbery somehow tied to history. This was a terrorist attack on a global scale.

"Hello, John. Are you all right?" Rachel asked.

He detected concern in her voice. "I'm okay, yes. I was nowhere near Paris when the attack happened."

"I didn't think so after you told me you were going to visit your young friend and his wife in southwest France. But just knowing you're over there worried me."

"Don't worry, Rachel. I'll be okay." Gibson paused before continuing. "But looks like I'm going to be over here a little longer than expected."

"This is what you do, John. I understand. Just promise me you'll be safe."

"I promise." Once again, Rachel demonstrated her amazing capacity to be understanding.

Next he called his department superior, Director Robert Smith, to inform him of an emergency leave of absence from his post in the San Francisco branch office. Director Smith was an old friend and confidant, and Gibson assumed Smith suspected there was more to his request than he conveyed. But Smith said nothing. He only added that if Gibson needed anything to let him know.

The offer meant a lot to Gibson, as he honestly didn't know what to expect from this new endeavor. He'd not really reflected on what he and Parker were offering to do. During their previous engagement together, they both had full access to the resources of their respective agencies. That meant full access to both the CIA and FBI. Now they really had nothing but each other, despite what Gibson said to Nivelle about having full access to FBI resources. And the case they were getting involved with was much larger than their previous collaboration.

Sebastian Parker had time and again proven to be resourceful on his own, but Gibson began questioning how effective the two of them would be on their own. One way or another, he was sure the journey would be interesting.

III.

Avignon, France

"GOOD TO SEE YOU, OLD FRIEND," Patxi Irionda said in French as he smiled and shook Garikotz's hand.

"You too, Patxi. Especially considering how things turned out," Garikotz responded. "I don't know if we could've asked for a better outcome."

"Yes, now the world will remember that there is such a thing as the Basque independence movement." Patxi poured from a bottle of Ricard into two tall glasses with ice cubes on the small patio table. Once the liquid level was just over the ice cubes, he stopped pouring. He and Garikotz each poured water into their glasses from a pitcher on the table, filling their glasses and changing the color of the liquid from light amber to pale green.

No one expected the Tour Montparnasse would be attacked. Everything had almost been too easy. The French security forces had been tight at other landmarks in the city. The Eiffel Tower, Notre Dame, the Louvre, Sacré-Coeur—all were watched closely these days.

Especially the fucking Eiffel Tower. That ridiculous structure scarring the Parisian landscape may have been the favorite potential target for the Islamist groups, but Patxi wouldn't have planned to attack that monstrosity and bring the tower down even if totally unguarded. He'd never do that favor for any self-respecting Frenchmen who despised the damn hideous thing.

After all, he wasn't French. He was Basque.

And Basques were strong, stubborn, and determined. These qualities always proved to be invaluable, as displayed by the success of the Tour Montparnasse operation. All went as planned. They had grabbed the world's attention.

Patxi was confident that every Basque alive with nationalist sympathies would praise what he'd done. Even if they stated in public they did not.

According to the latest report, the total count was over thirty dead and over forty injured. Those people were just in the wrong place at the wrong time. Unlucky for them.

The press release Garikotz sent out after through encrypted and untraceable sources announcing the return of ETA shocked the world. Declaring a return to war against the imperialist governments of Spain and France would not be enough. His words would become legendary in the annals of Basque history.

The world thought we were gone. Today our actions in Paris have reminded you of something that should never have been forgotten. Euskadi Ta Askatasuna: No rest until independence.

Immediately after the attack, there was a call to condemn Islamic militant groups in the Middle East or in Germany or in France or wherever. But after the world was informed that ETA was behind the attack, and not some jihadist movement wanting to claim the world for their prophet and religion, finally granting full independence to the Basques and ending the longest-running European conflict would be nothing compared to stopping the Islamist terrorists.

And Patxi knew Garikotz would use his methods and contacts to notify within ETA circles the leader of the group responsible. Then only a matter of time before Patxi was named military chief of a resurgent ETA.

"It may not be Basque, but I do like pastis. Especially on a warm evening," Garikotz commented, raising his glass to clink.

"Same here," Patxi replied, touching his glass against Garikotz's. "*Santé*," Patxi said to Garikotz before taking a drink of the refreshing pastis. Their entire conversation was in French, at Patxi's request. Even though they were sitting on the balcony of the hotel room he rented for the night under a false name, with no other hotel guests using their balconies around them, speaking in Basque, especially after the attack, may raise suspicion. This precautionary measure was likely overly cautious, as any random person overhearing them actually recognizing Basque would be extraordinary. There was a saying that Patxi was fond of regarding the obscurity of the Basque language. *The reason the devil could not tempt any Basque person was because the devil couldn't speak Basque.*

But if they were going to survive in this new world where everything was traceable, they would need to be disciplined. How much the world had changed in twenty years was amazing to Patxi. He'd already ordered no email correspondence or text messages among their team members and for all phone conversations to be conducted through landlines. All messages and conversations were to be delivered and conducted in person whenever possible. Cell phone communication between team members was absolutely forbidden.

When communication would be needed on operations, Patxi planned for all correspondence to be conducted through CB radios. There would be the risk of others being able to overhear anything on the radio waves at the time, but they would be untraceable. And most people wouldn't be able to understand Basque anyway, as Patxi planned to require all future communication at such times to be conducted. He didn't feel as strongly as some had at ETA's founding that the only ones to be considered true Basques, and especially those allowed to serve within ETA's cause for freedom, were those who actually spoke Basque. Witnessing a rapid expansion of the use of their ancient and proud language was certainly something he desired, but not at the expense of losing potential recruits who would be otherwise wholly devoted to the cause.

But, in his mind, the required use of the Basque language at certain times would not be to punish or dispel any members from taking part in operations. It was a question of strategy. If you're going to be overheard, be overheard in a language not many others speak or understand.

Patxi and Garikotz sat down in the two chairs at the table. The hotel was located near the center of the city above a long public square with Avignon's famed *Palais des Papes* looming majestically across the square. There were restaurants with outdoor seating in the square below and the evening air was fragranced with sage and lavender blowing in from the countryside on a slight breeze. Patxi chose Avignon for their meeting because the city was a good rendezvous location between Annecy and Perpignan, and conveniently accessed by train. But he also picked Avignon because, despite the herds of tourists, he liked the place. Even though it was sizeable city, Avignon managed to maintain a level of small city charm.

"We've come a long way, haven't we?" Garikotz asked in more of a statement than question as the two overlooked the square and grand palace, which for a period of history had been the equivalent of the Vatican.

A long way, Patxi thought. After his father was murdered by the GAL during their first wave of aggressions in France in the late 1970s and early 1980s, Patxi decided to join ETA himself. He didn't want to waste any time joining the youth groups who saw themselves as ETA in training, and he thought IK was a waste of time. He wanted to jump right into the thick of the fight, and the best way to achieve that goal was to join ETA directly.

His potential was recognized by those in the organization, but he was still young at the time. Instead of having him instantly join a unit, he was instead sent to Algeria to train for over a year at one of ETA's clandestine camps in the desert. This was a difficult time for Patxi, both physically and mentally. But he poured his grief at the loss of his father into his training, and he emerged from his time in the desert as a determined force, ready to lead the Basque people into a new era.

But his views were perceived as too extreme for the mainstream members of ETA and he was never allowed to move up within the organization as high as his ambition would have him achieve. He constantly felt held back.

Now was the time for something different. Now was the time for a new ETA. Now was the time for Patxi Irionda.

"How are the headlines?" Patxi asked.

"Just as we hoped. The world is afraid of us again."

"*Très bien*. And what news from our person?" Patxi asked, referring to their mole who'd infiltrated the French DNAT.

"*Rien*. They know nothing and have no leads on us. They are pursuing investigations with refugees based on videos they have of the people we used, but Aitzol and I ensured that there would be no way to trace them to any of us. The people we used weren't official, so identifying them is going to be very difficult."

"That was some fine work you and Aitzol pulled off." Patxi held up his glass of pastis to Garikotz and nodded.

Garikotz returned the gesture and both men took a drink. "Thanks are in order for the refugee crisis—the situation allows a perfect opportunity for us to exploit unsuspecting and untraceable recruits."

"That it is," Patxi agreed.

"Speaking of, should we put plans in motion for phase two of Nice?" Garikotz asked, referring to their next planned attack.

Patxi took a moment to consider before responding. Another attack so soon after their first could have drawbacks, but the upside had far more weight. Keep hitting while the fire is hot. This was the only way to properly announce the revival of a new, leaner, and more dangerous ETA. The only way to demonstrate their level of resolve.

"Let's move to phase two," Patxi decided.

"*D'accord.* I'll put things in motion. When are you planning to return to Lisbon?"

"Soon. In the next week or so."

"Okay, just let me know through our usual channels once there. I'll keep you informed of the status in Nice. Would you like to see the demands letter I drafted to distribute to media outlets?" Garikotz referred to a letter he'd carefully crafted demanding a free and fair referendum on the creation of a new independent Basque Country comprised of all three French Basque provinces and all four Spanish Basque provinces.

"Of course, but let's eat first. I'm starving."

IV.

Bayonne, French Basque Country

THE STORY OF HOW SEBASTIAN PARKER and Michel Michelena became friends always made Parker laugh. Their meeting happened while in lycée, Parker a foreign exchange student still learning French and Michel a tough rugby player who refused to speak English unless forced. An unlikely pair.

Back then, Parker was still Americanized enough to think drinking wine was only meant for adult dinner parties and that most of the time it came from a box in the refrigerator. He stuck to drinking beer when out with friends, already a special occasion each and every time. At the age of seventeen, back in the States he and his friends had to rely on fake IDs and the *hey, mister, are you heading into that liquor store* game.

Michel, on the other hand, always carried a slung bota bag filled with red wine when out with friends in Petit Bayonne. He'd tilt the leather wineskin and shoot a stream of wine straight into his mouth from his outstretched arms and never spill a drop. Parker would later learn that Michel made a point to always have a bota bag with him, regardless of being out for an evening or not. He even kept a bag in his backpack on school days. Michel told him that the wineskin was his grandfather's and he was merely carrying on the tradition of an old sheepherder. Parker liked the story.

But when the two first met, it was not obvious that they would end up liking one another.

The fateful encounter happened when their two groups of friends ran into one another at the Euskaldun bar in Petit Bayonne. Michel offered his bota bag to Parker, who promptly refused. Michel was initially offended, as he believed in the tradition that an offered drink from a bota bag should never be turned away, unless there are ill feelings involved. Since he'd just met the young American, he didn't think there was any ill will between them and he concluded, correctly, that not only did Parker not understand the potential offense he conveyed, but that he was also not used to drinking wine. He also assumed, again correctly, that Parker had no idea what to do with the leather pouch being offered to him even if he'd accepted.

Parker was still in the beginning stages of learning the French language and only knew enough to get by. He was at the point where he could understand quite a bit of what was being said, but his capability to produce French words and moreover sentences was still developing. Another month at least would pass before he experienced the magical yet proven threshold of dreaming in a new language.

Understanding the cultural impasse, Michel tapped Parker on the shoulder and gestured that he would demonstrate how to use the bota bag correctly. He stretched his arms outward, tilted his head back, and expertly streamed a line of red wine into his mouth. When finished, he looked at Parker and handed him the wineskin, accompanied with an encouraging slap on the shoulder.

Parker stared at the leather bag he was now holding. Michel stated his name and slapped his own chest as he handed over the wineskin. Parker had watched Michel's fine display, but was still uneasy about trying to perform anything similar. The entire group, both of their respective groups, was now eagerly watching him, no doubt curious to see what the American kid would do. He didn't really want any damn wine to begin with, but he clearly was on the spot. Even others around them were now anxiously watching to see how he'd perform.

Oh well, fuck it, Parker said to himself. He outstretched his arms, just as Michel had done. He tilted his head back slightly, just as Michel had done. And he gently squeezed the leather bag, just as Michel had done.

That was where emulating anything Michel had done ended.

The stream of red wine shooting from the bota bag didn't gently arc into his opened mouth. Instead, the stream went straight into his eyes and nose, covering his face in red wine. A chorus of laugher erupted around him. The bota bag had won the battle, and Parker was humiliated.

But even at a young age, his tenacious spirit would not be diminished. With his head turned downward to let the red wine drip from his face to the floor, he felt Michel try to take the bota bag back from him.

Parker didn't let go. Instead, he looked upward at the audience around him, laughing at his apparent stupidity. He grinned at them, making sure to look each and every person gawking at him in the eye. He then faced Michel directly and repeated the same self-naming gesture of announcing his name followed by a chest slap as Michel had done. After he did this, he unscrewed the cap from the bag and downed the entire remaining contents. When finished, he handed the wineskin back to Michel and slapped him on the shoulder.

Michel helped Parker walk later that evening and then stood guard while Parker vomited in an alley. That night both young men knew they'd found a new friend for life.

Now they were older, wiser, and probably a bit slower. Michel noticed Sebastian right away, seated at an outdoor café table. The young American he befriended so many years ago no longer looked quite so young, but he had aged gracefully. His hair was trimmed shorter now and, unlike many other Americans Michel encountered, Sebastian was trim and dressed well. But then again, there was always something different about Sebastian Parker. Not quite American, not quite French, not quite Basque. Something in between.

"You know, if you had told me one of those late nights back in the day that you would eventually end up back here, I would have believed you," Michel said in French as he approached, extending a hand to shake.

Parker beamed a smile at him as he rose to shake hands. "Chances are pretty good that I did say those very words, on numerous occasions, believing each time was the first time I was making such a prediction. And each time we were so wasted that we didn't remember I'd already said the same thing," Parker responded in French and hooked an index finger in front of his nose, a French symbol indicating inebriation.

They both laughed.

"Probably true. But if you had said that you would return and marry Alaitz and buy a house in the countryside—that I may not have believed," Michel replied.

"I don't think I would have either," Parker responded, his voice slightly trailing off as he spoke.

"*Putain*, we're here now though, right?" Michel slapped him hard on the shoulder.

His grin returned, Parker responded, "Yes, we are. If you don't mind though, I'd like to switch to English."

Utter devastation suddenly appeared on Michel's face. "Oh fuck, you can't be serious. You know me. I have no time for this ugly English language."

"Yes, I recognize your distaste to speak English, but I ask as a favor. And even though I am no champion for the English language, if you want to start comparing how languages sound, I'm going to have to say English sounds more pleasant than German or Russian."

"*Merde*, Sebastian. Okay, but you are buying me beers," Michel said.

Parker wasn't too concerned about their conversation being overheard, as he'd picked a very public and popular place to meet. But speaking in English would provide some deterrence to being overheard and understood. There were only a couple of other occupied tables in front of the café, but one never knew. And as it was Petit Bayonne, with a large number of Basque speakers, speaking in Basque would do them no good if he wanted to conceal their conversation even slightly.

A waiter appeared from the doorway of the café's interior. Before he was even close to their table, Michel ordered three *pressions*. "One for you, two for me," he said, reaching over to slap Parker's shoulder as he'd always done when they were teenagers. "So you said there is something you want to discuss about rugby. Are you finally going to stop being a little girl and try playing a real sport?"

"I'll leave the hard contact sports with no pads to highly intelligent people like yourself," Parker said quickly. Before Michel had time to process what he had heard and respond, Parker continued speaking. "But, yes, aside from always being a pleasure to see you, *mon ami*, I do want to ask you some things."

"What about?"

Parker clenched his jaw and looked away down the narrow street. "It's better you don't know what about."

"Ah...I see. I thought you were retired from *toute cette merde*." The waiter reappeared and set the three draft beers on the table in front of them. Michel smiled and picked up one of the glasses of beer, touched the glass against another while looking at Parker and saying *topa*, and then promptly downed the entire beer. When finished, he slammed the glass down to the table and picked up the other, repeating the same process.

"*Mon Dieu*, you are just as much a wild man as ever."

Michel shrugged his shoulders and unapologetically belched loudly. "I am what I am, nothing more. Are you going to drink your beer?"

Parker hadn't even touched the remaining full glass on the table. "You can have it, but I need you to tell me something first."

"Okay, *Alors quoi*?" Michel asked, greedily eying the remaining glass.

"Within the local rugby community, perhaps on one of the local teams, do you know of any active Basque nationalists?"

"Ah, Sebastian. You know this is not a good question. Many Basques, including myself, consider themselves to be nationalists and also love rugby."

"Yes, Michel. But there is nationalist and then there is the other *nationalist*. You know what I mean."

Michel's gaze moved from the glass of beer to Parker and the previous look of utter joy on his face was replaced with one of concern. "*Putain*...this is about Paris. Sebastian, *tu cherche la guerre là*."

Parker straightened himself in his chair. "I'm searching no war, only to find out if there are any radical elements you know of that still exist in the local rugby circles."

Michel eyed him questioningly. "I don't like this, Sebastian. It is no good. Think of yourself. Think of your wife. If *they* are back, they are not going to approve of you living in their neighborhood. And they are definitely not going to approve of you asking questions again."

"I'll worry about me and Alaitz. You don't need to make any assumptions. Just answer my question and we'll be done with this."

Michel's entire body tensed and his biceps bulged. He reached across the table, grabbed the beer, and quickly chugged it down. After he had slammed the glass back to the table, this time harder than before, he spoke. "Maybe."

"Maybe?"

"*Oui*, maybe. I don't know anything. Although I consider myself nationalist, I have never been political. I like to play rugby, drink, eat, and fuck women. There is another guy on one of the Biarritz club teams who I hang out with sometimes. He's a good guy. He's older than us, but you wouldn't think so by how he plays rugby, drinks, eats, and fucks women. For every one I bag, he gets two. He's impressive."

Parker interjected, "All very touching, but what does this have to do with what I'm asking?"

"I don't remember you ever being impatient," Michel said, looking away.

Parker could respond by saying that knowing of a potential threat to himself and family changed his general perspective in the span of a couple of days, but he didn't. "Michel, no one will know you said anything to me. I give you my word."

Michel turned back to face him. "This guy, sometimes when he gets really drunk, and I mean really, really drunk—like we used to get drunk when we were in lycée, he sometimes says things that have made me wonder."

"Wonder what?"

"Wonder if the movement is really dead as they say. I also am pretty sure he was a member in the past, so if there is still something alive, he could be involved."

"His name, Michel? I'll order another round."

"Aitzol. Aitzol Rubina."

Parker leaned back in his chair. "Thank you, Michel. But I have another inquiry for you."

"*Putain merde*!"

"Calm down. I'm going to take you to lunch after this. A proper Basque lunch. We're talking all the piperade and *poulet basquaise* you can eat, followed by *gâteau basque* and patxaran. "

Michel exaggerated exhaling through his mouth, forcing his lips to tremble. "*D'accord.* What else?"

"I need you to find whatever information you can on the whereabouts of someone. And I swear to you, if you uncover anything, your assistance to me remains between us and only I try to contact her."

"Her?"

"Yes, her...Graciana."

V.

Bayonne, French Basque Country

AN ANNUAL TRADITION SINCE THE MIDDLE AGES, 1424 to be exact, the Bayonne Ham Fair, called the Foire de Jambon, had always been one of Sebastian Parker's favorite festivals in the Basque Country. The festival showcased Basque cultural traditions and was held in the heart of the city along the banks of the Nive River, in and around the market building and square of the Halles de Bayonne, with the medieval spires of the Saint Mary's Cathedral towering above. And the festival's theme centered around something unique to the French Basque Country, and specific to the city of Bayonne. Jambon de Bayonne.

"A festival devoted to ham. I couldn't see this happening in the States. Maybe a festival to bacon, but it would be an afternoon, not four days," Gibson said. He and Parker walked through the stalls of the Halles sampling different hams from proud artisan producers with thick dried legs of ham hanging above them.

"See that bank over there?" Parker said, pointing across the square. "French police once arrested an ETA member right outside with a million dollars in his van. The million had been a ransom payment for a kidnapped businessman in San Sebastian. But the French police fucked up that day."

"How's that, if they caught someone connected to a kidnapping and also recovered the ransom money?"

"They acted precipitously."

Gibson didn't pretend to know the word, although he was sure he'd heard it before in his lifetime. "Not exactly sure what that means."

"They were too anxious."

"How so?"

"Banks here in the northern Basque Country were always suspected of laundering ETA's funds, but this was never proven without a doubt. That day, if they'd waited a little longer, the ETA member they arrested would have deposited the cash and, if they'd been smarter, they could have then tracked where the money ended up."

"Maybe don't remind Nivelle of that one unless you really want to tick him off," Gibson recommended and the two laughed.

They came to a table with a young man pouring tastes of Irouléguy red wine into clear plastic cups. Parker grabbed two cups from the table and handed one to Gibson. "What's amazing is that this festival has been going on since before the city's cathedral was constructed." He touched Gibson's cup with his own, saying *santé*, before tasting a sample of ham followed directly by a taste of the wine. His eyes momentarily closed. "This ham is just amazing. The rustic flavor and slight sweetness combined with the subtle spice they add—I've never had a better ham. Prosciutto in Italy is good and similar in style and taste, but prosciutto is not this. And one can make or buy prosciutto anywhere. Bayonne ham is very difficult to find outside of France and production is limited by law to this one region."

Gibson tried a sample of ham. "Damn good. Agreed. Back when I was in DC, I remember having some Virginia hams that I recall being similar."

Parker walked over to a stall and returned with another sample of Bayonne ham. "Similar in that they are cured pork, yes. But most of those hams are smoked, as curing meat without cooking is still something most people back in the States don't trust. There are some cured, unsmoked Virginia hams which are good, but they don't have near the flavor of these and always taste a lot saltier to me. Let's head outside to sit in the square," Parker suggested.

They emerged from the Halles to the open square to a festive environment. People were seated at dispersed tables and a band played traditional Basque music on a stage in the center of the square. There were stands on the perimeter selling food items and traditional crafts. Parker led them to one stand to buy a couple of sandwiches. They found a vacant table and Gibson sat down. Parker set his sandwich on the table, but instead of sitting himself, walked away without saying anything. Gibson watched him walk to another stand where he bought two glasses of red wine.

"When in Bayonne," Parker said after returning and handing one of the glasses to Gibson.

Gibson grinned and shook his head. *Same old Parker.*

He looked at the sandwich Parker insisted he try, saying that this was his favorite sandwich in the world. Gibson knew Parker had done his fair share of global travels and seemed to be quite the food connoisseur. His favorite sandwich in the world? Quite a bold claim.

Evaluating the sandwich he held, he couldn't understand how this could be true. To be labeled someone's favorite sandwich in the world, Gibson would picture some extravagant creation of exotic meats, vegetables, and condiments. This sandwich may have an exotic meat of sorts involved, but otherwise Sebastian's favorite sandwich didn't appear to be anything special. The sandwich was composed of thick slices of the deep red Bayonne ham between a baguette with only butter as a condiment.

"This is really your favorite sandwich in the world?" Gibson asked, holding the sandwich up on display.

"Yup." Parker bit into his own sandwich. He gestured for Gibson to do the same by pointing his sandwich at him.

"Okay, let's see what the big deal is about this sandwich." Gibson bit into his own. As he chewed he was surprised by how much character the simple sandwich offered. The baguette had a crispy exterior crust and a soft interior and was not chewy like baguettes he normally had in the States. The ham was flavorful and gamey. The butter was creamy. The combination of the three was outstanding.

"Excellent, I admit. Much more impressive than I would have thought bread, ham, and butter would be," Gibson said after swallowing a mouthful. "Doesn't beat my own personal favorite sandwich, but very good."

"What's your favorite?"

"There was this place in Little Havana in Miami that made the best Cuban sandwiches. When I was there on an assignment, an assignment you are familiar with, the local crew used to want to go there every day. At first I thought crusty bread, roasted pork, ham, Swiss cheese, pickles, and mustard was just a combination that I really enjoyed. But—" Gibson suddenly stopped talking, lost in thought, reflecting on his time spent tracking down a clandestine ETA member in Miami.

"But what?"

"I guess the more I think about it, the more I think that although I loved the sandwich at the time, and I still love it every time I have one, even if they aren't as good as in Little Havana, there may be more than sandwich involved."

Parker took a long sip of wine. "I think I know what you mean, but I want to let you come to a conclusion on your own."

In the past, Gibson would have commented on Parker's smugness, but he'd learned to ignore Parker's verbal jabs. Gibson assumed that at times they were intentional, other times unintentional. Either way, it wasn't worth one's time getting into spats with sharp-witted Sebastian Parker, who became even sharper when somehow instigated.

"What else was going on in your life during that time? Did you have a particular connection and fondness of Miami?"

Gibson shrugged his shoulders, realizing he was mimicking the very Gallic shrug he so often mocked. "Not really. A lot of people say they don't like south Florida, because of how hot and humid and how crowded it is. But I lived in DC for many years, and DC's just as hot and humid without the benefit of having the ocean within sight. In fact, with the way DC is located in a depressed area, the summers actually feel hotter. And as for crowding, the eastern seaboard of the US from DC to Boston is as crowded as anywhere."

Having lived in the DC area himself, Parker agreed with all of Gibson's observations.

Gibson continued. "I appreciated the diversity of Miami with all of the Caribbean and Latin influence, but, again, DC has its own influx of diversity. And the ocean is nice, but I've never been much of an ocean person. So I don't think it had anything to do with Miami." He took a drink of his wine. "I think it had more to do with the fact that at the time, I really was just becoming aware of how relieved I felt to no longer be married. The relationship between me and my ex-wife had been on a downward slope for some years before. She ended up leaving me for another man, and at first I felt some devastation. But about the time I was in Miami on that case, I came to see what happened as more of a blessing than anything. We were clearly never right for one another."

"*Et alors?*"

Gibson knew enough French to recognize that this was the equivalent of Parker asking *and so*? "*And so*, the taste of that sandwich just reminds me of feeling pretty good about my life at the time."

Parker smiled and raised his wine cup. "Bravo, John." They touched cups and drank their wine.

"May have helped that I also nailed that scumbag killer," Gibson added as afterthought, causing Parker to laugh.

"This city really has an old feel," Gibson observed after taking in their surroundings.

"Bayonne has quite a story of its own. During the Napoleonic wars in the early 1800s, there was even an important battle here known as the Battle or Siege of Bayonne," Parker responded.

"What's that area of the city called over there again?" Gibson asked, looking northward across from where the Nive and Adour Rivers intersected.

"That's Saint-Esprit. That area was originally founded by Portuguese Jews escaping the Spanish Inquisition. And what's interesting is that for some time in the late 1700s to mid-1800s, Saint-Esprit was considered separate from Bayonne. Saint-Esprit was actually considered part of the Landes Department to the north, and not part of the Pyrénées-Atlantique Department as this area is to this day.

"Why is there no Basque Country Department?"

Parker's eyes widened. The band playing in the square had taken a short break. If someone in the nationalist sentiment crowd overheard and understood, Gibson's question would surely receive a heated answer. After a prolonged moment before responding, he was about to answer when he heard a familiar voice behind him.

"Why not indeed?"

Parker turned around in his chair to see his friend Patrick Holm. "You come into the city and don't let me know? *Comment c'est possible?*"

"*Je suis desolé, mon ami*. A lot on my mind lately. And I know we keep saying that we need to get together for a game of *boules*. Just with the house, I've been busy lately."

Parker stood and the two shook hands. "And now you have company, I see," Patrick said, looking at Gibson.

"Yes, you remember…"

"Yes, I remember Agent John Gibson. How do you do," Patrick frostily interjected.

Gibson stood to shake hands with Patrick. "I'm good, thank you. And just *John* today."

Parker noted how neither said *nice to see you again*. The last time they met had not been the smoothest of encounters either. But Patrick had provided key information in their previous investigation regardless.

"Please, have a seat. Get yourself some wine and have a drink with us," Parker offered.

Patrick eyed Gibson suspiciously and then faced Parker. "Thank you, but I cannot. I was just having lunch with a friend and happened to see you sitting here and wanted to say *kaixo*. But let's get together for that game soon. Maybe we can even teach John how to play."

"I'd like that," Parker responded. Patrick walked away, his thick brown ponytail bouncing behind him.

Seated again, Parker returned to their previous discussion. "That's been a hot topic here since the early 1980s. A Basque Department was promised by the French government and then at other times by parties running for political power, but this never happened. It was and has been a topic of deep contention here for decades, and, frankly, I can understand why people here continue to be upset by the subject."

"Why never happened?"

"Originally, probably based along the lines of France not wanting to lose any more territory or possessions. The Basque movement started around the time that France was losing ground in places like Indochina and Algeria, so a form of protectionism sprouted. Even though granting a department would not mean granting separation, it could have been viewed as an initial stepping stone.

"After that, one could say that it likely had something to do with Franco-Spanish relations and that the French government promised the Spanish that they would not allow the creation of a Basque Department in France. Doing so would only further encourage the Basque separatists in Spain."

Gibson held up a hand to stop Parker. "But the Spanish Basques at least achieved their own department, right?"

"Yes, they did. They didn't get all they wanted, and the province of Navarre is still not included within the Basque department as was originally desired. But it has to be a slap in the face to the French Basques. Today, I imagine that the French government wouldn't want to allow a Basque department, as if it were to happen here, the action may instigate other culturally distinct areas of the country, and the country is divided enough all over the political spectrum."

Parker finished his wine. "Anyway, we should discuss something. You're probably not going to like this topic, so maybe I should get us a couple more glasses of wine first?"

Gibson finished his own wine. "Just get it over with."

"I have to leave for a couple of days." Parker held up a hand before Gibson could object. "And I can't tell you where I'm going. Just trust me that it's better that way. And I know you could track me if you really wanted to, but I'm asking that you don't. I need to do something on my own because if you are there too, we'll have no chance of discovering anything."

"So what do you expect me to do in the meantime?"

"Find and track Aitzol Rubina. I have a feeling that will also lead us somewhere. While you do that, I'll come from a different angle. Nivelle pledged to provide support, so you could call in that pledge."

"I intend to. But what if I need a local contact? What if I need you?"

Parker didn't have to reflect long on his answer. Always a firm believer in everything happening for a reason, he believed their chance encounter with Patrick Holm had been no mere coincidence. "I'll get you Patrick's contact info before I leave. You two may never be best buddies, but he'll respect you and help you if he can. And for every contact I have here, he has two. You can stay at our house. I've already discussed with Alaitz and all's good with her. Truthfully, I'd appreciate if you would stay there while I'm gone. She knows you'll be in and out, but I'd prefer to have your presence known."

Gibson inhaled deeply. "Okay. I don't suppose I can talk you out of whatever crazy-ass plan you have in mind?"

Parker grinned. "Have faith, *mon bon home.* My plans normally worked out for us before."

"*Normally*...but I recall a few times when they didn't," Gibson replied, dropping his eyes to Parker's shoulder where he'd been shot.

Parker instinctively touched the same shoulder as he adjusted himself in his chair. "I'll be fine."

Soon after, he suggested they return to Sare. He had a flight out of Biarritz early the next morning, and Lithuania was on the other side of Europe.

VI.

Vilnius, Lithuania

EVEN THOUGH HE'D TRAVELED throughout Europe, Sebastian Parker had never been to Lithuania. He'd been to other large cities in Eastern Europe: Warsaw, Tallinn, Prague, and other places. He expected Vilnius to be similar. As the Ryanair plane began a descent into Vilnius International Airport, passing over the outskirts of the city with its bland and blocky Soviet-style apartment buildings and derelict factories, Parker realized his assumption was mistaken. As he quickly discovered, Vilnius, and Lithuania in general, was a very different place.

From his college days studying European history, he was familiar with the country's uniqueness. During a high period in the 1300s, the territory of the Grand Duchy of Lithuania covered modern-day Lithuania, Belarus, Ukraine, and portions of Poland and Russia. At this time, the Lithuanian kingdom was considered among the most powerful in all of Europe. And if not for a brutal internal conflict between two brothers fighting one another for control, the kingdom would likely have been greater still and even more influential in European history. However, the ultimate result of the Lithuanian Civil War in the late fourteenth century was the creation of the Polish-Lithuanian Commonwealth, leading to the fall of the kingdom, and also leading to a greater role for the Polish element in the equation. This would eventually lead to the Poles breaking away from Lithuania and leaving the former kingdom with a tiny fraction of its once expansive territory and influence. Parker had heard that even though hundreds of years had passed, Lithuanians continued to blame Poland

and all the Polish for the dissolution of Lithuania's once prominent place in world affairs.

Although diminished compared to its heyday, Lithuania returned to the global importance stage in 1991 when the country declared independence, leading the charge in the breakup of the Soviet Union. The Soviets resisted, sending in tanks and soldiers, but this small country stood in the face of the giant and didn't back down. Perhaps the perfect exemplification of the famous, or infamous, Lithuanian stubbornness, Parker thought.

But the bygone Soviet atmosphere remained in certain aspects of Lithuania, beyond the housing and factories Parker noticed while flying overhead, as he quickly learned while arranging for a taxi into downtown Vilnius.

The first driver he approached replied in excellent English and with a distinctly unfriendly scowl that the cost would be twenty euros. Parker read that the airport was less than four miles from the city center of Vilnius, and twenty euros for a few minutes' ride was ludicrous, even in expensive places such as Geneva or London. But when he said the price was clearly too much and that ten euros should be appropriate, the taxi driver suddenly didn't understand English. When Parker repeated himself, the driver uttered what Parker could only imagine was a combination of insults in Lithuanian and waved a hand as if to shoo Parker away like a bug. He moved down the line of taxis waiting outside the airport terminal and experienced similar results with other drivers.

Finally, however, a driver smiled and said he would be happy to take Parker into downtown for ten euros.

Once seated in the back of the taxi, Parker said, "Thank you for being reasonable. The others were not budging on their ridiculous prices."

The taxi driver happily replied, "Oh, yes—they are not friendly, those guys. Once I return to the airport, they will of course call insults at me for taking you. But I do not care. I am used to such things."

"They insult you because you accept a fair price?"

"Oh, yes—they try and charge that much to all English speakers. If a Russian comes though, they don't even try to ask for so much. But they also insult me anyway and call me…what is it…oh, yes…they call me potato man."

"Why's that?"

"Because I am from Belarus. They do not really like us here and they call us potato people. But I do not really understand this, as the Lithuanians, they eat a lot of potatoes too. So they can call me that if they want to and laugh."

"I guess there are worse things to be called."

"Oh, yes…this is true! I am just thankful I am not Polish. They really do not like them and call them very bad Russian names."

"Do you enjoy living here?"

"Oh, yes. This may not be the UK or US or Canada, but Lithuania is better than Belarus. Belarus is no good. My family and I are better here. I think you will like here too, a young good-looking Englishman on his own. I am happily married, but I tell you, Lithuanian women, they are very beautiful."

Parker was about to correct the taxi driver to tell him he was not English, but he stopped himself. He didn't really know what nationality to consider himself anymore. "That's nice to know, but I'm married," he responded.

The taxi driver shrugged his shoulders in response. The thought occurred to Parker that he really ought to have responded that he was *happily* married, instead of just saying he was married.

As part of the deal with his friend, Michel Michelena, Parker swore that only he would know the whereabouts of Graciana Etceverria and that he would not tip off the authorities to her location. And only he was to go.

Michel told Parker he'd be watched, and that if any of these conditions were broken, his wife and home would not be safe. To make the point fully understood, Michel handed Parker two photographs which had been given to him as a warning to Parker. One was of Alaitz. The other of their farmhouse outside Sare.

He didn't inquire further on how Michel was able to infiltrate the proper channels to find out the information on Graciana and to then receive approval to allow Parker to approach her. Michel was an old friend, but he was also a connection. And even though he no longer worked in the business, Parker had learned that not asking too many questions with sensitive connections was best. ETA might be officially abandoned, but that didn't mean there were not still dangerous lingering elements and those who would be capable of doing harm to himself or his family if he broke the rules of the arrangement.

Michel told him that Parker's leaving the CIA was known, and most people appeared to agree that Parker was only trying to live a peaceful life in the Pays Basque. There were even some who openly praised him for marrying a Basque woman and adopting the Basque language and culture, despite his past job and nationality. These reasons proved to be beneficial for Parker's cause.

But Michel also hinted at something else. Something to do with Graciana.

Michel said he didn't know what it was exactly, but that he sensed Graciana had somewhat fallen out of favor with those remaining who identified as separatists. They made clear that they didn't want her apprehended, but also, at least under some conditions, they didn't mind identifying her exact location. They even told Michel the name of the restaurant where she worked in Vilnius.

But Sebastian Parker was in no hurry. He knew where to find Graciana, eventually. He'd taken an early morning flight from Paris to Vilnius after flying from Biarritz to Paris the evening before. After checking into a hotel near the old town's central square, he passed by the restaurant where he was told Graciana worked, and a small sign on the door said the restaurant did not open until five o'clock. He glanced at his watch. Just past noon. Plenty of time to explore the city.

He picked up a guide handout at the front desk of his hotel and began educating himself on Vilnius. Named after the Vilnia River passing through, the city had been the capital of Lithuania since the early 1300s. The location was chosen based on its central location in the Lithuanian territory of the time, the confluence of two rivers, and for defensibility based on the surrounding dense forests and wetlands.

The city's old town, considered one of the best preserved medieval centers in the world with narrow cobblestone streets and fantastic architecture, was declared a UNESCO World Heritage Site in 1994. A reminder of a Middle Ages heritage, the remnants of the city's fifteenth century upper castle complex perch above the city on a hillside, with the Gediminas Tower prominently overlooking the city. The old town was at one time surrounded by medieval city walls built in the 1500s with nine city gates and three watchtowers. However, the famed walls and towers and all but one gate were destroyed during Russian rule in the late eighteenth century.

But this was only a retouching job by the Russians, as they had already occupied, pillaged, and burned much of the old town during a the Russo-Polish War approximately a hundred and fifty years earlier. Not long after that conflict, the Swedish army had also had its way with Vilnius during a conflict known as the Great Northern War.

Vilnius had certainly experienced a fair amount of turmoil throughout its history, Parker thought. And he wasn't even into the nineteenth century yet.

During that time, in 1812 to be exact, that the city was again occupied by a foreign army, this time by French forces under the command of Napoleon Bonaparte. However, unlike preceding occupying forces, the French did not pillage and plunder Vilnius. Napoleon's *Grand Armée* was in fact welcomed into Vilnius while the Emperor was on his way to Moscow. He promised to restore the former glory of Lithuania by abolishing Russia's continued firm grip on Lithuanian lands. Napoleon relished the city's beauty and proclaimed Vilnius to be the *Jerusalem of the North*. Parker visited the Church of St. Anne, an impressive Gothic landmark in the city, and learned that Napoleon loved the church so much he stated that he wished he could take it back to Paris.

Unfortunately for Napoleon though, his last look at his beloved church would be while crawling back to France after being defeated by the Russian winter not long after. And with Napoleon's defeat, any hope of being independent from Russian control and domination was also repressed.

Parker walked the entire afternoon, stopping only once to enjoy a Lithuanian beer at a café on Pilies Street. Seated at an outdoor table watching people pass by, Parker was surprised by the beer. He'd never been much of a beer drinker, but he definitely knew the difference between top quality beer and everything else. Living in France, a country not known for beer reputability, he was often not overly impressed with any beer there. But the beer the young blonde waitress brought him after asking for a typical Lithuanian beer was delicious…not overly heavy, yet full of flavor.

"Do you like?" the waitress asked him. She was wearing a short skirt and tight shirt, and she was one of the prettiest women he'd seen in some time.

"Yes, I do actually. Very good."

"You sound surprised."

A little embarrassed, Parker admitted that he wasn't expecting there to be such good beer in Lithuania.

"We have very good beer," the young waitress said. "Maybe best in the world. We may be small country now, but once we were very big." Parker noticed her difficulty using articles in English.

"I've read that the Lithuanian territory used to extend all the way to the Black Sea."

The waitress beamed a smile at him in response. "I'm glad you know this. Most people who come here do not."

"Thank you for the lesson anyway. Nice to meet a waitress who knows her history as well as her beer."

"I do not really know too much about beer. I just know that we have the best. But I do know about our history and culture. I am sociology student at Vilnius University."

"Well then, what else is Lithuania known for, aside from formerly being much larger and having very good beer?" Parker asked.

The young waitress bit her lip and turned slightly to offer Parker a better profile view of her slender body. "Beautiful women," she replied suggestively.

Jesus, that taxi driver really wasn't kidding. Parker was unable to ignore that a much younger and extremely attractive woman was openly flirting with him.

"I get off from work in a couple of hours. Maybe you would like personal tour of city?" she added.

Blushing and forcing himself to look away from her sparkling blue eyes intently watching him, he struggled to reply. "Thank you for the offer, but I have an engagement this evening."

"What about tomorrow? I have day off," she quickly and eagerly countered.

He'd experienced women coming on to him in the past, but this was an entirely new experience. To have such a gorgeous young woman relentlessly pursue him was flattering and pulse inducing. Part of him wished he had come to Vilnius years ago, and he instantly felt guilty for the thought.

"That would be lovely…and amazing, I'm sure," he said as his eyes involuntarily moved down her body. "But I don't think my wife would be very pleased with me if I hung out with a beautiful Lithuanian while I'm here," he said, returning his eyes upward to hers and forcing a grin on his face.

She knowingly smiled at him in return and Parker assumed she was thinking that such details would normally not stop most. "Too bad, but thank you for the compliment. So if I cannot offer to show some of the best things that Lithuania has to offer, at least I'll bring you snack."

The young waitress returned a couple of minutes later with a small plate of something that looked like thin strips of thick bacon. After she set the plate in front of him, she stood by, clearly waiting for him to try.

Always an adventurous eater, Parker didn't ask what he was to eat before trying. As he bit into one of the strips, he confirmed that it was indeed some form of smoked pork, but the chewiness of the meat was not something he was familiar with.

"Smoked pig ears," the waitress offered as explanation. "In Lithuania, we eat all parts of pig," she added with a smile.

As Parker chewed on the tough meat, he couldn't help but admit to himself that the other best things Lithuania had to offer sounded more appealing.

Her hair was different, short and dark now instead of long and blonde. And seeing her dressed as a waitress was something new. But there was no mistaking Graciana Etceverria. On the taller side compared to most women, slim and lithe without looking too thin, long legs, and high cheekbones. As he did the first time he saw her in person, Sebastian Parker remarked to himself how Graciana was a very good-looking woman.

There was also something else, that something else that makes a good-looking woman even more attractive. Perhaps how she moved? How she carried herself? Whatever it was, there was something Parker found particularly sexy about Graciana.

An image of Alaitz flashed in his head as he watched Graciana from a distance. He felt a touch of guilt for his lingering looks and thoughts of another woman. But he considered how Alaitz hadn't been at all disappointed he was leaving for a couple of days. The feelings of guilt faded a little.

He was seated at a table alone in a corner of the restaurant where she worked. Before being seated by a hostess, he confirmed that he would be seated in the section of the dark-haired waitress. The hostess responded with a roll of her eyes she didn't attempt to hide. Clearly, he was not the only person to request being seated in Graciana's section. As the waitress led him to an empty table, she said something in Lithuanian. He correctly guessed this was a disingenuous wish of good luck instead of a traditional *bon appétit.*

Moments later, Graciana was standing by his table, pen and pad in hand. "*Labas,*" she initially said in Lithuanian. "May I take your order?" she then asked in English.

"Was it my clothing that made you think I was an Anglophone?" he asked in French, keeping the oversized laminated menu obscuring his face.

"I'm sorry, I don't speak French," she replied. "Can you please repeat in English?"

Keeping the menu raised, Parker repeated in English.

He heard Graciana sigh heavily. "No, of course not. But not many people who come in here actually speak Lithuanian. With the rest it is just easier to hope they speak English."

"And what about Basque?" he asked, slowly lowering the menu to reveal himself.

Graciana stood completely still. Her face remained expressionless. The slight narrowing of her eyes gave her away. She recognized Sebastian Parker.

"Don't worry. I'm not here to do you any harm. I'm alone and no one will know where you are," he quickly added in Basque, hoping to keep her from panicking. "I'm just here to talk with you."

"How do I know this is true?" she pointedly asked.

The inside of the restaurant was noisy, and a particularly loud group of Asian tourists was seated at the table closest to Parker. Although the odds of them overhearing, and understanding, whatever they said were slim, he continued speaking in Basque. "Because you almost got me killed."

Parker was taking a chance by directly addressing his attempted assassination in a Petit Bayonne alley, which had indeed nearly killed him. Letting Graciana know that he was aware of her knowledge of, and most likely of her participation in, the attempt on his life was a risk. Despite what he said earlier, she might react by assuming that he was there to bring justice on her. It was a risk.

But it was no different than his entire approach to confronting Graciana. If she wanted to run, she would do so anyway. And as he was truly alone, he'd have no way to find her again. If she were to run, not even those who Michel contacted would be able to track her.

At least now she knew he wasn't holding anything back. And he figured that, knowing her even a little, she would recognize his blunt honesty and believe him.

He was right.

"Don't speak to me in those languages anymore, okay?" she said in a hushed voice, despite animated outbursts from the adjacent table.

Parker nodded in agreement.

"I can get off in an hour or so. Will you wait?

He nodded again.

"I know you like wine, but I won't bother bringing you a glass of wine from here. I'll bring you a beer. Lithuanian beer is very good."

"No pig ears, okay?" he requested.

She looked at him surprised. "You've tried that?"

He nodded.

"I don't even think French people would eat those things. I'll bring you something that they call *balandeliai*. In English this means something like pigeons."

"Pigeons?"

"Yes, but really it's the same as stuffed cabbage rolls that are also popular in northeastern France." And before turning to walk away she said something he didn't expect. "I'm happy to see you." She revealed a slight smile for the first time since they began talking.

When they left the restaurant, passing by the hostess, Parker noted the total look of shock on the girl's face as she witnessed the highly pursued waitress leaving with someone. "I don't normally pay attention to anyone," Graciana said in French as they exited.

She pulled out a pack of cigarettes from her small purse and offered to Parker. He held up a hand and shook his head. She shrugged her shoulders and lit one for herself.

"Why, Graciana?" Parker asked in French as they strolled down the cobblestone road. The road was lined with low continuous buildings on either side; some were hotels and restaurants or shops and others looked to be large houses or apartments. Before she had time to answer, he spoke again, switching to English. "Oh, and you should probably let me know if I should be calling you something else."

"Lena."

"Lena? Interesting."

"Yes, short for Elana. My family is from Bucharest, but I was raised in the UK and I never learned Romanian," Graciana said with practiced proficiency.

"Okay, Lena. So why, Lena?"

"Why what?"

"Why did you say that you were happy to see me?"

She turned her head to peer at him as they walked. "Because I am. You may be some government asshole, as I learned after we first met. And you may be one those health-crazy Americans now who thinks everyone who smokes is bad even though you once did. But we had a nice time together, once on the side of a hill under the shade of a tree." She exhaled a cloud of smoke. "How do you say it: once upon a time."

Parker noticed a slight smile on her face once again. "Even though I quit, I don't judge people for smoking at all. I had a good reason to stop and now starting again wouldn't make any sense."

"My God, why not? Smoking is so good," Graciana said after blowing a thin stream of smoke into the air.

For a moment, Parker felt tempted to ask for a cigarette. But he didn't. "Yeah, believe me, at times it does sound great. But..."

"But you quit. I understand. I don't want this to turn into Oprah or something."

Parker laughed. "*Putain*, how do you know Oprah?"

Graciana shook her head. "You Americans—you have no idea how much your culture is thrown up all around the world. It's hard to ignore."

"Thrown-up?"

"Is vomited a better word to use?"

Parker laughed again. "No, thrown-up works. But I must admit that I'm not really that American anymore. I no longer work for the government and I live in the Pays Basque."

"*C'est vrai*?" Graciana suddenly stopped and Parker also came to halt. She tossed her cigarette to the ground and cupped a hand over her mouth with her eyes wide. She lowered her hand. "Fuck...I never slip up. Even when French tourists come into the restaurant and pretend to not be able to at least understand English."

"*Vraiement*?"

"Yes, really. Must be you," she said, moving a little closer. She looked directly into his eyes. Even though around nine at night, Lithuania's northerly location allowed for the day to remain still light outside until late on spring and summer evenings.

"I didn't tell you the whole truth earlier," she said with the same compassionate tone as in the restaurant when saying she was glad to see him.

"How so?"

"I was glad to see you because I liked you when we met. Although I normally like women more than men, I liked you. So I was happy to see you."

Parker was glad that while still light, the sunlight had faded enough so that she wouldn't see him blushing.

"But I was also happy to see you because, whatever you may have represented the last time I saw you, seeing you reminds me of my home. And I do not believe I will ever see my home again. So maybe for this reason I should also hate seeing you."

"I liked your other reasoning more," Parker said awkwardly, beginning to feel uncomfortable and excited by how close she was to him.

"There is another reason why." Just as suddenly as she stopped walking, Graciana turned and began walking again. She pulled out another cigarette from her purse and lit it.

"Why?"

Graciana blew a line of smoke and turned away. "Because I'm happy to see you are still alive."

"But didn't you want the opposite?" Parker said, trying to sound as if joking.

"*Mais, non…espèce de con.*" She turned and hit him in the shoulder. "I only wanted to knock you out that night in Petit Bayonne because you were trying to follow me and also because I was pissed off that you lied to me. I not only found out about who you worked for, but also that you were the *copain* of Alaitz Etxegaraya. Honestly, I don't know which made me more upset."

Parker was confused. The issue concerning Alaitz didn't surprise him. He recalled Alaitz having no kind words about Graciana when her name came up. But the second matter concerning the bullet he took was definitely something new. "What do you mean that you wanted to knock me out? There was no one else around in the alley that night."

Graciana pursed her lips and blew air outward quickly with a slight shrug. "That's what you thought. But apparently I inherited a trait even I didn't know about—being able to sneak up on people. When you were shot, I was right behind you, about to hit you on the head with a wine bottle."

"A wine bottle?" Parker jokingly asked.

"*Oui*, a *putain* wine bottle. Pay attention. This is important."

"Why is it so important?"

Graciana spoke quickly in responding. "Because I want you to know that I had nothing to do with whoever shot you. After you went down I had to run. I wanted to stay to help you, but I couldn't. I like you, but I wasn't going to get caught. *D'accord? Tu comprende?*"

"Yes, I understand."

"And you believe me?"

Parker responded faster than he would have expected. "I do believe you." He considered what had been said before continuing. "So you have no idea who shot me?"

"I have no clue. All I can tell is that I had nothing to do with it. But I knew I would be blamed. Right after I went into hiding. Then I was sent here. *Et voila*…here I am in Vilnius."

"What do you think of Lithuania?"

"Not a bad place. The Lithuanians are not my favorite, but I do admire their spirit."

"How so?"

"The Basque movement grew more determined when this tiny little country stood up the Soviet Union and declared independence. I have to at least respect that about them. But this city is nice, reminding me a little of Prague with less tourists and fast food *restos*. But I still love Prague. My favorite city in Europe. Have you been there?"

"Yes, I have. Prague is a beautiful city. Too many Americans and Asian tour buses these days, but still beautiful."

Graciana laughed. "Too many Americans—funny to hear you say that. Anyway, back to Vilnius. Even though Lithuania is a small country, this city is very multicultural."

"I read once that the Lithuanian language was not even the main one spoken in the city until the 1920s. Before then, Polish was the most spoken language."

"I doubt you read this in some guide. The Lithuanians are very proud and would never admit such a thing," Graciana commented.

"True—they left that part out in the guide to Vilnius my hotel gave me. But speaking of Lithuanians, from what I've seen, you would fit in better here if you had your long straight blonde hair again."

"Yes, but I'm Romanian, remember. Romanians have darker hair."

"Oh yeah, how could I forget?"

"Lithuania does have some good things aside from beer. Like mead. Have you tried?"

Parker remembered having had some sort of sweet mead once. "I don't remember caring for mead. Too sweet."

Graciana smiled at him. "That's not the kind of mead I am talking about. The mead they make here is like a Basque or French *digestif.* I'll take you to a place near here where we can try some."

"Wow, nothing like I was expecting," Parker said after he tried a sip. Darkness had finally arrived and a small candle was lit on the table. They were seated in the outdoor patio area of a bar. Various glasses sat on the table in front of them. Graciana had ordered what she described as a *samples* of different styles of Lithuanian meads and they had just tried the first in the line. Parker noted that the samples were actually fully poured glasses.

"That's more like calvados than the sweet honey wine called mead I've had in the past," Parker added.

"I don't know what *that* was you tried, but does not sound like this."

"Definitely not," Parker agreed, smiling. Their eyes met across the table and Graciana smiled back at him. *Merde,* he said to himself.

"So you drink this stuff a lot?" he asked, hoping to break the moment.

"No, I don't drink. I don't trust anyone or anything."

"I guess I'm the special occasion then?" *Damn, I shouldn't have said that.*

"Apparently. Now try the next one."

Parker obliged. The second mead in the lineup was stronger than the first and less smooth in its finish. "Do Lithuanians drink a lot from what you've seen?"

"Yes, but not mead, even though they make mead very well. They drink their beer, but the wine they drink, even the sparkling wine, is all very sweet. But I think that is only for special occasions. Normally if they are drinking, they have vodka shots."

"Vodka shots?"

"Yes. I've seen them do this many times. They take vodka shots while eating."

"Interesting. I guess, though, not so different from the French tradition of the *trou normand*," Parker replied, referring to a popular custom in the French region of Normandy where during large dinners a custom is to have a small dose of the region's famous Calvados apple brandy during the course of a meal.

"Yes, but one only has one *trou normand*, not five or six shots or more like they do here." Graciana took a sip of the second mead and lit a cigarette with the candle on the table.

"Good point." Parker picked up the glass of the next mead and turned the glass sideways. "You know, they really pour generous *samples*."

Graciana shrugged. "As I said, they like to drink."

"Maybe the whole drinking and vodka thing are all holdovers from having been under Russian Empire and Soviet Union rule for so much of the last few centuries."

"How so?"

"After the collapse of the Polish-Lithuanian Commonwealth in the late 1700s, Lithuania was under the control of the Russian Empire, notoriously repressive and even outlawed use of the Lithuanian language. Then during World War I, Vilnius, and all of Lithuania, was occupied by Germany.

"At the end of that war, in 1918, Lithuania finally gained independence. But then a new war broke out between the Poles and the Russians, and Vilnius traded hands between these two for the next few years. Lithuania managed to maintain its independence until 1939, when the Soviet Union invaded and occupied Lithuania. Soon after, Lithuania was annexed by the Soviet Union and some extraordinary 20,000 to 30,000 inhabitants of Vilnius alone were arrested by the Soviet secret police and sent to Siberian gulags. Also in a very short time period, the Soviets devastated industry in and around the city, probably in retaliation for the Lithuanians having ever wanted to secede from the motherland.

"But then, in 1941, the Germans betrayed their alliance with the Soviet Union and invaded Lithuania. Considering that Vilnius was known to have a large Jewish center, with something like forty percent of the population being Jewish, not terribly surprising that the Nazis had their eye on the city. They went to work quickly setting up a Jewish ghetto and deporting Jews to concentration camps. Estimates are that over two hundred and fifty thousand Jews from this city alone were killed. Nearly all of the Jewish population.

"Then in 1944, the Soviets took back the city and Lithuania, and held on firmly until 1991. So, this city has quite a history and Russia has always played a role. Even to this day, there are some people who fear that Russia will again try to take back all of the Baltic states, including Lithuania."

Even in the soft, faint light from the candle on the table, he could easily make out the blank stare on Graciana's face. "Are you sure you're not a history professor?"

Parker laughed. "No, no. I just love history. And, I stopped in at a museum today and learned some new things about Vilnius and Lithuania. The city guide I have said that the place is only open periodically with no real schedule, whatever that means, so I guess I was lucky."

"Yes, as was I, so I could hear your history lesson."

"You don't like history?"

Graciana picked up the third glass of the mead, saying this one would be the strongest, and drank before responding. "I like the present. There is nothing we can do about the past."

"True, but I said *history*, not the past..."

"They are different?"

Parker picked up the third sample glass. "Of course they are." He smelled the mead. The inside of his nose burned. "*Mon Dieu.* What the hell is this stuff?"

Graciana smiled at him as she dropped one cigarette to the ground and lit another. "The strongest one they make. Seventy-five percent."

"Whew...okay," he said shaking his head, setting the glass back down on the table. "Yes, they are different. History can define the present. But your past, for example, doesn't have to be your history."

"You want to know about my past?"

"I do," he honestly admitted.

"Then drink that glass and I'll tell you whatever you want to know." She eyed him mischievously.

Parker picked up the glass of mead. "Promise?"

"I promise. You can even ask me about having sex with women if you like."

He was glad he hadn't touched the drink yet. If he had, he would have surely spit up after hearing what Graciana just said. Doing his best to maintain his composure, he raised the glass slowly to her and drank the fiery liquid as quickly as he could. Flames spewed down his throat into his stomach. Holding back tears forming in his eyes, he looked directly at Graciana. "Okay, let's start from the beginning."

"I know who you used to work for, so I don't think I really need to start from the beginning."

"Good point, but we never honestly were able to find out much about you. I know you grew up in Mauléon with some sort of guardian and later moved to Hendaye. Your real parents were never identified. I know you joined Haika when you were only twelve years old. Aside from those things though, you've always been a bit of a mystery," Parker said, referring to the youth ETA-in-training group.

"What else do you want to know?"

Parker sensed a need to lighten the mood for a minute. "How about your middle name? Most people having some Basque heritage seem to have at least a couple."

"Only one. Amaia."

"That's a beautiful name."

"Thank you. Amaia is Maya in English. What's yours? All Americans seem to have one."

Parker grinned in acknowledgement of her quick turnaround question. "Mathew."

"Sebastian Mathew Parker...good that was your middle name. The boring American name doesn't fit your character."

"*Je suis d'accord.*"

Graciana took a drink of mead. "Do you want to know why I joined the movement?"

"You could have joined the separatist cause without joining the pro-violence side."

"You mean like your Alaitz?"

The mention of his wife made him feel a little defensive. "We're not talking about my wife."

"If you want to talk about other things, I want to talk about her too."

"Why?"

"Curiousity."

Parker sighed. "What do you want to know?"

"Are you happy?"

Parker involuntarily hesitated before answering. "Yes, of course."

"Why did you hesitate to answer?"

Parker shook his head. "I don't know. I mean, there are times when things are difficult with Alaitz, but I love her and always wanted to be with her. And now I am."

Graciana smiled. "Of course there are difficult times. Women are women. But I'm happy for you. You have something I'll never have."

"You shouldn't say that."

"Nice of you to say, but I know this is true. Anyway, what were you asking me *déjà*?"

"Why you didn't stay on the nonviolent side of the movement," Parker quickly responded.

Graciana shrugged and looked away. "They never accomplished anything, especially in the French Basque Country. You know this is true."

Although he didn't entirely agree with Graciana's assessment of the nonviolent Basque nationalist causes in the French Basque Country, she made a valid argument. Especially compared to the counterpart cause across the border in Spain, making substantial achievements.

"And save me the lecture on how everything that ETA or Haika or IK ever did was so evil. Centuries of repression of the Basque culture led to their existence."

The determination in her voice was clear enough to Parker that he would get nowhere in this argument. And if he made her upset, she would be less likely to help. He needed a different angle. "Did you know your parents?"

"Yes and no. But the answer to that question actually has a lot to do with why I joined the movement." She pulled out another cigarette and lit it from the candle. "I was born in Biarritz, then lived in Mauléon when I was little, and later moved to Hendaye. My mother was around for some time, from what I'm told, but I was really raised by one of her friends. I never met my father, and I don't even know who he was. But I know his leaving us when I was a baby was my mother's fault. He was an ETA member and he was killed for the cause. That's all I know. From the moment I was old enough to understand that he died for Basque freedom, I wanted to follow in his path."

"And your mother?"

"It was her fault that he left us, the *putain salope*!" she quickly responded, displaying the violent side of her personality he'd not personally witnessed before.

Parker slid one of the glasses of mead across the table toward her. Graciana grabbed the glass and finished the mead.

"My mother disappeared when I still very young. I only remember her a little. I found out later who my mother was and what happened to her." Graciana looked downward as she spoke.

"Who was she?"

"You know her." Graciana looked up at him.

"I know her?"

"Yes, you know her and everyone else knows her. She was an enemy to the cause, a member of that *putain* GAL hunting down our people and assassinating them in the streets."

Could it really be? Although the mead was starting to slow his capacities, he considered the possibility and concluded that based on Graciana's age, it could definitely be possible.

"I know you are intelligent enough to figure it out. My mother was the Lady in Black."

"*Putain merde*," Parker uttered softly in reaction to the stunning revelation. "But no one knows what happened to her. She simply stopped killing one day and vanished the next, never heard from again."

"That's what they wanted everyone to believe. But ETA never forgives or forgets. She may have tried hiding in Soule after what she did for the GAL, but she could never escape the reach of ETA. As far as I know, her remains are buried somewhere up in the Pyrenees. They found her eventually, but her death could not be made known to the world."

Parker admitted the scenario made sense. When the GAL killings in the French Basque Country ended, ETA would not have wanted the Lady in Black to be made out in the press as some kind of a symbol.

"Now you know my big secret. I am the daughter of an ETA martyr and a traitor assassin. How could I have possibly turned out any differently?"

"That's an extraordinary background, I have to say."

"But that leads us to the big question—why are you here? If you are looking to fuck another woman aside from your wife, I think you could have found some other a lot closer," Graciana said mischievously.

"That's not why I'm here."

"But why you are here then concerns me. Wanting to fuck me is one thing. But I told them I was done, no matter what may change in the future. ETA was always full of different factions going their separate ways. They may have even been trying to kill me when you were shot. I don't know. But I do know that if you are here, it proves that I'll never be safe. If someone is willing to give me up so easily, clearly I am only being kept in storage for later use."

Parker didn't want to admit out loud, but he agreed with everything Graciana said.

"So why are you here?"

"I think you can help us find whoever was behind the attack in Paris."

"At the Tour Montparnasse? I just told you that I'm done with ETA. I have been for a long time."

"Doesn't mean that you can't help."

"Didn't you say you were no longer working for that place? And who do you mean by us?"

Parker shook his head. "I'm not, and don't worry about the *us*. I'm simply trying to help stop another attack like this from happening."

Graciana breathed deeply before answering. "Yes, I agree. Causalities were always inevitable, but nothing like what happened in Paris.

The broader movement would never have supported such action. But, as I said, there were always lots of internal factions who disagreed."

"Exactly. Explaining why I'm here."

"I don't know how I can help you. I'm no longer involved, if there is anything to even be involved with these days."

"Think back. There had to be some extremists you knew who could be capable of resorting to this level of senseless violence. And I believe they would have been in France, not in Spain."

"If this is not for your job, why get involved?"

"I've always been sympathetic to the Basque cause. I love the Basque people and culture and want to see both survive. Even if one is for the return of radicalism in the Basque movement, it cannot be like this. Please, whatever you can think of may be helpful."

"What makes you think that I would want to help you? You know who I am and what I've done."

"That doesn't have to define who you are. And with those who continue to consider themselves associated with ETA since the announcement of the 2011 ceasefire, I'd be willing to bet that whoever was behind this attack, whoever is leading some rogue group, approached someone with a reputation for involvement in a high profile operation. Someone such as yourself."

Graciana sighed, closing her eyes and shaking her head. "I don't know...maybe."

"Maybe what?"

"Maybe he's involved. I don't know. After I came here, he sought me out to join what he called a new group. He said even if ETA appeared dead, he would not let it be. He wanted to carry on with fighting, but I told him I'm done. He was very persistent."

"Who?"

Graciana looked at him directly. "I'll make you a deal. A name for a kiss."

Parker held up his ring finger. "Sorry. Married."

"You can stay married—do you know how many husbands and wives cheat on one another in France? I would say this is more common in marriages than no cheating."

"I guess that proves that I'm not a real French husband then."

"*D'accord.* I would hardly call a little kiss cheating anyway, but if you want to be a puritanical American, *comme tu veux.*"

Parker's jaw tightened as he clenched his teeth together. Maybe he was being ridiculous. It would only be a little kiss. "Okay," he said with his eyes closed.

Graciana pretended to not hear him. "What was that?"

"I said okay. *D'accord*?"

Graciana smiled. "Patxi."

"Patxi Irionda?"

"Yes."

"That can't be," Parker remarked. In his previous position with the CIA as an analyst of Basque affairs, he'd been knowledgeable of most, if not all, of the known names and positions of ETA senior operatives.

"Why can it not be?"

"Because Patxi Irionda was killed in a failed bomb attack of an English bank in Bordeaux in the mid-1990s. This was during one of ETA's ceasefires, and it was believed that he was acting on his own to jump-start the return to violent actions."

Graciana rolled her eyes. "You government people. Everyone knows that was set up. One of the bombs was supposed to detonate at the front of the bank did not explode as planned, so in that case the attack was a failure. This was never allowed to be released in the press. But the second planned bomb in the car parked outside the bank did detonate, and detonated with a body inside of the car. But the body was not Patxi. So in that case, what he did was a success. I'm telling you, this man is very intelligent and very dangerous."

"Do you have any idea where to find him?"

"I have no clue. A person like that could be anywhere."

"Do you have any idea what name he could be using?"

"No."

Parker finished one of the glasses of mead. "That's a start—maybe, anyway. But that's more than I had to go on before."

"If you want to find Patxi, you should try and find his butch bitch friend Itxaso."

"Itxaso?"

"Yes, Itxaso Harinordoquy. I ran into her a few times and we never got along. I think she was jealous of me for being younger and better looking. She tried hitting on me once, but I would have nothing to do with her. And for a lesbian, she loves to lick Patxi's ass. She was always following him around and doing whatever he wanted. If he ever did form some new group, I have no doubt he kept her around. Patxi always used her for his operations in the past."

Parker was delighted. This was great news. He wasn't familiar with the name, but it was enough to start tracking. Then he was reminded of the deal he'd made earlier.

"Now that's two names, so I expect a real kiss, not just some little peck."

Fuck, Parker said to himself.

Sebastian Parker hadn't intended to share a real kiss with Graciana in fulfilling his bargain with her. He didn't intend to feel anything when their mouths met. He hoped he would feel nothing. This was not the case.

He offered to walk her home out of politeness, but Graciana didn't want him to know where she lived. But she did find amusing that he was actually concerned about her walking home alone at night, especially knowing her capabilities. As she thought when they first met, he was a good guy and someone she could even want to know better.

She believed she could trust Sebastian, but now that her location had been revealed, she needed to be extra careful. Even if Sebastian was true to his word and never said anything about their encounter, she was sure there were others who would not respect his wishes. The mead made her feel intoxicated, but not enough to slow her down. Immediately after her time with Sebastian was through, she would start to make her escape into total anonymity. It wouldn't take long. She could put anything she wished to take with her in one bag.

Sebastian Parker's arrival had proven to her that she could no longer maintain any ties to ETA, or whatever was left of the organization. Time to really disappear.

Completely aware of this, and therefore completely aware that this was the last time she would ever see Sebastian Parker again, she was willing to temporarily postpone her exit plans. At her insistence, she walked with him back to his hotel. Along the way as they walked, she placed her arm around his. She felt him stiffen at first in response, but he didn't pull away and gradually relaxed.

"I could come in with you," she offered when they reached the front entrance of the small hotel.

Parker touched her arm around his and turned to face her. He didn't want to give her some explanation about how he wished he could, but couldn't. Graciana deserved better.

He couldn't hide from the fact that he felt something in that kiss. When he'd casually started walking over to her seated across the table, he expected that he would simply lean down and they'd share a quick sealed lip kiss. But that was not at all how it happened.

Instead, before he was even at her chair, Graciana sprung from her chair, grabbed his shoulders, and passionately brought her open mouth to his. Instinctively, Parker's hands cradled her face as they embraced. As they slowly broke apart, their eyes remained locked together. Once again, Parker said *fuck* to himself.

"You're a special woman, Graciana. I hope you find happiness," he said, kissing the top of one of her hands.

Graciana was not an emotional woman. If she were, she might have gotten caught up in the moment. "Alaitz is very lucky," she said before brushing kisses on both sides of his cheeks.

And then she was gone. No good-bye. No nice to see you again. No I hope we run into one another again in the future. No maybe in another life.

He watched her outline vanish into the night as she walked down the street.

VII.

Biarritz, French Basque Country

AITZOL RUBINA WAS NOT DIFFICULT TO FIND. One call made by Agent John Gibson to an analyst in Washington, DC, was enough to get a known home address and basic background profile. The analyst found Rubina, whose full name was Aitzol Mugica Rubina, included in a list of suspected ETA members living or stationed in France. Unfortunately, there was not much else useful to Gibson in the profile. No known associations were listed for Rubina—no arrest record and no suspected crimes attributed to him. He was only listed as a person of interest. But from what Gibson could see in the records, Rubina had never been investigated.

Something didn't seem right. In Gibson's experience, terrorists always left some trail behind, even if obscured. Either Rubina was one extra cautious and careful son of a bitch, or he was involved at a high enough level to have others ensure his record had always remained clean.

Other details in the profile didn't appear to be important on the surface. Rubina had never been married, had an unknown family background, had worked at mostly manual labor jobs most of his life, and had once been a member of a semi-pro rugby team.

Rubina lived in an apartment building in the central part of Biarritz on the Avenue d'Ossuna. Once away from the waterfront area, which Gibson always thought of as a Miami Beach splattered with a touch of old-world class and elegance, the rest of the city didn't stand out as a particularly special place. Just another city. Nice and clean. But just another city.

However, it was a city located in the southeast corner of France on a spectacular jagged coastline, and the location experienced a warmer climate than most of the rest of the country and than anywhere north in all of Europe. After all, most of Europe experienced long, cold, gray winters. These factors made Biarritz a very popular resort, and he remembered Parker saying how the city had been this way for centuries. So really, Biarritz was not just another city after all.

Gibson sat in the car he'd rented at the airport when Alaitz dropped them both off the day before and waited for Rubina to emerge. Alaitz offered to let him use their car, but Gibson refused her politeness. Staying at the house without Parker was already enough to ask. And, besides, he had no idea what he was getting into. Being on a schedule or having responsibilities would only complicate matters if something happened. He couldn't risk it.

But parked outside Rubina's current place of work, a small agricultural packaging facility on the outskirts of the city, Gibson hoped something would happen. A long time had passed since he'd done surveillance work, and he'd forgotten how mind-numbingly tedious the job was most of the time. No wonder agents always had partners on stakeouts. At least they had someone to talk to that way to pass the time.

But nowadays, agents probably didn't need others for conversation. They'd just play around on their damn phones the whole time. Even though Gibson had a smart phone, reluctantly accepting the phone to begin with, he would never be one to spend hours staring at a small screen in his hand. Nor was he going to play games on the damned thing. He wondered what adults were doing playing stupid games on their phones anyway.

With a small pair of binoculars Parker gave him, Gibson noted Rubina step out of a back door of the facility for a few cigarette breaks. Actually, quite a few of the plant's employees seemed to pop out on a recurring basis to smoke. Clearly the antismoking movement having taken hold in the States hadn't caught on here.

At midday, noon exactly in fact, the plant appeared to pause for lunch. Some employees got in their cars and drove away. Rubina didn't leave. Gibson watched what he imagined was a daily routine.

Rubina didn't light up a cigarette this time when he stepped out of the building. And he now had on a pair of shorts. Rubina set a bag, towel, and bottle of water down on a bench and took his shirt off, revealing his muscular upper body. He then started running sprints back and forth within an enclosed courtyard area. He would run hard for thirty yards or so, stop and touch the ground, and then turn around and do the same thing. Over and over.

Gibson timed Rubina doing these sprints for exactly thirty minutes. At thirty minutes, Rubina stopped sprinting, and instead walked back and forth on the same line he'd just been running. During this pacing, he walked over to the bench and used the towel to dry sweat off his body. He grabbed the bottle of water and something else and returned to walking his line. To Gibson's surprise, he lit a cigarette while walking.

Once the cigarette was finished, Rubina went to the bench and pulled out a long sandwich from the bag and ate. At approximately the sixty minute mark, Rubina put his shirt on and stepped back into the building.

Maybe he was wrong about Aitzol Rubina. Any individual able to maintain such a rigorous routine was not someone who slipped up easily.

After spending the rest of the afternoon sitting in the car, Gibson imagined he was as grateful for the end of the work day as Rubina. Rubina drove straight home after work. Although nothing exciting, Gibson was glad for the change of scenery. He'd spent most of the day staring at a roadside billboard advertising new houses somewhere in the Basque Country's pastoral rolling hills.

Rubina pulled his car into the building's parking area and Gibson parked within sight of the front of the building. Gibson had grabbed a book from Parker and Alaitz's house and would pretend to be reading while he kept on eye on the front doors of Rubina's apartment building.

To his surprise though, Rubina reappeared only minutes later, dressed in shorts again and wearing a tank top. Gibson watched as Rubina started running. There would be no point trying to follow on foot. He was in good shape, especially for his age, but he'd never be able to remotely keep up with Rubina. And trying to drive a car following someone recreationally running was always a horrible idea. Unless one knew the exact route a runner would take, tailing a subject was virtually impossible and risked either losing them or getting marked. And that didn't even take into account curvy European city streets.

Having nothing else better to do but wait, Gibson decided that he'd try actually. But when he opened the book, he noticed that he'd grabbed a French book. He'd learned a few words and phrases in French, but was nowhere near being able to read the language. He uttered one of the French words he did know very well: *merde.*

He'd had enough sitting in the car anyway and he noticed a small café across the street from Rubina's building. The tables in front of the café were all occupied, but as long as he could stay somewhere inside near the front windows, he'd have no problem keeping an eye out for Rubina. And a beer sounded delicious.

Typically, he'd not have a drink while working or on a job. In the past, he would have never even considered doing so. But Sebastian Parker had worn off on him, at least a little. As he approached the café, he noticed a small sign above the doorway. Café des Pyrenees.

The inside of the café was not as busy as the full outdoor tables would imply. Two young men were seated in a corner not talking and instead staring at their phones. Two middle-aged men were seated on stools at the café's wooden bar not talking and instead staring into their glasses of pastis. And one old man was standing at the bar instead of sitting. He had a half full glass of white wine in front of him.

A portly bartender stood behind the bar, more interested in watching a soccer match on a small television than his customers. A young waitress appeared periodically to check on the tables outside and then quickly retreated through a back door to go somewhere else. A menu of food items was scribbled on a chalkboard on a wall. Inside the café there was a smell of meat cooking somewhere and cigarette smoke coming in from the outdoor table smokers.

Gibson walked up to the bar. The bartender either didn't notice him or pretended not to. Gibson waited patiently for a minute, considering that perhaps the bartender was caught up in the soccer match and would register the presence of his new customer once there was a break in the game. But the bartender remained unmoved, his eyes locked on the small television.

Gibson's presence did not go unnoticed though. The elderly man with the glass of white wine called out to the bartender in French, lambasting him for not attending to his patrons.

The bartender muttered something in response. They continued an exchange of words and gestures Gibson couldn't follow. But he'd heard one word the bartender initially said. *Américain.*

Apparently he'd found what had to be one of the few anti-American establishments in Biarritz. The old man continued to berate the bartender until the bartender looked in Gibson's direction, not bothering to actually say anything.

"*Une pression,*" Gibson said. He hoped he'd not too badly butchered the pronunciation for a draft beer that Parker taught him long ago. He knew how to add *please* in French, but based on the bartender's attitude, he didn't bother including the pleasantry.

The bartender scowled at him, but filled a glass from the beer tap and set the glass in front of Gibson. "*Cinq euros,*" he rudely stated, still scowling at Gibson.

"*Mais non! C'est criminale ça, putain*!" the old man exclaimed, continuing to point out to the bartender than even the chalkboard said that before six o'clock all draft beers were four euros.

The bartender reluctantly gave in and said the cost was *quatre euros*. Gibson firmly planted a five euro note on top of the bar. "Keep the change," he said in English.

The bartender grinned and took the money without saying a word. He turned back to face the television. The old man laughed and patted Gibson on the shoulder. "You are American, *oui*?"

"If that means I get overpriced for beers, then no," Gibson responded, making sure to speak louder than he normally would so the asshole bartender would overhear.

The old man laughed again. "My name is Jean-Claude. If you would like, we can talk a little in English."

Gibson liked the old guy. Despite his age, he had a twinkle in his eyes that let the world know he was still around.

"Sure, I'd be happy to talk with you. But do you mind if we move over by the window?"

The old man looked at him curiously.

"I'd just like to see the sun a little," Gibson offered as explanation.

Jean-Claude grinned at him. He was missing a few teeth, but his smile was genuine. "Sure, as long as you are in the sun and not me. As you can see, I've spent enough time in the sun." He pointed to one of his leathery sun-spotted arms.

"I'm John," Gibson said, offering his hand.

Jean-Claude shook his hand with one firm pump. "I've always liked Americans. You came to help us kick the Germans out of France twice," he said as they walked toward a group of tables at the front of the café next to the window. He pointed to one of the tables that was higher than the others with bar stools. "Do you mind if we stand at that table? I sit all day at home and will soon be lying down forever, so I prefer to stand when I can."

"I don't mind at all," Gibson agreed, glad to have the excuse to remain standing. "And you French helped us too to kick the English out of America."

Jean-Claude grinned again. "*Mon Dieu, quel bon gars*!" he said, lightly slapping Gibson on the back. He held up his wine glass to Gibson and they clinked and drank. "But I'm not just French—I'm French-Basque," Jean-Claude clarified after setting his wine glass back down.

"French-Basque?"

"Yes, that is correct. French-Basque." Jean-Claude proudly touched his chest. "My parents were both Basque, but they were part of a generation forgetting how important speaking Basque is to our people. They believed learning French and then English was important, but not Basque."

"So they did not speak Basque?"

"No, but I do. I learned, because Basque culture must never be lost," Jean-Claude emphatically replied, taking a drink from his glass. "I love Basque culture so much, I fought for it." He inched closer to Gibson and added: "I was once a member of IK. Do you know IK?"

Far better than you imagine, Gibson said to himself. IK stood for *Iparretarrak,* the name of the radical and violent Basque separatist group active in southwest France for a few decades of the later twentieth century. The organization was known by some as ETA of the northern Basque Country, but it had other, less glamorous labels. Such as being called ETA's unloved sibling.

Although the organization managed to cause some trouble, IK never had the popular support of ETA and never had a political wing such as ETA managed to always somehow maintain, even when the Spanish government outlawed the parties. And without any large population centers as in the Spanish Basque Country, IK had difficulty recruiting. Ultimately, IK had achieved next to nothing in the quest for Northern Basque Country independence from France, and some believed that IK's existence actually hurt ETA's efforts, as the emergence of a violent separatist group in France likely contributed to the loss of the so-called ETA northern sanctuary in France. But Gibson would, of course, say nothing of the sort to his new acquaintance.

"Yes, I do know IK. I believe your former leader Philippe Bidart is still alive." Parker had explained Bidart's role as leader of IK to him in the past.

Jean-Claude grinned warmly. "Ah yes, Philippe. An old friend of mine. He was a good leader. Do you know he said once to the press that the only reason he spoke French instead of Basque was so that the public would understand what he said?"

"No, I hadn't heard that one. I know he's supposed to be very charismatic."

"Yes, this is true. You know when the French were looking for him after what he did in Pau, he was seen all over the southwest eating in the nicest restaurants. And the whole time he was moving from safe house to safe house, sometimes going up into the Pyrenees and staying at campsites and even at abbeys which sheltered him. No one wanted to turn in Philippe Bidart. It took them six years to catch him." Jean-Claude raised a finger to the air to exemplify his point.

"But there was always something more about Philippe. He was as in touch with the past as with the present. He talked about Basque resistance going back to the time of the Romans, then during the

French Revolution, all the way until modern times. He could walk into a room of doubtful people and change their minds in minutes."

Gibson told himself to remember to ask what the earlier reference to Pau was about. As for what he knew of Bidart, Bidart's charisma may have been as detrimental as beneficial. He was reputed as such a polarizing figure that he led to internal fragmentation within IK.

Gibson was curious to hear more about IK from this old member. He knew some of the background from what Parker had told him, but in their last investigation together and even in his western United States monitoring of potential radical Basque nationalism elements, the focus had always been on ETA. IK was always there in the background, but more of a sideshow.

"I'd like to hear more about IK if you'd like to tell me," Gibson said.

Jean-Claude eyed him curiously and moved backward a couple of paces. "You're not a *flic*, are you?"

Gibson recognized the colloquial French name for a cop. "No, I'm not a *flic*." Technically not a lie, he thought.

Jean-Claude nodded his head. "That's good. We can be friends then."

"Are you concerned about your past?"

"Oh, no. I was, how do you say..."

"Exonerated?"

"Yes, exonerated. That is the word. I was exonerated for my past."

Gibson didn't need to ask for further details. If the former leader of what became regarded as a terrorist group was living life freely, it was more than possible that others were too.

"But you never know. Maybe one day someone comes and wants to do me *mal* for something I did back then. Not that this would do them much good. I'm old now. They would only hurry things along."

Gibson hoped he had such a good outlook on death when he reached Jean-Claude's age.

"We were never as sophisticated or as deadly as ETA, even though people wanted to label us that way. ETA had dynamite. We had homemade bombs. We targeted symbols for things we did not like. Tourist offices. Realtors who only had the *roast beefs* as clients. Golf courses. Fast food restaurants. But we were never the same as ETA. When we bombed the Biarritz tourist office, we went in and evacuated all of the employees before the bomb went off after we saw them not leave when we made a warning phone call. We were pro-violence, but we were not pro-killing. And we only became pro-violence after Mitterrand and Defferre lied to all Basque people by turning their back on promises to create a Basque *departement.*"

"Do you believe IK was effective?"

Jean-Claude was pensive before replying. "We received their attention. That is for sure. Did you know that the French national police opened a special unit in Bayonne to investigate *les affaires basques*?"

"No, I did not know that," Gibson lied. He'd been in the very offices Jean-Claude referred to. And he knew the establishment of the unit had been more instigated by ETA members in France than IK activities.

"We blew up their building once," Jean-Claude said with a laugh, making Gibson think that Jean-Claude was remembering a personal effort. "We may not have achieved our own department as was our primary goal, but we accomplished other things."

"Such as?" Gibson asked, trying not to sound condescending.

"We made known to the world that there was a French Basque Country just as there was a Spanish one. We made known to the French Government that we would not be ignored. We helped to resurrect Basque pride in the Pays Basque. Today there are Basque elementary schools and road signs in Basque just as in French. These things did not exist when we started our campaign."

"Do you recall there being much interaction between IK and ETA?"

"They didn't respect us, I think. Even though we almost pulled off some bigger events than they ever would. And what Phillipe did at Pau. Nothing that ETA or anyone ever did compares to that."

His curiosity now piqued, Gibson had to ask. "What happened at Pau?"

"We broke two of our comrades out of prison without firing a single shot, without hurting a soul."

"How did you do that?"

"Our commando unit kidnapped the prison director's daughter. Then we had her call her father saying that she needed his help with something at her apartment. When he arrived—*plop*! We had him. But we didn't hurt either of them, this I promise." Jean-Claude proudly touched his chest.

"Then we used the director to get us into the prison. Three of us dressed in gendarme uniforms we had stolen earlier and we said we were conducting a prison transfer. Prison transfers for Basque prisoners happened very often back in those days, so since we were in uniform and with the director, not one of the guards questioned us. We walked right in, and walked right out with our comrades. One of us signed *IK* at the clerk's register when we left, which they didn't notice until later when they realized they had let two of their highest profile prisoners walk out of the front door. It was a touch of genius, I tell you. No one ever proved that he planned the escape and no one knows who all was in that commando unit. But only Phillipe could have planned and executed an operation like that."

Even if he'd tried, Gibson would not have been able to ignore Jean-Claude's choice of pronoun use as he described the story. This reminded him of being in an interrogation room when a suspect suddenly decided to gleam in delight at whatever they had done instead of trying to hide their guilt.

"What do you think happened to IK?" Gibson asked.

Jean-Claude waved a hand in front of his face and feigned disgust. "IK's end was a combination of a few factors, *à mon avis*. Not only were there some people who did not agree with Phillipe's tactics, but also the French started arresting more of us. We even had a member go missing from a campground in the Landes who was seen being arrested by French police then never seen again.

We always believed that the organization was infiltrated with police spies who pretended to be Basque. You have to remember that it is more difficult to identify who is Basque than who is not here in the north than in the south. And there were rumors of police informants in the villages where many of our members lived and where we hid our arms.

"Again, unlike in the south, even back then there were more foreigners living among us, even if they were only around part of the year. But in a small village, it is not difficult to notice things."

Jean-Claude paused, appearing lost in thought. "Although I am surprised," he added.

"Surprised by what?"

"Surprised that there was never another Phillipe Bidart. Back in the day, there was always a great hope and fear that one day there would be. Considering how after the breakup of IK the radical movement in the north was largely limited to Basque youths carrying out their own *kale borroka*, I don't think I was alone in thinking, and hoping, to one day see a new leader rise."

You have no idea how close that came to be, Gibson thought. Jean-Marie Uhaldes, better known as Lopé, who he and Sebastian Parker helped the French DNAT track down and capture, could have very easily become the next Phillipe Bidart. The US had been disappointed to not be granted extradition of Lopé to face trial in the States, but the French effectively made sure that Lopé would spend at least the majority of his remaining life in a prison far from the Basque Country. Last he'd heard, Lopé was stowed away in prison in some French overseas territory. The French kept his arrest and sentencing as quiet and out of the press as possible, explaining why even someone as aware of Basque affairs as Jean-Claude was not familiar with Jean-Marie Uhaldes. People knew about the Haika 4, but Lopé's leadership role of the group was always downplayed. When considering the potential rise of a new Phillipe Bidart, Gibson completely understood France's careful handling of the situation.

"I hope to one day see a return to the struggle for our own department, and maybe even for a unified Basque Country between the north and south, but I do not believe this will be in my lifetime. Although either could happen before long, I don't have much time left, you see."

"So what do you think of what happened in Paris? A resurgent ETA has claimed responsibility."

"That was not ETA," Jean-Claude replied indignantly. "Not even they would do something so cowardly."

Interesting, Gibson thought. "These are confusing times, that's for sure."

"This is true. And there will always be memories of the struggles here, even in a place so calm and peaceful as this," Jean-Claude added. "Just out there," he said, pointing to the metal bistro tables in front of the café, "the Lady in Black assassinated two ETA members by throwing a firebomb on them."

When John Gibson returned to the house in Sare, there was a note in the kitchen from Alaitz. The note said she'd gone to bed early, but that there was some piperade for him in the fridge he could warm up for dinner. He'd asked that she not go out of her way for him while Parker was away, but this was now the second night in a row that she'd cooked for him.

Although he didn't expect the gesture, he was not disappointed. He had not eaten anything for dinner and was famished. As he'd noticed the night before, Sebastian and Alaitz did not have a microwave in their home. He warmed up the Basque egg specialty loaded with peppers, onion, tomatoes, garlic, and slices of jambon de Bayonne in a pan on the stove. There was half of a baguette on the counter near the stove, and he broke off pieces of the bread to soak up the juices of the cooking piperade. He and Rachel Dowling had eaten at all of the Basque restaurants in San Francisco and he'd tried piperade at each of them. But none of the piperade he had there in expensive restaurants was as delicious as the piperade Alaitz probably made as an everyday dish.

Aitzol Rubina returned from his run and did not leave his apartment building again. Gibson sat in the café watching for him, switching to coffee after a beer, until nine in the evening, when he decided he'd had enough surveillance for one day. The realization struck him on the drive from Biarritz to Sare, turning precarious after he turned off the main highway onto small winding country roads, that he didn't have the time or ability to conduct proper surveillance on his own. If Nivelle wanted to invest in the coverage, he would have the resources available to conduct proper surveillance.

But Gibson didn't want to alert Nivelle to anything until he was sure they had an unmistakable lead. Parker had a way of digging up good intelligence, but Gibson couldn't deny that the tip on Rubina was purely speculative. Nivelle may have been a pain in the ass at times, but Gibson respected him professionally and recognized the amount of pressure that must have been falling hard on Nivelle. Because there was a connection to Basque separatists, at least as claimed, a lot of people would be looking to Nivelle for results. Nivelle had enough on his plate at the moment and Gibson wanted to be absolutely confident in a lead before reporting anything to him.

If they were going to get anywhere on their own, they were going to have to get people talking. And remembering a recent encounter with an old friend of Parker's and a prior informant during their last investigation triggered a thought. Gibson needed to talk to Patrick Holm.

Of course, meeting with Patrick would be better and more productive with Parker also present, but Gibson hadn't heard from Parker since he left. He hoped he was okay. Time and again, Parker had proven himself to be resourceful. But he'd also proven that he could get himself into trouble.

"Somehow, after running into you with Sebastian the other day in Bayonne, I had a feeling I was going to be seeing you again soon," Patrick Holm said unenthusiastically as he opened to the door to his house. He didn't invite John Gibson to enter. "Where is he, anyway?"

"I don't actually know," Gibson honestly answered. "He had a hunch about something and has been gone for a couple of days." Gibson hadn't received any messages from Parker, even though he told Parker to do so on a normal basis while he was away.

"So you thought a good idea would be to come see me by yourself? You are aware that I don't like you, right?"

"I'm aware. But if you just have a few minutes, I'd like to get your thoughts on something."

Patrick stared at him without responding. "My wife took the kids to the beach and I'm supposed to meet them there. But I suppose I can offer a few minutes to a friend of Sebastian's." Patrick opened the door wider.

"Thank you. I appreciate this," Gibson said as he entered the house.

"You can thank Sebastian. If I turned you away, I'd never hear the end of it."

Patrick led them to the kitchen. When they were seated at the table, he spoke again. "I'd offer you coffee, but I really don't have much time."

"That's fine. I'll get right to the reason for my visit, seeing as how you dislike me so much. Parker—*Sebastian*—and I have offered to help try and find out who was responsible for the Paris attack."

"And you thought I would be able to assist you in that endeavor? Whatever Sebastian has told you about me, I got out of the movement a long time ago, shortly after the last time I saw you, in fact."

"You got out because you didn't believe in the cause any more?"

"No, I still firmly believe in the cause. And while I know you're going to think negatively of me for saying this, I'm not entirely opposed to the attack in Paris. The movement for Basque independence has been quiet for too long."

"A lot of innocent people were killed," Gibson stated.

"That part is unfortunate," Patrick nonchalantly offered.

Gibson felt his fists clenching underneath the table. If the conversation continued down this path, undoubtedly things were going to lead to Patrick making some bullshit statement about unintended casualties being normal in the name of a cause. And that would lead to Gibson getting pissed off and punching Patrick in the teeth.

Gibson realized he needed to alter the course of discussion quickly, but before he could, Patrick continued speaking.

"Do you know that when France suddenly decided to start expelling and arresting Basque refugees here, when the French prime minister pledged cooperation with the Spanish government, saying that France would not be a rear base for so-called terrorists operating on Spanish soil, at that time France was the second largest source of foreign investment in Spain? And that same prime minister stated that if he had been in the role of his Spanish counterpart, he would have supported the GAL activities. Can you fucking believe that bullshit? The prime minister of a democratic country publicly admitted that he would have supported a group of assassins conducting an illegal secret war. There are even reports that the French government contributed to the GAL by reporting on the locations of refugees in France. I'm telling you, it's fucking madness and this madness is never going away. Maybe the Spanish and French should have offered more when ETA agreed to the ceasefire."

"Maybe. But what I'm interested in is now, not in the past. I'm curious to know if you know Aitzol Rubina?"

"I know him."

When clearly Patrick was going to offer nothing more, Gibson asked: "Do you believe he could have any ties to extremists?"

Patrick laughed. "Where the hell do you think you are? The Basque community is very connected here, and everyone knows someone who could have ties to extremists."

Gibson felt his fists clenching again. He began to think that this visit was a bad idea and a waste of time. He'd been in enough interrogations throughout his career to know when someone was not saying the whole truth. From the moment Patrick heard Rubina's name, his demeanor changed and he appeared tenser. Whatever Patrick was withholding, Gibson began to doubt he'd be able to coerce it out of him.

"What do you want with Aitzol?"

"He's a person of interest. That's all. I'd just like to know if you know anything in particular."

"In particular as in whether or not he was a member of ETA?"

"That would be a start."

"I have no idea. Maybe. Who knows? A lot of Basques here were supporters of ETA in one way or another."

"So does that mean that you believe ETA is finished?"

"You can't kill an idea. Maybe ETA as the organization used to be is no more, but that doesn't mean ETA is gone forever. And just because some pledged to stop fighting, doesn't mean that all of them did."

"And Rubina?"

"I don't know him very well. I just know he's a tough-ass rugby player. Did I used to see him at rallies and community meetings related to Basque issues? Yes. Does that mean he was ever ETA? No. I really don't know anything more. So if that's all that brought you here, then…"

Gibson finished the sentence. "Then we're done."

VIII.

French Basque Country

"YOU ACTUALLY WENT TO SEE PATRICK ON YOUR OWN?" Parker asked. Gibson had picked him up at the Biarritz airport and they were driving to Parker's house in Sare.

"I thought maybe he'd be able to help," Gibson replied.

"Did he?"

"No. I think there was more he could have told me about Aitzol Rubina, but I didn't get the impression that he was deliberately withholding anything major. I know he's your friend, but I think he was just being an asshole and that my attempt was a waste of time."

"Probably true. But it wasn't a total waste."

"How do you mean? I told you he didn't tell me anything."

"No, but he did tell me something."

"How's that?"

"After you went to his house yesterday, Patrick called me."

"What did he say?"

"Aside from the fact that he doesn't like you?"

"Yes, aside from that. And the feeling is mutual, by the way."

Parker laughed. "Aside from that, he told me that for as much of an athlete as Rubina is, as you've seen yourself from what you told me about observing his lunch sprints and after-work runs, he's also apparently a huge weekend partier guy. Patrick told me that Rubina has a reputation for going out to bars and discotheques with guys half his age and picking up girls even younger."

"So what's that give us?"

Parker grinned knowingly. "An opportunity."

"An opportunity?"

"Yes. It's Friday, so we can expect Rubina will go out on the town tonight. We can drive back to Biarritz later and wait for him to leave and follow him.

"Sounds good. How about now telling me where you've been?"

"Lithuania."

"Lithuania? What the hell was in Lithuania?"

"Someone. *Who* doesn't matter and I'm sworn to not tell you or anyone anyway. But I have a couple more names. When we get to Sare, let's call Nivelle."

Gibson didn't like not knowing the full story, but he was familiar with Parker's stubbornness. And if he had some solid leads, how he'd come by the information wasn't all that important. At least for now.

Parker called Capitaine Nivelle once he and Gibson arrived at his house. Nivelle sounded pleased with their efforts. However, he recognized that following the lead for the recently undeceased Patxi Irionda would be difficult.

Nivelle was familiar with Irionda and the bombing in Bordeaux that had supposedly killed him. But without knowing what name he was going by since his alleged faked death, tracking him down was going to be a long shot. Any person who faked their own death and had been able to keep it a secret for decades was not going to pop up easily. All three of them agreed on this point. Nivelle said he would have his team investigate, but this was a cautiously opportune lead. Something else was needed to complete the puzzle.

Parker's other name, Itxaso Harinordoquy, was far more promising. Nivelle had one of his people search the DNAT database for her while they spoke, and within minutes Harinordoquy was identified as a suspected former ETA member. She was tied to having participated in numerous high profile ETA attacks, but never convicted of any crimes. Her present whereabouts were unknown.

Nivelle was encouraged by the possible connection. He pledged to have his people try and track her down using the full extent of his resources, including contacting other intelligence agencies in surrounding countries. The European Union may have removed borders in theory, but in practice every country was still its own. And that included having their own intelligence forces, which may or may not openly exchange information with neighboring countries. One way or another, Nivelle was confident he'd be able to find wherever Harinordoquy had chosen to hide.

Gibson didn't like the idea of mentioning their lead on Aitzol Rubina. He forgot to mention his hesitation to Parker before they called Nivelle, and then Parker spoke so quickly Gibson had no opportunity to stop him. Nivelle called out to someone again with a name to be searched, and just as before, he quickly received a positive confirmation. This one had an address assigned to the suspected former ETA member. An address in Biarritz. The same address on Avenue d'Ossuna Gibson already knew.

Nivelle offered to send people to watch Rubina, but Parker quickly suggested that since the two of them were already nearby, having them conduct surveillance on Rubina, instead of Nivelle having to reassign personnel to the task, would be the most convenient option.

Gibson wanted to smack Parker across the back of his head. From a logistical view, Parker's suggestion did indeed make sense. But he didn't like feeling forced into the position. Now he felt locked into it. They had, after all, pledged their full support to Nivelle. Nivelle added that his offer to take over the surveillance would still stand, unless Gibson and Parker had other leads to pursue.

Nivelle also attempted to pry out of Parker how he'd come by the names of his leads, but Parker stood firm in his resolve to guard the names of his contacts. Much to the chagrin of Gibson, Parker told Nivelle that Gibson didn't even know all of his contacts.

Nivelle finally gave up and abruptly ended the call, apparently having made the decision all worthy conversation had ended. Parker shrugged his shoulders.

"Guess his highness was done with us," Parker said. "I'll make dinner for us to have with Alaitz when she returns from her mother's and then you and I will get back over to Biarritz to watch Rubina."

"Isn't that going to be too late? Won't he already have left his apartment by then?" Gibson asked, thinking that Parker's ignorance at methods of surveillance were to blame.

"Oh, he'll probably be out by then, yes," Parker replied as he walked away in the direction of the kitchen.

Gibson followed. "I don't understand. How are we going to watch him if we don't know where he'll be?"

Parker pulled down a thick frying pan from a group of pans hung from hooks on one of the kitchen's walls. "Oh, we know where he'll be."

"We do?"

"Yes, the same place he frequents every Friday and Saturday night," Parker casually said as he pulled out a basket of fresh green beans from the refrigerator.

"The same place he goes..." Gibson started to say, but didn't have to finish the sentence. Obviously, Patrick Holm told Parker where Rubina would be. The smug, lying sack of shit, Gibson thought.

Parker placed the basket of green beans in the sink and spoke without turning around, apparently sensing Gibson's frustration. "Oh, get over it. You need me for this shit," he said. "Now if you want to go to your room and lie down for a few minutes, I'm going to get a quick dinner around."

The recommendation wasn't a bad idea, Gibson admitted. If they were going to be chasing after the same athlete he'd been watching the last couple of days, they could be in for a long night.

The music was too loud. There were too many people inside the bar. Despite no smoking allowed, smoke was freely pouring in through the front entrance from the herd of smokers standing outside. The music hurt Gibson's ears; the crowd of people made him anxious; the smoke hurt his lungs.

Aitzol Rubina was somewhere in age between himself and Parker. Although he expected Rubina was closer to his end of the age spectrum. Regardless, Gibson thought this was no place for anyone over thirty. Most of the bar's patrons looked like they were barely out of high school. Even the ever boyish-looking Parker appeared among the oldest of the bar's patrons.

Seated across from him at a darkly lit wooden booth, Parker picked up on Gibson's thoughts as they surveyed the room. "I know—a lot of young people. Very young people. There's no twenty-one or older requirement in France, remember. And, don't worry, even I feel too old to be in here," he commented in a louder than normal tone to account for the music volume.

"But *he* certainly doesn't," Parker added, lowering his head to a table across the room from them where Aitzol Rubina was engaged in a lively conversation with a group of guys. All of them were broad-shouldered and younger than Rubina. Parker assumed they were rugby players.

Before long, Rubina was trying to start a conversation with a group of three young women at the bar. Based on their looks and clothing, Parker thought they were Italian. Whatever Rubina tried, the attempt failed. Soon after approaching the women, he was walking away from them with his head hanging in exaggerated shame back to his group.

An hour passed and Parker was bored. He'd finished two beers, while Gibson was still sipping one.

While Parker was staring into the bottom of his empty pint, Gibson said, "I'm surprised you haven't had three by now," in his own above-normal tone.

Parker looked up at him from the empty glass. "Yeah, yeah. Just trying to tone things down. Though some booze sure would make this experience go by faster, and be more enjoyable. So would smoking."

"Hey, you offered us to do this, don't forget. You should have checked with me first. I'd have told you that surveillance is assigned to rookies for a reason."

"Sorry," Parker reluctantly offered. "Seemed easier in the past."

"You mean like that time at that Basque village festival when you identified the pelote player?" Gibson asked, referring to their contribution to the capture of Peio Camino, one of the infamous Haika 4.

Parker nodded. "Yes, like that time."

"Or the time in Paris?" Gibson said, referring to the capture of Lopé, leader of the Haika 4.

"Yeah, like that time too."

"Both pure luck," Gibson said, downing the rest of his beer. "And they spoiled you. True surveillance can take weeks, months, years."

"We don't have time for that. Whoever was responsible for Paris is not going to wait long to attack again."

"Why do you think that?"

"Because if you've waited years to make a comeback, you don't do a single show, you book a comeback tour," Parker said with his eyes fixed on Rubina across the interior of the bar. "And if some element of the former ETA is trying to reignite the movement, one attack is not going to be enough. I guarantee they're already engaged, planning their next attack."

"Well, we're here now, so this is what we can do."

"Just sit and watch and hope for something? Hope to see Rubina start talking with someone I recognize? Or try to get close enough to overhear his conversation to see if he's dumb enough to blab about the attack?"

"That's the job," Gibson leaned back in the booth, confident his young friend was learning his lesson for volunteering their services too quickly.

"Fuck that," Parker replied.

Before Gibson was able to get in another word, he watched Parker make his way through the crowd of people standing around the bar in the direction of Aitzol Rubina. *What the hell does he think he's doing?*

What the hell am I doing? Parker said to himself as he meandered through bodies to Rubina. In truth, he had no idea what he was going to say to Rubina once he reached him. He imagined that most rugby players of any nationality would not be the most welcoming to being approached by other men.

Then Rubina was directly in front of him. He was shorter than Parker, but Parker thought Rubina's shoulders were about as wide as his own torso. Whatever happened, Parker hoped he didn't end up taking a punch from this stout *mec*.

Before Parker had time to formulate a plan, Rubina abruptly stumbled backward as one of his counterparts playfully pushed him. Parker didn't have a drink in his hand to spill, but a woman standing next to him did. The force of Rubina's solid frame slamming into him jolted his stance. One of his arms knocked the woman's drink directly down the front of her shirt, which happened to be a low-cut blouse, revealing a perky set of breasts. Breasts now glistening and doused in vodka and soda.

The woman held her hands outstretched as if she'd been shot in the chest. Rubina and Parker glanced at one another. Parker grinned at Rubina and then turned to the woman and spoke in French. "I am so sorry. I will be happy to buy you another drink, and my friend here," he held a hand outward, presenting Rubina, "he will have no problem cleaning you."

The smack to the side of his face came faster than he'd have expected. It stung like hell, but at least he hadn't had to take a blow from Rubina. The guy's body felt like a truck ramming into him earlier. The woman proclaimed all French men to be pigs and huffed away with a friend.

"Maybe I should have told her I'm American," Parker said to Rubina as the two faced each another. He silently cursed himself for speaking English. Now there was no way he could fall back on a fabricated story about his origins.

Rubina erupted in laughter and clasped a hand on to Parker's shoulder. "And I should have said that I'm Basque. Maybe then she would have let me dive into those beautiful tits!"

Parker couldn't have anticipated the encounter better, even if he'd planned it. Rubina instantly liked him and welcomed Parker to join his group by putting an arm around Parker's shoulders and pulling him along.

One thing Parker would have planned, however, was for Rubina to be more cooperative. As he soon learned, despite Rubina's joyous openness with him and seemingly everyone, laughing and joking and drinking without a care, he was remarkably tight-lipped. Every time Parker tried to bring up anything remotely political in nature, Rubina quickly shot down the potential discussion by changing the subject.

When Parker bought a round of shots for the group, he proposed a toast to an independent Basque Country. When he did, Rubina held up a hand signaling for the group to hold off. "*Mon ami*, I know it's customary for the one who buys the drinks to make the toast, but I suggest something less serious," Rubina said with remarkable clarity considering that Parker had seen him consume four drinks back to back.

Sensing that he needed to lighten the mood, Parker changed his toast. "To beautiful women in our beds!" His suggestion was openly received by the group.

Later, when Parker was separated for a moment with Rubina after he engaged the rugged rugby player in a discussion on the similarities between American football and rugby, he tried again. "Quite a way for ETA to make a return, don't you think?" he fished, hoping Rubina would take the bait.

"*Je ne sais rien*," Rubina replied flatly, shrugging his shoulders. He didn't appear the least bit nervous or apprehensive. Parker was about to continue when one of the other rugby players roughly put his arms around Rubina's neck and pointed to a group of young women just entering the bar wearing tank tops. The two exchanged a few words and then began swaying in the direction of the women.

This was going to get him nowhere, Parker thought. From the very little interaction he'd so far had with Aitzol Rubina, Rubina was clearly more than one would expect from someone who at first glance looked like the only achievement he'd had in life was to have his nose broken a couple of times.

For the first time in at least an hour, he looked around for John Gibson. Although he was sure Gibson would understand he was trying to do what he could to help, Parker felt guilty for having left him on his own in a place where he was clearly not comfortable. He spotted Gibson still sitting in the booth where he left him, with a half full pint of beer in front of him and his eyes pointed downward at a pinkish newspaper.

"Where the hell did you find a *Financial Times*?" Parker asked as he sat down again at the booth.

"She brought it," Gibson said, nodding in the direction of a passing waitress carrying a tray of drinks. "When she first said something to me and I told her I didn't understand, she switched to English. She said she'd seen an English newspaper behind the bar that she could bring me if I were interested, so I took her up on the offer.

It's from a couple of days ago, but better than sitting here pretending to not be watching you get drunk over there."

"First off, I didn't get drunk," Parker started to say, but then corrected himself after a hiccup. "Okay, maybe a little drunk. But all in the line of duty," he added with a grin. "But secondly, if you weren't paying attention, what would you have done if I'd gotten into trouble?"

Gibson set the newspaper down. "You're a big boy. You'd figure things out." Although, in reality, he'd kept a close eye on Parker the entire time. But there was no need to spoil his fun. "I hope you were able to come up with something. Because not only have you revealed yourself to our lead, but now you've also revealed me to him too."

Merde, Parker said to himself. He realized how correct Gibson was and how he should have walked by him pretending to not know him, yet somehow indicating they should leave.

"We were sitting together earlier. He could have seen us then anyway," Parker said defensively.

"Maybe. Doesn't matter now, because since you came back and sat down he's looked over this way quite a few times.

"*Putain merde.*"

"Don't worry. It's fine. I told you, I've put in years of surveillance. As boring as surveillance is, there is an art to it and you don't learn overnight. But unless you want to come up with some brilliant story about who I am and risk spooking our lead over there, I recommend that we get the hell out of here. Now."

Parker agreed and they made an exit once Rubina had his back turned to them while trying to impress the newly arrived group of women at the bar.

On the drive back to Sare, Gibson driving, Parker admitted his failure and apologized. "I'm sorry. I kinda fucked up back there, Gibson."

"Don't apologize. You took a risk because you thought you were right. But you need to learn that Sebastian Parker is not always right all the time," Gibson told him.

Maybe the alcohol was to blame, Parker thought, but Gibson's words sunk deeply into him. He felt his eyes closing while Gibson was saying something about calling Nivelle in the morning to take him up on his offer to put an assigned detail on Rubina.

Alaitz's voice woke him. "Seriously, Sebastian?" This wasn't her pleasant voice. This was her angry voice. "You leave for somewhere I don't even know and then come home and get drunk on your first night back?" As she spoke, she pulled open the window curtains in their bedroom.

Parker used a hand to block the bright sunlight from his face. "I didn't think you cared that I was leaving, or where I went, for that matter."

"Maybe I did, maybe I didn't."

Parker was tempted to comment on the irrational tendencies of females, but decided it was better not to. "I didn't want to drink so much, it was just…"

"Let me guess: You had to for whatever you are up to with John?"

"Yeah, actually, that pretty much sums the circumstances perfectly." Parker nodded approvingly.

"So then what is the explanation for the bottle of Izarra on the table?"

"Ah, yeah." Parker smiled, remembering that he and Gibson had indulged in a nightcap once arriving back at the house.

Alaitz shook her head as she paced in front of him, but he sensed that she wasn't really that upset. He moved up in the bed to press his back against the headboard. "Listen, Alaitz, I know things have been a little weird between us lately. Maybe the whole house and settling down thing happened a little too fast. I can see that. And I know it's difficult for you to face me helping Gibson. I can see that. But I just feel like this is something I need to see through, as if what we started together before was never quite completed."

Alaitz stopped pacing and appeared to relax, sitting down on the side of the bed beside him. He leaned forward and hugged her from behind. "I have to make one call with Gibson, and then you and I are going to spend the day together on our own. We can go over to hike our trail above Saint-Jean-Pied-de-Port." The trail he referred to was one of their favorite hikes and one they often hiked together, especially when they were younger. One time Alaitz had surprised Parker by removing her clothes in front of him and they made love in the open air on the side of the mountain. That afternoon was one of his favorite memories, and he grinned like a schoolboy every time passing the turnoff spot on the trail.

"Oh, you want to go there, do you?" she friskily replied, affectionately grabbing one of his arms. "But does that mean you also want to stop by my mother's?"

His first impulse was to say *hell no*. Instead, he said, "Sure, if you would like."

She grabbed his arm a little tighter. "Good answer, but I was only joking. I saw her yesterday. Even I can only take so much of my mother."

Parker wisely chose to not say anything.

"And as far as your call, I'm pretty sure John already made it. He stepped outside earlier with his phone and I heard him talking to someone."

"Really? What time is it anyway?" His normal wake-up time was around 6:30 am. So Alaitz's response was shocking.

"Past nine."

Mon Dieu. Being away from his old overindulging self really made a difference, he thought.

"Now get your cute ass out of bed. You're going hiking with your wife."

Parker watched Alaitz leave the room before moving. He smiled as he felt the sunlight touching his face. Temptation was one thing, but really loving someone was an entirely different matter.

IX.

Lisbon, Portugal

PATXI IRIONDA HADN'T GONE BY HIS REAL NAME for years. Only those in his innermost circle still knew him by it. To the rest of the world, he was dead. Not even his wife knew his real name.

Before staging his death in Bordeaux, he started a life under a new identity in Lisbon. His wife was oblivious to the operations of the company he started and his connection, both past and present, to ETA. As she'd always been. This was partly because Patxi deliberately didn't inform her of his involvement with ETA, and partly because she was content to stay home with the children and not ask questions about what her husband did for his career.

She knew of his Basque nationalist sympathies, but that was all. And since she didn't speak Basque, he never had any concern of her overhearing his conversations with others regarding sensitive matters. She didn't speak Spanish either, but Portuguese was similar enough to Spanish that he never risked discussing anything important in Spanish when she was around.

He didn't have to waste time trying to pick up some woman at a bar or taking one out to dinner and pretending that he cared what she had to say whenever he wanted to get laid. He never understood Garikotz's obsession with being single. Garikotz always said he was too devoted to the cause to have time to deal with a woman or family. While Patxi found this noble, he also thought it was crazy. Men have needs and those needs must be addressed, in his view. If they don't have some sort of outlet, they'll become too focused and potentially irrational. He trusted his old friend Garikotz with his life, but at times

Garikotz's obsessive devotion worried him. He hoped the day would not come where Garikotz's commitment blinded him to his surroundings to the point of getting himself arrested or killed.

Patxi didn't see why one couldn't be completely devoted to the cause and still have a family. After all, if Basque nationalists stopped having families, there would be no continuation of the Basque cause. And for him, the family situation worked out. His family was never a priority and was more of an obligation. He was just glad to have had two boys. One day, when they were old enough, he would reveal to them who their father really was and how he was more than the owner of a profitable import company.

Although these two components of his life were very much connected.

Prior to his *death*, he ran an established company in Bilbao, brokering some legitimate, but more not-so-legitimate import transactions. He used his contacts within ETA to become the organization's primary supplier of weapons, running transactions through groups operating in Libya and Algeria. The ability to conduct affairs in Arabic had always been advantageous, helping to enable embezzling part of the funds he used to bring in guns and explosives for the organization. The way he viewed the situation was that since he was responsible for supplying the organization's weapons and doing so through his own company, putting himself at personal risk, it was only natural that he should be entitled to part of the proceeds. After all, even if he was a high ranking operative within ETA, he still needed to earn a living and appear as a legitimate businessman.

This model continued to work effectively, even after the ceasefire announcement. In fact, it proved to be even more profitable. Previously all of his gun-running activities were solely for the ETA cause. But after the ceasefire, this revenue stream came to a screeching halt. And while he did skim part of the money he funneled through the organization to purchase weapons, his devotion to the cause kept him from being too greedy. With his primary financing mechanism gone, Patxi had to turn to other buyers. Ironically, his sources of supply continued to increase, with instability in Northern Africa allowing groups to more freely operate. And there were always more people to sell guns.

But Patxi Irionda considered himself a revolutionary at heart and he wouldn't sell weapons to just anyone. He chose his clients selectively and now sold most all of his weapons to rebel groups in Syria and the PKK in Turkey. The profits were enormous. In recent years he'd amassed a personal fortune, which he was now using to fund his own personal quest to revive ETA and the greater Basque nationalist movement.

Paris was a success. No doubt. More attention was being paid by the world to the Basque cause now than ever before. There was a lot of negative reaction, of course, but nothing more than expected. This was the only way, he was sure. If ETA was to make a comeback, there was no returning to the hit and run and hide tactics of the past. The organization needed to announce its presence and demand results. Paris had made that point. Now Nice was going to confirm it.

Patxi lived with his family in Castelo, one of the oldest and chicest neighborhoods of the city on a hillside above the rest of downtown, with the São Jorge Castle looking down from the top of the hill. Itxaso Harinordoquy lived with her partner in the nearby neighborhood of Mouraria. Mouraria was not nearly as fashionable as Castelo and was long considered a slum area, but had recently become an area of revitalization. Lisbon was a pleasant place to live, Patxi thought. He didn't consider Lisbon or Portugal to be his home, but he appreciated Portuguese culture.

There had once been a remote ETA operatives base here, but after the ceasefire the base had been disbanded. There were still at least two etarras left in Lisbon though: Patxi and Itxaso.

Patxi invited Itxaso for a talk. He asked her to meet him. He liked thinking of his grand plans while strolling around the grounds of the former castle. The castle had been an impenetrable fortress in the Middle Ages, and he felt connected to the power of the place.

Even though they lived within a twenty minute walk from one another, Itxaso and Patxi rarely saw each other. Not Itxaso's choice. She would have liked to spend much more time with Patxi. Although she was not physically attracted to him in a sexual way, she was attracted to his brilliance, determination, and devotion to the cause. Maybe if he were a woman she'd be attracted to him in other ways?

Nonetheless, she idolized Patxi and felt indebted to him. It was Patxi who first identified her talents and then harnessed them to their fullest potential. Without Patxi, she'd never have achieved anything and wouldn't have moved up in the ranks of ETA. She would have been nothing without him.

And it was Patxi who first suggested she move from Bilbao to Lisbon. He told her the move would be best for their long-term relationship. She didn't know what he meant, but it didn't matter. In her mind, whatever Patxi said was fine.

Since moving to Lisbon, she'd worked as forklift operator at the port. A good job and she didn't mind the work. She liked being in a position normally held by males and proving that she could do better. But the job was merely a means to live. Her passion was with the cause of Basque independence, and she'd been devastated when the ETA leadership announced a ceasefire.

Patxi assured her that just because some of ETA announced they were giving up, this didn't mean the struggle was over. There would come a day when they would make their voice heard again. That's what he always said and she believed him. If anyone could revive a movement, Patxi could.

When he first contacted her to begin planning for the Paris attack, a fog was lifted. She had purpose once again. Paris led to their plans for Nice, that hideous stretch of French coast lined with suntan-oiled foreigners. She hoped the meeting Patxi called for today was to tell her all the final arrangements were made and that soon they would hear news of the attack in Nice.

She couldn't wait to have the world feel the impact of the explosives she'd intricately designed and orchestrated along the Nice beaches. The way she synchronized the explosives would create chaos, with beachgoers running back and forth believing they would be running away from danger and to safety, only to discover that they had run back into an explosives area. Itxaso's masterpiece was only waiting to happen. In a hundred years, people would still be trying to analyze the genius of the attack. Some people would be killed. But their deaths would be justified by the normal ETA line: they would be consequences of the conflict.

She recognized that everything was a team effort. As with all things, Patxi initially thought out the overall plan and oversaw the effort like the manager of a company. Garikotz was the strategic thinker. However, unlike in Paris, Patxi had not involved Aitzol in the Nice plan at all. This was strange, as the four of them worked so closely with one another as a group for years, and Paris had been executed perfectly. But questioning Patxi was not her place.

Patxi knew best.

It was a glorious summer afternoon in Lisbon. The day was hot, but a cooling breeze blew in from the Atlantic. On such days, Patxi savored walking the grounds of the São Jorge Castle. In the open air above everything else, he could think more clearly. Normally he preferred solitary walks, but he hadn't spoken with Itxaso lately and needed to keep her close. Especially since his closest group of friends and collaborators, their group of four to be remembered as the saviors of the Basque movement, was about to be reduced to three. An unfortunate reality, but one Patxi Irionda anticipated all along. History had proven that no great achievements occurred without sacrifice. No groups, no matter how big or how small, were able to change history without suffering some loss of their own.

The sight of Itxaso approaching on the paved sidewalk meandering through the castle's wooded park distracted his thoughts. He held a great deal of respect for her. She was the kind of person to never back away from anything. Itxaso had progressed into a position normally only achieved by antisocial men as an explosives expert, and she didn't give a damn if anyone knew she was a lesbian. She didn't go out of way to express herself as some other gay women or men may do, but her clear sense of confidence exhibited a person completely comfortable with themselves. Although she had short hair, as always, it wasn't super short. And, as always, she wore jeans and a T-shirt. But her appearance never tried to announce her sexuality as he'd seen with others. She was just herself.

Itxaso beamed a smile. Patxi knew that she looked up to him, but knowing this didn't make him feel awkward. True leaders needed to be comfortable being idolized by others.

"This is a surprise, but I'm glad you asked to meet," she said in Spanish and leaned into him. They exchanged cheek kisses. "I've been thinking of you a lot. I haven't been able to congratulate you on our success." Having spoken too boldly out loud without gauging their surroundings first worried Itxaso for a moment. Patxi would note her mistake. She quickly glanced around, making sure there was no one nearby.

Patxi sensed her nervousness. He placed a calming hand on her shoulder. "*Está bien.* Just us."

Itxaso's tense body relaxed. She exhaled deeply. She wanted to remark how at times she forgot herself in his presence, but she didn't want to embarrass herself any more.

"And thank you. But also commend yourself. Without you, the operation wouldn't have been possible," Patxi added, now with his other hand on her shoulder, looking directly into her eyes.

Itxaso blushed. This was the only man in the world who could make her blush.

"Come, let's walk. There's something I want to talk to you about." After they walked a few paces, he continued. "Although I would love to talk about our success, and our success in the near future, we need to talk about something very serious."

Itxaso wasn't sure what to say. She couldn't imagine what Patxi was referring to. Nervousness moved through her body. Patxi would always look out for her; she knew he would. But whatever he was going to say didn't sound like it was going to be good.

"I fear that we may soon be compromised," Patxi gravely said, stopping at an overlook of the city.

"You know for sure?" Itxaso asked, coming to a stop.

"No, I not for sure. But there's a strong possibility, and I wanted you to be aware in case the situation arises and you have to make hard decisions." Patxi assumed Itxaso was astute enough to figure out he referenced the possibility that at a moment's notice, she might have to abandon her Lisbon life. Her apartment. Her job. Her lover. Her life there.

"But how? We were so careful."

Patxi began walking again and Itxaso followed. "We were. Any comprised situation would not be through any fault of ours."

"*No comprendo.*"

"There's a strong possibility we will be in a compromised situation, as there is a strong possibility that Aitzol will soon be apprehended for questioning in France, the place I told him he should leave long ago and he didn't listen." Patxi had indeed repeatedly suggested Aitzol leave the French Basque Country and settle somewhere less conspicuous over the years, but Aitzol adamantly refused to even consider the possibility. Patxi even considered recently ordering Aitzol to leave yet again, but he didn't want to be viewed as an absolute ruler in his leadership. Leaders rose to the occasion, but they didn't abuse their position. If Aitzol wanted to stay with his life in Biarritz, that would be his fate.

Even though this stubborn arrogance of Aitzol annoyed Patxi severely as he planned out his grand scheme, Aitzol's position became an asset he could keep on hand. Just in case. And that *just in case* situation had presented itself.

Itxaso shook her head as she considered the possibility of Aitzol's arrest. "But even if they question Aitzol, how would they ever suspect him or be able to tie him to anything?"

"I don't know," Patxi replied, revealing only half of the truth. Although he didn't know how Aitzol Rubina had been identified, he did know who was responsible. His mole within the French DNAT tipped him off on Aitzol's identification as a strong person of interest potentially tied to the Paris attack. The same mole also was able to give him the name of the person credited with having marked Aitzol as a suspect.

It was an American named Sebastian Parker who lived in a Basque farmhouse outside the village of Sare. The American was married to Alaitz Etxegaraya. This Parker had been responsible for the Haika 4 disaster a few years ago. Everyone knew that Parker once worked for the CIA and had close connections with the French DNAT.

Specifically with the despised Capitaine Jean-Pierre Nivelle, an infamous enemy of the Basque people.

But Lopé and his group of young followers were never supported by ETA in their actions to attract support from the American Basque population for the Basque cause in Europe. Their intended goal may have been a good idea, in theory, but it was juvenile from the start. Lopé actually approached Patxi for help before executing his plans and Patxi laughed at him, calling him a young fool. Even if possible at one time to solicit both financial and moral support from the Basque-Americans, that time had long passed with those so-called Basques forgetting their homeland after they grew accustomed to the easy life of America. And any so-called operation in America was sure to only bring negative attention to the Basque separatist cause.

ETA's most clever minds, chief of which was Garikotz, effectively were able to disassociate the Haika 4 and their actions from ETA. They were painted as they were: rogue kids wanting to taste blood. For that reason, the actions of Sebastian Parker were not considered as severe against ETA as may have been imagined. Especially after he married a Basque girl and moved to the Basque Country. Patxi and others eyed Parker as more of a curiosity. And Patxi even held respect for this Basque, French, Spanish-speaking American who, by some accounts, was more conversed in Basque history and culture than most Basques.

"I don't know how they came to suspect him. But DNAT is watching him and I'm told it is only a matter of time before they make a move," Patxi conveyed to Itxaso.

"Shouldn't we warn Aitzol then?" Itxaso asked, looking worried.

"No, he would panic and do something stupid. Like maybe lead them to Garikotz." Patxi's answer was partially honest. Aitzol was strong, brave, and dedicated. But he was not the most intelligent.

"Aitzol would never turn us in. They could torture him to death before he would say anything."

"*Si*, I have no doubt this is true."

"Then why are you concerned?"

"Because I have a feeling that they may get something out of him, even if not directly, which will lead them here. And, more specifically, lead them to you."

"But the plan?" Itxaso wondered aloud, considering that as far as she knew, there was some work to be done before ready to initiate.

"Already taken care of," Patxi assured her.

After meeting with Garikotz in Avignon, Garikotz made the final arrangements to have Itxaso's explosive devices planted all along Nice's waterfront. Just as they'd done in Paris, they used illegal immigrants, the untraceable gifts that they were.

Everything was actually in place now for the attack. All that was needed was for the devices to be remotely armed and set off. But Patxi didn't offer all of this information to Itxaso. He kept things simple.

She didn't know the heightened role for Garikotz in the operation. She didn't need to know. And she didn't need to know that he had deliberately not involved Aitzol in the operation. In fact, Aitzol knew nothing about the planned attack in Nice. But that was not to say that he was not aware of a planned attack somewhere else.

"How would they be led to me?" Itxaso wondered aloud.

"Because you have known, traceable involvement with ETA in the past, and it would not take a genius to find you here if they have any help."

"So what do you want me to do?"

"Nothing yet. But I do want you to prepare yourself. They may catch Aitzol, but we can't let them catch you. *Claro*?"

As he spoke, Patxi questioned the honesty of his words. Although he didn't overly enjoy the circumstances, he'd planned for the detaining of Aitzol Rubina, sooner or later. And if needed, Itxaso would be expendable as well. She would be more of a loss than Aitzol, but he could replace her. *Being a leader was hard, but the cause needed him.*

Another hard decision he made earlier that day was that Sebastian Parker represented a significant threat to him and his plans. Commendable as he might be, especially for an American, he was still a looming threat. His name was often mentioned in circles involving those remaining loyal to the cause. Just to loosely monitor him. Now things had changed for this Parker.

Patxi was confused why Parker would actually be involved, as his sources informed him that Parker parted ways from the CIA, and this was made known by his wife's influential, and loud-mouthed, mother. But for whatever reason, the decision to become involved was a mistake.

Parker should've been content to be allowed to live in peace in the Basque Country. Now it was clear to Patxi that he wasn't an exile. Like Capitaine Nivelle, Sebastian Parker was an enemy. Using his handwritten message system, which would have instructions delivered to Garikotz in Perpignan, he instructed Garikotz to discreetly return to the Basque Country and keep an eye on someone. Just in case.

Patxi also instructed Garikotz to watch Parker's wife, Alaitz.

Just in case.

X.

French Basque Country

JOHN GIBSON TORE OFF a piece of bread to dip into the sauce of the cassoulet he was having for lunch.

"You know, I'm normally not one to be health conscious. And I'm definitely not one to turn away a real French baguette any time of day, but you may be having the one French or Basque or Spanish dish that really doesn't require any more carbohydrates."

Gibson's eyes dropped to the steaming aromatic bowl of beans with chunks of vegetables and meat in front of him. Parker was probably right, but he didn't care. Once back in San Francisco, he'd put himself on a temporary diet and devote extra time to walks in the city with Rachel. The thought of her made him smile inwardly. He missed her, but missing someone was good. After his ex-wife left him, he'd experienced a long period of indifference to women, and even a certain aversion to them.

Having a significant other in his life also made him more sensitive to others. Parker opened up over lunch at the restaurant with outdoor seating overlooking a golf course with a backdrop of the Pyrenees. He mentioned that they were just outside the limits of Biarritz at a place called Arcangues. This was hard for Gibson to believe, as the rolling countryside setting was very separated from any city development. But it was not difficult for him to believe when Parker told him that the golf resort with vacation homes lining some of the fairways had been a favorite target of ETA and IK in the past, as they both conducted their own *vacation wars* on the Basque Coast at times.

On a more personal level, Parker also mentioned how he and Alaitz had been experiencing difficult times recently.

"Do you think maybe you should be more involved with your wife than with this case?" Gibson asked as delicately as his normal stern character allowed.

Parker took a sip of his glass of rosé and pensively replied. "We just had a nice afternoon yesterday together. That's good enough for now. Alaitz has always been a flame in my life and I've always had to be careful to not get too close too quickly or I'll get burned, even if she doesn't intend to burn. I think I was starting to forget that important lesson, having gotten too caught up in the whole settling down thing."

"Sounds reasonable."

"Besides, her mother was coming over today, and another lesson of mine is to never let myself get talked into spending too much time with her mother."

Gibson laughed. "It's good," he said, smiling widely.

Parker shook his head and casually shrugged. "What's good? Being driven crazy by my aggressive, nosy, pestering, ultra-opinionated mother-in-law?"

"No, no, no," Gibson replied, waving a hand in front of him. "Maybe that's good too, in a way, now that I think about it. But what I'm really talking about is just seeing you like this, so much more…"

"Mature? Established? Toned down?"

"Sure, all of those things. I wouldn't say you're a different person, but this is all definitely a new side to you."

"Yeah, yeah," Parker said, rolling his eyes.

"Okay, maybe not so different at times," Gibson teased.

"Very funny. But truth is that I know all of that's true and I know it's all for the best. However, I'd be lying if I didn't say that I sometimes miss being that other guy. Sometimes I think he had a better time."

"You mean the reckless, unpredictable partier who smoked too many damn cigarettes and drank too damn much?"

Parker sighed heavily, staring into the remnants of the local river trout with yellow string beans he'd had for lunch. "Yeah, that guy. He was a lot of fun."

Gibson watched his young friend and for a moment felt concerned. "He was also unhealthy and a punk at times. I like seeing this new and improved Sebastian."

Parker looked up from his plate. "Thanks, John," he said with a grin. "We should get going though. About time to meet up with Nivelle at the Biarritz gendarme station."

Gibson glanced at his watch and saw that Parker was correct. Nivelle called him that morning asking them to meet him at the *other* Biarritz police station, adding that Parker would know what that meant. From the tone of Nivelle's voice, Gibson believed Nivelle had good news to share.

"By the way, what did Nivelle mean by the *other* police station?" Gibson asked Parker as they drove into the heart of Biarritz.

"The French government never really officially declared open war against Basque separatists. Ex-president Chirac once famously said that France would not be a back yard for terrorists, but there was always a fine line between rhetoric and practice. The last thing the French wanted to do was to provoke their own Basque provinces. It was always a dilemma for the French to keep in mind."

"And so?"

"And so, publicly distinguishing separate police and gendarme annexes to existing facilities devoted to the sole purpose of Basque affairs was not something the French government wanted to do. So you would never see such places publicly labeled, but everyone knew they were there. The Basques even bombed the Bayonne annex a few times. The one we went to where they were holding Peio, who's now sitting in a prison cell outside Lille in the northernmost area of France. He'll be there for most of the rest of this life. Nivelle will make sure of this," Parker said, referring to another captured member of the Haika 4.

"Ah, yeah. I remember that little stout tough bastard who loved playing that pelota game. Anyway, so not the Biarritz one?"

"Biarritz has always been an interesting case study in Basque affairs. Biarritz has never been wholly accepted by the Basques as one of their own, even though it has a Basque name of Miarritze. But Biarritz represents the center of tourism and foreigners to the French Basque

Country. Although exactly for these reasons, the city is also never entirely rejected. I think most nationalist Basques see Biarritz as a necessary place in their land, even if they don't necessarily claim the city. But, economically, the city is arguably the most important revenue stream generator for the French Basque Country. The Spanish Basque Country has a vibrant Spanish market surrounding the area contributing to the regional economy. This is a clear contrast to the French Basque Country, where you have this huge expanse of pine forest separating the French Basque Country from the regional commercial hub of Bordeaux. So even though some French Basques want to spout off about how Biarritz isn't truly a Basque place, if they ever want greater economic autonomy from Paris, Biarritz is absolutely necessary."

Gibson eyed Parker reflectively for a prolonged moment. "Somehow I forgot how you can sound like a history teacher at times."

"Yeah, yeah. That was more of an econ lecture than history. Anyway, my point is that Biarritz is a special case and the annex here for Basque issues is even more conspicuous than in Bayonne. And, no, the complex was not a target that I'm aware of."

Gibson understood what Parker meant by less than conspicuous when he saw the building. The building was a nondescript place on a side street and could have been the home of any business or office. Yet once one stepped inside the door, the interior was entirely different than the outside. An armed guard stood just inside the doorway, out of sight from the outside. After nodding approval for Parker and Gibson to proceed forward, they mounted a spiral staircase to the second floor. The guard gave them a room number after Parker said they had an appointment with Capitaine Nivelle, but the number wasn't necessary. Gibson thought most of the rooms in the building appeared to be unoccupied, and the noise of voices from a room at the end of the hallway was easy to follow.

Entering the room, Gibson was surprised even more.

In the middle of the room there was a table. At the table sat Nivelle and Aitzol Rubina. They both looked relaxed and like they were having a normal conversation. A guard was standing at the entrance to the room, but otherwise the scene was casual.

Rubina instantly recognized Parker and peered at him menacingly. “And I thought you were a good guy,” Rubina said to Parker in English.

“I am a good guy. I like to think so anyway,” Parker said as he shook hands with Nivelle.

“Let’s keep this friendly,” Nivelle suggested. “After all, as I’ve explained to Mr. Rubina, this is all just a conversation to help us investigate potential connections with what happened in Paris to here in the Pays Basque. Mr. Rubina’s former association with the ETA is known and he does not deny this. But as I’ve explained to him, we are simply having a conversation,” Nivelle stated, looking at Rubina the entire time.

Parker and Gibson sat down at the table. “So what are you?” Rubina asked, his eyes fixated on Parker.

“I’m Sebastian Parker, just as I introduced myself to you the other night.”

“You are more than that. Otherwise you would not be here.”

“True. Let’s just say I’m a friend of his.” Parker glanced at Nivelle. They shared a look of startled recognition that Parker even associated their relationship as friendly.

Rubina spoke in Basque. “He has friends?” he said, laughing at his own joke.

Parker kept a straight face, not revealing that he understood.

“As I was saying to Mr. Rubina, we are just curious if he may have any knowledge of those responsible for the attack in Paris, as we believe he is still in contact with certain elements of the ETA organization who may still consider themselves active participants,” Nivelle commented.

“You may deny if you want, but the struggle is not over,” Rubina sternly stated.

“A ceasefire was declared and has been respected,” Parker said.

“You cannot kill a dream, despite a piece of paper a few may sign.”

“Does that mean you agree with what occurred at the Tour Montparnasse?”

“I didn’t say that. I only say for you people to believe that the dream of Basque independence will ever disappear is ridiculous.”

"Does that mean that you don't know anything about who may be responsible for what occurred at the Tour Montparnasse?" Nivelle asked.

"I have no idea."

"And if you did, would you tell us?" Gibson added.

Rubina turned to look at Gibson before responding. "Oh yes, I remember seeing you the other night. The old guy sitting alone reading a newspaper at a bar. Hard to miss. I suppose you are just a friend of his?" Rubina asked nodding in the direction of Nivelle.

"More like professional colleague. And I also am a Special Agent for the American FBI. My name is John Gibson."

Rubina smirked. "FBI? Since when did the FBI get involved in Europe?"

"Let's just say I'm here as a personal favor to Capitaine Nivelle. And law enforcement is the same everywhere around the world, despite political borders. But what you all did in Paris was far beyond the law. It was cowardly and a disgrace to the Basque people and culture."

Parker and Nivelle shared another look. This one acknowledging Gibson's clear progress in the knowledge of all things Basque.

Rubina's expression remained unchanged. "I don't know what you mean by *you all.* Unless you mean all Basque people who want what is rightfully theirs."

"Rightfully theirs at the expense of murdering innocent people?" Parker asked.

"If that is what gets people's attention," Rubina coldly replied.

"So you're saying you were involved with the attack in Paris?" Nivelle quickly asked.

"I did not say that," Rubina answered. "I said that perhaps such things are necessary."

"Necessary for Basque independence?" Parker asked.

"Perhaps."

"So you're saying that you know who was involved?" Nivelle asked.

"No, I am not saying that."

"Would you tell us if you did know?" Gibson asked.

Rubina looked directly into Gibson's eyes. "No."

"I didn't think so." Nivelle stood up from his chair and looked downward at Rubina. "But let me lay the situation out for you. From the moment you step outside this door, we're going to be watching you. And we're going to ask more questions and find out everything there is to know about you. If you are truly not involved, I'll apologize myself. But I think you are. And I think eventually we're going to have something on you. We're not the Spanish here. I'm not going to detain you for no reason and coerce you to talk as they are known to do with you Basque terrorists.

"But that may change any day. The President has called me personally asking for results, and he's not a patient man. And I promise you this: if you are involved with this group in any way, we will catch you. I will catch you. And we'll put you away for a long time. You will take the fall with the rest of the cowards. And I wouldn't be surprised if there are calls for bringing back the guillotine.

"However, if you were willing to cooperate, I can guarantee your fate will be much less severe than the others. All you need to do is to help us a little. Give us some names. Tell us where to look."

"Tell us where next," Parker interjected, receiving an icy glance from Nivelle. Parker shrugged in response.

"Yes, as *my friend* here mentions, you could tell us where next," Nivelle continued.

Rubina calmly shook his head. "I don't know what you are talking about. I may have ETA sympathies, but I have never been arrested for being a member. You cannot prove anything."

"Maybe, maybe not. But *franchement*, I don't give a damn about whether you are or are not or were or were not an ETA member. I only care about tying you to Paris, and I think we'll be able to do so. And soon," Nivelle replied.

For the first time since entering the room, Parker noticed a slight look of concern on Rubina's face.

"What makes you so sure?" Rubina asked.

"That's the question you should have been asking from the beginning," Gibson chimed.

"Yes, that's true. After all, how do you think we've been led to you? Seems strange to me that for such a secretive and careful group, somehow we were able to find you. I wonder how that could be?" Parker added.

Aitzol considered what the younger American was saying. It dawned on him that the fact he was being questioned was indeed strange. Everything had been done according to the plan and there'd been no mistakes or missteps. Could he have been sold out? Did the others plan for him to be the fall guy?

Garikotz first had the idea to target the Tour building, but it'd been Patxi's idea to use immigrants to help carry out the attack.

There were so many of them these days, filling *les banlieues* of all the major cities of Europe. Most of them were not legal and trying to claim refugee status to legally live in Europe instead of whatever *bordel de merde* place they came from. In the suburbs of Paris, there were in particular a lot of desperate people from somewhere in the Middle East. Patxi only needed a recruiter.

When considering who the recruiter would be, Aitzol had been the perfect choice. Aitzol was a people person and, in particular, a guy's guy. A real *mec*. He was a perfect choice to send in to recruit young men from a culture where male dominance was accepted as normal.

Patxi sent Aitzol to the Paris suburb of Saint Denis with instructions to find and lure a few young men, six in total, with a promise of legal residency papers. All for doing one day's work. But they were to have no idea what the actual job would be, only to know that they would have to do something when contacted. If they asked how such a thing could be possible, to receive such rewards for only one day of work, Aitzol was to say they would be doing something of great importance. That was all. If they continued to question, Aitzol would say there were hundreds of others he could find to take their place. And the truth was—there were hundreds, if not more, desperate men who would do anything asked of them to get legal immigration status.

Furthermore, Aitzol was to target younger men in particular. Younger men were always more radical and less rational, something that played perfectly for them in the situation, Patxi told Aitzol.

Aitzol was to remain in contact by untraceable cell phones with his recruits, constantly assuring them that their troubles were to soon be over. Just before the day of the attack, Patxi would have Aitzol come back up from Biarritz to Paris to meet again with his group. At this time, they would be given their specific instructions.

There was no way of not revealing to the six young men that they were to be involved in an attack, but Aitzol assured them they would be safe. All they had to do was send a message from the cell phones given to them from the top floor platform of the building and then leave. The bombs would not detonate until an hour later. Aitzol promised them. They would have more than enough time to descend from the top floor on the elevators to the metro station and be long gone before any explosions.

This, of course, was a blatant lie.

Being of Middle Eastern descent, the young men would be easily identifiable on the building's security cameras after the attack. Eventually, the French authorities would be able to track them down. Once arrested, they would give up Aitzol immediately to try and save themselves. Even with a fake name and no traceable mobile phone account tied to him, there was too much of a chance that Aitzol could somehow be linked to the group.

Aitzol had done his job. And he knew he had done his job well. But the attack wouldn't have been possible without Itxaso's involvement. She specially designed the explosives they used. The three bombs would not be armed until they received a signal from a transmitter, a transmitter she installed in six mobile phones. Only three were required, but it was agreed that planning for potential complications was better than not achieving their objective. Failure was not an option.

The explosives themselves were planted long before. Garikotz had come up with the idea of having the bombs placed in the floor of the viewing platform. The explosives needed to be small, but Itxaso could handle that. Garikotz had found out about planned construction on the flooring of the platform, and Patxi only had to bribe the construction crew foreman to get what looked like little boxes installed within the replacement flooring on the platform.

If the foreman had any suspicion of what he was asked to do, no one would have noticed. He appeared pleased to take the suitcase of euros handed to him. Even so, Patxi couldn't leave a potential tie to him. Aitzol was tasked to take care of the loose end. He even managed to get the money back.

Just another casualty of the war for Basque independence.

So where did this all leave him? The more he thought about what was happening, the more he admitted his being sold out could be a possibility. Patxi was upset about Aitzol never leaving Biarritz. Aitzol knew the plans for the next attack were already underway, and for some reason Patxi didn't involve him. This hadn't bothered Aitzol before, but now that he was the one being questioned by the French DNAT and the American FBI, including being questioned by the historic adversary of the Basques, Nivelle himself, he began to feel less certain of his status.

Could Patxi have really been behind all this? Or Garikotz? He'd followed Patxi blindly for years, knowing that Patxi's number one concern was himself, even if Patxi constantly repeated that he was only interested in the cause. And Garikotz was always scheming. Who knows what that one could have thought out in his grand plans? Was there a possibility that Aitzol had been designated as the scapegoat?

"I can see you're having second thoughts." Nivelle walked behind Rubina so that he was standing over him. "Why don't you take a few moments to keep thinking before you leave?"

"I am not having second thoughts. I am thinking about how I would like to see you three on the rugby field."

Nivelle grinned across the table at Gibson and Parker. He placed both of his hands on the back of the chair next to Rubina's head. "That'd be better than seeing us from the other side of a prison cell. And this is where you're going to end up."

"I believe I have been cooperative enough for one day. Am I free to go?"

"*Bien sûr*, you are free to go." Nivelle patted Rubina's shoulders and moved away.

Rubina pushed his chair back from the table, causing a loud screech, and began to get up. Parker suddenly remembered the name Graciana gave him. Itxaso. Seeing how Aitzol Rubina would react to him mentioning the name was worth a chance. "We'll just have to talk to Itxaso and see what she has to say."

Rubina halted midway as he was about to stand fully erect, clearly hit by hearing Itxaso's name. He quickly decided that he couldn't deny his association with her. If they did any searching of his history, they were bound to find a connection between him and Itxaso. But how the hell did they know her name? Something wasn't right. And if they already knew of his connection to her, he couldn't deny it now, as this would evidence that he was lying from the start. And if they knew about Itxaso, he would be even more suspicious that someone was talking. Someone was giving them up. Or was someone just trying to save their own ass? Could it be Garikotz? Aitzol doubted that Garikotz could hold his ground. And despite whatever Nivelle said about not using torture methods to interrogate people, Aitzol didn't believe the *connard flic*. Nivelle's name wasn't common among the Basques as the French government's anti-Basque leader without reason. Stories about Nivelle and his personal war against Basque nationalists went back decades.

"That's a long trip to Lisbon just to try to find an old friend of mine," Rubina offered as he fully rose and stood facing them.

"Lisbon?" Nivelle questioned.

Aitzol wanted to kick himself as he realized that they didn't even know she lived in Portugal. He didn't respond and instead started for the door.

"Why *try* to find?" Gibson asked.

"Because I don't know where she lives. I just know she lives there." Rubina opened the door and stepped into the hallway, closing the door behind him.

After he left, Nivelle, Gibson, and Parker looked at one another. Nivelle spoke first. "That will greatly narrow down our search. I'll have my people start tracking addresses for her in Lisbon. If you two are willing, I'd trust you to go to Lisbon to question her first. As you know, Agent Gibson, sending my own people into another country to question a suspect gets complicated, especially since the French and Portuguese don't always see eye to eye. But if you two were to pursue the lead on your own and report back to me, I can start the motions to get permission to have her detained if we believe it's a credible lead."

Parker and Gibson exchanged a look that they both knew meant they were taking a trip to Lisbon.

"Of course, this all assumes that we'll be able to locate her," Parker said.

"*Bien sûr.*"

"But aren't you concerned we could spook her and trigger that we're on to this group, if she is involved?" Parker questioned.

"Of course, that is a concern. But now that we have her name and a relative location, we should be able to keep track of her once we do find her. Once we have an address, I'm also going to call my counterpart in Lisbon and request assistance with surveillance of her. I'll let this person know you two will be there with my compliments. I cannot guarantee you will have any support from the authorities, but considering that Agent Gibson is with the FBI, I expect you will receive the normal courtesies."

"What are you going to do about Rubina?" Gibson asked.

"I'll keep my people on him. And I'll bring him in for questioning again. Let's see how long he can hold off, as I think he knows something, even if he's not directly involved."

All three men nodded in agreement. "I guess we'd better get ready to go to Portugal," Gibson suggested to Parker. "I hope Alaitz isn't upset with you for leaving again so soon."

"Me too," Parker replied.

"Where did your husband go this time?" Zurina Etxegaraya asked her daughter, Alaitz, making no attempt to conceal the contempt in her tone. They were walking in one of Saint-Jean-Pied-de-Port's public squares, and the wide open space was filled with temporary stalls and tables for the weekly market.

"*Maman…arrêt.* I told you already that I don't know. He just had to go somewhere."

"I thought he quit working for that place?" Zurina questioned, referencing Sebastian Parker's previous employer, the American CIA.

"He did. But he's offered to help try and find who is responsible for the Tour Montparnasse attacks and had to go somewhere."

"So he left you alone when you have a visitor staying with you," Zurina stated more than asked as she picked up a red bell pepper from a stall to examine the vegetable more closely.

"*Maman, ça va*. John is very respectful and I barely noticed he was around while Sebastian was gone. And this time he left with Sebastian anyway."

"Regardless, *ce n'est pas normale*. And your husband is foolish for getting himself involved with these people. This could be dangerous, for both of you." Zurina tossed a few peppers into her shoulder bag and handed some euro coins to the seller.

"These people are something different than in the old days. Who knows what they are capable of doing," Zurina added as they continued walking.

She noticed a wispy middle-aged man a couple of stalls behind them who she believed was possibly following them, as she'd noticed him the entire time they were at the market, always watching them and staying close. But Zurina didn't say anything to her daughter. The whole business with Alaitz's husband was troubling, and she figured she was being a little paranoid. But she couldn't help feeling that they were being followed. Ever since her early days in the Basque Country troubles, she'd learned to keep a watchful eye on those around her. Back in those days the Spanish were sending their mercenaries across the border and killing and kidnapping anyone they believed even remotely connected to ETA. No one could imagine how tense life in the French Basque Country was during those times.

Zurina thought she was too old for anyone to care about what she did or may have done connected to the Basque movement twenty years ago. But her daughter had always dangled on the fine line of being viewed as a radical. And her choice of husband—that of course could be a concern. Who knows what he used to do for that damned place? The Americans always pretended they had no involvement one way or another with any of the Basque troubles on either side of the border. But who knows if that was ever really true?

Yes, she decided, the wispy man was definitely following them.

Dembora demmborary darrio. (*After one climate comes another.*)
—Basque proverb

Saindu man, otso hazana.
(He has the look of a saint and the actions of a wolf.)
—Basque proverb

Part IV.

(Present/*Le Présent*)

I.

Lisbon, Portugal

"I THINK YOU'LL LIKE LISBON," Sebastian Parker said to John Gibson as the plane landed at the city's Portela Airport. "It's a unique place that doesn't receive much attention, especially compared to other Western Europe cities. And I honestly have no idea why not. Lisbon's a fantastic place."

"How so?" Gibson asked.

"To begin with, Lisbon is older than most other cities, including London, Rome, and Paris. So there's a little history to the place. And it has all the things people rave about with other cities, such as a pleasant Mediterranean climate, centralized parks, grand public squares, interesting architecture, great cuisine, and distinct neighborhoods. Lisbon also has a really hilly downtown, which I think is pretty cool and you should appreciate, as you live in San Francisco. To me, Lisbon is almost like a more spread-out version of the Montmartre area in Paris. Part of the city's mystique is that Lisbon is also the westernmost point of continental Europe, almost as if destined to be a point where Europeans left Europe for other worlds, with the Portuguese being one of the first European powers to venture around the globe. This turned out to be the case. The city also has a North African feel at times from centuries of rule by the Moors. You find this in some southern Spanish cities too, but this influence feels somehow more ingrained here."

"I've heard that it's kind of a rough place," Gibson said, purposefully lowering his voice despite the fact that the only passengers sitting near them were a couple of teenagers wearing headphones.

"Every big city in the world has rough areas. Been to the Tenderloin district at night in San Francisco?" As Gibson knew him to do, Parker continued talking before hearing an answer to a question he'd asked. "But as far as Lisbon is concerned, sure, I admit that this city is probably a little on the grittier side. You have to remember that for decades Portugal was like the poor kid in the corner of Western Europe. When I first came here, this place reminded me more of a developing country than an advanced economy like others in Western Europe. So I guess that adds a little more exotic flavor. Another touch of the exotic is that the Portuguese colonial influence from around the world is strongly felt here, most noticeably in the cuisine."

"I think the only Portuguese food I know of are those skinny spicy sausages you see in grocery stores in California," Gibson commented after a flight attendant welcomed the plane's passengers to Lisbon.

Parker laughed. "*Linguica*. Yes, that's the Portuguese sausage that is smoke cured and has garlic and paprika mixed in. But I promise it tastes better here than from Safeway. We'll go for a feijoada while we're here and you'll have the best linguica of your life."

"Sounds good to me."

"But any time you've had a port style wine, you've had something Portuguese inspired, as port wine originated here. And even though people make these fortified wines all over the world now, technically they are only supposed to be called port if from the Porto region of Portugal."

"Interesting, but I've never really liked sweet wines. Maybe they are better here too?"

"I'm sure they are better than the ten dollar bottles you can find anywhere in the States. But in general I'd say that people either like those kind of wines or they don't. I'm also not a fan of sweet wine. But don't worry, as the Portuguese make some outstanding regular wine and we'll find some to try later."

Gibson was tempted to remark that they were there for work, but realized this wasn't entirely true. "That sounds good, but let's get some work done too." The plane came to a complete stop. People stood up to retrieve their bags from the overhead compartments, to stretch their legs after being seated in crammed positions, or to anxiously await escaping the confines of the plane.

Gibson pulled down Parker's bag from the overhead compartment and handed it to him. "Hopefully we don't have to wait long for an address from Nivelle's people."

Parker wasn't looking at him and was instead staring at his phone, which he'd just turned back on. He looked up at Gibson and grinned. "No waiting." He held up the phone for Gibson to see.

"Bingo," he said, grinning back at Parker.

Parker laughed. *Who the hell says bingo anymore.*

After they passed through the Nothing to Declare doorway, Parker and Gibson were surprised to see a young man in a police uniform holding a piece of paper with their names written on the sheet.

"What the hell?" Gibson said as they approached the young police officer.

"*Bom dia, senhores. Venham comigo, por favor,*" the officer said to them.

Gibson turned to face Parker. "I understood the *por favor* part."

"He's asking us to come with him. Under the circumstances since we don't know what we just stepped off a plane into, probably not a bad idea," Parker offered.

"I suppose so. He does look serious." Gibson nodded to the young officer and his stern expression.

Once in the back of a marked police car, the officer asked the name of the hotel where they were staying. Parker booked a couple of rooms for them at a small hotel near Rossio Square in central downtown.

Parker asked the driver in Portuguese where he was taking them and the officer replied that he was under orders to take them to their hotel where they were to wait to be contacted by Chief Superintendent Barros. The officer added that Barros was the commanding officer of the Lisbon metropolitan area. Although Parker was unfamiliar with the hierarchy of the Lisbon police forces, by the way the young officer made a point of adding the distinction and the tone of his voice, Parker assumed the position was of exceedingly high rank. Apparently he and

Gibson were being considered as very important. Whether or not that turned out to be a good or bad thing, they'd have to wait and see.

Parker conveyed the message to Gibson.

"I didn't know you speak Portuguese," Gibson responded.

"I don't. Not really anyway. But by knowing French and Spanish, Portuguese is not the most difficult to at least understand quite a bit. Speaking is another matter, but I can get by with some words and phrases I know and then say things in Spanish or French when I don't and hope there's some familiarity."

Soon after leaving the airport, they entered the city's downtown area on a wide avenue, eventually turning onto much smaller side streets. The Portuguese police officer stopped the car in front of their hotel, only distinguishable as a hotel with a small sign posted above a doorway. The Hotel Lisbon.

"Wait here for further instructions," the police offer said in English, surprising Parker and Gibson.

"How long do you think we will have to wait?" Parker asked.

The police officer shrugged in an absent way that would make any Frenchman proud.

"Then can I give you my mobile number and you can pass the number on to the Chief Superintendent or whoever? That way we don't have to sit around waiting," Parker suggested.

The police officer gazed at him as if Parker had asked a ridiculous question. He finally spoke, apparently after deciding that his obvious look of confirmation was not enough to be understood. "Of course, you are not under arrest. You may do as you like." The police officer made no effort to conceal his annoyed expression.

Parker nearly spoke in response, but held back. They were unofficial guests involved with an international investigation that had the world's attention, after all. But knowing that Portugal had been ruled by an oppressive right-wing government until the mid 1970s, Parker wanted to reply to the police officer that in places with a repressive police force past, he found it always a better idea to exercise caution before making any assumptions. Not wanting to start their short visit off on a bad note though made Parker hold his tongue. Maybe Gibson was right that he'd changed. In the past he would not have given a damn about protocol.

The police officer took Parker's mobile number and sped off without saying another word. Standing on the narrow sidewalk in front of their hotel, Parker and Gibson exchanged a glance that asked the same thing. *What the hell did we get ourselves into?*

Despite the strange arrival, Parker and Gibson made a swift recovery, starting with a large local beer at a café near their hotel. Parker insisted they enjoy a beer before heading out into the streets of Lisbon.

As soon as they were seated at a small outdoor table, Gibson assumed he was about to receive a typical abbreviated history lesson from Parker. He was correct.

"As I mentioned when we were landing, Lisbon was ruled for centuries by the Moors. There was actually a crusade in the eleven hundreds by Christian armies to free the city and bring Christianity here." Parker almost remarked that Lisbon was similar in that way to the other city he had recently visited, Vilnius, but caught himself before admitting to Gibson where he'd been. Of course, with Gibson's capabilities, if he really wanted to know where Parker had been, he could easily find out. Perhaps he already had, but Parker saw no need to test the waters. For multiple reasons, he didn't want to talk about Graciana.

"But before the Moors, there were Germanic tribes who'd taken over the area after the fall of the Roman Empire. During Roman times, Lisbon was an important city at the edge of the empire and played a key trading post role. The Moors conquered the city in the seven hundreds, so they were here for quite a while. After Christian forces took over the city, a lot of Moorish architecture was destroyed or converted. What wasn't decimated in an earthquake in 1755, along with most of the city at that time. There's one enclave of the city, the Alfama district, retaining the most Moorish influence. This area was mostly spared from destruction during the earthquake because Lisbon the area was so densely built, like traditional North African cities, that it was able to withstand the quake." Parker paused as two large beers appeared on the table. As soon as the beers were set down, the waiter stepped away into the street and lit a cigarette.

"Miss smoking?" Gibson asked, watching the waiter.

Parker glanced in the direction of the waiter. "Not really. I'd be lying if I said having a cigarette doesn't sound good sometimes, but then I hear a little voice reminding me that it wouldn't be." He turned to face Gibson and lifted his beer. "To Lisboa."

Gibson raised his own beer. "To Lisboa."

They both drank and Parker continued. "So this earthquake—in the States there's always talk about the devastation to your current home city. While that earthquake was of course terrible, San Francisco in the early twentieth century was nowhere near the global importance of Lisbon at the time of its own leveling earthquake. The Lisbon earthquake was so bad the event scared the hell out of all of Europe and made its way into novels of the time. The city was absolutely decimated, with a quarter of the population killed.

"This earthquake was such a notable event because Lisbon was a jewel of Europe at the time, though on the downside of a reign of importance. Because the sixteenth century, the century before the earthquake, was when Lisbon really experienced a golden era. The city was the hub of commerce between Europe and colonies around the world. And that world had a large Portuguese presence in places including Africa, India, the Far East, and then later Brazil. To this day, the port outside of Lisbon is one of Europe's busiest."

"What about after the earthquake?" Gibson asked. When he first met Sebastian Parker, these little history and cultural lessons annoyed the hell out of him. Over time though, he'd come to appreciate the body of knowledge within his young friend. Parker could still take things too far, but being around him was enthralling in that one could feel Parker's deep appreciation for everything around him. Food, wine, architecture, history, culture, languages, geography—no matter where he was, Parker managed to soak it all in.

"After the earthquake the city was rebuilt, but most of its medieval charm vanished with the rebuilding. Still though, this city has a unique feel. You'll see when we start walking around."

"Which I hope is going to be soon and that this is not going to turn into one of those all-afternoon occasions," Gibson said while looking at their beers on the small table.

"No, no, no…nothing like that. I'm actually anxious to walk around myself. It's been a long time since I was last here." Parker paused and Gibson thought he might be done with the history lesson before Parker suddenly spoke again. "Something else interesting about this city is that during World War II, Lisbon was the only major neutral city on the Western European coast. So not only was it a primary point of debarkation for people trying to escape the madness enveloping Europe, but also a haven for spies from both sides. And something about the city's grittiness lends itself to that past."

"Okay, now I'm interested. Let's finish these and head out." After he spoke, Gibson picked up his beer and finished it. Sebastian Parker tipped his own glass to Gibson with a grin and did the same.

Parker and Gibson stood overlooking a panoramic view of Lisbon. The red tile roofs of the city were on full display, with the prominent castle on a hill in the background. They'd walked for over two hours throughout the city, walking up steep hills alongside vintage yellow trams, which Parker called *elevadores*, climbing the same hills. There were yellow electric trams running throughout the city and they all looked like they were at least fifty years old, but the *elevadores* were even smaller and older looking. John Gibson considered himself to be in good shape for his age, but after a while he began to wonder why they were not taking one of the *elevadores* up the city's steep hills.

But Parker was right: the views from various overlooks they stopped at were spectacular. Especially the one where they now stood on the ramparts of the former castle perched above the city.

Walking up the hills of Lisbon was an interesting experience for Gibson to compare to trekking the hills of San Francisco. The inclines were similar, and, from what he'd seen, San Francisco was one of the most European feeling cities in America. But there were differences for sure. Not only did Lisbon have the historic presence, causing one to reflect on the centuries the roads and buildings had witnessed, but Lisbon also had something distinctly unique, as Parker suggested.

Many of the buildings were brightly colored, reminiscent of a tropical location. But the paint was noticeably peeling and there was more graffiti on building walls than anything Gibson had seen living in DC or San Francisco. And although the peeling paint and graffiti were distracting from the beauty of the city, somehow they seemed normal components of Lisbon's overall presentation.

"Napoleon actually invaded Lisbon with his armies and they pillaged and destroyed whatever they pleased," Parker commented. As he spoke, the thought occurred to him that the Napoleon experience was in stark contrast to what the city of Vilnius experienced. There they had welcomed him into the city with open arms and he fell in love with the *Jerusalem of the North*. Apparently, he'd not felt so fondly of Lisbon.

Parker was about to propose another café and beer refreshment stop when Gibson's phone vibrated in his pocket. Gibson glanced at the caller identification screen and saw that Capitaine Nivelle was calling.

"Nivelle, what the hell is going on?" he said right away. Although he didn't mind spending some time with Sebastian and getting a personal tour of an intriguing European capital, putting the reason for being there completely out of mind wasn't possible. He may have loosened up a lot in recent years, but his strong sense of duty would never entirely disappear.

"I regret. I regret. I should have called you earlier. But as I will inform you in a moment, I have been very occupied," Nivelle replied.

"I need a better explanation than that. We did fly all the way down here."

"*Je sais. Je sais.* And I called ahead as I said I would to respectfully inform my professional colleague of your visit. *Mais...*"

"But what?"

"Ah *bon*, Detective Gibson. You are learning a little French after all."

"Flattered. Now continue, *s'il vous plait.*"

"Apparently, our Portuguese friends were very pleased to enlist themselves in our investigation. So much so that they have already apprehended this woman you went there to question. They are questioning her now. I regret, but this is beyond me. It is their jurisdiction."

"Goddammit, Nivelle. You and I both know, that could tip off the rest of them and give them a running start to jump into hiding."

"*Oui, oui, je suis d'accord. Mais...*"

"But?"

"But there's nothing we can do about this situation now. It is out of my hands. She is their suspect now, and if we want any information from her, we need to cooperate. I'm told you are to be contacted by a..."

"Yes, we know. We've been told that too."

"Ah *bien*. Then everything is okay."

"How is everything okay? We flew down here to try and catch an unsuspecting culprit. Now we're not even sure we're going to be able to talk to her."

"*Oui, oui*, that would be unfortunate. *Mais...*"

"But?"

"But all is not lost."

"How do you mean? From where I'm standing, this whole trip was a waste of time."

"*Eh bien, oui*, that may be so. But since you have been gone, Aitzol Rubina has changed his mind and decided to cooperate."

Gibson ignored the confirmation of his suspicion and instead focused on the more compelling statement. "How has he cooperated?" When he spoke the words, Parker's eyes widened. "And why? He appeared dedicated to silence the last time we saw him."

"*Why* is irrelevant," Nivelle sternly replied. "But as for how, he has informed us of the next planned attack location."

"Where?"

"Le Mont-Saint-Michel."

"Mont Saint-Michel?" Gibson slowly repeated.

Nivelle noticeably sighed by blowing air into the phone and Gibson pictured him rolling his narrow eyes. "Ask your young friend. Anyway, I must go. Do what you can down there. If you can get nowhere, come back to France. I will find use for you." Nivelle abruptly hung up.

"What an asshole he can be," Gibson said to Parker as he held the phone up to punctuate his point.

Parker shrugged in agreement.

"What's that place, Mont Saint-Michel?"

"It's a medieval monastery and town on a hill in the Normandy region at the end of an inlet. The place is daily cut off from land by tides and is also one of the most highly visited locations in France. Because of its narrow roads and geographical location, it would be a deadly target for an attack."

"So you think this could be a real threat?"

"Sure, I don't see why not. Or at least I don't see why Nivelle would not treat it as such. There's no connection between the Basque movement and the Normandy region, but there has been a slow burning separatist movement in the Brittany region to the south that has a historical connection with Basque separatists. So from that angle, I guess there could be a connection."

"But then why was Paris a target then? That's a long ways from the Basque Country."

"True. But after the French started cracking down on ETA members hiding in France and IK's activities, Paris became a remote base for both. The entire population of the French Basque Country is under three hundred thousand, so a place like Paris with over two million is a lot easier to hide out in."

Parker's phone began vibrating in his pocket as he spoke. He answered and after a brief exchange told Gibson that the Chief Superintendent was going to meet them in front of their hotel. "Guess we need to put our city tour on hold and head back," he added.

Patxi Irionda couldn't believe that Itxaso was being questioned by the Portuguese police. How had she been identified? Had Aitzol ratted her out? He was walking fast with his head down along the São Jorge Castle ramparts as he considered the possibilities.

He knew from his source inside the French DNAT that Aitzol had without a doubt revealed the next attack location, or at least what he believed was the next attack location. This was unfortunate that Aitzol would betray him, their group, and the entire Basque people with such cowardice, but not overly surprising. Patxi had long thought that Aitzol merely acted like a tough hard ass.

Good thing he'd excluded Aitzol in the plans for Nice. The French authorities would be investigating the false lead for days. Mont Saint-Michel was a perfect decoy. It was going to be a nightmare for the French to evacuate such a popular tourist attraction, especially in peak holiday season, and to then search for nonexistent explosive devices on the island. Even though a small area, there would be a million places one could hide explosives, and the French would be wasting their time searching them all.

Everything was brilliant, but he couldn't take full credit for the idea. Garikotz had mentioned Mont Saint-Michel as a possible target before they had decided on the Tour Montparnasse and Nice.

Patxi wished his concern ended there, as the false information on Mont Saint-Michel would keep anyone getting close to them distracted, giving them time to initiate the Nice attack. But Itxaso's incarceration was potentially a major problem. He wasn't worried about her being able to identify him. None of his team members knew his Lisbon identity. If Itxaso talked, she'd only be able to reveal that he lived in Lisbon. That's all she knew. But, if forced to talk, she could reveal their plans for Nice and identify Garikotz.

All of them were prepared to go to prison if they were caught and become martyrs for the cause. Patxi made certain that each one of them understood the consequences of their actions and ensured they accepted if caught, and not killed, they would spend the rest of their lives locked up in a cell a long way from the Basque Country. Each one said they were prepared for these outcomes and Patxi believed all true to their word.

The more he considered potential outcomes, the more relaxed he became. Because even if they were somehow able to coax their plans for Nice out of Itxaso and stop the attack, the entire world would still know of the planned strike. Although this scenario would not be as pronounced as an actual attack, this would be an acceptable outcome. He smiled to himself at this victorious conclusion.

Just as he was looking up from his deep thoughts, he walked directly into another person walking on the castle's rampart path. The man, appearing to be in his mid-thirties, was walking with another older man. The younger one looked French, but the older man was without a doubt American based on his appearance and the fit of his clothing. Americans were always easy to pick out in a crowd, even if they didn't speak.

"*Desculpe,*" Patxi excused himself to the one he'd walked into.

"*Não faz mal,*" Parker replied, saying the equivalent of "no worries" in Portuguese.

Patxi changed his mind. The younger one may have looked French, but after hearing his accent speaking in Portuguese, Patxi was sure he was also American. Even Americans he'd encountered who spoke French, Spanish, or Portuguese very well were never able to fully lose their accents. Patxi nodded and continued walking by. At least he was a polite American and one who tried to at least learn a few local language phrases when traveling. In his experience, both were rare traits for American tourists.

Chief Superintendent Barros could have been the Portuguese brother of Nivelle, Parker thought when they first saw him. He was tall, thin, dark-haired, and even had Nivelle's pencil-thin mustache. But being the Portuguese version of Nivelle, his complexion was darker and his eyes more deep-set than Nivelle's. He also wore a brown fedora hat, a look Parker had not seen Nivelle try to pull off.

Barros exited from a parked car nearby as they approached the entrance of their hotel. There was no doubt in the mind of either Parker or Gibson that this was their guy. He strode with the confidence of a man knowing someone was always watching out for him. In this case, a uniformed officer remaining seated in the car, watching every movement of the Chief Superintendent.

Barros calmly approached them and spoke in accented English, "I believe you know who I am."

Similar arrogance to Nivelle, Parker thought.

Before Parker or Gibson had time to speak, Barros continued. "Let us go into your hotel and have a glass of wine together while we discuss the situation." He nodded at the entrance of the hotel.

"Actually, our hotel doesn't have a restaurant or bar. Not even a sitting area," Parker commented.

The expression on Barros' face displayed both disappointment and pity for these two foreigners who either could not pick a decent hotel or were too cheap to pay for one. "Ah, I see. We can step right inside that hotel then." Barros pointed across the street to the entrance to a larger hotel. The hotel clearly had a restaurant within.

Once inside and seated at one of the tables next to the front window, Barros called out to a waiter in Portuguese, asking for a specific bottle of wine. "As I was saying earlier, I know that you know who I am. And I know who you are. So we can skip the formalities," Barros said matter-of-factly.

Gibson quickly jumped on the opportunity to speak first before Parker had a chance to say something offensive. "Thank you for taking the time to meet us. As you know, we came here to assist in the ongoing investigation, based on our particular experience with the potential subjects."

Barros smiled, but it wasn't a friendly smile, Parker thought. "*Sim*, you came as a courtesy…not on an official assignment. And from what I understand, you, Senhor Parker, do not even work for your former organization anymore."

Parker was tempted to comment that he could always be a contract employee, but didn't respond after he felt Gibson firmly step on his foot under the table.

A waiter appeared and set a white wine bottle and three glasses on the table. Beads of water rolled down the sides of the chilled bottle. The waiter poured wine into each glass and walked away.

"Vinho Verde," Barros said, raising a glass to Gibson and Parker. They responded by each also raising a glass. Once they had all taken a sip, Barros described the white, slightly sparkling wine. "This wine is a Portuguese specialty. Refreshing and low in alcohol, perfect for hot summer days."

"Yes, all you said before is correct," Gibson remarked, wanting to return to the conversation at hand. "But let me stress again that we were specifically asked to come here based on what we can offer."

"*Sim, sim.* Yes, I understand this, Senhor Gibson. But this is Portugal and you were asked by the French. It is not…how do you say in English—oh yes, it is not the same thing. Why does one say the word *thing* in English so much?"

With concentrated effort, Parker didn't acknowledge Barros' unrelated question on word usage in the English language. "So are you saying that if you knew us better and had invited us personally, then there would be no problems?" Parker asked before Gibson could stop him.

"No, Senhor Parker, I am not saying that," Barros replied with the same unfriendly smile Parker noted earlier.

"Be that as it may, we were told that if we encountered jurisdictional conflicts, they would be addressed at a higher level," Gibson added.

"Yes. I regret to inform you this is not the case."

"Does that mean you're not going to let us even talk to Itxaso Harinordoquy?" Parker quickly asked.

"Yes, that is precisely what I mean. Senhora Harinordoquy is at present our concern. If we are able to ascertain that she is involved with the attack in Paris, a more open collaboration will, of course, be established between my unit and that of Senhor Nivelle. However, at the present time, there is no evidence from what I see that Senhora Harinordoquy has anything to do with the Paris attack."

"Then why would you hold her?" Gibson inquired.

"It has long been suspected that once they were run out of their hiding place in France, the ETA terrorists established an extensive network here in Lisboa. In the past, my government may have not looked too hard to uncover if these rumors were true. Portugal and Spain, as you may know, have a long history of not trusting one another. But these days, we are getting along much better, and even if it is said that the ETA is dead, if we can show the Spanish we are attempting to find any of their enemies who may be here, this would be seen as a good gesture to our neighbor."

"So you are holding her merely for political posturing?" Parker asked and then took a long drink of wine.

Barros stared at him for a long moment. "I suppose one could say it that way, if they really wished to do so."

"I suppose one could also say that this wine of yours kind of tastes like kids' grape juice, if they really wished to do so," Parker replied.

"Grape juice?" Barros questioned.

Gibson sensed he needed to step in again before Parker dug them into a hole. "There is no way we can see her?"

Barros turned away from Parker and looked directly at Gibson. "*Não*, with all respect, Senhor Gibson. This is not going to be possible. I am sorry that you were led to believe there would be no conflicts of interest. However, if it is any conciliation to you, I can tell you that it would do you little good to see Senhora Harinordoquy anyway."

"What the hell does that mean?" Parker asked.

"It means that she is not saying a word, Senhor Parker."

"Nothing?" Gibson asked.

"*Nada*," Barros confirmed. "I would be surprised if we get anything from her. She is tougher than most men. But in holding her as a potential suspect in an international crime, we have time to investigate her further. Maybe we will uncover something."

Barros finished his glass of wine and said that he had to leave for another appointment. He wished them a pleasant stay in Lisbon and invited them to finish the rest of the bottle. Once he was gone, Parker suggested they go out to dinner.

Parker was surprised to see on his phone's display screen that his mother-in-law was calling. She never called him. They had just finished eating huge bowls of steaming feijoada with various meats, beans, carrots, and cabbage in a heavy broth, and Parker was in the middle of comparing the dish to French cassoulet when his phone rang.

He apologized to Gibson, saying that if he didn't answer he would never be forgiven. To be polite, he stepped away from the outdoor table and walked into the large adjoining open public square. He stepped into a typical European summer evening scene. There was a central fountain and sculpture in the center of the cobblestone covered square. Children screamed and chased one another while their parents walked slowly behind. A group of teenaged Asian tourists were seated around the edge of the fountain laughing and taking pictures of one another in the dim evening light. The square was lined with the outdoor seating of restaurants similar to the one they had picked and most tables were occupied. The air was warm and fragrant.

He answered the call and said hello to his mother-in-law.

"You need to come home," Zurina sternly stated in English.

"Why?"

"Now. Do not ask questions."

"Why?"

He heard Zurina sigh heavily. "Not that I should have to explain why a husband must return when something concerns his wife, but Alaitz is being followed."

A jumble of thoughts immediately flashed in his mind. *Could the agency be keeping tabs on him? Could this new group have already identified him as a potential threat? Did his trip to see Graciana have repercussions? Could Nivelle have ordered for Alaitz to be watched while Parker was in Lisbon? If so, was Nivelle using Alaitz as bait?*

"I'll be on the first flight home," he said after rapidly considering the possibilities. "Did you get a good look at whoever was following her?"

"No, unfortunately not, but I know he was following her."

Parker reflected on how a decade ago it could have easily been someone tracking Zurina, considering her past affiliations with the separatist movement. But he had to believe that she was too old for any vendetta now. However, precisely because of her past, he didn't once question her assessment. He knew that Zurina had to keep a watchful eye over her shoulder for decades and would be more capable of marking a tail than most intelligence agents.

"Are you with her now?" he asked.

"Stupid man. You think I would leave my daughter alone after I notice her being followed?"

Parker smiled. This was one time when he was glad to have a former nationalist militant as a mother-in-law.

"I made an excuse after dinner of having indigestion so bad that I could not drive home. The same comment I make after I eat your cooking. But those times I am not lying."

Parker rolled his eyes. Even with the insult, he was glad she was there at the house with Alaitz. "Okay, stay there. I'll call you when I'm able to find a flight and will get a taxi from the airport. So keep your phone on."

"Of course I will keep my phone on," Zurina huffily replied and hung up before Parker could say anything more.

When he walked back to the table he said, "I'm sorry, Gibson, but I need to go back to Sare immediately. I'm going to head back to the hotel and then to the airport and get on whatever flight I can to get back to Biarritz. I know how non-enjoyable that sounds, so if you would like to stay here and fly back in a couple of days, I completely understand."

"Why do you need to go back so quickly?" Gibson asked.

"Alaitz may be in danger. Her mother says she's being watched."

Gibson picked up the napkin on his lap and tossed the cloth on the table. "We're both going."

II.

French Basque Country

"I DOUBT NIVELLE'S PEOPLE ARE INVOLVED," Gibson said as Parker gunned the rental car they picked up at the Biarritz airport into second gear.

"Why?"

"He may be a bureaucratic asshole at times, and you and he may not be best friends, but I don't think he'd do such a thing as put a tail on you, much less on your wife. You may think he's a prick, but I think deep down he likes you, in a way. After all, if not for him, I wouldn't be here in the first place."

"That's true," Parker grudgingly admitted. Agreeing with Gibson was troublesome for two reasons. For one, it meant that he agreed that perhaps Nivelle wasn't such an ass. More problematic, though, was the fact that if the tail on Alaitz wasn't Nivelle's, who was behind it?

The other options were far worse, as he and Gibson already concluded that there would be no reason for the CIA to be keeping an eye on Parker or his family. Although he had played a key role in the agency's credit for assisting in tracking down the Haika 4, he'd never been a high level operative. Definitely not justifying keeping an eye on in suspicion of his future loyalties.

Parker hadn't even been an operative. He was just a bright and capable desk officer happening to have the perfect skill set for a particular case. That was it. And once over, Parker got out. There had been no ill feelings, and no ultimatums for him to stay. After he recovered from the gunshot wound, he informed his supervisor that once he'd finished with cleanup requirements for the investigation—

the paperwork, the reports, the signatures, the statements, the interviews—he was going to resign.

Of course, more people than just his supervisor were shocked by Parker's announcement. And there were some who questioned his judgment after his performance on the Haika 4 assignment, proving himself to all and displaying that, if he so desired, he could become a full-time field operative.

But this was not what Sebastian Parker wanted. Alaitz stating that she desired them to be together, both spiritually and physically for once, made up his mind.

And now, from the little information he obtained, she was in danger.

"Also because of Nivelle, we know that you were in someone's headlights to begin with. So maybe whoever is hanging around Alaitz now is part of that group. By the way, you never really answered me when I asked if you thought there was any reason you'd be watched," Gibson pointed out.

Parker took a sharp turn onto a narrow country road. "I told you that I retired from the agency. I haven't done anything remotely suspicious. Not until I started asking around about the Paris attacks anyway. I know it seems really fast if that is what's brought me to their attention, but we can't rule the possibility out. Because possibly they were already watching me, if Nivelle's intel was accurate. From what we know so far, we're most likely dealing with a very tight group, and they appear to be organized and calculating. Considering that, there's every possibility that they could have found out about me making the recent inquiries, especially now, if we've in fact found two of them with event in Lisbon."

"What about what's-her-name? The one from our last case? The pretty blonde? Nivelle never caught her and she could still have a plan to get you back for helping stop her and her friends and—"

"It's not Graciana," Parker interjected, offering no further explanation.

Gibson took the hint that this was apparently a sensitive subject. He reminded himself to mention this part again later when Parker wasn't so on edge.

After getting to the airport in Lisbon following Parker's call with his mother-in-law, the best option they had was to wait until the next morning for a direct 6:00 am flight to Biarritz. They spent the night in the airport, and Gibson, accustomed to decades on the job where he had to find sleep whenever he could, did manage to nod off a little on an uncomfortable bench. He hadn't seen Parker, on the other hand, even sit down. Parker paced back and forth with a look of deep concern on his face. Gibson was not used to seeing Parker so tense. The five hour flight between Lisbon and Biarritz put them back down in the French Basque Country around 11:00 am. It was a Saturday, so Alaitz would not have to go to work in the morning, Parker mentioned.

Considering how her mother stayed over the night before, as she did on occasion according to Parker, his mother-in-law and Alaitz would most likely walk to the village market in the morning and then make lunch at home. After arranging for the rental car and driving to Sare from the airport, Parker estimated they would arrive just before noon, probably about the time his wife and mother-in-law were sitting down to eat.

Parker contemplated calling his mother-in-law once they landed in Biarritz to let her know they were on their way. But Gibson advised him not to. If they were being watched, since his mother-in-law was with his wife, better for them to believe Parker was still in Lisbon. Parker reluctantly agreed.

"So I suppose that leaves us with two alternatives: either some ETA-related faction is considering revenge, or this new group, whoever they are, are on to you."

Parker nodded in agreement as he drove, both his hands clasped tensely on the steering wheel.

"Thing is though, most likely someone is just keeping an eye on you, and apparently your family, for whatever reason. In my experience, groups don't have the resources to devote members to surveillance."

"What are you saying?" Parker asked without turning his eyes from the roadway ahead.

"I'm saying that chances are that when we get there, we'll find no one keeping an eye on your home and this won't be as serious of a situation as it sounds."

"We'll find out soon enough. We're on the outskirts of Sare now."

"How close are we to your house?"

"About three kilometers." Not hearing any reply from Gibson, Parker added, "just under two miles."

"Your house is a bit off by itself, so if anyone is watching, we should be able to notice. Is there any place where you could stop away a little so we can survey the perimeter first?"

Parker made a noise that slightly resembled a laugh. "*Survey the perimeter.* You've loosened up a lot since we first met, Gibson, I'll be the first to admit. But there are times when you still sound like some general from an old black and white war movie."

"If we're talking about your family, safe to call this is a goddamn declaration of war," Gibson stoically replied.

Parker turned to glance at him before responding. "Damn good point." Turning back to look at the road, he added, "To answer your earlier question, yes, there's a hill on the road leading down to our house. If we pull over to the side of the road before then and walk up the hill, there are some trees on one side which should provide coverage."

"*Provide coverage.* Now you're sounding ready for battle too. I like it."

Bantering with Gibson relaxed him some, but once they walked up to the top of the hill to peer in the direction of his house, the tenseness returned even more fiercely than before. There, less than a quarter mile down in the direction of the house, a car was parked on the side of the road and the outline of a person sitting in the driver's seat was obvious. So much for Gibson's theory on not being a serious situation.

The more Garikotz watched her, the more his contempt grew for the woman. First of all, she was Basque and should have known better than to marry an American. He could understand why some Basque men who went to live overseas married into other nationalities, although the best of them waited for Basque women to arrive. But seeing Basques marrying foreigners in their own homeland was sickening. Marrying French or Spanish was acceptable, yet still frowned upon. But definitely not English, Germans, or Americans. Even worse that the American she married was known to at least formerly work for the American CIA. And now he was living among them. In their own homeland.

Patxi's instructions were vague. *Keep an eye on the American's wife.* That's all the note delivered to him stated. Garikotz agreed with the system he and Patxi devised, that of exchanging handwritten notes instead of traceable emails or phone calls. They transferred messages using an overland trucking company Patxi owned tied to his importing business, but this was one time when Garikotz thought Patxi could have included a little more detail.

Garikotz wondered what the hell the instructions implied for him to do. Was he supposed to rough her up when he had the chance, to remind the stupid American to mind his own business and stop meddling in affairs which didn't concern him? If this American was truly retired, he should remain retired. He was already extremely lucky to be allowed to live freely in the beautiful Basque village of Sare, in the heart of the Basque Country. To have a beautiful old *baserri* in the Basque countryside. To have a beautiful Basque wife.

This is the life he should have had for himself, Garikotz thought. Not some *putain* American. Most of the time Garikotz remained on the sidelines and let others do the deeds he meticulously planned. And that was probably what Patxi had in mind, once again. To use Garikotz's mind and someone else's muscles. Normally that role would have fallen to Aitzol, but with Aitzol still being questioned by the police, as far as anyone knew, Patxi would have to find someone else. But Patxi was resourceful. Such a thing wouldn't be difficult for him.

Patxi always found a way, and ever since ETA stopped recruiting, there was a countless supply of angry young Basques looking to do anything to reassert the struggle. After the next attack, they would begin the next phase of their plan. This phase was to recruit a new underground army.

Therefore, he knew that he was too important to their plans, too important to the future of the Basque separatist movement, to be involved with something so unimportant as threatening a *salope* traitor.

But he wanted to.

At times such as this, reason abandoned him. He only saw a threat to the Basque cause. And threats had to be dealt with. Nothing else mattered. He had to keep watching this woman. He had to wait for his opportunity to do something. But he could keep watching and waiting while getting out for another smoke.

Knowing his wife was being watched pissed Sebastian Parker off. Actually seeing the person who was watching her infuriated him.

"We have to call Nivelle," he quietly said to Gibson as they looked in the direction of the parked car down the road.

Gibson agreed. Parker didn't want to leave his watch on the vehicle in case the person inside decided to make a move on the house. But calling Nivelle to get his support, in the form of sending official gendarme officers to help, was the most sensible course of action. They would have no authority if they approached the person in the vehicle, and Gibson was nervous about what Parker might do if they conducted a direct confrontation. Parker was as agitated as he'd ever seen him, and combined with a sleepless night, there was no predicting what he might be capable of doing.

Gibson walked backward from their overlook on the hill and called Nivelle's cell phone. Nivelle answered after a few rings, but he didn't say hello.

"You do realize that we are conducting a massive closure and search effort of one of France's most visited tourist attractions today, *non*?"

"Yes, but this is an emergency," Gibson replied, overhearing loud voices around Nivelle on the other end of the line.

"More so than making national news as we are here, *j'espère*?" Nivelle condescendingly answered.

"Yes, I realize that. But we returned from Lisbon early. We got a tip that Parker's wife is being followed. We may be looking at the culprit now who's taken position outside Parker's house."

"Why is this my concern?" Nivelle asked with annoyance prevalent in his tone. He was not only annoyed at the situation, but also with Capitaine Roman Guerin who had been, against his wishes, sent from Paris to assist Nivelle in the Mont Saint-Michel investigation. They were essentially equivalent ranks, and Nivelle had to be careful with how he handled his aggravating counterpart who seemed to be there more to discredit Nivelle than find anything related to the investigation. Guerin had remained a menace to him since their early DNAT days in the 1980s. He wasn't even assigned to Basque affairs these days, yet somehow he still managed to weasel himself into certain situations and always seemed to know the moves Nivelle was making.

"This is your concern as Parker volunteered to help you. And if this tail on his wife is true, I'd say there's a high likelihood that's the reason."

Nivelle sighed audibly into the phone and Gibson overhead more shouts and loud voices in the background. "What do you want from me?"

"We need to move in and question this person. But if we move on our own, you and I both know it's not going to do any good. We don't have authority, and if the person exhibits any suspicion, we're not going to be able to hold them without your help."

Gibson heard Nivelle calling out orders in French. "*Oui! Oui! D'accord*, Gibson. I'll have two officers come to assist you. *C'est bon*?"

"Yes, *merci*." Before Gibson could ask how long it would take for the officers to arrive, Nivelle hung up.

Gibson walked back to Parker and informed him of the call. Parker was unconvinced that Nivelle would live up to his word, especially considering the current circumstances. Remembering to make a call to send out a couple of officers for routine questioning would be easy to forget when dealing with a national crisis with international implications.

Gibson told him they had no choice but to wait for backup. Moving in too early on the suspect could end up not only in the person escaping, but worse, would let whoever was behind everything know they were onto them. Keeping the element of surprise was essential, Gibson insisted. They had to wait for Nivelle's people.

Parker remained unconvinced. He mumbled something to himself. Gibson assumed they were curse words, but he had no clue in what language.

After an hour of waiting, Parker couldn't wait any longer. How could he stand by and watch while this person might be just waiting for a glimpse of Alaitz to take a shot at her? He couldn't.

He waited for a moment when Gibson had his back turned and made a quick move to start for the vehicle. Parker figured that once he was away, Gibson wouldn't call out to try and stop him. He didn't enjoy doing something he knew would upset Gibson, but he couldn't sit by and do nothing any longer.

Parker didn't look back. He just walked straight down the road. As he got closer, he couldn't make out if the individual was a man or a woman. Whoever was in the car had their hair pulled back into a ponytail.

When he was less than twenty yards away, the person opened the car door and stepped outside. Parker now saw that the person was an older man with a ponytail. For a moment Parker froze, thinking the person had seen him and was getting out for a confrontation. But the man didn't even look in his direction. Parker watched as the man pulled out a pack of cigarettes and lit one, still staring in the direction of his house. Parker started walking toward the man again, though he tried to step lightly.

He had to think quickly. In his haste to break away from Gibson before he could stop him, he hadn't developed a plan. Now he was right on the bastard. Just as Parker was about to say something to announce his presence, Garikotz turned at the sound of approaching footsteps.

Startled, the cigarette hanging from Garikotz's mouth fell to the ground as his eyes met Parker's.

Parker took in the man's appearance instantly and tried to form a profile. He was probably in his early fifties. But he was still trying for a youthful appearance with long straight hair in a ponytail and black-framed, round glasses. He was fairly tall, roughly the same height as Parker, and very thin. He didn't look like an assassin. More like a pseudointellectual who would be more comfortable in a café.

Then it struck him.

Parker knew who was standing in front of him. This was Garikotz Auzmendi, a former top ETA strategist. He had been on lists of suspected ETA members for decades, but Auzmendi was notorious for never being directly tied to any attack or illegal activity, even though most believed he orchestrated many of ETA's highest profile actions. But more than operational strategy, Auzmendi also had a reputation of being one of ETA's main political advisors, apparently a top voice within the entire organization, even if he was never a face for it. Auzmendi wasn't a front-lines guy—he was a behind-the-scenes force. That made him even more dangerous.

Auzmendi was surprised for sure, but Parker noticed that Auzmendi had no clue who had just walked up on him. This gave Parker an advantage.

Parker decided to play the role of a local out for a walk. "*Bonjour.* Sorry to startle you," he said in French. "Just out for a stroll," he added, nodding down the road past his house.

Garikotz leaned down to pick up his fallen cigarette. "*Bonjour. Il n'y a pas de quoi.*"

"Are you having car trouble?" Parker asked.

"No, no, just enjoying the countryside," Garikotz responded, offering nothing further.

Parker needed an excuse to hang around. He asked if he could bum a cigarette. He hadn't smoked a cigarette ever since a dark night in Paris when Gibson had *convinced* him that smoking was bad for his health. But he had no choice. Auzmendi clearly wasn't offering to strike up a friendly conversation.

Garikotz handed him a cigarette and Parker leaned forward to let him light it for him. As he did, he quickly glanced inside the car and saw a pair of binoculars on the passenger seat. He wasn't sure which part he despised more, being so close to this piece of shit threatening his wife or having to fake enjoying smoking a cigarette. He tried not to inhale. The cigarette tasted horrible.

"So you said you are just out for a walk?" Garikotz asked.

"Yes, I live in the village and like to walk on these roads. I feel more connected to the land when I do. So you are just enjoying the countryside?"

"Yes, I am."

"You should go further down the road in the direction of the mountains. After this house," Parker pointed at his own house, "there are not many more and the landscape opens up even more."

"Maybe I will," Garikotz replied.

"This is a beautiful house here though, don't you think?"

"Yes, it is. I would like to own this house myself. Do you know who lives here?"

"No, I actually don't know for sure. Some young couple maybe I heard."

Seeing the noble Basque farmhouse in this idyllic setting caused a resurfacing of some of the jealous feelings Garikotz experienced earlier. This should be his house. Not some damn American's. "A Basque woman and her fucking American husband," Garikotz blurted out in contempt before he could stop himself.

"Not all Americans are so bad," Parker said in English.

Garikotz's eyes widened in shock. How could he have been so foolish? This was *the fucking American*! He moved quickly to try and reach into the open front window of the car.

Parker tossed away his cigarette and lunged forward, catching Auzmendi before he could reach whatever he was after. He grabbed him by the shoulders and slammed him into the car. "Who sent you, Auzmendi? Why are you watching us?" Parker didn't even recognize his own voice. The open threat to Alaitz was bringing out something foreign in him.

Garikotz reacted quickly. Sebastian Parker was clearly stronger than him, but Garikotz had dealt with and defeated stronger men than himself all of his life. He was a strategist and could find ways to achieve victories. And right now he had to think fast.

Garikotz considered claiming ignorance, sticking with the enjoying the countryside angle. Maybe say he was bird watching. But he quickly dismissed the idea. His cover was blown. He had fucked up by not paying close enough attention to his surroundings. He should have never stayed in one spot so exposed for such a long time. He left himself vulnerable to being spotted.

Now he had to figure out how to escape. Parker may have pinned him against the car, but the younger man, acting in passion, made the mistake of getting his face too close to an adversary with a burning projectile. Garikotz brought his head forward and aimed his cigarette at one of Parker's eyes.

Parker narrowly avoided having the burning cigarette rammed into his eyeball. But he couldn't avoid the cigarette being pushed into the side of his face instead. The moment the end of the cigarette pressed against his skin there was a sizzling noise. He cried out in pain and involuntarily released his grip on Auzmendi, staggering backwards.

Garikotz used the separation of space between them to reach inside the open front window of the car and grab a small revolver. He pointed the gun at Sebastian Parker, ready to fire.

"You are an enemy of the Basque people. I should kill you for that alone," Garikotz threatened.

Parker prepared himself to be shot, and maybe killed. It didn't matter. Once Alaitz heard the gunshot, she would look outside and see what was happening and call the police. They would catch this asshole and put him away. Alaitz would be safe.

Instead of hearing a gunshot though, he heard a loud authoritative voice demand: "*Déposez votre arm maintenant*!"

In the melee between him and Garikotz, neither had noticed a vehicle speeding down the hill with two uniformed French gendarme officers in the front seats and John Gibson in the back seat. Now the two police offers had their guns drawn, pointed directly at Garikotz Auzmendi.

Garikotz knew there was no way out now. And as dedicated to the cause as he was, having devoted his life to it, he was not ready to die. He slowly set his gun on the ground, already contemplating what he was going to say once they began questioning him.

Parker and Gibson were seated outside the back of Parker's house. The two French gendarme officers took Auzmendi away in handcuffs. Parker had a conversation with them, but the dialogue was in French and too complicated and too fast for Gibson to make out anything. Parker then immediately tried to call Nivelle, but said the line went straight to voicemail. He didn't leave a message.

Parker then explained to Gibson how the two gendarmes were aware of why they were there and knew the potential magnitude of the arrest they just made. Parker informed the gendarmes how his *belle-mère* could identify Auzmendi as having stalked her daughter. They were going to take the suspect back to the regional station in Bayonne to hold and await further instruction from Capitaine Nivelle. They were aware of Parker and Gibson's special relationship with their superior officer, but Parker told Gibson that under no circumstances were Parker and Gibson going to be allowed to question the suspect until permission was clearly granted by Capitaine Nivelle. Until then, they would have to wait.

Considering that Nivelle was currently investigating a possible terrorist attack of equal or greater magnitude than even the recent Paris attack, and considering that they had not really slept in a day and a half, Gibson suggested they return to Parker's house to rest and wait to hear from Nivelle.

Parker wanted to follow the officers back to the Bayonne station and wait for Nivelle's contact there. But the exhaustion he felt settling in, especially with the adrenaline beginning to drain after the removal of Auzmendi, allowed Gibson's rational reasoning to win the argument.

"It's actually fortunate that you were almost shot again," Gibson commented, trying to keep a straight face. "In that moment, any jurisdictional questions were erased, and the French officers had probable cause to arrest that bastard."

"Garikotz Auzmendi is his name, as I informed the gendarme officers. I'm sure whatever form of identification he has on him says differently."

"You know him?"

"Not in person, but I know that was Auzmendi. I tried keeping tabs on him back when I was with the agency, but he was always a slippery bastard. And thanks, by the way, for your apparent concern for me even though I just had a gun pointed at my chest."

Gibson waved a hand in front of his face. "You were fine. That guy looks like he's never actually fired a gun in his life. He probably would have missed."

"Too bad he didn't miss me with his damn cigarette," Parker said, lightly touching around his upper cheekbone where Auzmendi burned him.

"That must be painful."

"Hurts like hell, like the end of the cigarette is still searing into my skin."

"Want a smoke?" Gibson joked.

"Hell, no," Parker said with a smile and the two laughed.

"You sure you don't want to head into a clinic or something to have that checked out?" Gibson asked more seriously.

"Home medicine will do just fine. Alaitz knows how to make a mountain Basque ointment which should do the job."

"You're going to end up with a nasty scar. He got you pretty good."

"A reminder of my contribution to trying to stop this new madness before getting any worse." As he spoke, Alaitz walked outside from the house carrying two bottles of beer. Seeing her, Parker added, "And a reminder of the love for my wife." Alaitz handed them each a bottle and smiled at Parker.

So far he'd only told her an abbreviated version of the recent events that led to him almost being blinded by one of ETA's former top strategists outside their home. Alaitz thanked him for running to her rescue, but Parker sensed that she wasn't too concerned hearing that she'd been under surveillance. The fact that she didn't at least display more gratefulness bothered him a little, but he tried not to let it get to him. She was the woman he married, he reminded himself.

"Mother and I already had lunch awhile ago, but I'll make you both Sebastian's favorite sandwich and you can have it out here," Alaitz said, returning inside the house.

Gibson now knew what the favorite sandwich was going to be and was anxious for one. He hadn't eaten since the night before. His stomach growled at the prospect of food.

As was the one they'd had in Bayonne at the ham festival, Parker's favorite sandwich was delicious.

The two old friends and partners ate their sandwiches in silence, staring off at the line of the Pyrenees in the distance.

Once they were done with the sandwiches, Alaitz and her mother came outside with small plates of gâteau basque, Parker's favorite dessert. Zurina handed Parker his cake, affectionately patting his back and saying to him in Basque that he was a good husband.

Once again, Gibson thought Parker's favorite was far from an elaborate culinary creation. The cake was like a dry cookie cake with pastry cream inside. But again, the simple creation was delicious.

After they finished the cake, Gibson noticed Parker starting to nod off. Gibson felt like he could fall asleep in the chair himself. He suggested they both try and get some sleep. With all that Nivelle was doing, some time could pass before they heard from him. In the meantime, the police were not going to release Auzmendi. Parker resisted at first, saying he'd be fine after a coffee.

Moments later when Parker jolted himself awake after feeling his head fall forward, he agreed. But only if Gibson promised to keep his cell phone on and nearby.

Gibson promised, saying he would let Parker know as soon as Nivelle called.

Parker opened his eyes, expecting that less than an hour, two at most, had passed since he lay down on top of the bed's covers and closed his eyes. If that had been the case, it would still be early to mid-afternoon. But the level of daylight he saw out one of the bedroom windows was not midday sunshine. The soft light was that of dusk.

He checked his phone, lying on the covers next to him. He saw that sure enough, the time was after eight in the evening. He'd slept for around seven hours.

Parker sprung from bed and felt lightheaded for a moment. He could easily fall back to the bed and return to slumber, but Nivelle must have called by now. Gibson had taken pity on him and let him sleep instead of waking him up.

Parker wasn't upset with Gibson for having done so, as he knew that Gibson would have only been looking out for Parker's well-being. But now that he was awake—time to get back in action. He wouldn't be able to relax knowing that someone else might come next. He didn't care if he would have to wait all night for Nivelle to let him talk to Garikotz Auzmendi. He needed to know why he and his family were being tracked.

He heard voices coming from the downstairs of the house. Gibson was awake and discussing something with Alaitz. He didn't hear his mother-in-law's voice and wondered if she'd left. For once, he hoped she was still there, as he didn't want to leave Alaitz alone if they were going to head into Bayonne.

When he walked down the stairs to the house's ground floor, he saw the three of them, including his mother-in-law, seated at the dining table.

"There's my hero," Alaitz said when she noticed him. "We thought you may sleep through the night, so I didn't want to wake you for dinner. We just had some paté de compagne, saucisson, bread, and soup. I can warm up some soup if you would like."

Food did sound good, he thought, but Parker didn't want to delay any longer getting his chance with Auzmendi. "*Merci, chérie,* but Gibson and I should be going. I'll take a paté sandwich with me though if you wouldn't mind making me one."

"You may as well take a seat and have some soup too," Gibson suggested. "No need to rush."

"We need to go. Thank you for letting me get some sleep, but Nivelle's going to be expecting us."

"No, he's not. He hasn't returned any of my calls. So, as I said, no need to rush."

"You haven't talked to him yet?" It didn't seem possible that Nivelle would try keeping them from Auzmendi, especially after they wasted their time on a trip to Lisbon and then delivered a prime suspect on a platter.

Gibson shook his head slowly. "Nope. And I've left him numerous messages. But, somehow, I think he's preoccupied at the moment."

"How so?"

"It's all over the news," Zurina said.

"What's all over the news?"

"Whatever he was after at Le Mont-Saint-Michel was not there," Alaitz explained. "It's made the national French news, and your colleague has been identified as having been behind the entire operation. They closed off the whole place for a day and didn't find anything to indicate there would be an attack."

"That doesn't mean that there would not have been," Gibson clarified. "It just means that there were no explosives planted anywhere for a timed explosion like what happened in Paris."

"Yes, but it still makes someone look like a fool to shut down such a place over nothing. And to do this in peak tourist season...*oh la la*, there are going to be some very angry people," Zurina commented.

"He was acting on a lead, and this result is better than the alternative," Parker exclaimed, surprised to find himself defending Nivelle.

"He was in a difficult position. Do too little and risk not being able to stop an attack. Do too much and risk being completely wrong," Gibson added.

"With everyone in the country and world, really, watching," Parker commented. "I actually feel a little sorry for the *mec*."

"Me too," Gibson admitted. "And knowing that he's just been humiliated and is probably taking a lot of heat right now, I'd say we should cut him a little slack on getting back to us. As it turns out, possibly the best lead he has in this case is being held in Bayonne. Knowing Nivelle's determination, it's only a matter of time before he's back down here."

Parker knew Gibson was right. He didn't like the obvious situation, resulting in waiting around even longer to hear any word from Nivelle. But that was how the scenario was going to be, and they had no control over the situation.

"Okay, guess I'm having soup," Parker said.

Capitaine Nivelle didn't let himself give into the defeatism he felt following him. What happened at Mont Saint-Michel, or what hadn't happened was the more accurate way to describe the resulting situation, was a disaster.

And there was no way he could hide.

The whole affair had been his operation. He put the entire island on high alert, forcing closure of one of France's most popular tourist attractions. Eager to please the politicians breathing down his neck for results after the Paris attack, he had his public relations officer let media outlets know that Nivelle and his team were about to foil another major attack. Of course, they still might have by showing strength of force and rapid response capability to a threat. But no one else would see the result that way.

They would only see failure to find anything remotely suspect. A mere spectacle and waste of time, money, and effort, as they were calling the operation on national news. There was even footage that a damn cameraman managed to capture of Nivelle holding up a hand and briskly passing by a group of questioning reporters.

Calls from Paris were being made to his mobile phone, but he didn't bother answering. He knew who was calling. They would demand answers. He simply didn't have any. Except to say that indications were that they were dealing with a group, or at least a leader of a group, far more clever than anticipated.

Nivelle expected whoever this leader was would be a calculating individual. And clearly this person was comfortable taking innocent lives in the name of their cause. But this most recent move by the leader indicated Nivelle was after someone more devious and, ultimately, more dangerous. If Nivelle was right, then the leader purposefully misinformed one of the group's members of the next attack location. If true, that would mean the leader expected, and maybe intended, for the piece of *merde* they were still holding in Biarritz to be caught. And the leader expected that same piece of *merde* to talk. If true, this was a level of deviousness Nivelle had rarely, if ever, encountered during his long career.

And if true, this could indicate that the leader had intended for all of this to happen. Perhaps even though Rubina was expected to talk, this was not supposed to happen so soon? Perhaps this mighty leader who thought they were so intelligent had overestimated the resolve of Rubina? Perhaps more time was supposed to elapse? More time to ensure that the true plans for a new attack were not uncovered while Nivelle wasted his time in Mont Saint-Michel?

If all of this were true, then there was still time to stop the next attack. Furthermore, all was not lost. His gamble of enlisting the help of the two Americans apparently paid off once again. Rubina may have been a designated misleading target, but he was still somehow tied to the Paris attack, and that was a minor victory, however one considered the situation. Of course, the national news providers were still unaware of this success, but eventually they would know the truth.

And now his Americans delivered him a promising new suspect.

Unfortunately he could not show them respect by allowing they immediately join his interrogation of the suspect, but Nivelle felt compelled to get answers. After Mont Saint-Michel, he couldn't allow another mishap. This time he needed to be certain. This time he needed more to move on than the word of a terrorist. He'd be lucky to recover from the Mont Saint-Michel affair as things currently stood. Another embarrassment and he'd be done for sure.

As soon as it was clear that there was nothing to be found on Mont Saint-Michel, Nivelle left a contingent of men to remain in Normandy and seek out any possible evidence linked to the supposed planned attack. He wasn't confident that they would uncover anything, but he couldn't rule out the possibility.

Historically, the Basque radicals had found a welcome set of like-minded friends with Breton separatists just to the south of Normandy. Once the GAL's actions convincingly conveyed that the French Basque Country was no longer a safe haven for *etarras*, the region of Brittany became a new favorite destination in France. The Breton separatists had never risen to the level of the Basques, but they had always been organized enough to keep Paris nervous. Not hard to imagine that a level of cooperation still existed between the two groups. Even a possible *new* connection between the two groups needed to be further investigated.

But as soon as Nivelle was informed of the capture of a known ETA member in France with possible ties to this new group, he called for helicopter transport back to the south. And now he had that known ETA member seated in a chair in front of him.

Garikotz Auzmendi had already undergone thorough questioning by Nivelle's men before Nivelle arrived. And he was about to be subjected to the same line of questioning by Nivelle himself. Standard protocol for questioning a suspect. Just keep asking the same questions until they get their lies crossed.

Nivelle always looked forward to the moment when a suspect realized they'd just fucked-up and given a different answer to a question they'd been asked repeatedly before. Lawyers would often say this was the interrogation technique of exhausting a person until their minds became clouded, but Nivelle didn't give a damn what any lawyer would later say about their interrogation of Auzmendi. The national security of France was at stake, and Nivelle was charged by those at the highest level of the government to come up with answers and prevent any future attacks.

Many years had passed since he authorized the use of *other* interrogation techniques, but he was not opposed to resorting to such methods if his hand was forced. He didn't want to have to use such methods though, and he hoped the smug-looking Garikotz Auzmendi seated across the small table was as smart as he looked and could sense that the rules of interrogation were about to be tossed out the window.

Nivelle had softened his demeanor in recent years when dealing with suspects. He eased up on the steely presentation and attempted to reach some common ground with suspects to help along their confessions. But he had no time for that game now.

"Who are you working for?" he directly asked in French before even sitting down across from Auzmendi.

Two of his men stood by the doorway behind him, their hands crossed in front of their bodies, waiting for any order he gave. He picked these two men specifically, as he believed they would have no problem taking the interrogation to the next level if needed.

Auzmendi slyly grinned at Nivelle. He carefully pulled out a cigarette from the box in front of him and, with his handcuffed hands, used a lighter to light one. He exhaled with smoke surrounding his face. "I don't work for anyone. More appropriate would be to ask me who I am *working with* instead of *working for*, since you and your *txakurras*"—using the Basque pejorative word for dogs—"seem to think

I am somehow involved with what happened at the Tour Montparnasse. Speaking of, these two morons have not explained to me on what authority you are holding me against my will."

"Cut the bullshit. We know you were ETA in the past and that you were high up in the organization. And if the organization still exists in some clandestine form, there's no reason to not suspect you're still involved. And that alone, suspecting you of being a member of an outlawed terrorist organization, is enough to hold you. The fact that you are a suspected member of such a group believed to be currently operating in France, that just gives me even more authority to hold you, amongst other things." Nivelle grinned slyly back at Auzmendi.

Auzmendi didn't flinch or show any distress at Nivelle's meant-to-be-mildly-threatening suggestion. He calmly took another drag from his cigarette and blew a thin line of smoke, aiming the stream of smoke just to the side of Nivelle's face. "You've proven my point. If you believe I am who you say I am, you should have asked me who I am working with, instead of who I am working for," he calmly stated.

Nivelle laughed lightly, but not because he thought Auzmendi was funny. He was laughing so he didn't reach across the table and slam this *fils de pute*'s face into the table. "Why were you stalking Alaitz Parker?" Nivelle asked, shifting direction.

"What a shame," Auzmendi said after reflecting on hearing Alaitz's last name.

"Shame?"

"Yes, a shame that this Basque woman not only betrayed her people by marrying a foreigner, but then by also disgracing her family by taking his surname."

"She's still a Basque woman, no matter who she marries or whatever surname she takes."

"Maybe to you. You are not Basque."

"No, I am not. Maybe if I were, I would understand why it would be acceptable to stalk an innocent woman."

Garikotz grinned again. This one is more astute than the others, he thought. The infamous Nivelle. But he said nothing and merely stared blankly ahead.

Nivelle leaned back in his chair. "Let's just say, for argument's sake, that you really were just randomly stopped on the side of a country road for no reason, with no car trouble—yes, we checked your car in case you were wondering—at a spot which is not necessarily scenic. So you were not stopped to take in a view, nor is this a place to stop for any other reason. There are no trails or picnic areas anywhere close by. In fact, the only reason one could perceive of someone stopping there is to have a full view of the old Basque farmhouse down the hill. An old Basque farmhouse that happens to belong to Alaitz Parker and her husband, Sebastian Parker. And let us not forget that when you were apprehended, my officers also noted that there is a witness who would be able to identify you and your suspicious conduct around her daughter. So connecting you to stalking Madame Parker and causing moral harassment is not entirely difficult for one to do. And, as a criminal such as yourself should know, moral harassment is a crime in France and can put you in prison for minimum a year."

Auzmendi was about to say something in response, but Nivelle continued speaking. "Let's just say you were parked there for some other reason and you were never seen, where was it again?" Nivelle turned his head slightly to ask his men behind him.

"The market in Saint-Jean-Pied-de-Port," one of them replied.

"Ah yes, the market in Saint-Jean-Pied-de-Port. So let's say you were *not* seen there and you were *not* found suspiciously parked outside a private residence with binoculars in the front of your vehicle, as if they were being used for some purpose. Let's just say those things are inadmissible. If so, we are left with a couple of other serious offenses to discuss."

Auzmendi snubbed out his cigarette in an ashtray on the table.

"Assault," Nivelle added.

"Is protecting oneself a crime?"

"Possession of an illegal firearm certainly is."

Auzmendi shrugged his shoulders and sighed. "What can I say? There are a lot of dangerous criminals around these days. I felt I needed to arm myself."

"What a piece of shit explanation," Nivelle responded. "Did you have anything to do with the attack in Paris?"

"No."

"You know, as a terrorist suspect, the rules on how long I can hold you, they really don't apply."

"Your point?"

"My point is that I don't believe you. And I don't believe you are as brave as you think you are. And I think you are going to break eventually, so you may as well save yourself from some *private* time with these two behind me."

"Is that a threat? The Spanish authorities are known for their appalling mistreatment of Basque nationalists, but the French have always been considered more humane. Has something changed?"

"So you admit you are a Basque nationalist?"

"I've never denied this," Auzmendi smugly responded.

"Are you a Basque terrorist?"

"I am not a terrorist."

Nivelle grinned at Auzmendi. "Okay, Mr. Basque Nationalist. Here is what has changed. No cowardly terrorist act on this level in the name of Basque nationalism has ever been committed on French soil. Now that it has, maybe our attitude for suspected Basque terrorists will change. At one time you people believed that France was a safe haven, but then we started sending you back to Spain or arresting you and putting you in prisons far from the Basque Country. That was when your people had to start going elsewhere for your safe havens, places like Mexico and South American countries where you set up your ETA *embassies overseas.* I've heard estimated that over a thousand of your people were living over there during the height of the conflict years. Perhaps you should have gone as well?"

Garikotz ignored Nivelle's suggestion. "I do not need any lessons on the history of my people in France. You people have been trying to assimilate us into your culture since the time of your Charlemagne. And we Basques wanted nothing to do with your silly revolution. We were all considered noble and your *putain* revolution wanted to strip everyone of titles and culture and ties to the church. Thousands of us were deported or killed by your enlightened revolutionaries, as they were suspected of treasonous activities or coercion with Spain. And if that was not enough, there were even attempts to rename our cities and villages.

"Then that little chubby emperor of yours lied to the Basques, telling them he was considering uniting the Spanish and French Basque regions together as their own, only to conveniently forget such promises after he used Bayonne as a base of operations for his schemes in Spain. And after one of your prime ministers promised and failed to grant Basque independence, another one promised and failed to grant autonomy, as the Spanish had allowed."

Garikotz could have continued, describing more recent failed promises of the French government to all Basques. Such as a recent UMP president's failed proclamation that he would move Basque political prisoners home to the French Basque Country from the distant prisons where they'd been sent. And the Basque nationalist movement had then seen some hope for greater autonomy in France with the election of the current socialist president, only to have such hope crumble yet again. Garikotz felt himself getting angered. This *putain flic* was not going threaten him. He didn't care who the fuck he was. He pulled out another cigarette.

"Thank you for the fascinating history lesson, but, frankly, I don't give a damn. What is important to me is now. And at present we already have your friend, Aitzol Rubina, and he's talking. He's looking to make a deal to save his own ass. You would be wise to do the same. Maybe you can avoid spending the rest of your life in prison."

Garikotz wasn't sure what to believe. But this *flic* could threaten him all he wanted. Garikotz was never going to say anything revealing about their operation and plans. And once they gave up with their interrogation, they would eventually let him go. They were probably going to rough him up a little, but he'd be fine. He'd devoted his life to the cause. A few bruises were not going to alter his life's purpose.

They would have nothing on him. They'd have to set him free. Even if they could hold him for an extended period as a suspected terrorist, everything was much more public now than in the past. They wouldn't be able to hide him away in some far-flung detention center for weeks, holding him on bullshit charges. Even with the so-called ETA ceasefire, there were still organizations like Etxerat, closely monitoring all actions by police forces against Basque nationalists and maintaining records of where political prisoners were kept. Only a matter of time before his incarceration would be noted and the activists would begin lobbying for his release. He could endure whatever they would subject him to until then. They had nothing on him. *Espèce de connards.*

"And, just so you know, as we speak, my men are searching your apartment and business in Perpignan," Nivelle commented.

Let them search, Garikotz thought. They would find nothing. They could even search his computer and mobile phone and they would find no emails or text messages implicating him in anything. Their rule about no electronic correspondence was genius. In this age of incredible technology, the way to beat the technological system was to avoid it altogether. Leave no traceable records. That's what Patxi always said.

But wait…

Garikotz felt his stomach falling and he thought he might vomit. *Putain merde!*

There was the map. The map showing the different locations for the explosives set around the beaches of Nice. The map wasn't the most detailed, by any means. More of a rough sketch Garikotz made in order to direct the different groups of immigrants he'd hired to bury the explosives. But the map would be enough to arouse suspicion when found. He knew keeping the map was a bad idea, but he just wanted to keep some little piece for posterity of their brilliant plan. Would they find it in his apartment? He knew right where the map was, inserted into the pages of his old copy of the great Basque novel *Ramuntcho*.

But he couldn't remember if he'd left the book out on his desk after he inserted the map page, or placed the book back on the bookshelf. One way or another, chances were the map would eventually be found, as even if he'd put the book back on the shelf, the government goons would thoroughly search the home of someone suspected of being connected to the Paris attack. And even incompetent government goons would be able to recognize the curve of Nice's Promenade des Anglais on Garikotz's map. Depending on when the map was found, sooner or later, Garikotz would be implicated.

If the map was discovered before Patxi gave the order for the coordinated Nice attack's execution, the locations would be investigated and the explosives uncovered. If the map was not found until later, after the attack, assuming that Garikotz was still being held, then the map would be a direct indication that Garikotz was involved.

Either way, Garikotz realized he'd screwed himself.

He was not, however, one to deny his own wrongdoings. He only had himself to blame. If this meant a lifetime in prison as a martyr for the Basque movement, so be it. Garikotz wasn't going to turn his back on his brothers and sisters to try and save himself time in prison. He was already in his early fifties. His life was nearing an end anyway. Whether he would be released at age eighty or ninety didn't matter. He'd devoted his life to this purpose. He'd denied himself a wife and a family for the cause.

Perhaps spending the rest of his days in a prison cell would be a fitting way to end his life after all. He'd have all the time in the world to solely dedicate to reading and writing. Maybe he could even write what would surely become a modern-day treatise on the Basque struggle. Perhaps this would be his legacy. His legacy to the Basque people.

And he wasn't surprised to have been caught after Patxi ordered him to watch the woman. Garikotz had never been a field operative. He didn't have the skill set. Patxi knew this and made the mistake of assigning Garikotz to a field assignment. Patxi didn't make mistakes often, but this was one of them. But Garikotz didn't, and would never, blame Patxi. No matter what happened to him. They may have been a team in planning and strategy, but Patxi was the leader—his leader. He always had been and Garikotz would do as his leader ordered.

Nivelle interrupted Garikotz's thoughts. "Your butch lady friend, Itxaso Harinordoquy, has also been picked up in Lisbon. I don't know what is going on with her, but somehow I imagine that she will talk soon. The Portuguese police have a reputation for being a little rough, as you probably know."

Hearing of Itxaso's capture was more concerning than that of Aitzol. Aitzol had never been much more than muscle, but Itxaso and Patxi had always been close. Garikotz wasn't worried about her talking, but he was worried that if they found her in Lisbon, Patxi could also be in trouble.

Garikotz always warned Patxi that the two of them living in the same city was a bad idea. He now hoped he'd been wrong. The rest of them could be caught, but Patxi needed to stay free. Only Patxi could reenergize the Basque cause.

Garikotz realized there was nothing he could do, and any more talking could jeopardize their plans for Nice, or Patxi, or both.

"Do what you will. I'm done talking," Garikotz said plainly, staring directly into Nivelle's eyes.

"*Quelle saloperie d'espèce de putain merde du con!*" Parker exclaimed after being told by Capitaine Nivelle that the interrogation of Garikotz Auzmendi had already commenced and Auzmendi refused to talk.

"My French isn't good enough to have understood any of that, but I imagine it wasn't good," Gibson dryly commented.

"No, it was not," Nivelle confirmed, not looking pleased at Parker's reaction.

"You only have this bastard because of us, and only because this fucking piece of shit was stalking my wife. And then I almost have him burn my goddamn eye out with his cigarette. And now you're saying that I'm not even going to get a chance to confront him?"

Gibson fully understood Parker being disappointed and upset, but his professional instincts leaned more toward Nivelle's position. Nivelle was investigating one of the worst terrorist attacks ever in France, and he had to be under an immense amount of pressure to find culprits. At times such as these, keeping in mind personal matters was hard. And while Parker may have been correct in all that he was saying, he was out of line.

Without Nivelle, they wouldn't have ever even been allowed into the facility where Auzmendi was being held in Bayonne. And based on the way Parker was speaking to him and the clear look of contempt on Nivelle's face, they were not going to be staying long unless Parker cooled down.

"Come on, Parker. Nivelle's just doing his job," Gibson said, trying to convey with a glance that Parker needed to back off, and quickly.

Nivelle rolled his shoulders backward and said nothing, still looking like he could easily have Parker tossed out the door.

Parker noticed Gibson's look of concern. He inhaled deeply through his nose and turned away. After a few seconds he turned back around to face Nivelle and Gibson. "*Je m'excuse*," he said to Nivelle.

Nivelle responded in English. "Understandable. I agree that you and Agent Gibson have been very helpful. I will take you to see Auzmendi, but nothing you say can be admissible," Nivelle said pointedly to Parker. "I may be willing to stretch some rules for this case, but obtaining any kind of confession via a civilian, and a foreign one, *c'est trop*. Agent Gibson at least is still officially in law enforcement. So if you ask any revealing questions of Auzmendi, direct them through myself or even Agent Gibson. I don't want some *avocat* in the future trying to *casse les couilles* over improper procedure."

Parker agreed to Nivelle's terms. His first concern anyway was to find out why his wife was being followed. If this also led to more on the case, *tant mieux*.

Nivelle was actually curious to see how the two of them would interact. Auzmendi may have claimed he was done talking, but if anyone could get him to talk, it could be this young American who Nivelle could never decide if he despised or slightly admired. One thing he was sure of, though, was that he respected Sebastian Parker. Even if Parker's insolent ways aggravated the hell out of him, Nivelle respected that Parker was a natural at the art of interrogation, even if he was unaware of this inner ability.

Nivelle had witnessed Parker's skills before with their collaboration on the Haika 4 case. He'd been able to get people to talk who would have remained silent for anyone with professional training. Nivelle hoped the same proved true this time, because Garikotz Auzmendi did just as he said he would and refused to say another word. Nivelle felt the pressure on his shoulders to come up with something positive. He needed something quickly.

If Parker couldn't get anything out of Auzmendi, the time to resort to other tactics would be upon him. Nivelle still didn't want to have to use hard interrogation. Everything these days was inadmissible for some violation or another, even if he had so-called emergency authority to operate however was necessary.

All it would take would be for some bad press to emerge regarding the mistreatment of suspects under Nivelle's watch. And if some *lèche-cul* politician felt they had something to gain in dragging someone down to appease the masses, Nivelle's head would be sent to the guillotine. He had no grand ambitions in life beyond serving his role to the government and to France, but he didn't want to spend the rest of his career and life shamed for doing what had to be done.

As he led Gibson and Parker through the corridor to the room where Auzmendi was being held, Nivelle began to feel better about calling them in after giving up on getting anything else out of Auzmendi. Perhaps setting Parker loose on Auzmendi was the best thing he could do. Parker promised to keep his cool when confronted with the suspect, but Nivelle knew him better.

Parker was someone who lived through the passion they felt in life, with that passion leading them for better or worse. In another life, Parker could easily have been on the other side of the fight against the Basque terrorists. And such a person would be unable to keep themselves completely calm when face to face with someone who undoubtedly wished them harm. Now that he'd had time to reflect further on the situation on the walk through the corridor, Nivelle was counting on Parker not being able to keep his word to remain calm.

Nivelle knocked on the door. The door was opened from the inside by one of his men. Auzmendi was seated at the table in the middle of the room, calmly smoking a cigarette. Nothing about his expression exhibited worry or fear. He smiled when he noticed Parker walk through the doorway.

"And they say you are out of the law enforcement game, but you being here proves you are not," Garikotz said in English, still smiling at Parker. "All you *txakurras* are the same. You say that you retire or change jobs. You get married to a Basque woman you don't deserve. And you get a Basque farmhouse you don't deserve. But you cannot leave the only life you know. I guess this is the same for some others too." Garikotz knocked a piece of ash from his cigarette into the ashtray. "Now you are different from others though," he added, grinning and raising a finger to his cheek.

This is perfect, Nivelle thought. Every word spoken was now being recorded in the room and Auzmendi just admitted that he recognized Sebastian Parker. That immediately tossed out any defense he would have attempting to justify a random coincidence of being stopped in his vehicle outside of Parker's home.

Parker calmly sat down across the table from Garikotz. The burn on his face was covered with a bandage Alaitz put on him before they left the house. He felt his searing skin as he watched Garikotz ash his cigarette. "If it was only the two of us here, I'd take that and make sure not to miss your eye," Parker said in Basque, smiling back at Garikotz.

"What's stopping you from trying?" Garikotz taunted.

Parker felt his blood pressure rising and he balled his hands into fists under the table.

"*On parle en Français ici*, messieurs," Nivelle ordered before Parker could respond.

Gibson recognized the direction to speak in French. "Or English, if nobody minds," he suggested, causing Garikotz, Parker, and Nivelle to turn to look at him.

Garikotz laughed. "Yes, yes, why not? Let's speak English for the American who doesn't speak a word of another language."

"*Va te faire foutre*," Gibson steadily replied.

The two guards at the door broke their restrained demeanor and chuckled. They stopped as soon as Nivelle shot them an icy look.

Parker was too upset to laugh or smile, but he was pleased with Gibson's performance.

"*Bravo*," Garikotz remarked, nodding to Gibson. "And for proving me wrong, I'll grant you the favor of speaking in English."

"*Merci*," Gibson said.

"So, what shall we talk about in English then? McDonalds? Disney World? Hollywood? Baywatch? Jerry Lewis? Sylvester Stallone?" Garikotz asked.

"Stalking," Parker replied.

"Stalking?" Garikotz asked with a surprised look on his face.

"I'm willing to bet you know the meaning of the word," Parker flatly replied.

"Yes, I know what the word means. But as I've been telling these *cons*, I don't see how this applies to me."

"You were parked on the side of a rural road for no reason, conveniently across from my house."

"I was having car trouble."

"You didn't appear to be having trouble with your car. And his men," pointing to Nivelle, "found nothing wrong with your vehicle."

"I stepped out for a cigarette. You know, smoking while driving is dangerous." Garikotz touched his cheek again and grinned at Parker.

Parker didn't flinch. "With a pair of binoculars and photographs of myself and my wife in your car, and a gun."

Nivelle and Gibson quickly glanced at one another, sharing a thought. Neither was aware of any photographs in the car.

Garikotz had a similar thought. He did have a file with photographs of this American's traitor *salope* wife, but he couldn't remember if he'd left the file in the car or back in the safe house room where he'd been staying. But if this cocky American knew about them, they must have been discovered in the car. *Merde.* He was confident he could hold strong for as long as he had to, but he couldn't hide that pieces were starting to align against him.

Parker knew he had Auzmendi struggling. He'd taken a chance at saying they had found photographs in the car. From the slightly confused expression now on Auzmendi's face, he knew his guess had been effective.

"Why my wife? Don't you guys have better things to do these days trying to restart your little war?" Parker asked.

"There is nothing to restart. A dream can never die. And the Basque people have always been dreamers. Dreams took our fishermen across the Atlantic long before any Italians."

"Why my wife?" Parker repeated.

"I don't know what you're talking about."

Parker realized he needed to change course in his questioning. Auzmendi was clearly going to stand firmly with his denial, at least for now. He'd tripped him up on the photo comment, and it would be enough for Nivelle and his men to continue with later, but something about Auzmendi's smug demeanor irritated the hell out of Parker. He didn't want to let up.

"Where's Patxi Irionda?"

How could he possibly know of Patxi? Garikotz asked himself. "Who?" he said aloud.

"Don't play dumb. You heard me. Patxi Irionda."

"Ah, Patxi Irionda. You must be confused. Patxi Irionda died in an accident in Bordeaux long ago."

"Yeah, I've heard that story. But you and I both know it's not true. He's alive and he's somewhere and I believe he's behind all of this. Did he order you to watch my wife? I'll bet it was him. And I'll bet it was because we're starting to catch all of your little group of geriatric revolutionaries trying to relive your glory years."

Garikotz grinned coyly and pulled out another cigarette. "An interesting theory."

"What name does he go by now?"

"I do not know what you are talking about."

"I was told by one of your own that he's still walking the streets today."

"Who told you?"

For a moment, Parker hesitated. Revealing her name would be going against his word. Saying her name would be betraying her. But he had to. "Graciana Etceverria."

Nivelle and Gibson shared another glance. Different from before, however, this shared glance was more of concern than appreciation.

"That is a name I have not heard for a while," Garikotz said. "The only member of the Haika 4 never captured. You have been to Eastern Europe lately?"

Damn, Parker thought. Where Graciana had been sent was obviously known throughout the ETA ranks. And if Irionda had been able to trace things back to him, eventually Irionda would put the puzzle together and figure out that Graciana helped him. He hoped she'd already left Vilnius. If she hadn't already, she would soon be in serious danger.

"We're not discussing where I've been, we're discussing where we can find Patxi Irionda."

"When one of our own betrays the rest of us, it's not good for that person. That was very foolish of that little *salope* to tell you anything, although I am impressed you were able to find her. But…"

"But what?"

"But you will be the last person to ever find her, I promise you. Because if this person you think is still alive and she is the only person who could verify it is him, I would not think she will be—what is the word—*findable* for long."

"You'd better start explaining yourself," Nivelle ordered Parker after they left the room.

"It was the only way to get information. And it's turned out pretty well for us. We never would have had the lead on Lisbon or the name of Patxi Irionda without her pointing us in the right direction. We wouldn't even know that Patxi Irionda is not deceased without her."

"Where is she?" Nivelle demanded, stepping closer to Parker so that they were face to face.

"The deal was that I not reveal her location. You asked for my help and that's what you got. I gave my word."

"*Va chier* with your *putain* word!"

Gibson stepped in to separate the two. He was disappointed that Parker hadn't told him of the true reasons for his earlier solo trip, but it wasn't entirely surprising. Parker always had his way of doing things.

"*Putain de bordel de merde*! She is a wanted terrorist! I could arrest you right here and now for withholding information." Nivelle felt his blood boiling. Marie-France's daughter had finally resurfaced. Just the mention of her name brought up the painful memory of her mother destroying his heart so many years ago. After that experience he'd never allowed himself to get too close or invested in any woman. None of them could be trusted. And he wanted to put Graciana away for good so that wherever her mother was in the world, she would know that he was responsible for putting her daughter in prison. This was a revenge he deserved. Even during the Haika 4 investigation, he'd personally wanted Graciana's capture most of all once she was identified as one of the members of the group. And it had been a slap in the face and just another reminder of her mother's cruelty that her daughter was the only member to evade them.

"Wouldn't matter. She has a new identity and she'd be impossible to find again. Wherever she was is irrelevant, because she'd be somewhere else by now."

"Are you able to contact her?" Nivelle asked.

"No, I have no contact info for her and I wouldn't be able to ask again. I doubt anyone knows where she would be now anyway."

Nivelle turned away in disgust. He tried to compose himself and separate personal emotion from the moment. After all, while the capture of Graciana Etceverria would be notable, there were more important things to worry about. Just as he was about to say something else to Parker, one of his young officers came running down the hallway. The young officer stopped in front of them, catching his breath.

"What is it?" Nivelle asked in French.

"A map. We've found a map in his apartment in Perpignan," the young officer replied, pointing to the room where Auzmendi was being held.

"A map of what?" Parker asked in English for Gibson.

After a nod of approval from Nivelle, the young officer continued in English. "Locations on the beaches and waterfront. Reports are that these appear to be locations for explosives for some coordinated attack."

"*Mon Dieu*, and during peak tourist season," Nivelle exclaimed. "Where?"

"Nice," the young officer replied.

"Prague? Why the hell are we going to Prague?" Gibson asked Parker.

As soon as Nivelle was informed of the map found in Garikotz Auzmendi's Perpignan apartment, Nivelle said he needed to get to Nice. He was clearly still displeased with Parker, but said they would reconvene to discuss further after he returned.

Parker suggested that he and Gibson take a walk around Bayonne before driving back to Sare. Parker also suggested that he go alone to

Prague, but Gibson was not going to let his young friend go off alone on another reckless, albeit effective, venture. Especially now that a very dangerous individual was known to be after Parker.

"I think that's where she'll have gone."

"What makes you think so?"

"Just call it a hunch."

"And what makes you think we would even be able find her? You said you didn't have any way to contact her, and I'm assuming that Prague is a pretty big city. You said you don't even know her new identity."

Parker didn't say anything in response at first, but Gibson noticed a grin extend across his face. "I never said that."

Gibson grinned in return. *Nice, Parker,* he said to himself. "I'll let Nivelle know, but I'm sure he'll be preoccupied after their big discovery," he responded.

Eskualdun, fededun. (*He who is Basque is a believer.*)
—Basque proverb

Herriak bizi behar du. (*The people must live.*)
—Basque proverb

Part V.

(Present/*El Presente*)

I.

Prague, Czech Republic

OVER A DECADE HAD PASSED since Sebastian Parker had last been in Prague. Despite the fact that the city was clearly much more of a popular tourist destination than in the past, he thought Prague had managed to retain its charm. The castle still overlooked the city below from a lofty perch. The countless church and tower spires filled in for the role of skyscrapers across the urban landscape. Prague was known as the City of a Hundred Spires, but he'd read that the actual number of spires rising above buildings and other structures was more in the realm of five times that.

The majority of the streets were still cobblestone and the majority of building rooftops were still a reddish hue. The Vltava River still languidly bisected the city, crossed by some of the most picturesque bridges in all of Europe. The charming mix of Gothic and baroque buildings still lined the many public squares, and every block revealed some new historical marker. All was still there, even if obscured by the throngs of tourists and tour buses. Parker recently read that Prague was now among the most visited cities in Europe.

"So how do you think we're going to find her? This has to be a city of around a million people," Gibson commented after they checked into a hotel near Old Town Square and stepped outside into the warm summer evening.

He'd debated leaving his gun in the hotel room's safe—traveling internationally with a sidearm in one's carry-on bag was not overly difficult with a FBI badge. But having to conceal the weapon while walking around in a hot and humid climate was more of a challenge.

He figured there was no real reason to bring it along, as they were only searching for Graciana and were removed from any potential threats. But decades of instinct warned him otherwise.

"One point two million is more accurate," Parker responded and started walking away.

Gibson followed him. "Impressive as always, Sebastian. But that doesn't do anything to address my doubts."

Parker didn't stop walking, but turned slightly to let Gibson see him shaking his head in mock disbelief. "Haven't you learned by now to trust me?"

Gibson realized he was joking, but the question cut into him. Because he did actually trust Parker. "So what's your big secret this time? Even if you think you know the name she's going by and still have some connections around the world, we're talking only a couple of days at most. If she's even here like you think, you and I both know that it's a long shot that anyone would be able to trace just another young European woman in just another huge European city."

"All valid points."

Gibson waited for more of an explanation. None came. "Nothing more?" he inquired as they walked underneath a stone archway over the road that looked like it had been there since the Middle Ages and probably had.

Parker abruptly stopped and turned to face Gibson, not caring that in doing so and also stopping Gibson, they were interrupting the flow of people walking along the sidewalk. "I want to be upfront with you right away—she never told me she was coming here. I just know that she left Vilnius and I have a strong suspicion she's here."

"A *strong suspicion*?"

Parker shrugged. "Yeah, sorry, but that's what I've got. I could be wrong, but I could be right. Anyway, I just wanted to be straight with you in case we don't find anything."

"Don't you think you should have mentioned that earlier? If so, I may have reminded you that you left your wife alone and that this is crazy."

"Nivelle promised to put a detail on Alaitz and I believe him. He's an ass, but true to his word. He knew that we would be pursuing our own leads, so it will not be out of the ordinary for his post person to let him know we're not around. And besides, whatever is going down in Nice is going to keep him more than busy. In fact, I would not be surprised if we see something on the international news later tonight. I'm sure he can't wait to make a positive announcement after the Mont Saint-Michel debacle, and I can't blame him. Irionda's orchestration of that charade was brilliant."

"That same brilliant orchestra director may also be after your wife."

"Conductor."

"What?"

"The director of an orchestra is called a conductor."

Gibson shook his head. "Jesus, Parker. You're one of a kind, kid."

Parker didn't laugh. "Yeah, let's hope I'm right. Because if we can find Graciana, I have a feeling that this will lead us to finding Patxi Irionda. A guy that faked his own death and has lived a clandestine life for years doesn't let someone betray him and get away with doing so. I may have been in his crosshairs before and Alaitz with me, but now I promise that they are fixed directly on her."

After walking a half hour, Parker suggested they stop in at a café for a beer. Gibson was not opposed. They had no clear agenda on this assignment. The way he saw it, they were merely having a look around. Thankfully, Gibson still had his gun with him. Being a law enforcement officer of the world still had some merits for times of trouble.

Parker ordered them two beers and they toasted to Nivelle's success in Nice. Parker always liked Czech beer. Maybe Czech beer wasn't as good as the Lithuanian beer he'd recently discovered, but it was still better than the light beers of Spain, France, and Italy. And better than the darker beers of Germany, Belgium, and the Netherlands. As for beer in the States, he'd never really been impressed. Somehow despite so many options, they were either too light or too heavy.

"Parker, you need to understand something. I may be off duty, but I can't ignore that you are seeking out someone wanted in connection with a murder in the United States. If we find her…" Gibson's voice trailed.

"We both knew that we would have to face this if we found her when we came here," Parker reluctantly offered.

"You clearly have a connection to this woman. I don't understand, given all that's happened and that she may be responsible for that sore shoulder of yours that will never be the same. But I understand if you've given your word and I don't like the thought of having to ask you to betray that trust. Even if you're no longer officially in the law enforcement arena, you're still involved, and giving your word to someone is a hard thing, even if to a criminal."

More of a criminal of circumstances than anything, Parker said to himself. Just a kid trying to get involved in a dying struggle for a culture and a people. She was led astray by a charismatic figure and the rhetoric of radical extremism. The same recipe lured kids astray around the world, the same today as throughout history. Maybe even worse these days, though, with the world's population having more young people than adults.

Gibson wouldn't understand that logic though. He was a good man and was good at his job, but he was stuck in the past. A past when things were more black and white. A past when there was a more defined line between good and bad, good and evil. The world of today was different. The lines were far more vague.

"Let's cross that bridge when we have to," Parker suggested. He could see that Gibson was not pleased with his response and spoke again before Gibson could say anything. "And if this all results in Graciana being arrested, I'd prefer that to her being killed," he admitted to Gibson. And to himself.

"So why and how do you think we can find her?"

Parker finished his beer. "For all her good looks, Graciana is a worker and self-sufficient. If she's here, she already has an under-the-table waitressing job in a restaurant somewhere. As attractive as she is and considering she speaks multiple languages, anyplace would have scooped her up as soon as she walked through the door. A place like Prague is a gold mine for restaurant owners hiring attractive girls from Eastern Europe and the former Soviet countries. Most of the waitresses will speak their native Russian or Ukrainian, in addition to some level of English. But Graciana would impress by being able to speak not only

English fluently, but other popular tourist languages, such as French and Spanish."

Gibson stared into the remains of his glass of beer. "But again, how does that help us find her when we have nothing to go on?"

"She's a smart girl. She'll know to stay away from local restaurants. Tipping is not customary anywhere in Europe, so being a local waitress is not to her advantage. Being in a tourist trap *resto*, she may get stuck with the occasional table of non-tippers, but chances are that if she gets into a nicer and more popular place, she'll end up with boatloads of American men willing to try real absinthe at her encouragement and leaving a nice amount of dollars on the table."

"So where are you thinking? There must be a hundred places that could fit that description in this downtown area, if not more."

"Actually, more like twenty. I already did a search," Parker said, holding up his phone to Gibson. "I figure we'll be able to cover them all in a couple of nights and we're already down one. Next time the waitress comes by, I'm going to start asking around to see if anyone knows of a new foreign girl having started."

This cannot be happening, Patxi Irionda thought. Although he was prepared to become a martyr for the cause, and for the rest of his crew to become the same, he didn't believe they'd all be captured. And now because of Garikotz's mistake of keeping a map of the target sites, the Nice attack was ruined.

He'd anticipated Aitzol being caught; the rugby *bourrin* had taken too many blows to the head over the years and wasn't the brightest to begin with. This explained why he'd planned for Aitzol's potential arrest by feeding him the bogus Mont Saint-Michel information. The loss of the Nice attack was unfortunate, but wouldn't be a total loss. After the embarrassment at Mont-Saint-Michel, Patxi was certain the fact that another attack had been averted would make huge headlines around the world. Almost as effective as confirming after Paris that the Basque movement was alive and thriving. Almost.

But Itxaso? How the hell had they found her? And Garikotz? The capture of Garikotz was a shame, but Patxi assumed Garikotz had done something to stick out and make himself a target.

Aitzol could pin them all to Paris, but he'd not be able to help track any of them down, even if the *connards* managed to coerce him to blab even more. But Itxaso and Garikotz—both could lead to Patxi in Lisbon. And there was now another threat just revealed to him by his man on the inside in the French DNAT. That little blonde *salope* had sold out her people. She had to pay for her treason.

He had to move and he had to move quickly. As long as he was on the move, they wouldn't be able to track him down. He'd tell his wife and kids that he was going away for another long business trip. He had a network of safe houses and contacts strung all over Europe. First stop was Vienna.

After the first couple of places, they all began to look the same to Gibson. Parker explained that they were historic, traditional pub style and beer hall Czech restaurants. The menus often had pictures of food items and were available in a wide variety of languages. And they all seemed to share being heavy on meat and potato type dishes, and every menu had some sort of goulash prominently displayed on the front page.

Parker's inquest became routine early in their evening. They would enter a restaurant and Parker would quickly survey the interior to view the wait staff. After being seated, he'd attempt to strike a friendly conversation with every waitress or waiter he could. They would order a couple of Czech beers, and if Parker didn't believe he reached a certain comfort level with their server by then, he would delay his questions until after ordering food.

Initially, the tour was an enjoyable experience, but as the evening wore on, Gibson began to feel bloated from all the beer and heavy Czech food. He was relieved when Parker concluded they had given enough effort for the night. They returned to their hotel and agreed to begin with those restaurants on Parker's list open for lunch the next day.

The little blonde *salope* wouldn't be able to hide from him. If only Aitzol had carried out his assignment years ago and eliminated

Graciana Etceverria instead of shooting the American, then none of this would have happened. At that time, Patxi ordered Graciana to be taken out when she was the only one left of the so-called Haika 4. The hit hadn't been approved by ETA's leadership chain, but Patxi knew the best plan was to take out Etceverria before she was caught by the French and exposed ETA's recruiting techniques to acquire new soldiers for the cause. At the time, the majority of ETA's new recruits were coming from their sponsored youth groups, such as Haika and Segi, but this was only known within the organization itself. Etceverria's arrest would have exposed this ultraimportant lifeline. As usual, the leadership had been afraid to do what needed to be done. Even back then Patxi was able to see the bigger picture that other senior members of the organization apparently couldn't comprehend.

Aitzol had disappointed him by missing his mark. How difficult could it have been for a trained killer to take out one skinny girl? Patxi forgave Aitzol for a mistake that must have been influenced by other factors. Perhaps the American jumped in front of Graciana as Aitzol was firing? He'd never known what happened, but considering his recent unimpressive performance, Patxi looked back on the event as just another example of Aitzol's incompetence. So much for the supposed training Aitzol received, as clearly the training hadn't turned him into a lethal killing machine.

Like usual, if Patxi wanted something done his way, he was going to have to do it himself. He'd have no problem finishing off Graciana Etceverria. Once he knew she was in Prague after being contacted by his DNAT mole, he'd be able to find her. Patxi had an extensive network of contacts and he'd be able to have her tracked down. He knew her new identity since being put into exile, and identities were always searchable these days.

Only a matter of time.

So far so good, Graciana thought. Since relocating to Prague from Vilnius a few days ago, she'd been able to find a room to rent in a shared apartment and already had a job. Online sites made finding rooms or apartments to sublet easy these days, and moving itself was not difficult for someone whose possessions could fit in a couple of bags. As for finding a job, she'd been hired by the first restaurant she tried.

She'd known right away what to look for—some overdone touristy place where they'd be all too happy to bring on another attractive server who could also speak a few different languages. The though occurred to her that she should use a new alias, but since the manager said her status would be *unofficial*, she wasn't overly concerned.

As she walked from the bus stop into Old Town for her second night of work she considered how she would be fine with staying in Prague. It was a beautiful city and there would always be work. And her manager let the employees eat for free before their shifts, as long as they showed up early enough to also have time to change into their costumes before the doors opened.

"Seriously, how certain are you that she's even here?" Gibson asked Parker as they approached the first stop of the day on Parker's list.

"A hundred percent," Parker quickly replied.

"Just because she told you she may move here? She's a wanted criminal and is accused of international terrorism," Gibson replied, unconvinced. "Why would she possibly be honest to you about her future living plans?"

Parker stopped to face him. They were standing in the middle of the wide Old Town Square, near the Jan Hus Memorial and surrounded by some of Prague's most recognizable buildings: the Our Lady before Týn, with the church's signature high Gothic tower, the majestic baroque Church of St. Nicholas, and the unusual architectural combination of structures making up the Old Town Hall. When Parker turned to confront Gibson, the fascinating medieval astrological clock on one of the Town Hall's frontages was directly behind him.

"Because aside from those other things, she's still a woman, and women like men. Part of the time in her case, anyway," Parker said, hoping he was not going to have to explain things further on the matter.

He didn't. Gibson could sense Parker's awkwardness and apparent discomfort at making this revelation. He wondered if more happened on Parker's trip to Vilnius than just a conversation. She was, after all, as he recalled, a very attractive girl. But he didn't say anything else. Whatever happened was now up to Parker to deal with on his own.

But he hoped his young friend hadn't done something foolish. Gibson could see how Parker adored his wife and she him, even if they did have issues getting along at times. And he'd been playing with fire without doubt when confronting this other woman on his own. All women have the potential to manipulate men. But this one was the especially dangerous type—beautiful, unpredictable, and cold-blooded. And European. Every European woman he'd ever encountered was even more unpredictable than women of any other region of the world. He hoped Parker's concern for Graciana's safety was based on a sense of responsibility for having exposed her to elements who would do her harm, rather than another reason.

Parker sensed that Gibson was questioning his motives. "Totally not what you think. I love Alaitz," he stated. Parker then added another statement, easing Gibson's apprehensions. "But by helping me, helping us, and helping Nivelle, she put herself in a lot of danger. The world just witnessed this group mercilessly kill innocent people in Paris, and it sounds like they had something even more devastating planned for Nice."

That morning, news had broken in the world press of the discovery of a plot to detonate a massive amount of explosives at various locations along the most popular beaches of Nice. Details were still not being made public due to the ongoing investigation, but the fact was known that the planned attack was directly linked to the Montparnasse Tower attack and to elements of ETA.

"This Patxi Irionda is clearly capable of anything, and there's no way he's not going to take Graciana out if he's able to follow the trail back to her."

"Okay, fair enough. Let's just hope we're successful. All we've achieved so far is gaining weight from heavy food and beer."

They both laughed, glad to have the mood lightened between them again.

He had her. Prague. There had been no hits on where she might be living, but after an afternoon meeting with an associate in Vienna,

Patxi knew where Graciana Etceverria had a job. She'd probably thought that the job was entirely off the record and thus under the radar of being traced, but the stupid girl should have known better. Prague was no longer really Eastern Europe, where such things could still be possible. Even if not entirely legitimately registered, the names of employees were still recorded. She'd ended up at some sort of medieval theme restaurant on the edge of the Old Town and Lesser Town areas of the city. He'd pay the place a visit tonight. Even if she wasn't there working, he'd get her address from the manager, however he had to.

The local associate also provided Patxi with a small snub-nosed revolver. The little gun wasn't much of a weapon, but it would do the job and was easy to conceal. He planned to be standing right next to Graciana when she died. And after the news of the French uncovering his plans for Nice, Patxi was feeling especially spiteful toward the person who'd identified him. The way things were now quickly spiraling out of his control, Patxi was starting to admit that martyrdom in the form of spending the rest of his life in prison was becoming more of a reality.

But he would not go without getting his revenge. Other events may have been out of his hands, but he'd be damned if he let that little blonde *salope* be the cause of his capture.

Graciana Etceverria died tonight.

Another long day with nothing to show for their efforts. But Gibson wasn't overly disappointed. Even if they were getting nowhere with the search for Graciana Etceverria, he was still experiencing a remarkable new city and enjoying spending time with his young friend. They spent the day walking the streets of Prague, with Gibson allowing Parker to serve as tour guide. And while conducting their tour of the city, they continued their search of restaurants on Parker's list.

But now they were at the last place on the list, a pub style restaurant in the city's castle district, and their search hadn't even resulted in a potential hit. Parker tried hard to question his mark at every place they visited, asking each person he centered on the same series of varied questions. Did they know of any new hires lately? Specifically of a young woman? Perhaps a European woman? Perhaps a short-haired woman? Perhaps a woman with a Romanian sounding name? Perhaps a woman by the name of Graciana?

For once, Gibson entirely understood the conversations occurring, as Parker asked all his questions in English. Parker commented once to him that if he spoke Russian, he could probably get by speaking it as a native Czech speaker would recognize much of the vocabulary. But as English was now so widely spoken in Prague, especially the areas popular with tourists, conversing in English was just as effective. Gibson was used to Parker speaking French, Basque, or Spanish. Even on their recent trip to Portugal, Parker conversed with a few locals in what he called his attempts at Portuguese. So to be able to fully understand what was being said him now and not have to guess based on body language and a word he'd pick up on now and again, or wait for the translation after from Parker, was a most welcome change.

Having some positive tip from the last waiter would have also been a welcome change. Instead, all of Parker's questions were met with shakes of the waiter's head. Gibson noticed Parker's own head begin to hang some after the waiter walked away from their table. That was it. At least, according to Parker's list. Gibson was tempted to ask if there were perhaps other places Parker hadn't considered, but he decided this would only be adding insult to injury.

Parker may have never been a field agent, only an unwilling one of sorts based on the circumstances into their investigation of the Haika 4 murder in San Francisco leading them to France and Spain. But what Parker had always been was a top-notch researcher and investigative analyst. Even if he was no longer working in the intelligence world, the skills that one acquired from prior service would never diminish. Although Parker may have flashed his phone at Gibson and pretended there was nothing elaborate to show, Gibson was certain that Parker had carefully vetted his list of potential places before finalizing the list. To question him now would only be insulting.

Besides, their string of good luck, beginning with their previous collaboration, had to come up empty at some point. The Parker-Gibson team had been damn fortunate on numerous occasions. But after spending his entire career in law enforcement, Gibson knew every good luck streak eventually ended. Gibson thought of a way to cheer Parker up.

Earlier he'd seen some people seated near them order absinthe drinks. He'd never tried absinthe, but knew enough from seeing it mentioned in movies to recognize the infamous green fairy. He'd heard that some form of absinthe was now legal in the States, but knew that for years it had been illegal. He said he needed to use the restroom, and on the way, when he was sure that Parker would not see him, he stopped their waiter and ordered one absinthe. He returned to their table, unable to hide his grin.

"What the hell are you smiling about? *Nous sommes foutus et nous avons rien.* We're done and we've got nothing," Parker gloomily remarked.

Gibson didn't respond, but nodded behind Parker. Their waiter was walking their way with a tray. On the tray was one glass, one small bottle of a green liquid, one spoon, a small bowl of sugar cubes, and a bottle of water.

Parker's frown turned slightly upward as the waiter stopped at their table and began setting the tray's contents down in front of him. "Thank you."

"You're welcome. Thought you needed a little lift and just assumed that you like that stuff."

"I do actually. You know pastis in France came about because once absinthe was outlawed, some smart people came up with a similar tasting drink, just without the potential hallucinogenic aftereffects. You don't want one?"

"No, thanks. I'll just watch you defile yourself. One of us needs to stay mostly sober, just in case."

"Just in case…I like that. Always ready to kick ass."

Gibson grinned. "Something like that."

Parker walked Gibson through the absinthe ritual of first pouring the dark green absinthe into the glass, followed by placing the flat slotted spoon on top of the glass and placing a sugar cube on top. Next he slowly poured water over the sugar cube so that the cube gradually melted and fell into the powerfully strong alcoholic liquid waiting below. When the water hit the absinthe, a small reaction occurred, resulting in a milky blend in the glass. Then the spoon was dropped into the glass with the remaining grains of sugar and stirred. Finally, one took a sip of the notorious elixir.

"*Putain merde.* That's some strong stuff," Parker proclaimed.

Parker described the drink as tasting like black licorice dipped in pepper sauce, very hot pepper sauce. Gibson smelled Parker's drink and his nose burned. Parker said tasting the drink burned his throat and he could feel the heat of the alcohol travel southward into his body.

"You really like it?" Gibson asked.

Parker downed the rest of his glass in one drink and Gibson noted that he didn't even wince. "Yeah, unique. Just don't drink too much or you'll become an obsessive painter and cut your own ear off."

"Van Gogh?" Gibson asked.

"*Très bien,*" Parker said, pleased that Gibson answered correctly, but not feeling overly joyous based on the situation. "Some people also like to light absinthe on fire before they drink it, but that's all show. Anyway, what do you say we get out of here and check out the view from up by the castle?"

Gibson agreed and downed the rest of his glass of beer.

Once outside the restaurant, they noticed the evening air had turned much cooler. They walked up a steep cobblestone roadway lined with streetlamps and a tall stone wall on one side to the top of a hill where the Prague Castle was perched. The entire city stretched out in front of them in a soft glow of lights and steeples rising above low lines of buildings with a great river passing through the center.

Gibson thought how even though he enjoyed the skyline of large cities with towering skyscrapers in the States, he had to admit that there was something special about every European city he'd visited. And their nighttime skylines were just as impressive. Maybe even more, if he was being truly honest with himself.

Parker was also thinking to himself, but not about the fantastic beauty of the city presented in front of them. Earlier he'd been frustrated. Now he was just disappointed.

From an early age, he had understood that he would never be physically imposing. He would never be the boy in class who everyone was afraid of making upset. When he was a little older, he would never be some strong athlete. And when he was really big, he'd not be one of those guys who looked like they could beat anyone up. But from an early age, Sebastian Parker recognized that he wanted to be an imposing figure. And if not a physically imposing figure, he'd be imposing in other ways. That was when he began developing his own personal combination of his three C's: cleverness, charm, and confidence. But the first C was letting him down in a big way. Apparently, now was time to admit failure.

The trip to Prague was a waste. Obviously, Graciana deceived him into thinking that she'd come here. Obviously. She'd played him from the beginning, knowing that he'd believe her and lead whoever here. She could be anywhere. Tallinn? Riga? Minsk? St. Petersburg? Kaliningrad? Kiev? Bucharest? Warsaw? None of them would surprise him. After picking up some Lithuanian language and culture, she may have even just slipped over to a more obscure place in that country, like Palanga on the Baltic Sea. Graciana was gone and he was a fool to believe he'd even partially figured out the motives of an accused murderer and terrorist.

Gibson interrupted his thoughts by saying that after the long day and evening of walking the streets of Prague he was ready for bed. Parker agreed and they began the walk to the other side of the river and their hotel. On the way, while passing over the Charles Bridge, still crowded with people even this late, Parker told Gibson that he was going to go for one more drink.

Gibson offered to go with him, but Parker insisted Gibson return to the hotel and get some sleep. He said that in the morning they'd contact Nivelle and let him know they'd struck out and were heading back to France. Gibson agreed, but reluctantly. He was so tired, that he didn't have much argument left in him. He didn't have the youthful legs and stamina of Sebastian and they'd walked all day. Even his gun in its holster pulled heavily on his shoulder. To keep his weapon concealed he'd had to wear a jacket on a hot summer day.

When they crossed the bridge and their hotel was just a block away, Gibson asked where Parker was going. Although he didn't know why, as it didn't really make any difference. He had no clue how to get around the city. Parker said he was going to go back to the overdone medieval place they had gone to the night before. The place where he'd told Gibson he was nearly positive they would find Graciana. But they didn't find her there.

The entire city was a maze to Gibson. Even after walking around for two days, if he couldn't see the castle or the river, he didn't believe he'd be able to figure out his orientation. But he did remember the restaurant Parker was talking about. And he remembered the place was not too far from their hotel, just down the same street in the direction of one of the large squares. Not that it mattered. He just wanted to head to bed. He wished Parker good night and told him to behave.

As Parker started walking in the opposite direction, Gibson said, "Don't be too hard on yourself, kid. It was a good try."

Parker turned and said thanks and then continued walking away. The thought occurred to him that he'd been nearly positive they would find out Graciana working at the medieval style restaurant. The restaurant was one of the top tourist attractions in the entire city. The staff dressed in period dress from the Middle Ages, and the entire setting was designed to look like a medieval tavern with stone walls, candles, solid rustic wood furniture, and even tableware fashioned to resemble the forks and plates and cups of centuries ago. The restaurant was a sprawling place, with multiple rooms, but Parker thoroughly searched the interior the day before when they visited.

But he was no longer searching for Graciana Etceverria. He just wanted to have one more drink before fully accepting defeat and turning in for the night. And he wanted to go somewhere lively. Despite his diminished mood, the thought of going to some gloomy, quiet bar was not at all appealing. One more drink, yes, but not six more, as may turn out to be the case in the fitting setting. And besides, the medieval place was just up the street from their hotel. He wouldn't have to walk around hoping to come across some jewel of a suitable place. Maybe the cheesy touristy place would even cheer him up a bit.

From the moment the doors opened for dinner guests, Graciana hadn't stopped moving. Vilnius had a lot of tourists, but nothing like Prague. There was more of every nationality: Germans, English, French, Poles, Russians, Scandinavians, Italians, Spaniards, Dutch,

Japanese, and Chinese. But a major difference was that in Vilnius, one rarely came across American tourists. The situation was the opposite in Prague.

Tourists from the land of fast food and big houses may have not outnumbered those from other European countries or those combined from Asian countries, but it was close. And the Americans here were no different from the Americans anywhere. Loud, overweight, obnoxious, and clearly not able to hold their alcohol. They also must have believed that just because they were in Eastern Europe, all women were secretly whores or ready to be mail-order brides. In only her second night on the job in Prague, she'd had her ass pinched a few times and been proposed to while passing by tables occupied by Americans.

Americans. She'd really only met one in her life she found interesting, and she found him very interesting. Sebastian Parker. Although she wasn't sure he really counted as an American. Her thought was punctuated by two American middle-aged men wearing expensive shirts and jeans they were too old to be wearing asking her if she did private after-dinner shows. Everything in her wanted to slap both of their bloated faces. She wanted to keep this job for a while, as she was going to make a nice chunk of money in this tourist joke of a place.

The place clearly relied on tourists, and these days any persistent unhappy patron could vilify a restaurant on all of the online forums saying how they were mistreated and that others should never consider frequenting the place. Such reviews could be devastating, especially considering how accessible information was these days, when a tourist could be walking by and see the sign of a restaurant and instantly find reviews of the place on their mobile devices. Considering how these two chubby assholes were dressed, she assumed they were at least mildly wealthy in America. They also looked like the sort of pricks who took being offended like a couple of bitches. And even though she knew she could find another job easily, she had made more money last night than she would have made in five shifts in Vilnius. And there would be ten other young pretty women from some Eastern European country at the door to take her spot. So she just smiled and replied in Basque telling them to go fuck themselves.

One of the more spry older men of her grandpa and grandma table suddenly rose, waving a hand to catch her attention. She knew what the old guy was going to ask before he said anything. Where was the bathroom and did one have to pay? He'd heard that it costs money to use every bathroom in Europe.

Graciana pointed him in the right direction and assured him that he would not have to pay.

What a night. If every night was going to be like this, and she'd been told to expect so except for the deepest months of winter, she would soon have some real money saved.

She didn't care about settling in anywhere. Once she had dreamed of doing so in her homeland, on her Basque Coast, but now everything was different. She had even considered Vilnius to be a temporary place, despite assurance from ETA command that she would be safe there for as long as she wanted. And now here in Prague things were the same. The exception was that now she was out from under the watch of others. She was on her own. However, ETA would always have eyes, and she'd never be safe again. But perhaps she'd be safer out of Europe. Once she had enough saved, her next stop would be somewhere where no one cared where she came from. Somewhere where she could begin a new life. She'd always thought Madagascar sounded nice.

But she'd have plenty of time to think about her future later. For now she needed to work and keep making money. One thing about these annoying Americans was that they tipped, and not just leaving a few extra coins on the table after getting change. They left real money.

Each room had a string of stone arches between them, and the rooms were divided to different servers, but some tables were situated so that one could easily see into another room. But she was so busy that she couldn't even glance away from her own tables to notice if people at other tables were staring at her.

Even with that ridiculous Middle Ages costume with a red bonnet on her head and that equally ridiculous red gown, there was no mistaking Graciana Etceverria. To hide a woman like Graciana would require much more. She'd have to entirely conceal her pretty face and completely hide her svelte body. Patxi Irionda always thought she was a beautiful young woman. He might have regretted ordering the hit on her a little had she not turned down his advances.

Now, stealthily watching her from his table across the restaurant, Patxi once again felt an urge to have Graciana…he'd have to settle with just killing her instead. There was no time to waste here in Prague. He needed to take care of this loose end and get back to addressing his current dilemma, the dilemma of the Basque movement. Would he return to hiding to let things settle for a few years and slowly rebuild? Or should he stick with his attack, even if this meant capture or death?

At first, he was concerned that she would recognize him right away, giving him no choice but to take immediate action. But she'd glanced in his direction a few times and clearly not noticed him watching her.

And she was not escaping her fate tonight. Once she left the restaurant, he planned to follow her and take care of what should have been done years ago.

Enjoy this, Graciana. Enjoy being drooled over by men, he thought. *This is the last time.*

What happened could be a line out of a storybook. He walked in. He saw her. She saw him. There was a shared magical moment. It was perfect.

Only, it wasn't perfect. Sebastian Parker was not there to sweep Graciana off her feet and spend a lifetime of love and adoration with her. He was there to warn her.

Graciana didn't know why Sebastian was there. She only saw someone she believed she'd never see again stepping into her restaurant. She made no effort to hide. If he'd come this far, there was not time for any more games between them. There would be no other reason for him to be in Prague and in her restaurant. He was here for her.

Parker brushed by the hostess who spoke at the entrance of the restaurant. She said something, but he didn't hear her. His gaze was fixated across the room into the adjacent chamber-like room where Graciana was waiting tables. He noticed her instantly. That bonnet and gown couldn't hide her beauty. Even from a distance, he had no doubt it was her.

He walked past the hostess into the chamber room. Graciana noticed him just as she was setting down a round of drinks for one of her tables. For a moment, the connection between them was magnetic.

Without uttering a word, Graciana approached him, reached for and grabbed his hand, and led him to a small two-person table in the corner of the chamber room. They said nothing as he sat down, but the glance they shared spoke paragraphs: *He was there to see her. She was very happy to see him. Now sit there and be good. Wait until she had a free moment.*

Parker understood completely. There was no reason for Graciana to suspect he was there for any other reason. It didn't even matter anymore that he was right all along and that she actually was in Prague, and actually did work at one of the places where he'd predicted. All that mattered at the moment was that she was here. What happened next? He wasn't entirely sure. But he knew there was no way he was alerting Gibson of her presence. As much as he respected Gibson, Parker couldn't betray his word. And definitely not his word to Graciana.

He couldn't explain the sensation, but there was some sort of bond between them. There had been from the moment they met at a Basque youth music festival. Parker hadn't necessarily felt a sexual attraction for her, but there was an unmistakable attraction all the same. And he was feeling that sense of attraction once again, although this time mixed with a sense of urgency.

Parker sat patiently waiting for her to have a moment to talk. At one point, she set a large beer on the table without Parker asking for one. She threaded her way with birdlike agility through the tables, carrying trays of food and drinks, careful to avoid the sudden unpredictable movements of diners not paying attention to their surroundings. Parker noticed that the gazes of many of the men in the room tended to follow Graciana's movements. There was even some older guy in another section of the restaurant staring her down. This one kept a menu in his hand, pretending to be reviewing the restaurant's offerings, but Parker noticed the man's eyes fixated on Graciana. The older man was too far away and too obscured by a shadow to make out his features. Although the man was slightly suspicious looking, Parker didn't consider him an overt threat. Just another fantasizing dirty old man.

He felt her hand gently touch his shoulder before he heard her speak. Her touch felt nice, but made him uneasy. "Hello, stranger. This is a nice surprise," she said in French as she moved in front of him so he could see her.

"Nice costume," he responded, unable to avoid noticing how the red dress Graciana wore clung to her slender frame with a plunging neckline accenting her slight cleavage. "Not sure about the bonnet though."

Graciana laughed. Could he really have come for her? It had been so long since she'd been interested in another person, woman or man. And now one was here. Sebastian Parker was here.

"I came here yesterday and asked about you—or asked about someone fitting your description going by one of a few possible names—but was told no one like you worked here. I've been to around twenty other places in Prague looking for you."

This is too good to be true. Actually searched Prague for me? "This restaurant is a big place and a lot of people work here. This is also only my second night," she offered in English as explanation.

Parker suddenly felt foolish. *Of course!* He should have thought of the possibility earlier. This was one of the largest tourist oriented restaurants in the entire city. "I really need to talk to you."

Graciana liked the sound of this, as she was anxious to hear what he had to say to her. "The restaurant closes in an hour," she suggested in Spanish.

"I will wait. We can go for a walk."

Graciana would rather he said they could return to his hotel, but a walk would be okay. She imagined any walk would end at his hotel room. She leaned down and kissed him on the cheek and then was off to attend to her tables.

A table of four men on multiple rounds of beers had been intently observing the entire conversation between Graciana and Parker and they cheered when she kissed his cheek. Parker blushed and took a long drink of his beer. A very long drink.

The thought occurred to him that in the hour before Graciana got off, he could easily walk back to the hotel, wake up Gibson, and return to meet up with her.

But Sebastian Parker didn't move from the table.

That was him. The fucking American helping the goddamn French. Sebastian Parker. Patxi knew him from the photographs he'd seen of Parker in the past. How the hell did he know Graciana Etceverria was here in Prague? The little *salope* must have told him that she was coming here after leaving Vilnius. No matter—if Parker got in Patxi's way, there would be two killed tonight instead of one. Patxi wasn't going to delay his plan just because this *putain* American was once again meddling in affairs he should have long ago turned away from.

Although he'd assigned Garikotz to watch the American's Basque wife, with the fool getting himself caught, Patxi had not been entirely sure how he intended to strike at the American. His original thought had been only to have Garikotz track the woman's routine patterns, so that if they needed to send a threatening message, the task would be easy to handle. Killing the American now would make things more complicated. The killing of an unknown young woman with false papers was one thing. The killing of an American with ties to both the American and French governments was quite a different matter.

Patxi watched Graciana and the American conversing. He'd noticed how Graciana looked at him differently from the way she looked at other men. She also acted flirtatious around the American. When the restaurant began to close and patrons inside began to slowly leave, Patxi took a position opposite the entrance of the restaurant. There was a café with outdoor seating where he sat at a table and waited for Graciana to leave so he could follow her.

Patxi wasn't going to let anything stop him. If the American had to also die…so be it.

"You look more like yourself again," Parker said in French to Graciana as she appeared from a back room of the restaurant, changed out of her period costume. Now she was dressed in a pair of tight jeans and a tank top.

"Thanks, now let's get out of here," she replied and they stepped outside into the night. As they did, Graciana put on a hooded sweatshirt she was carrying. The summer night was still warm, but the temperature had considerably cooled off.

Parker didn't have a destination in mind, but they were walking in the direction of the Charles Bridge. Even though it was after ten in the evening, there were still tourists on the streets.

"So why are you here in Prague with me, Sebastian Parker?" Graciana asked in English as they walked.

Parker's answer was not what she hoped for. "To warn you," he flatly stated in Basque.

His words were like a shot to her heart. She didn't respond immediately, letting the effect of his response sink in. Of course, he was not there for her. How could she have ever thought there was a happy ending in her future? Her life had always been in turmoil. There was no reason for her to think anything would ever be different. Adolescent notions of love and romance had no place in her world. She was on her own. She always would be.

"Warn me of what?" she finally asked in English, accepting reality.

"Patxi Irionda. He's going to find out, if he hasn't already, that you helped me."

"So?"

"Graciana, the man faked his own death years ago. He's obviously going to be ticked off at the person who's revealed that he's not so dead. Add on that he's now suspected to be the leader behind the group responsible for the Tour Montparnasse attack and the planned Nice attack, and he's really to be after the person responsible for identifying him. And that person is you. A person that is capable of fabricating their own death and living a secret life and organizing all these attacks, that's the kind of person who doesn't let things slide. You know as well as I do—he's extremely dangerous and he's going to take this personally. And with the ETA network throughout Europe, even if you left Vilnius unannounced, we have to assume he'd be able to track you here."

Graciana considered what Parker said to her and admitted there was some truth in his words. But she didn't care. She wasn't going to live a life constantly running and hiding.

By her silence, Parker assumed Graciana was taking the threat seriously. "Graciana, you have to leave. I don't know where, but you have to go. Prague is going to be too easy to trace you to."

"Would you want to know where I go?"

Parker hesitated before responding. Graciana spoke again before he could speak. "It's okay, you don't have to answer," she offered.

"Listen, Graciana. You have to take this seriously. You need to leave and you need to leave now. Tonight. If that means leaving with me, then at least we'll know you'll be safe."

"With you?"

"Yes...but that would mean..." Parker awkwardly began to reply.

Graciana finished his thought. "That would mean a French prison for me, somewhere far from the Basque Country."

She was right, he said to himself. Although there was no way she could know that Gibson was also in Prague, she knew that Parker was working with the French and would not be able to conceal his association with her any longer. Especially if he was offering to accompany her personally back to France. The only way she'd be safe in that scenario was if he delivered her into Nivelle's hands. And with Gibson involved, he'd definitely not have a chance to consider any other option.

"You'll be alive and you'll be safe. That's all that matters," Parker said, turning his head away from her as they walked. They had been so engrossed in their conversation that he'd not even noticed they were now about halfway across Charles Bridge.

Graciana stopped and turned Parker by his shoulders to face her. Even in the soft light from the bridge's lamps, she noticed the look of concern on his face. "Sebastian, I appreciate you coming here and your concern for me. I really do. This is all very touching and reminds me of something I'll never have. But for as much as I would like you to save me, you cannot. No one can. I can look out for myself. I always have."

Graciana moved closer to him and placed her hands gently around his face. She leaned forward and kissed him on the lips. "Alaitz is very lucky," she softly said as she pulled her lips away from his. She lowered her hands and moved away from him.

As Graciana stepped backward, Parker was about to speak, but he noticed someone moving toward them out of the corner of his eye. The next few seconds unraveled as if in slow motion.

Nearby on the bridge, a group of teenagers were posing for pictures and giggling. A young couple holding hands walked past them. A man approaching extended a gun pointed directly at Graciana. Before he could move, Parker saw the raised gun and a flash come from the silencer-encased barrel. The man fired three shots, directly into Graciana's torso. Graciana's slight frame was pummeled by the close-range shots. Her body slammed backward into the stone side wall of the bridge.

The man turned the gun at Parker and spoke. "You should have never crossed the Basques."

Just as Parker braced himself to be shot, he heard a gunshot from somewhere behind him.

The gun the man was holding dropped to the ground and the man himself stumbled, dropping hard on his back in the middle of the bridge. The young couple had dived to the ground nearby and the kids down the bridge were screaming in fear. Parker looked backward and saw the shot behind him had come from Gibson, now slowly approaching with his gun drawn.

Parker grabbed the gun on the ground and approached the man lying in the middle of the bridge. As he got closer, he recognized the features of Patxi Irionda he'd seen in photographs of the supposedly deceased former ETA member. And he noted that he'd already seen Irionda earlier at the restaurant without making the recognition.

Parker could see that Gibson's shot had struck Irionda squarely in the chest and the man was bleeding out profusely. There was no way he'd survive more than a couple more minutes. Parker crouched down near Irionda's head. Irionda was breathing heavily and coughing, but even in the dim light from the bridge's lamps, Parker could see the hate in Irionda's eyes looking upward at him.

"Those who kill innocent people in the name of the Basques don't deserve to call themselves Basque," Parker firmly stated.

Patxi Irionda tried to respond, but exhaled his last breath before he was able to formulate words.

Parker heard Gibson approaching and knew he was now standing next to him. Without saying anything, Parker raised the gun he'd picked up to hand to Gibson and went to check on Graciana.

Parker's steps were heavy and he felt his heart sinking as he moved closer to her. She was lying with her back on the ground and Parker didn't see any sign of life as he approached. But when he was right next to her, he saw her eyes were open. She was breathing slightly.

Graciana smiled when she saw him. She knew she was dying, but she was glad he was there. At least she wouldn't die alone.

Parker leaned down and grabbed her hand. She wasn't going to last much longer. "Graciana, I'm very pleased to have met you," he said in French. "And I wish things had turned out differently and better for you." It wasn't romantic love he felt for the dying woman, but he did care for her.

She curled her body as best she could manage to try and be nearer to him. "Basque stories don't really have happy endings," she slowly said, feeling an emptiness closing in around her. She raised her other hand and touched his face. "But maybe things will be different now." Graciana's hand fell and he felt the grip of her other hand loosen and slip from his grasp.

"*Bonne nuit*, Graciana."

"After I got back to the hotel room, I sat back on the bed and just nodded off a little. Then I woke up and something just felt off, more so than falling asleep in my clothes. I looked over and saw that I'd only been out for an hour or so. I knocked on your door, but when you didn't answer, I remembered where you said you'd be, so I thought maybe you needed rescuing from yourself. I walked down there, just in time to see you leaving with a young woman," Gibson explained as he stood over Parker, still kneeling next to Graciana's now lifeless body.

Parker touched her face and leaned down to kiss her cheek. Then he slowly stood. There were no more screaming tourists, or anyone else on the bridge. But sirens were ringing out in the summer night.

"Right when I was going to approach, I noticed him watching you and thought it would be best to hang back," Gibson continued, gesturing to Irionda's still body. "When I got to the bridge, that group of teenagers got in my way and I didn't see this one draw his gun until he'd already fired."

The sounds of the sirens grew closer. Flashing lights began to appear on either side of the river, bouncing off the stone walls of surrounding buildings. There wasn't much time to get their story straight. Gibson set the two guns on the ground. Although he had faith the local police authorities wouldn't start shooting right away once they arrived, he didn't want to take a chance of making them nervous. He also took his FBI badge out, able to be easily seen.

His involvement would not be so difficult to explain. He was with the American FBI working with the French DNAT. The situation was sticky, but not unheard of, especially not in these days of global terrorism concerns. Although the Prague authorities would undoubtedly be unconvinced initially, a call to Nivelle would clear things up.

Nivelle would explain that he commissioned the help of Gibson based on his previous engagement with the French DNAT. And in times such as these, when a terrorist threat could occur anywhere in Europe, it was of the utmost importance to stop any more attacks from happening. After all, if a known terrorist was in Prague, perhaps the next target was the Prague Castle or some other landmark tourist attraction? Gibson was sure Nivelle would handle everything.

Of course, the Czechs would claim they had some role in the overall operation to track down wanted terrorists in their own capital. He imagined that if his involvement became known, the FBI would also issue some statement that the agency was involved in the investigation from the start, offering the assistance of the American government in a time of European crisis. That was just the way things worked.

Justifying Parker's involvement would not be as simple, but Nivelle could fall back on the same explanation. In times of fear, details often blur.

"I suggest we keep your name out of this as much as possible. Even if this most current threat is now neutralized, this whole thing shows how another threat could come again in a few years. And if so, your involvement here will put you, and your family, in even greater danger," Gibson suggested.

"Fine by me," Parker agreed, knowing Gibson was absolutely right.

"Let me do the talking when they get here. I'll state right away that we need to keep your name out of any reports. My credentials should be enough, but if not, I'll enlist Nivelle's help."

"Thanks, Gibson."

"No problem."

"No, I mean, *thanks*," Parker said, motioning to Patxi Irionda's body. He extended a hand and the two shook.

Now they heard loud yells coming from policemen running down both ends of the bridge.

"We'd better assume the position," Gibson advised. The two of them slowly placed their hands behind their heads and descended to their knees. He added: "Hell of a way to spend a vacation."

Facing one another, there was enough light from the lamps on the bridge for each to see that they were both grinning.

As the sound of shoes pounding against the stone bridge from the police officers grew closer, Parker's thoughts drifted from the long explanations and reports ahead of them. He thought of Patxi Irionda's body spread prostrate on the stone bridge behind them. He thought of Graciana Etceverria's small curled body nearby. Together, these two radicalized Basque separatists represented the old and the new versions of ETA. In a way, the old and the new had come together.

And they died together.

WANTED BASQUE TERRORISTS KILLED IN PRAGUE

PRAGUE, CZECH REPUBLIC: Authorities in Prague are reporting that two wanted members of the Basque terrorist organization *Euskadi Ta Askatasuna*, better known by the acronym "ETA," have been tracked down and killed in a joint French-Czech operation with US support. The suspects were killed in a gunfight with law enforcement officials on the Charles Bridge while resisting arrest.

The successful operation is being hailed as an excellent example of international cooperation in the combat against global terrorism. The French president stated: "The recent attack in Paris and the foiled attack in Nice were not just planned attacks against France. The targets were clearly chosen based on their popularity with visitors from around the world. Therefore, these attacks should not be seen as attacks against just France, but as attacks against all free people."

One of the ETA members killed in Prague has been confirmed as Patxi Irionda, believed deceased since a 1996 failed bombing attempt in Bordeaux, France. Through a joint operation between French, Spanish, Portuguese, and Czech authorities, it has been revealed that Irionda's death was staged in order to evade arrest by Spanish or French authorities for multiple assassinations of prominent Spanish politicians and military officers, and the 1990 bombing of a Barcelona supermarket.

Irionda reportedly adopted a new identity in Lisbon, Portugal, and ran a successful importing company operating throughout Europe and the Mediterranean. Allegations of the company's connections to illegal arms dealers and militant groups are under investigation. It has also been reported, but not confirmed, that Irionda lived with a wife and two sons in Lisbon. His wife, according to reports, had no awareness of his previous name, connection to ETA, or the suspicious dealings of his company. Irionda is believed to be the leader of the group responsible for the recent bombing of the Tour Montparnasse in Paris and was planning another major attack in Nice.

The other ETA member killed in Prague is reported to be Graciana Etceverria, also a known ETA member living clandestinely. Etceverria was wanted by the French and American governments and was suspected of being a member of the infamous Haika 4 group which brutally assassinated a Basque-American politician, José Aldarossa Arana, in San Francisco in 2010. Etceverria's recent whereabouts and connection to Irionda or the recent and planned attacks in France are not known at this time. However, unconfirmed sources have stated that Irionda's purpose in Prague was to recruit Etceverria for a future attack.

French media outlets have also reported that two other suspected ETA members, Aitzol Rubina and Garikotz Auzmendi, have been arrested in France in connection with the recent Paris attack and planned attack in Nice. Rubina and Auzmendi both are suspected of participation in a number of crimes in both France and Spain in the past thirty years. French authorities have not released the location where each suspect is being held, but unconfirmed sources have indicated that the two men are being held in separate facilities outside of the department of the Pyrenees-Atlantiques, the French department within which the three provinces of the French Basque Country are located.

Another suspected ETA member believed to be associated with the Paris attack and Nice plot has reportedly been arrested in Lisbon. However, no details of the individual or circumstances are being released by the Portuguese government at this time.

The Spanish and French prime ministers have issued a joint statement assuring that there is no evidence to indicate that recent events will result in a resurgence of violence by terrorist elements within the Basque separatist movement. No direct mention of ETA was made in the statement.

The Basque nationalist political party in Spain has stated that in no way should the 2011 ceasefire agreement be considered broken by recent events. The party claims to have no direct connection with ETA, but will not state that the organization no longer exists. However, sources from within the party speaking on the condition of anonymity have told news outlets that the group responsible for the recent resurgence in violence was a rogue group operating on its own without knowledge or approval by mainstream elements of the Basque separatist movement.

The French government announced yesterday that it will reconsider the question of a referendum to allow voters in the French Basque Country to decide if they would elect to become a separate department. The creation of a Basque Department in France has been discussed numerous times in the past. The announcement has been met with joyous reaction in the French Basque Country; however, skepticism remains. When asked his thoughts of the announcement from Paris, the leader of the Unified Basque Front, a French nonprofit group advocating for Basque cultural rights in France, stated in Basque (later translated): "Great. But I'll believe it when I see it."

Also in France, Capitaine Jean-Pierre Nivelle of the French DNAT, whose unit is being heralded as responsible for thwarting the planned attack in Nice, has been promoted to a director level within the French domestic intelligence security agency. Unconfirmed reports from Paris claim the French president himself insisted on Nivelle's promotion after the recent turn of events, despite a disappointing false lead pursued by Nivelle's unit at the French landmark, Mont Saint-Michel, which received international coverage.

American FBI Special Agent John Gibson was also personally awarded the *Légion d'honneur* medal by the French president during a publicized ceremony at the Élysée Palace. Agent Gibson was previously involved in the international investigation of the Haika 4 group. Agent Gibson's exact role in the recent investigation has not been disclosed, but inside sources have indicated that in cooperation with Capitaine Nivelle's DNAT unit and Czech forces, Agent Gibson was involved with the attempted apprehension and eventual shooting of Irionda and Etceverria in Prague. The FBI has issued a statement commending the "above the call of duty" actions of Agent Gibson. Unconfirmed sources have informed news outlets that Agent Gibson has stated that he plans to take early retirement from the FBI once returning to the United States.

There are also unconfirmed reports of another individual having been on the Charles Bridge at the time of the shootout with Irionda and Etceverria. The identity of the person remains unknown, and Czech authorities have declined to respond to inquiries.

Amaiera
La Fin
El Fin
The End